MEMOIRS
OF *A*
TRANSFERABLE
SOUL

A Novel by
W. Town Andrews

FIRST EDITION SOFTCOVER
ISBN: 1622530462
ISBN-13: 978-1-62253-046-5

Editor: Lane Diamond
Cover Artist: Richard Tran
Interior Designer: Lane Diamond

EVOLVED PUBLISHING™

www.EvolvedPub.com
Evolved Publishing LLC
Butler, Wisconsin, USA

Printed in Book Antiqua font.

"But there might be such a thing as a man's soul being loose from his body, and going out and in, like a bird out of its nest...."
George Eliot in "Silas Marner"

Am I writing this? In a borrowed hand, yes — a hand, in many ways, unlike my own.

A hand that wrote verse:

> I stand within a circle that I drew
> Drawn upon a plain far, and wide
> And using all the colors that I knew
> I tried to paint everything inside.
> But even in my circle things I see
> Colors that weren't placed upon my brush
> And misty, distant things are telling me
> I was drawing with a stick, upon the dust.

***

Though I was still a young man, the events had taken their toll. I didn't know what was wrong with me, but could see its depth in the doctors' eyes, and feel its invasion wedging into my flesh, my bones, my brain, my spirit—my very soul. It had been weeks since I'd felt any of that effervescence, the liveliness that the truly living take for granted. Indeed, *feeling itself* had slipped away, eroded by the steady draining drip of will, of being, of vitality, and even identity.

The cause of my troubles—the elusive it—remained a mystery.

Specialists, generalists, homeopaths, allopaths, osteopaths—the doctors could find nothing, with their sapless eyes, useless despite their book learning, med-school training, years of experience, and diagnostic puzzle solving. The best hope came at first from the Immunology subspecialties, then when their toxic antigen trials failed, the Rheumatologists. I suffered through so many fleeting diagnoses: *Granular Lymphatic* this, *Cherg-Slaughter's* Syndrome that, *Sclerofascia, Selenioluposa, Peripheral Neuropathy, Pseudoleprosic Exzemoid Scrofulosis* and *Systemic Planar Cystoids*. I couldn't help but wonder if diagnosticians had little white plastic circular slide rules, where they lined up concentric batches of Greco-Latin prefixes, roots, and suffixes to bring fresh, new, and interesting combinations to their mystery patients.

My fear rose not so much because of the knowledge that I was dying, but because of the lack of knowledge about what, specifically, was killing me. The medical establishment—and increasingly, as I became more desperate, the medical *dis*establishment—simply didn't know. With my mystery affliction, bad news became good news because, as so many tests continued to come back negative or inconclusive, I began to develop a little hope. At first. In time, as I continued to deteriorate, I actually began to *hope for* dire results from some test, *any* test, rather than continuing to suffer through the mystery. After all, spinacanulastenosacorpuscula could be approached with several singular or combined therapeutic ideologies, whereas an unknown mystery ailment could be treated with....

No treatment. No cure.

At some point, denial vanished, and that unspoken residual resentment drained away too.

Yet the will to survive is so relentless, so inescapable, that it can't be denied if there is still some mechanism for keeping the flame alive—even if the vessel for continuing, for survival, for life itself, is non-living....

...or, more specifically, *formerly* living.

PART ONE

A SOUL UNTETHERS

Chapter I

Room 312, bed B; I had the window bed.

Mike, the inhabitant of bed A, had the bathroom side of the suite.

It hardly mattered, as neither of us was in any condition to appreciate a window, or a bathroom, for that matter. We were both bedbound, a jolly pair of bedpanners, catheterized and crash cart at-the-ready.

Chester Valley Manor was a medical facility of a hybrid nature, not quite a hospital, yet not a mere clinic. Nominally a nursing and rehab center, it occupied the former dilatory mansion of Sumner Westlaw Wood, a 19th-century industrialist who made fortunes mechanizing the textile trade, mostly in wool. A century ago, the estate came alive annually in the spring and summer months with extended family and guests in its 80 rooms and sprawling grounds. It featured badminton, horseshoes, croquet, parties, banquets, and balls—pianos in two parlors, a conservatory, a recital space, and a screened gazebo. I knew this from reading a large, framed copper plaque on the dark-panelled wall in the vestibule by the main entry. Nowadays, Chester Valley's population consisted of a mixture of retirees that could no longer care for themselves, and younger accident victims recuperating for a week or a month... and a few odd cases for the one unusual service this particular convalescent home was known for: its diagnostic specialty. Chester Valley Manor had a knack for odd cases.

Because of its location in the heart of the suburbs and its high caregiver-to-patient ratio, it was also, unofficially and quietly, reputed as a palliative center. People who would shudder at the connotations that the word *hospice* carried would come to Chester Valley to idle their way through their final days—although, perhaps more often, the shudders were being shuddered by the middle-aged children of the elderly "guests" who had to do the actual dying.

I had come for the diagnostics, perhaps desperately so, because the toney diagnosticians at the more prestigious facilities in Center City had already taken their stabs at my raw marinade of symptoms and declining vitality—all attempts ending skewers unskewed and kabobs unshished. Now, even here at the quirky and less varnished Chester Valley, as time passed these beyond-the-line crayoners of the maligned margins of medicine, these unorthodox infiltrators of organ systems and circulatory circuitry remained stumped. As one after another of these diagnosers examined, inspected, and tested my vitals and systems, theories were inflated, floated, batted around, and, one by one, popped.

I had come a few miles west for help, but it seemed I would stay for the end.

CVM, aside from not being a modern building, couldn't even truly be called a modern facility—not *thoroughly* modernized, in any case. One would not have chosen *antiseptic,* or *astringent,* or *stark,* or *clinical* to describe it. The manor still had the feel of a cavernous home, or even more so, an estate hastily converted to medical rehab use for wartime or sudden pestilence. Closets had dark-stained walnut louvered doors, in patient rooms with matched recessed bookcases and carved chair moldings lining the walls, windows ornately trimmed but treated with olive green blinds. Fluorescent tubes in the corridors lit darkly striated walnut floors.

I figured Mike, my roomie, to be in his late sixties, with a complexion that increasingly matched the blinds. I hadn't found out what ailed him, and it was too late to ask. When things got that bad, one didn't bring the subject up. If *he* did, well... that would be another matter. Our chatter, never lively, had consisted of a few phrases and half sentences for a day or two, then a few grunted exchanges. Now, he no longer talked even a little, just a gurgle now and then. His family, what remained of it, came and went every couple of days; those wet/dry, half-guilty visits when it's too late for meaningful—but not for emotional—interaction. A daughter in her thirties who made it into town post-coherence but was secretly glad—and I liked her—and a limping older brother who looked in corners, studied the closet, stared at the ceiling—I had the feeling he was checking out the place for his own reasons. Trying it on for size. I'd overheard family members discussing a living will, a DNR order—Do Not Recessitate. Mike was coasting down his last, lonely hill.

When *it* happened, I was *relaxing.* I call it that, because I've never really thought of myself as a meditator. For years, when I was still working, and working on my *myselfhood,* and was married, and still read novels and nonfiction and clever magazines named after big eastern cities, and consumed entertainment, and had conversations, and was invited places, and collected glass and porcelain insulators, and slept regular... but was just starting to notice an odd decline, spells of dizziness, emeryboard dryness in the eyes and sinuses, numbness in my fingertips, throbbing joints, increasingly frequent headaches, often striking in the middle of my deepest sleep.... As all this developed, I transitioned slowly from everyday American pastimes, spending more and more time seeking diagnosis, trying to undo or reverse whatever illness had infiltrated my body. I saw doctors, of course, but increasingly — as they told me that either there was nothing wrong, or that whatever *was* wrong had no name yet, much less an obvious path of treatment — I began to look beyond the doctors.

I had a second row of alternatives, after I'd gotten past the smiling and frowning doctors, first-row non-specialist GPs, and internists with their efficient reception women out front behind sliding glass windows and computerized appointment systems. The second row consisted of chiropractors and fallen medics, the puncturists and pressurists, the tick specialists and thyroid quasidocs, cranioskeletals, metabolists, and the clinical psychologist that whispered to my spine. And because I'd tried all the specialist referrals, and exhausted all the avenues covered by my HMO plan, I had no choice but to wander in the second row.

I found a sleep psychiatrist there who suggested I learn to relax. So, I would listen to delta-wave saturated loops, and concentrate on my breathing, and play mental flutes, and I did learn to withdraw *myself* from my *self* — mindfullness to cultivated mindlessness. Although none of this had any impeding affect on my accelerating decline, it helped me cope. It helped me cope with the physical pain, and the pain of losing my connection with the living, and my high-voltage insulator collection.

I began to pick and choose more discriminatingly my activities in the second row. I increasingly avoided therapies that pulled and prodded and straightened and released, instead steering deeper into the ether, because, as my world dimmed, as my joints inflamed and my energy ebbed and my miasmas gravitated and my brain sank, coping became more important than physical improvement. Not least because coping seemed achievable, whereas improvement remained elusive at best, and always proved fleeting when occasionally realized.

On this July evening, a few days after the Independence Day holiday, solidly into summer, I'd been a resident in Chester Valley Manor for over a week. The ancient oscillator ceiling fan in our room, hanging just below the ceiling on the wall opposite our beds, kept us company with its droning. Its scanning vigil, like a lighthouse, beaconed incessantly left, then right, then back again in a 270-degree arc. Yes, a modern medical facility lacking central air, or maybe it had central air, but relied on fans for air circulation in the patient rooms. It really wasn't that hot, and we had our window open. Sounds of the night—crickets, distant traffic on West Avenue, the occasional Septa, Conrail, or Amtrak train—joined the sounds of treatment and convalescence, briefly winning our ears each time the fan reached the quieter extremes of its oscillation.

I was deeply relaxed.

It must have been late, but not too late—certainly past visiting hours—and relatively quiet on the floor, patients and staff staying put. For me, that was a good time to do my relaxation exercises. From other rooms came steady but faint garbling dialogue from televisions, occasional bursts of laugh tracks, faint beepings and buzzings of medical monitors.

Some minutes into my routine, I had reached a level where I was beyond conscious relaxation, beyond focusing on breathing or other inducing mechanisms. Sometimes I used visualizations, imagined music, muscle contractions. I was floating beyond that, and I became aware of something. Actually, it was more of an awareness of a *nothing*. Better yet, awareness of an *absence*.

Mike Lindner was gone.

I was tempted, briefly, to rouse myself, blink and flex, and look over at the other bed, but I resisted. I was *very* relaxed. I realized that he was gone, but not in a physical sense.

I checked it out another way. Until that moment, I didn't realize I could do such a thing, but I just sort of floated over. I wasn't seeing. I didn't actually have a sense of looking or listening to perceive the presence or absence of my roommate—more of a feeling. No, it was more of a *mental tendrilling*. I floated my sphere of consciousness into the space right above where his had been. I drifted over his body.

I didn't break my state of tranquility, but I managed to quickly check my normal perceptual senses, in order to confirm what I knew with another sense, which I was very tuned to at the moment.

Mike wasn't breathing.

I didn't exactly look down on him, and didn't really experience a visual sense or approximation. It was more of a general, cross-sensual perception—a wee bit of seeing, and equal wee parts of feeling, hearing, and those other bundled and ephemeral senses we often don't name except to call them intuition.

I got closer.

He was so still, so serene. His skin had no glow, his vital rhythms had gone static, and the tides of his various internal fluids no longer waxed and waned in the constant cycles of the living. His flow had ceased. Mike had ebbed his last ebb.

I must have gotten too close, somehow. I certainly didn't intend it, but I was fascinated to be experiencing something so intimately, something so private, something we're certainly — *normally* — destined to experience only once, and that *once* at a moment when there's to be no further time for reflection, sharing, or discussion. Perhaps it seemed a morbid fascination, but I wasn't experiencing it vicariously. I was *in* the moment, exploring a reality that seemed incomprehensible, and I was drawn to it.

At any rate, I got too close or something, and felt a pull. I resisted for a moment, then decided to continue exploring. I let the pull... pull.

Thwock.

I no longer floated. I was re-anchored.

Then I coughed, my reverie broken, and took a gasping breath. My sphere had settled, and at first, I figured I was just coming out of my trance state.

I turned my head and looked up at the oscillator fan, turning on its stalk, turning and fanning, blowing. But it — *the fan* — was in a different place, to the right instead of to the left. I turned my head a little further, and looked at the figure on the bed next to where I lay, and....

There *I* was, lying on my back, so still that it appeared I was barely breathing at all.

I was *in* Mike, looking through *his* eyes.

"Mike?" I said.

What had happened then became clear, not so much because the fan was on the right or because I was looking at myself lying on the window bed, but because I heard my voice, spoken through Mike's vocal chords. Weird, it didn't really sound like Mike at all. It didn't sound like me either. His mouth, his muscles, his tongue didn't feel at all right to me, and *Mike* emerged more like a cross between *Bike* and *Sprocket*. Still, some essence of this odd voice *was* me.

I had not intended to occupy Mike's empty husk, but he was definitely gone, and I had definitely, though inadvertently and involuntarily, taken occupancy.

I sort of panicked a little — I certainly hadn't been *that* relaxed — and I think that's partly what caused the problems. Had I been able to stay relaxed, I might have managed to reverse course, to slide back out and reawaken myself, properly *in* myself. I might have then had a little *wow* sigh and a *whew* chuckle, then begun the task of distancing myself from the incident, and engaging in the inevitable rationalization:

That didn't really happen, it was just an unintended phantasmal imagining....

Instead, it had jarred me out of my delta wave, and instead of raveling back, spooling back onto my own spiritual reel, here I was in Mike's bed... wearing Mike's flesh.

The idea made my... er, made *Mike*'s skin crawl.

I pushed off the covers, sat up, swiveled and stumbled toward my bed, toward *me*. Mike's knees and hips didn't work for me any better than his lips and tongue had for him. I held out my arms and stared at them, and took another step closer, so that I was close now to the other bed where my own form lay silently.

"Get back!" I said — it sounded like *Wet mags!* — willing myself to cross back into my own corpus, but I just lay there peacefully respiring.

Then I panicked for real. "Help! Help!" *Melt! Melt!*

I leaned on the side of my bed and looked out the window at passing cars, but the headlights were blurry. Mike's eyes worked no better than his knees or his tongue, lips or hips. Did Mike wear glasses? I didn't know. I straightened up, turned, and walked — or tried to — tripped over a corner of a bed, and lay sprawled on the linoleum. I reached out, flailing, found a wheeled IV stand, and used it to pull myself back to my knees.

The next few minutes had blank spots.

I hadn't thought things through, of course, but how does one think things through when in a predicament so frightening, so impossible, so harrowing as *this*? One doesn't. So I simply reacted.

After the blank spots, I was walking down the hall, a little darker and narrower than your typical hospital hall because this was a converted mansion, after all. I held onto that IV stand, or another one, and supported myself with it, mincing and stumbling down the hall toward the nurse station. In my other hand, I held a bunch of carrots, with the greens sticking out the fat end and everything.

Every few steps, I stopped and cried out. *Melp! Melp me!*

I heard *me* clearly and felt proud that I actually enunciated a word, even just one word, rather than nothing but quasi-intelligible syllables. My voice was faint, however, as if muffled, and, proud or not, it brought me no *melp*.

The distance from 312 to the nurse station was only about 30 yards or so, but in a devastated and over-palliated body with a mismatched soul... well, that 30 yards became like 300.

I finally turned the corner, from where the patient hallways had the lights dimmed for the evening, into the relatively well-lighted nurses' station, with its counter and desks and monitors, and stopped and looked at the nurses.

Two of them, or perhaps a nurse and an assistant, looked back at me all regular-like, as if silently asking, *May we help you?* Then they looked at each other—my vision had cleared a bit by now, and I could make it clear up even more if I squinted Mike's eyes a little—and looked back at me as if I had a polar bear slung over each shoulder.

"Mr. Lindner," said the little dark-skinned one, "What are you doing—"

"—Out of bed, in the hall?" The other one, the nurse in charge, finished the question for her. "Oh Mr. Lindner, you look terrible."

They both jumped up.

"I'm not Lindner," I said, but it sounded like *Llama Linda,* or perhaps *Mama Mia.*

They came over quickly.

Oh good, here's help! Then I fell over.

The ladies sort of caught me, and I ended up in a seated position, with them on either side of me. I held out the carrots and said, "Put me back, please. Put me back."

They heard me all right, but they misunderstood. "Oh yes, Mr. Lindner, we'll get you right back into your nice bed."

"No, no, nurse," I said, gesturing with the carrots. "Not Mike, *not Mike.*"

She really was trying to understand—I saw it on her face. She listened, and then focused on the carrots that I was waving in her face. She tried to reason out what I was trying to tell her: "Not your, not your... your *carrots?*"

"No, no, no, nooooooo." I cursed the carrots. Where had they come from, anyway? I looked at the carrots, the Bugs Bunny carrots, and in frustration tore at them. I broke them and tore the greens off, then shredded the leaves, and the bits and pieces flew here and there. Finally, I started to scream, but my scream faded and my vision dwindled to a little white dot, like when you turn off an old black-and-white television.

Thwock!

I was back in *my* bed. I opened my eyes and looked at the ceiling, at the oscillating fan, and then over at the bed next to me. Yes, it was empty.

"No, no, no, noooo," I said. "It must have been a dream. Must have!"

Then I heard the nurses, not quite *screaming*, but sounding very, very... *distraught*... from 30 yards down the hall.

Chapter 2

It took a while, but I finally grabbed a few minutes completely for myself, and really took stock. Usually, they handled deaths on the floor quietly—you might even say dignified. These were not the usual circumstances, however.

Rehab nurses, and care providers in general, do not rattle easily. They see a lot of pain, a lot of desperation, consistent doses of sorrow and despair. They cope with patients that try them, deceive them, and connive to outwit them. Even through all that, they consistently manage to maintain control over their patients, and to a lesser extent, over attending relatives and other visitors. Still, one might expect that if a patient died on the floor in the hall, right by the nurses' station, while mutilating organic carrots and barking like an Airedale with a harelip, the care staff might be thrown off their death-coping routine.

And if the patient had already been dead for 45 minutes when the Airedale-with-vegetables incident happened, any clinging shreds of expectation and protocol they might normally have called upon would certainly centrifuge off and whirl away in the out-of-control spin of my unscripted, out-of-body, postmortem performance.

This had been a bit more... *eventful* than the average death incident at the home, though after the initial event itself and that fairly hysterical aftermath, the staff pulled themselves back together and did manage to get routines re-established pretty quickly.

The nurse came to talk to me—Ellen was her name—after which they brought Mike back to the room, in a stretcher, just long enough to get him back into his bed. Then they wheeled the bed out. They might have parked him somewhere, or taken him straight to the morgue, but having a living roommate—me—they didn't want to leave him in 312.

First Ellen, then later an administrative guy named Carsoner, asked me about Mike. I told them both that I was asleep, and didn't see or hear anything, not until I heard the screams. First, the hoarse, harsh screams of a man, followed by the near-screams of distraught nurse Ellen and the assistant. I said nothing, of course, about my involvement.

After all that, sometime around midnight, things grew quiet again. I had the room to myself, and I could think about what had happened.

It really had been frightening, and strange, and nightmarish in the purest way. I didn't like it, hadn't wanted to do it, and didn't know how it had happened. I didn't really want to relive it, or think about it, and really didn't want even to *wonder* what I *really* had done — what inadvertent technique I had stumbled upon. I wanted to put it behind me as a freak occurrence. I wanted to forget.

But as I lay there, in the bed where I'd lain for a week and a half, steadily growing weaker and falling further from human routine, having steadily less appetite for all normal human needs, including nourishment, mental activity, social interaction — as I lay there, looking around, feeling myself, my mind, my body, I realized something. There had been a change.

I felt better. In fact, I felt *a lot* better. I felt better than I had felt in weeks, maybe months.

I pushed the covers off, tentatively swung my legs out, pushed back on the bed, and rested my heels on the smooth hardwood. I hadn't been on my feet for several days, so I wasn't steady. After resting my weight against the side of the bed for ninety seconds or so, I pushed off, stood a few feet from the bed, and....

I couldn't help but smile. I reached back to retie my gown, and walked out into the hall.

When I reached the nurse's station, Ellen took one look at me and jumped up. "Christ, not again!"

I had to play dumb. "What?"

"You okay?" She paused, looking at me hard, then took my arm and supported my shoulders with one of hers.

"I like it," I said.

She seemed relieved. "Never mind. You must be feeling better, Mr. Resurrection."

"Yes," I said. "My relaxation techniques are improving my energy level."

She steered me back to my room. "You sleep. You've had excitement enough for one evening. You can get some exercise tomorrow. We'll bring the physical therapist to you in the morning. You've been in bed too long to be doing this without help. Your medication must be starting to work."

I lay in my bed, not sleeping, and wondered. Was it the meditation? The penicillamide?

Or had I somehow restored my own vitality by sending my spirit for a twenty-minute vacation in a dead man's body?

Chapter 3

The next day, I felt a little worse—better than I'd generally felt recently, but not as good as I felt right after my unusual out-of-body experience. It might have been because I hadn't slept well. Not terribly surprising, that, given the events.

I continued to doze throughout the morning, and my favorite shift started at noon.

It may sound odd—a *favorite shift*—but it must happen a lot, for folks who must endure lengthy, or frequent, hospitalizations. The sameness of hour after hour could weigh you down, with the days and the nights passing one into the other, on and on, in a little room that always looked the same, with the noises and routines of health facilities being pretty much the same around the clock.... One seizes upon whatever handles are available for gripping onto something bright or meaningful—even something as simple as a workshift.

My favorite shift started at noon. That's when Natalie worked.

She brought me my lunch. She didn't have to do that, as the diet orderly traversed the hall distributing daily meals with the tray cart, but sometimes Natalie made this gesture. Gesture? No, more than that... a *flourish*.

"Look at you!" she said.

Having dozed much of the morning, I sat up and worked on the *Jumble* in the Daily News.

She wore her green hospital scrub pants and her usual medical smock, a lineny, tunicky, gaily-printed, short-sleeved top nothing the like the straight whites of years past. Today, it had a pattern of little lavender honeysuckle bouquets alternated with crossed baguettes.

I hadn't seen her wear the same tunic twice, or hadn't noticed if she had, also possible given my usual tunnel of fatigue and pain.

"Aw, you're a picnic today!" I smiled and put down the news.

My smile amplified hers, and her dark eyes and white teeth sparkled at me as she shook her black hair back, set my tray on the rolling tray table, and slid it over my lap.

"I don't think I've seen you smile like that since the day you got here," she said, her slight accent sounding like something from Eastern Canada, perhaps from childhood. Her lips pursed and her eyes narrowed as she studied my face. "You *must* be improving."

"Maybe it's Dr. Jidalco's protocol," I said.

"I had my doubts about that cocktail, but I'm glad to be proven wrong!" she said.

I thought about that. It reminded me of Mike, and I briefly thought about keeping what I said next to myself, but I couldn't help it. "I thought you'd been wrong about Mike, yesterday morning, but you were right, after all. What you said."

She looked at me funny. "Mike? Poor Mike, I heard. Yes, but...?"

"You chided him yesterday, with your bright and sunny, 'Oh, Mike, you'll be up and about before you know it!'"

Natalie put her hand over her mouth, eyes wide. "Oh, I did say something like that! How *awful* of me!"

"Well, you couldn't have known he'd summon up his final ounces of strength to get up and walk down the hall and terrorize the nasty night nurse one last time."

"Oh, Ellen's not so nasty. Is she?"

"She's all business."

"Speaking of which, I've got to make the rounds and dock some charts. I'll be back for your vitals after you eat. Eat well, and keep this up!"

She whirled out of the room, and for the first time in a week, I actually felt buoyant enough to *enjoy* watching her wide hips swinging into the hallway.

Chapter 4

I wheeled myself down the hall to the elevator.

I had talked Natalie and the OT into privileging me the wheelchair. Patients with mobility were allowed—encouraged even—to navigate the facility, get some exercise, fresh air, and participate in scheduled activities.

When I'd arrived at the facility, I'd not been at all mobile, and until last night, it had been downhill from there, so this was my first foray out and about. I'd wanted to do so afoot, but after nearly two weeks bedridden, I couldn't walk far, at least not without stopping and resting often.

It's surprising, when one gets no physical activity other than rolling over in bed, how fast you lose muscle stamina, strength, even the wind to walk more than a few dozen steps.

So this was good. I felt somewhat autonomous, able to wheel myself around without somebody pushing me. Getting some of my stamina back proved a value-added side effect to last night's event. I intended to get the hang of the place, and the wheelchair, a new vehicle to me. Up to then, I'd either been capable of walking, or completely weakened. This was my first time in the in-between status that wheelchairs serve. I'd never needed to learn about the wheels, the footrests, the brakes, how to set them to get in and get out of the seat.

Natalie had gotten me a chair, but an OT had to show me how to use it. It was kind of fun in a way, something of a *guilty pleasure*, but in this instance, more like a *childish pleasure*. I remembered wanting to play with wheelchairs at various times as a child—an uncle with a broken leg when I was 8, a visit to a friend getting an appendectomy when I was 11—but I'd been discouraged from it or scolded when caught.

"That's not a toy, sonny!"

This time, the childish aspect was brief, as I still didn't feel well enough or energetic enough for juvenile joy. I had other reasons, however, to roll quietly and slowly around the facility—things I needed to find out.

And places I needed to find.

I asked myself a lot of questions, the kind I could ask nobody else, and the answers, in some cases, could only come if I had access to certain places. And certain objects.

Some of the questions, I hesitated to ask, even of myself. I wanted to somehow skip straight to the answers, but there is a kind of question whose answers don't just come twirling out of the mind and tripping off the tongue. I thought of these as *research questions*, which would take some digging, or special resources or conditions.

Could I do it again? Could I move my spirt again?

Could I go in *and* out *at will?*

I'd gone *in* to my roomate's cooling husk unexpectedly, even accidentally, and I'd left suddenly under stress, and then had somehow found my way back to my own trancing body. I'd completed both actions without intention, without knowledge, and upon reflection, I could recognize no clear technique to the accomplishment. It had been artless, but it had occurred, and I felt better afterward — indeed, improved, revitalized even — after only 15 minutes or so.

Would I feel even better if I stayed for an hour?

Are there any dead people in the facility? If so, where are they kept?

My research questions, stuff I could only learn through investigation.

I couldn't exactly bring up such topics in casual conversation in the activity room, where a group of elderly patients were watching *All My Children* and drinking hot chocolate. Nor could I do so out in the breezeway at the entrance, where another group sat in wheelchairs and on bench swings smoking Carletons and Newports and Camels.

Old smokers tend to be primarily women. I wonder why that is?

I rolled back to near the elevator, loitered around until I was the only one there, and pushed the call button. I wanted the carriage to myself, for multiple reasons. I wanted the practice, because these little elevators were tricky for wheelchair users, and I really needed to learn to access all the floors. I also wanted to sneak around, and when you have company in a supervised facility, even in as casual a setting as an elevator, they always seem to want to know what you're up to, where you're going, and often even wish to accompany.

The problem? If somebody else, somebody who travels afoot, is there to operate the elevator, there's no problem. If you're by yourself, and in a wheelchair, it's one of those weird challenges, like cutting your own hair or kissing your elbow.

If you push the button, and wait, and then the car arrives, and you just wheel yourself in frontways, then the floor number buttons are behind you and you can't reach them without spraining your neck, and there isn't enough room in the little compartment to conveniently make a full turn.

If you push the button and wait patiently, watching for the arrival light and bell, then the door opens and you quickly turn your wheelchair to back in, by this time the door has closed and the elevator has gone on to pick people up on another floor.

So, you've got to plan ahead, and it probably looks weird—you're waiting for the elevator with your back to it, staring into the nonexistent distance like an old one-legged salt on a Nantucket whaling barq or something. If somebody comes along, one glance and they think you're one of the oddballs, and there are plenty of that sort in places like Chester Valley Manor. Of course, if a fellow wheelchair jockey shows up, they just nod. They know.

So eventually, after some practice—and by *practice* I mean, actually, considerable frustration while I learned all those details one at a time—I got in, had access to the elevator controls, saw all the buttons, and was by myself, so I could study the layout—three patient floors, an office floor—the fourth—and a basement. The basement was my first choice. Carefully and silently, I wheeled past the maintenance office and workshop, housekeeping headquarters, a flatwork laundry, and several unmarked locked doors near the end of the hall where the exit to the loading dock led out. I'd have to come back and see if I could get access.

Nobody really bothered me, but when a housekeeping supervisor looked like she was about to, "Exercise!" I said as if winded, and gave several vigorous strokes to my wheels to get out of earshot as quickly as possible.

I rolled back to 312, parked, took my noon nap after lunch—no new roommate yet—and woke up groggy and stiff.

Am I already losing my hard-gained ground?

It was time to get friendly.

Back on my trusty steed, I took a fast roll down past the nurse station to the elevator, rode down with a visitor, which made it easier, and headed for the furthest point I could—first floor, west wing, PTHQ, where the physical therapists had their mats and therabands and graduated barbells and photocopied exercises. I took a quick look, but didn't linger long.

This floor had patient rooms too.

I took my time meandering down the halls, stopping long enough to look in doors, to look at the names by the doorframes, to see the little clippings and family snapshots on the cork panels, to nod hello when eyes looked out from the beds and bedsides, but hopefully not long enough to seem especially nosey.

Art Chumley's voice rang out, "Got anything to drink, boy?" and I rolled on.

Hazel Rathley's daughter and son, sitting at her bedside, tracked my progress, and Hazel gave me a little finger wave from her bed when the others weren't looking. A week ago, when I'd been worse, utterly bedridden at the time due to an unusual intravenous arrangement that had my legs up, and she'd been better, Hazel had wandered into *my* little room and introduced herself by promptly opening my closet and ruffling through the few articles of clothing I had on the perma-hangers in there. She'd ignored me when I tried to say, *"What the...?"* After a squeaky *"Hey!"* and a push on my nurse-call plunger, an aide came in.

He'd immediately scolded the old girl. "Hazel, Hazel, you've got to stay out of strange mens' closets!" He'd then shooed her out of my room.

These were the relatively hale and healthy.

Randale T. Owens was very quiet, in a room that looked well lived-in, but he appeared to be beyond living well. I'd have to watch him. I didn't allow my gaze to linger over his lifestuff, his caseboard, his signs of personality. It felt awkward, as if my curiosity were inappropriate, considering... considering that I was effectively casing the joint, and the *joint* was Randy.

There were others, older of course, and younger too. Younger ones tended to be short termers, accident victims, sometimes facing major structural operations like joint replacements, but not always. Sometimes the younger convalescers seemed to have other disabilities too—sundry physical problems, plegias, low motility. I felt even queasier considering these, and rolled on.

I canvassed the east wing, and then moved on to the 2nd floor, where I managed to eavesdrop a key bit of post-mortem intelligence. As I prepared to roll nonchalantly past the central nurse's station, I heard the indistinct chatter of an in-progress conversation. I slowed and hung back before passing the wall's edge into view of the nursing team, but edged as close as I could to improve earshot.

Little bits rose louder than the other words. "...so nice that nearly all of you...very peaceful...." Then the other voice said, "...so wonderful with them all," and especially, "...nice touch."

I kept listening, zoning out a little as the tones of the voices indicated continuing exchange of platitudes and sympathies, but then, my attention snapped back when the tone changed.

"Yes, the gentleman, I believe... your uncle? ...yes, arrangements... underway, but we'll take good care of him until, well.... Yes. Don't worry. Yes, all the details... taken care of."

I practiced my in-place spin, where you spin the left wheel back and the right wheel forward, like the treads of a tank, and headed back to the elevator.

It was nearly four-o'clock, and if the shifts for the support departments in the basement level were similar to those for the nursing staff, I'd need to move quickly, but I needed to stop by 312 first.

Chapter 5

A minute before 4:00 PM, I rolled down the hall on the basement level with my earbuds on but nothing playing, slowly moving past the unmarked doors that I'd noticed the day before. The earbuds were to create the impression of a patient self-propelling his chair while preoccupied with his exercise and tunes.

Having passed all three doors, I did a quick turn and rolled past them again. It was a little bit like musical chairs, except instead of waiting for music stopping, I was waiting for a door to open—any door.

On my fourth cycle, I heard indistinct but audible sounds, and readied myself without changing my pace or my seeming preoccupation. Then the far west door sounded metallically, its knobset and latch activated, and it swung open.

Although the door was behind me, I didn't turn my head or pause in my rolling stroll. I waited until the person exiting had passed me, and then I quickly yet quietly threw my wheels in reverse and rolled backwards right next to the wall, trying to cover the five or six feet as fast as possible. I managed to reach the door just before its autocloser swung it shut, and still looking ahead at the departing back of the patient tech, I quietly slid my right elbow back off my armrest to block the door open.

I listened. No noise came from inside the room, which I hoped meant no living occupants remained to interfere with my plan. The fellow who'd just left had almost reached the elevator, so I snatched from my jacket pocket the rolled gray washcloth I'd retrieved from my room on my way down here, reached back and dropped it over my left shoulder. It fell right where I wanted, so I resumed my forward rolling, letting my elbow slide out from between the door's edge and the doorway, and the door resumed its autoclose, but did not click. It only made a muffled *whump* when it closed on the wadded terrycloth.

I headed toward the man, a young fellow with a crewcut and a tired face, waiting for the elevator.

When it softly dinged its arrival bell, he said, "Going up?"

I maintained the headphone ruse, not responding, but I was close enough to see that he was talking to me, which also meant that from his perspective, he was close enough to see me see him, so I waited an extra half second to make it seem real, then pulled off one of my earbuds and shook my head. "Think I'll do another lap. Less foot traffic down here."

He nodded and got on the elevator.

When the door had closed and the hum of its motor signaled its ascent, I executed my fastest spin and zipped back to the jammed-open door. The laundry and other housekeeping supply rooms and administrative sections were down here too, just a few yards down the corridor, so I had to be quick while there was no foot traffic. Muffled voices came from further along the hallway, so I just kept moving, rolling to the door. I stopped at just the right angle to swing it open and slide through with almost the same motion, hand on the knob, pulling myself to a roll and assisting with my left hand on my left wheel. Then, as the door started to close behind me, a quick spin and I already had my hand on my pinch grabber—an essential tool of the infirm. Just before the door shut on it, its yellow plastic beak seized my rolled washcloth and pulled it out of the way. After a soft but firm metallic click, I was alone in the room.

I hope I'm alone.

After feeling around the doorway and switching on the fluorescents, I pushed the brake levers on the chair. Their steel shoes bit into the soft solid tires and park-braked my chair right in front of the door. An inconsiderate means, perhaps, but toward an end of worthwhile design: to slow down any possible intrusion.

I pushed myself to my feet and shuffled over to the drawers. I actually had to navigate around a central stainless steel, guttered table, but I doubted they used it for much other than brief postmortems, as this center was not equipped for any detailed forensics. That was good. I didn't want to be interrupted, although I wasn't planning to do anything. *Literally.* All I wanted was a few quiet minutes' communion.

The room contained eight drawers. The hum of the refrigeration provided a low background of steady white noise. Only one of the drawers held an occupant, which I could tell because it was the only one with a white card in the ID slot. Although I wanted to get on with it, I was also torn about it, so I opened one of the other, empty drawers first. I was stalling, dawdling, but it gave me an idea—I could hide my wheelchair, fold it up inside a broom closet or something, and then come back and slide into one of the empties and really take my time.

That creeped me out, so I quickly discarded the idea. I was just getting started with this stuff, and wasn't even sure I could pull it off it again. At this point, some nineteen hours later, I wasn't even entirely sure it had happened at all, the incident with Mike—or what was left of Mike. *Something* had happened, yes, and the nurses knew *something* had happened, but with each hour that passed, I grew less and less certain that it was what I'd thought it was at first.

I just didn't know. I needed to try again.

I read the tag on the drawer; his name was Manuel. I opened it, unzipped his cocoon, and looked at Manny—white hair, mustache. I'd never seen him before. I'd never seen him... alive. I knew this more with my heart than with my eyes—a feeling, an intuition. I felt no connection with him. Still, I left the drawer open, went and sat in my chair, reached up and switched off the light, and relaxed. I cleared my mind, letting the white noise blanket the internal drone.

Half an hour later, I switched the light back on, stretched, rose, went and zipped Manny back into his cocoon, closed his drawer, switched the light back off, quietly opened the door back up, wheeled myself quickly into the corridor, and headed back up to 312.

None of my questions were answered, not with conclusive, useful answers, anyway. I had reached my deepest, fullest stage of relaxation. I had even managed to feel as if I were extending my aural center across the room, past the metal table, hovering near the refrigerated drawers. It was like extending a pseudopod—maybe it's called an ectopod—but it was as though a wall blocked my path, one with no window or door, just smooth, impenetrable stone. I could not connect to Manny. I felt no connection with him. I had never seen, spoken to, listened to, or even *heard* Manny.

My first willful, conscious attempt to cross had been thoroughly unsuccessful.

Yet even in failure, there are gains. I had a feeling that the conditions were wrong, that I *had* gained an answer of sorts, and that perhaps the difference between Mike and this Manuel was that I had at least been acquainted with Mike. Some connection, some sort of familiarity, or at least some minimum level of cognizant interactivity, might be a requirement. I'd also been able to carefully examine the the latches on the doors to the basement body rooms, and they were fitted with simple knobsets, not deadbolts.

For an hour or so after dinner, I made the rounds, but I was distracted, thinking these things over, and was really getting tired, and hadn't found any new leads, so I retired early.

I resumed my turns around the wards the next morning, even more fatigued than the night before. With my energy flagging, my vitality redraining, and my confidence and optimism at low ebb, I finally found a clue to what I was looking for. I had zeroed in on a new target, a recent casualty of all our modern life extension efforts failing again, as they always did, of course, eventually.

Nobody gets to stay, indefinitely. Nobody.

This time, lots of family mingled around, so I had to wait until they'd completed all their farewell stuff. Then the body was ready to be moved, having completed his sojourn in the American *dying* industry, ready now to passively travel to the next intermediate stop on his way to immersion in the American *death* industry.

Joseph had been a good guy. I had ended up seated next to him at a Tuesday afternoon bingo activity a few days into my stay at the Manor, and we had looked at each other with that mutual squint that meant we were both thinking there's something familiar here, and neither of us could quite put a finger on it at first. As it turned out, we remembered when we had sat in adjacent upholstered recliners at an IV therapy clinic a year or so ago, getting supplements and enzymes dripped into our veins.

Once we remembered that, which took a while, we remembered what we had chatted about that afternoon as we received state-of-the-art infusions for fibromyalgia and chronic fatigue — baseball, the DH, its plusses and minuses. I did the minuses, and he did the plusses. In the end, we agreed that the plusses were good for the players and to some extent the revenues of the teams, while the minuses were bad for the fans, for strategic interest, and the purity of the game.

That afternoon at the bingo tables, we compared notes again. The infusions had been no lasting help to either of us. Now, just under two weeks later, surrounded by his family and in a deepening palliative buzz, Joseph had passed.

I needed help from my friend. I didn't think he'd mind.

This time, I managed to cross, and compared to my first sudden, shocking, and unintended experience with my roommate Mike, this time the incident was much less... eventful. For the most part, most of the way through, it wasn't even interesting, and I was actually glad of that. This was my research, and I was methodical about it, testing, evaluating, ticking off my research questions one by one. I waited until the transit morgue was left unmanned — by the living, anyway.

It was cold in there, and being in a drawer... well, think *claustrophobia*, and then amplify it a bit, a big bit, by the presence of a dead guy. This time, I knew the guy, which made it creepier. It made it personal.

I wheeled myself down there, waited until I was alone in the corridor, and used a plastic credit card shim to jimmy the door. I closed it and locked it, then went and found the right body door, opened it, and unzipped the bag enough to have a quick look.

Hi, Joseph.

Then I went back, hunched down in my chair, and relaxed.

Over the next half hour, I quietly asked my research questions, and my cold, quiet friend gave me the answers. I didn't move. While my body was slumped in a wheelchair, my spirit lay feet outward in a long steel drawer, in a cold basement room. Janitors, maintenance workers, and housekeepers toting linens milled around in the halls, so where was I going to go?

Here were the answers:

Yes, it seems there *is* repeatability. With adequate preparation, I could occupy vacant flesh at will, *if* I had some connection with the subject while living. Not sure yet how extensive, how deep the relationship needed to be. Joseph and I were acquaintances, perhaps even well acquainted, as much as two people could be who had met twice.

And yes, once again my time outside myself had rejuvenated me. This time, I stayed for half an hour, and felt even better than I had after my twenty inadvertent minutes with Mike. I couldn't risk more time, still nervous about being found out, and being nervous may have affected the quality of my relaxation and the depth of my recharge. I was a little "in and out" of my subject this time, and indeed, my first occupation, with Mike, was no walk in the park either, though it *was* a stroll down the hall. Well, maybe a bit of a *lurch*, with banging off the walls, as it were.

This time, though, with this second occupation, the hardest answer, the toughest research question, came unexpectedly, and created a bit of a panic: *How do I get out?*

I was nervous, so after staying about as long as I could stand, lying there quietly — which seemed longer at the time, in the moment, but turned out to be about a half hour — I decided it was time to go.

I said to myself, "Okay, let's move this along," and sort of shook and flexed the muscles and the mentality, gearing up the will for departure and return to my own enfleshment, and....

Nothing happened.

I'd made pretty much the same physical, mechanical, and mental preparations as when I'd failed to cross the day before—body drawer open, bag unzipped, wheelchair parking brake on, parked right in front of the door, mind cleared, relaxation maximized. I visualized the whole scene, though it was dark in the room except for the little indicator lights on the few pieces of plugged-in equipment lining the walls, a thin slice of light around the main door, and a faint green coming from an exit sign above the door frame. I visualized it, though I didn't actually look at it. I'd been staying still, occupying Joseph's shell, with my eyes closed, my mind also staying, as much as possible under the circumstances, tranquilly still and relatively serene.

Then, I visualized myself rising, untethering, hovering, achieving the separation, moving back to my own breathing form.

Still nothing.

Then, I quickly became less and less serene as the uneventful accumulated eventlike characteristics. I could still think, and I needed to do so.

I need to think.

My mind was not in my brain. It was twelve feet removed from my oblongata and my medulla and my stem and my left and right hemispheres and my cortices, but in my limited experience so far with this astral experimentation, my mind seemed to work much as it would normally. True, some portion of my thought stream and background mentation had focused on maintaining my out-of-body coordinates, but it didn't seem like a big deal to think at the same time.

So, I thought... back to the other night, the night with Mike.

How did I do it then? How did I return?

Well, it was much like how I had gotten *into* Mike in the first place. I hadn't planned that either, hadn't thought about it. I just *was*. I just *did*. And when I left and went back to my own self, I just... *thwock*... was back—*snap*, just like that.

Yet there were circumstances, differences, between then and now.

Then, my prostrate self lay back in my bed, and my mind, my intending center, was thirty or forty feet away, in the hallway. *Now*, I sat in a wheelchair twelve feet away from my intentional being.

That's a difference.

Maybe it was like a rubber band, between my body and my mind, and when the distance got long enough, the rubber stretched tight and... *snap*, I was compressed back into my body.

Am I too close?

That didn't quite feel right, though it felt at least partly possible.

I had planned to, other than taking brief occupancy, leave Joseph alone and at peace. I didn't want to make him move. I hadn't wanted to move Mike either, but I had panicked. Now, I seemed to be stuck, and I really, really didn't want to be stuck. I needed   to figure this out.

I summoned more will, more intent, more *oomph,* more of that living essence we might call vitality, into Joseph's still form, and I managed to move his left hand. Then I opened his eyes. It was dark. I turned his head, looked around, flexed his fingers, and reached up through the small, unzipped opening in the body bag. I managed, with some effort, to push against the cabinet face and actually extend the drawer a few inches.

The body bag stumped me, though. Lengthening its opening should have been like unzipping a winter coat, or maybe more like a heavy-duty rain slicker, but my fingers—Joseph's fingers—felt like swollen sausages: boneless, greasy, fat and inarticulate. I couldn't get them to grasp the tab of the zipper, much less hold the heavy vinylized fabric and pull the zipper open. I made a noise, vocalized reflexively, trying to swear. It came out about as clumsy as the futile digital efforts.

It gave me an idea, though. I wanted to test the proximity angle, get up, get farther away from my living body. That would be a challenge, even if I could get out of the drawer, and it was risky, the room being so small. I could use Joseph to push my wheel chair to one corner, and then stumble him over to the catty corner, but that would still be about 16, 18 feet. Would it be enough? It didn't really matter if I couldn't get the body bag open.

Icy nervousness washed over me, and I shivered and spasmed in Joseph's drawer.

I summoned air into Joseph's lungs, expanded his chest, and pushed down with his elbows to let as much air and expansion take place as possible. Then, I let it back out forcefully through the vocal cords, as fast and hard and loud as I could. It generated an inchoate, non-syllabic holler of purely meaningless inexpression, and I felt something happen, something like a leavening of my existential link with Joseph.

Then his lungs were empty, and I remained there in the drawer.

I started to panic again, and drew air back in sharply, and repeated the harsh, inhuman, bellowing, almost Howard Deanian scream, knowing it was likely to bring unwanted attention, but knowing I had to keep going, had to get out.

Thwock!

In a whirling sensation I became a rising wisp, *lifted and separated,* twisting up and out of the drawer and back into my own wheelchair. I tried to get myself unsubmerged out of the relaxed state, which normally couldn't be done quickly—because... it *just can't*—but I managed to start wheeling the chair even while still groggy, trying to open my eyes.

Somebody behind me, at the door, said, *"Is everything all right in there? Hello?"*

I needed it to be *all right,* but nothing would be *all right* while the body bag and the drawer remained open. Nobody came in, though, probably because the housekeeping and maintenance workers that came and went constantly in these basement halls didn't carry keys to the undertaking rooms. They probably didn't really want to have anything to do with what went on in there, and now would be no different.

"We're fine," I said over my shoulder, as I zipped Joseph back into his cocoon. "Just dropped the...." I looked around for something to have dropped, fishing around in my mind for a creative technical term. "...the *spine pliers* on my toe. Just wrapping up here. We'll be done in five minutes."

I counted on the possibility that there wasn't much interplay between whomever I was talking to and whomever routinely came and went in this room, the body orderlies or funeral drivers. That, and the possibility that very large pliers are used in cadaver work.

Spine pliers?

I shut the drawer quietly, sat back down in the wheelchair, and wheeled over toward the door.

From the hall, the person said, "Okay, just want to be sure you're all okay."

Try a little dark humor? Why not.

"I'm fine. The others in here... well, they're not complaining, either."

"Better you than me," said the voice. Then, receding, he added, "Have a good evening!"

I waited three minutes, and let myself out.

Chapter 6

My heart raced as I rode the elevator back up to the third floor. Natalie would probably advise me that that fast a heart rate was risking trouble, but by the time I'd wheeled myself back to Room 312, it had calmed down a bit. Natalie must have been making rounds because she wasn't in the nursing block when I went past. Probably just as well, because she'd likely notice my recent exertion. Nurses are trained observers, and of course, it's harder to hide things from those we're fond of, anyway.

I wheeled into my room and discovered that I had a new roommate, but I also realized that I felt even better now than I had after Mike. This was working. I had found a therapy that actually reversed the ravages this illness had perpetrated against my body. Furthermore, it was repeatable, and measurable, and in my current setting, quite... available. Even more important than improving how I felt, it improved how I *felt* about how I felt. I'd developed some hope, whereas two days before I'd felt nothing but despair.

The only problem was that I couldn't tell anybody.

This wasn't something I could easily keep a quiet secret. It was so bizarre, so gruesome, so medically anti-intuitive — some might even say ghoulish, though I wouldn't, not after what I'd recently learned — that I would have to overcompensate and develop some sort of conventional cover, perhaps even several decoying covers or obfuscation layers, because it was so effective. This kind of breakthrough would demand some sort of explanation, and the additional scrutiny would certainly veer toward exposing the truth.

That terrified me.

Credit would have to go to some existing protocol or protocols, and I was receiving several. Occam's razor suggested that I steer the eye of evidence to lock its gaze on the most obvious, although I was receiving both conventional but cutting-edge autoimmune disorder treatments, as well as several alternative and new age medical and non-medical interventions.

I couldn't exactly conceal my progress, but the best thing, for now, would be to underplay it, to keep under-reporting my improvement, and to control my own subjective reaction and outward appearances. I'd keep to the wheelchair, although I felt improved enough to walk quite well for short-to-medium distances. After the obligatory, *"How are you today?"* I might be tempted to reply reflexively, *"Fine"* or *"Great,"* but I'd stick with *"Okay,"* or *"Ehh,"* the common, nursing home verbal shrug, for the time being.

Based on my two experiences thus far, I had a rough equation for the duration and effectiveness of the treatments. For every minute I spent in possession of one of my departed acquaintances—or that I spent lodged outside of my own skin—I seemed to gain one to two hours of robustness in my own physical and psychological sphere. It wasn't *exactly* like that; there was some decay, so to speak, in the effect. About halfway into the gained time of wellness, I would start to feel the fatigue, the joint pain, the brain fog creeping back in, and would have to begin planning my next treatment. Diminishing returns.

Chapter 7

"We think it will both help you gain even more benefit from your treatment, and help us better understand what is working, and what isn't," said Dr. Wade. He held my chart and stood between me and my new roommate's bed.

Dr. Jidalco nodded his agreement, the point of his beard pointing at his feet, then my feet, then back, as he stood at the foot of my bed.

My new roommate, Dale, was out getting a test or a treatment somewhere.

I looked from one to the other and said, "I'm not sure I understand why we need to change anything. It seems like what we're doing here is working maybe, sort of, and I'm afraid that if we mess with it... well, you know."

I resisted being too specific about anything. I actually had mixed feelings about what my team was suggesting.

Several days had passed since my session in the basement with Joseph. I'd been getting around the facility — a lot. Even when feeling well, I tended not to be the most social of people — nor was I a complete recluse — but now, I was a moth *and* a butterfly. For evening activities, when the Manor brought in little entertainments, I played the moth dancing in the light. I attended a singing and juggling magician one night. On another early evening, when medical events used the meeting spaces provided by the Manor, I attended a session — where most of the audience had come from outside — on the astonishing recent increase in the incidence of autism in children. The post-lecture discussion was the interesting part, because the parents in attendance blamed everything from innoculations to television to video games to terrorism to fluoride to partisan politics to the loss of prayer in schools. One lady actually sounded somewhat credible and old-fashioned when she suggested those washed and tumbled baby carrots might be responsible.

Daytime was more about the business of living and healing, and dying — services in the chapel, training sessions, advocacy, dietary programs. I butterflyed from one end of the facility to the other, top to bottom, with occasional visits to the basement lair to see if any new "transients" had arrived.

No such luck.

A lot went on, day and evening, if one sought the light and heat in these actute-care environments. I was a seeker.

Most of the activities provided opportunities to meet people, see people, and increase my bank of potential friends. One never knew whom would be next to *move on*, and I had to be ready.

And I had finally managed to get in one more quick one, sort of like a *take-out*, or *on the run*. It was yesterday, before this meeting with the doctors, and this time, I was able to make quick work of a little unexpected window of opportunity.

I'd been meeting a lot of people on my rounds of the various events, but my *best* candidates weren't exactly out and about, bopping into the magic show and piping up in mental-illness presentations. My best prospects lay quietly ebbing in their rooms.

Dolly had Alzheimer's, and must have been close to 90. I'd been hanging out in the breezeway one early evening when her daughter — out for a smoke — and I had struck up a conversation. I'd been a smoker once, and had quit not so much for my health as because the inhalation of the nicotinic fumes no longer gave any pleasure. When I was exhausted with a splitting headache and unyielding ligaments, somehow nicotine didn't make things better, or carbon monoxide and those 834 other distinct chemical byproducts.

Anyway, she had Dolly along in the wheelchair, and although the old girl was quite close to delirium, we made eye contact. Even when I couldn't make any strong connection otherwise, such as through conversation, I always tried for eye contact.

Eye contact *is* a conversation of sorts. People that can't really talk well anymore, or even just temporarily, or babies that are pre-verbal, or invalids with limiting appliances or instruments blocking their speech or hearing.... Well, they do compensate with other means of communication — eye contact more than anything, and after that, gestures: hands, shoulders, posture. People are inherently communicators, whether they can speak or not, and the eyes speak, and they listen.

I looked at Dolly, and she looked back at me. She was frail, her trimmed white hair brittle and thin, her papery skin laden with veins and dry patches, but her eyes were still deep brown, almost black, though her eyelids were lined with the wrinkles of a long and well-lived life. She was tired, and confused, but she looked at me, and I looked at her, wishing I could help somehow. Her gaze held and exuded knowledge, and somehow, as her eyes held mine, I knew that she knew, that she felt two things: the desire on my part to help, and my sympathetic yearning. The other thing she knew? She knew I was also looking for some help from her. She didn't know how — how could she? — but I felt the same yearning from her.

She *wanted* to help *me*.

The next morning — yesterday — she got her chance. She'd passed away in the night, and I'd run into Maisie, her daughter, on her way to the breezeway for a smoke, a much needed smoke after the long vigil of the night — her first smoke as an adult orphan.

I knew from experience the way cigarettes sometimes served as life's punctuation marks, as mileposts.

Dolly still lay in her room, and they wouldn't move her until after some other family had paid their last respects — a brother and a grandchild. After giving Maisie my condolences, and seeing her light up a second one, I rolled up to Dolly's room in Two East, and just poked my chair in briefly. She was alone, still and silent in death, and someone had pulled the sheet up to cover her head.

I backed out, wheeled my chair a few feet toward the hall-end window that was beaming the early sunshine in, and sat quietly. Dolly's room was near the end of the hall, so there wasn't much traffic.

I had managed to close my eyes, and got in a good ten, twelve minutes. It was my first time visiting in the shell of a female's body. In these circumstances, it didn't seem to matter much which gender the subject was. Even so, I didn't really have any opportunity or inclination to try out anything that would have been gender related. Once I got in, I stayed there quietly with the sheet over my face — her face. I didn't test Dolly's intuition, her maternality, or her superior left-brain creativity — there was nobody to flirt with.

People arrived, and I slipped quietly back into my own self, and left them to their grieving and respect paying.

So Dolly had helped me with the increased strength I needed for this session with my medical team.

Perhaps it was a little of a cat-and-mouse game. It seemed the doctors were playing out a bit of their own professional agenda, trying to pawn it off as all "what's best for you, the patient." Of course, they had no inkling of my own little bit of hidden agenda, either.

If only they knew! Cat and mouse. Which is which? A little of both.

It wasn't as if I could really refuse to go along with their idea. I really couldn't buck the system.

Jidalco, my rheumatologist, and Wade, my GP internist, wanted to move me to a hospital. Jidalco did, at any rate. Wade may have been a little less enthusiastic about the transfer.

"You see," Dr. Jidalco reasoned, "we don't know what causes many autoimmune diseases, and even when we find effective treatments, we're not always sure, or even a *little* sure, why they work. And when they work at all, it's very inconsistent. It can be a miracle for one patient, and for another, ineffective, or even seem to make it worse."

"We're not sure I even *have* an autoimmune condition," I pointed out, repeating something Jidalco had told me, and which I had discussed many times with Wade.

The two doctors looked at each other. Jidalco's beard pointed at Wade, then at me.

Wade took up the thread. "There's a theory that all these great variety of AI illnesses — the arthritics, the Lupus, the Cherg-Strauss, the Scleroderma, the common, the rare, and all the as-yet-unnamed or even unrecognized disorders, like yours perhaps — well, this theory says that there are no autoimmune diseases. Rather, there is one big autoimmune umbrella, and what we now recognize as distinct diseases or disorders are actually all variations of the same underlying imbalance or immunosystem flaw. Furthermore, they theorize that not only is it *not* rare, it's omnipresent. Everybody has it, just as everybody gets old. It may even be closely related to the mechanisms of aging itself. I call it a *flaw*, but it may not even *be* a flaw. It might be a necessary feature of some unrecognized interrelation of immunity and aging."

Jidalco stopped combing his beard with his fingers and pointed it at my feet again, which meant he was actually looking somewhere up above my head as he spoke. "In many cases, we take a shotgun approach, especially in non-responsive and undiagnosed or idiopathic cases like yours, because without a named variant that we can apply precedented best practices to, our only choice is to try various protocols that have worked on cases or symptoms that may show similarities to your unnamed bundle of pathologies."

*Specimen. Specimen! Specimen. SPECIMEN. **Specimen.** Specimen.*

It kept running through my head now as he droned on. *Specimen.*

They wanted me to go to the hospital, not to give me more care, better care, but to study me. They wanted to find out what was happening. Which of their shotgun shells was lowering my WBCs, abilifying my bilirubins, declensing my lymph nodulations, and depronating my decathetated squat assessment.

I *knew* what was happening, the *why*, and as much as what I knew could be of great interest to these doctors and other clinical professionals, they might not even believe it. They would most certainly resist seriously considering the possibility.

I'd been toying with sharing my findings, because it was hard keeping it all to myself, but I had to be careful — *very* careful.

It isn't the time, and these aren't the guys... I don't think.

I told them I'd think about it. There could actually be some advantages to moving my gig — my little treatment development system — to the larger, busier hospital setting. However, I had sort of found a rhythm at the Manor, knew my way around, and had a supply of treatment candidates — not a reliable supply, not a convenient or steady or *easy* supply, but this was a center for palliative and hospice care, with its infallible — if intermittent — supply of quiet death that seemed to be serving my needs.

They might have been concerned that I was improving so rapidly that they might lose me altogether.

I was thinking the same thing. What if I felt good enough to be discharged, to go home?

The idea was a little scary, since there would be no ready supply of the dead or dying in the average apartment complex or workplace — at least not in the decent neighborhoods where I cared to live and work.

When Wade and Jidalco showed up again during the next morning's rounds, I felt run down again, but they were clearly determined to move me to County. What could I do? I needed some autonomy. I needed access to departing and departed patients, and I needed to stay in the game, at least while I was figuring out this new mode of survival. There would certainly be... *possibilities*... in a 700-bed hospital that I hadn't experienced in a 60-bed nursing and convalescent home.

Still, I didn't just completely surrender. I worked out a little deal.

Months ago, I had worked through and drained this year's annual deductible, but then I had rapidly spent my way through my plan threshold in several weeks. I was down to 75% coverage, and the bills were accumulating. In return for my availability and consent to studies, their research funding would cover the balances that I would have to pay, eventually. I hadn't worried much about it, about a big healthcare debt, when I thought I was dying. Now, it had become a concern.

By that afternoon, I was in the med transport, making the 15-mile cross-suburban journey to County Hospital. Fortunately, I could sit and look out the transport window. My previous transport, to the Manor, had been flat on my back in an ambulance. I hated riding like that, able to see only wires, poles, and tree canopies.

Now, I watched people, cars, buildings, parks, children, junk, and strip malls.

Miles of scenery that I'd seen hundreds, even thousands, of times looked different now, with this new perspective. My newly acquired awareness of the death that surrounds us all, resting and burbling behind veils, screens, and walls; of the way the ultimate fate of all flesh, the final and unavoidable human disposition has become sanitized — it takes a heightened perspective to bring it back into focus. The outward signs, outpopping manifestations of grief and love and memory, such as those little roadside memorials for car accidents, elicited a new feeling from me now — the white plastic crosses, stapled polaroids and pink ribbons and silk flowers, and flasks of Captain Morgan, teddy bears, maybe a bag of pork rinds....

I'd never realized how many funeral homes sat between Wynneboro and West Gruber.

As so often occurs when one rides and thinks, I lapsed into reverie, and mused about how I might make a life of my affliction and this new lifestyle it required.

Could I move to San Francisco, keeping watch from the footings of the Golden Gate bridge, waiting for the steady stream of suicidals that I'd heard use that romantic and scenic russet span for their last despairing drop? I could walk them out on the pedestrian walkway, getting to know them a little, as I would need that for my purposes later. Would they wonder why I wasn't trying to talk them out of it?

No, wouldn't work.

How many would-be suicides took that walk and chickened out when the bay wind blew the cold fog against their shaking will, when they saw the whitecaps and jolly boardsailers below? And the whole matter of the bodies; how many of them simply washed to unavailability out to sea, or sank or became shark snack, or most often, probably bits of all three—a bit down to the bottom, a few bits drifting off sunsetward where the Pacific stretches and stretches blank and pacific, and a bit of a scavenged snack. I'd end up racing from the bridge to the shoreline, and trying to learn to meditate while riding a kite board, or chasing the Coast Guard cutters or the marine ambulances that do manage to pick up the floaters.

As I tripped through these reveries of possibility, the snag, the catch, the thwarter, was so often *that single inescapable requirement that I had to have at least some small acquaintance with the departed.* I couldn't just linger in mortuaries, or unlicensed west-Philly funeral homes, nor wander around war zones, or get a job servicing the refrigeration equipment in hospices. Having ready access to dead strangers wouldn't help me, the constraining inconvenience being that I had to *know* my decedent.

I couldn't impersonate a grief counselor, or become one, for the same reason: by the time they came on duty, it was too late to get acquainted with the mourned.

I mused thusly as the transport motored along, my mind deep in relaxed concentration, poking at ideas that might allow escape from what looked like an inevitable pattern of precarious health facility exploitation, when I felt myself pulled, yanked even. My eyes were closed, and the sun had been shining on my face—I had felt its warmth—but now, immediately and jarringly, all was different.

What's happening?

It was pitch dark, the air cloying, and I was suddenly not in myself. I snapped open my eyes and nothing changed—the same darkness, but eyes-open darkness. Upon my body, I felt stiff clothing, and when I moved my fingers—stiff fingers—I felt cushioned satin.

I remembered panicking before, when the surge of panic had jolted me loose. *Mike.* Well, I *needed* to panic again. I drew a rough lungfull of that dankness and screamed, hoarsely, through inelastic vocal chords— not a word, not even a thought, just a simple bellowed exhalation of fear and expulsion.

Snap!

I shook myself again and felt the sun on my face, and opened my eyes as the transport accelerated and pulled forward when the light turned green.

I saw the black hearse then, crossing in front of us, turning, passing, and dwindling behind. A casketed inhabitant rode off now, back the way we had come.

I wonder if the driver heard his passenger scream.

I would have to be careful. If not somebody I knew — perhaps even knew well — the idea played through my mind that it could have been somebody I'd been acquainted with or... hell, maybe somebody I simply made fairly significant eye contact with in an elevator five, ten years ago.

Maybe it wasn't so hopeless, after all. Still, I would have to be careful when falling into relaxed reveries out and about, especially when near funeral homes, mausoleums, and medical centers — and hearses.

I'd spent most of my life in Southeastern Pennsylvania.

It made me wonder. In a young adult's life, somebody in their late twenties, thirties, or early forties, reasonably social, working, living, partying, attending, representing, public transportation, business meetings, interviews, walking through crowds, parks, concerts, sporting events....

How many strangers does the average person meet, see, or have meaningful eye contact with? 10,000? A hundred thousand? Probably somewhere in between. There must be some kind of gathered research on this somewhere.

When you stand in an auditorium, or on a soundstage, and give a speech or do a routine or a skit or sing a song; when you look out across a sea of heads and see there eyes of 2000 people, 4000 eyes, and they look back at you.... Is that meaningful enough?

As we waited on a July day at the intersection of Old York Road and Sumneytown Pike, I closed my eyes and blocked out the sounds of traffic, and the motor. I concentrated not on relaxing this time, but on remembering. I remembered those five seconds, just moments ago, when I had been suddenly and unexpectedly resheathed in that hearse. I relived that five seconds and felt around inside there, or rather looked within *and* beyond the five seconds, to examine my own recollection somewhere behind them — deep, very deep. I knew it was there, and looked for the thread that led back out, back to a past connection between me and... somebody, however brief. Perhaps I'd been close to that somebody, or maybe that somebody had just, improbably, rolled past me again on perhaps their last ride. Gradually, the feeling of darkness and quilted satin left me, and I felt a sense of thread unspooling, like sparkling monofilament whirring out of a spinning reel, and a picture began to take form.

It's a carnival night one summer, on fire-company fairgrounds, many years ago. I stand on dusty, beaten down grass, accompanied by the calliope sound of cheap thrill rides as other kids walk by with cotton candy. I'm eight years old, playing a wheel game, putting quarters down on numbers, cards, and suits. The big white upright wheel with all the nails on it spins and the metal clicker click-click-clicks, *and I win. I play hearts, and I win. I play again, and win again. I have a big mound of quarters, and the people I'm with need to move on. It's not my own family: I'm summer-visiting family friends.*

A man, not an old man, but a wise-ass type, probably one of the firemen, says, "Get this kid out of here. We don't need hot streaks like that." He's wearing suspenders, has gray eyes and round glasses, and combs his hair straight back.

Is it him?

Everything started to blank out, until....

Then there was more, as though remembering the scene itself brought back more of it, more continuity.

He raises his chin, then offers a quick headshake, like saying, without saying, "Get out of here, kid, your people are leaving." He isn't staffing the booth, and he isn't a player; he's just hanging around.

I resent his unneeded involvement. I've never felt like such a winner, not like this.

I put three quarters down on even. He shakes his head and walks off, and I know he's going off to find Mr. Healey, Chad's dad. Chad Healey is at my side, my pal, and he's with me, but he knows this can't go on forever, even though I want it to.

"C'mon," he says, "that guy's getting mad. We should go."

"I'm winning."

I lose on that spin, and quickly gather up my six bucks worth of quarters in the front of my T-shirt, and give Chad a handful. We run off to find his family, and his mother is a little ashamed that I've won so much.

As we walk off, a man looks at me – a different man. He's been watching, I can tell, but this is the first I've seen of him. He possesses a peering, judging look on his face. He's large, middle-aged with dark brown hair, and walks with a cane. He leans on it as he watches us, especially me.

A siren blasted, and an ambulance passed us. Now back in my transport, I startled, and came up fully from the depths as we arrived at County Hospital.

I studied the memories, examining them. At first, I had thought it was the jerky guy, the first one, the wise-ass guy, but it wasn't. *It was the man with the cane.* As we'd walked past him, he said, "Kid, you're too young. They shouldn't let you enjoy that so much."

I'm sure he had more to say, but then we were gone, off to buy some popcorn balls and ice cream with my winnings.

It was him.

I would never have remembered that night, if I hadn't just visited that human husk, found the thread, and followed it back deep into my own past.

Did it mean anything? Not really, but I couldn't stop thinking about it, all the same. All those years ago, I had walked away a winner. But as Bret Harte said, the only sure thing about luck is that it will change.

Chapter 8

I needed *an hour*.

Snatches of relief, fifteen minutes of Mike, twenty minutes in the Manor's morgue, good old Dolly, and the others as short or shorter, had created an *appetite*.

That's not the right word, nor is dependency, *but* sustenance *might work. Yes....*

These brief sessions were in actuality *sustaining* me, bolstering and supporting my fragile health. Somehow, I needed to arrange an extended session, see what benefit I could get from a real, solid hour or more of restorative possession. I had more research questions, and perhaps the answers lay in getting more than a briefly snatched body, more than a transient treatment of short and furtive duration.

So, in my new surroundings, newly submerged within the bustling, big sea of systematic healthcare; hundreds of specialists and a thousand support workers and technicians; all the departments and the equipment; shipping and receiving and plant operations; maternity and geriatrics; birth and death; joy and sickness; relief and hope; loving and living and dying.... I began to plot my next treatment. It needed to be *more* — lengthier, deeper, more energetic.

I had a private room in the new state-of-the-art wing of County called *Sanctuary* — not *The* Sanctuary, just *Sanctuary*. The main comfort fixture in this new-agey unit, other than my amazing hospital bed, was a clever bench sofa that could convert into a night cot for family. This was not your old-school box-shaped hospital room. With its warm homey pleated drapes, a big bed, swooping contoured satin mauve walls, polished hardwood floors, and vaguely apartmentish appointings, this medical cocoon was meant to be, nay, *designed* to be, a nurturing, healing environment. It deserved substantial credit for being far more pleasant than what it replaced, those familiar modern, 50s, 60s, 70s clean, clinical white-walled, square-cornered hospital rooms. Ironically, though perhaps not so surprisingly, it felt not entirely unlike the converted 19th-century mansion summer-home setting I'd just left at The Manor.

Sanctuary was just one part of a huge health campus, with wings that still had the "old-fashioned" modern shared rooms and cold-cube architecture, with steel-doored locker closets and venetian-blinded windows. The main complex had six floors, with adjoining medical office buildings, nearby but disconnected outpatient surgical centers, therapy centers, sleep specialty centers, and whole buildings devoted solely to colon scopings.

Modern hospitals like County are like icebergs. You see all the public spaces, the patient-serving departments, the outward-facing features and services; ER, OR, Acute and Intensive care, a high-security psychiatric ward, patient wings, cafeterias, coffee shops, atriums and courtyards, radiology and nuclear and imaging, maternity, EEG and EKG, and so on and so forth. But there are yards and yards of corridors that are off the public map, that are "below the waterline" and not really obvious to the public.

I needed to explore both above and below the waterline at County. I couldn't look as if hurrying, but I couldn't really afford to waste a lot of time either, because except for ten seconds banging on satin and screaming with the lungs of a man who'd worried about me developing a gambling habit three decades ago, I hadn't had any life-force sustenance for nearly four days. Enveloped in a health-care cornucopia, there woulda-coulda-shoulda been lots more opportunities to fill my unusual new needs, but County was a bolted-down, multi-system, thousand-part machine, whereas the Manor had offered a quaintness and informality that allowed certain laissez's and leeways. Here were locked doors, patrolled sections, and security-coded departments.

My energy and vitality were draining, and I probably had something like twenty-four to thirty-six hours before my joints started giving out and my extremities started jittering. And the headaches....

My first instinct was to go straight for the meat and potatoes — well, the meat, anyway — and find the hospital's morgue and forensic medicine sections.

My already weakening state made this a searing temptation, but really, what was the point?

It's certainly sure to be quite a party, but... I won't know anybody there!

I had to start thinking of my circumstances as more like a romantic — or even baldly sexual — equation. As eager as I was to find my next treatment partner, I couldn't simply locate the fridge bins and help myself to a cold one.

Just like you don't just hop into bed with a lady without *some* preliminaries, I couldn't cut to the chase and hop across the ethereal synapse and occupy a cold decedent on a gurney in the iceberg's bowels down in the facility's loading dock area, just like that.

Phase one: I had to do my socializing, needed to make some friends. I really wanted to figure out how to just occupy any old cadaver, but at this point, I knew from my brief experience, and my developing instincts about the limits of my odd capability, that I required some acquaintance, however slight.

I needed to make the rounds, because in order to befriend the dead, I needed to court the dying.

Of course, it would be most efficient if I learned what I could about the floor plans and the locations of key departments. I needed to prioritize my attention upon the best wards, departments, and treatment areas for dire and terminal cases. Who would be most familiar with those particular surrounds and systems, and know the ins and outs best? Simple: the chronic patients and their peeps. Staff would know too, but unlike nurses, PAs, and techs, all of whom would be reluctant to share "inside baseball" with nosy patients, the inmates and their supporting resources would be eager to share their hard-won knowledge of *the ropes.*

I didn't go wandering off right away, as it wouldn't look right. I was a patient, after all, even if a studied one and no longer an acute one at this point. Still, I spent a couple hours in my suite, N222, resting and studying the hospital welcome folder. I familiarized myself with the breathless publicity on this new patient-centric paradigm, and made some notes on where I might find key nodes of interest.

When my nurses had been lulled into thinking I was simply another quietly ebbing patient, I slipped into my wheelchair, took the long way out and around the long loop to the main crosscorridors, and headed two levels down to the atrium lobby to begin my reconnoitering.

I approached the big circular greeting desk, huge at probably twenty feet across, with a hollow wheel of shiny wood-grain countertop.

A single occupant sat there, a middle-aged lady with short, permed, black hair, a bulby nose, and a helpful smile above a powderblue jacket. She sat in front of a countersunk touchscreen.

"Is there a chapel?" I asked after we exchanged the preliminary greetings.

Of course, I already knew the answer, but I was laying groundwork, leaving impressions, creating my personal brand for my stay at County.

"Well, something like that," she said, clearly not happy to have to equivocate. "They call it *The Tranquilitorium* now."

"*Really?*" I said, exaggerating my eyebrow raising and chin stretching, "Oh, I see, yes. Now we have *holiday events, fellowship sessions,* and *tranquilitoriums,* instead of *Christmas receptions, services,* and *chapels?*"

Nothing wrong with this, of course—much more inclusive, more all-embracing, than the old way—though with some wavering clarity sacrificed and charm lost. Again, I was new here, and wanted to leave an air of righteousness and spiritual harmony in my wake.

She smiled, obviously well trained in health care and institutional reception: don't agree, don't disagree, don't engage, and don't disengage; just provide information without editorial inflection.

"Is there a map of the hospital?" I asked.

"We do have a floor plan." She reached down, and then placed a brochure on the wood-grain in front of me.

In my wheelchair, the counter sat roughly at my eye level. The fanfold brochure was green and cream, slick and shiny, and about the thickness of a small gas station road map. Its cover image displayed walking doctors in white lab coats with clipboards and stethoscopes in the foreground, a phalanx of them—a woman, two men, three more men, and men and women receding out of focus into the distance.

I took it back to N222 and, sitting on my crescent windowseat, opened it.

Chapter 9

Two days later, lying in the Blodwynn room, I tried to feel my way to a place one floor down and slightly to the east.

Blodwynn tranquilitorium, a public/private space on the 2nd floor, had navy brocaded stuffed chairs, a couple of Grey Poupon vinyl sofas against the walls, and some A/V equipment tucked into one corner. It was nice, quiet, infrequently used, and situated not quite directly over the morgue, but pretty darn close.

My head was throbbing. My extremities were numb, my joints spasming, and my brain fogged with fatigue.

I had spent the past two days trying to be social, seeking the friendly dying, and casing the place to find where they kept the bodies — all the little details I needed to continue my investigations and clandestine treatments. All the while, I needed to humor the doctors, dodge the nurses and orderlies, and tolerate the useless official treatments, tests, and evaluations.

Being social among the ailing can be a challenging bit of a tiptoe. Not only are they *not* in the mood for chitchat, but they wonder why the hell you *are*. You're not, of course, and if you try to fake it, you're just an ass, plain and simple, adding irritation and annoyance to the pre-existing discomfort brought on by dire ailments, invasive treatments, and hand-wringing relatives.

Yet said relatives often felt more inclined to talk, even listen, as more often than not, their expiring kin weren't saying much, and they *needed* the release that conversation gave them. Sometimes, they became my go-betweens, my introductions, or simply unwitting advance men, providing some valuable details for when my chance arose to cultivate a new short-lived friendship.

All this cultivation took time and energy, though, and as the minutes, hours, and mealtimes passed, I began to drag, to feel the weight of time upon my strength and stamina. I needed to separate myself from myself. I needed the rejuvenating jolt of a session, a solid, time-spanning session, in the cold frame of a recently deceased.

The task of finding treatment partners was much harder here, despite its being a big hospital. Focusing on the morbid, which had become my job, really, brought to my awareness several important *factors* and *circumstances.*

Factor: 17 admissions die in this facility every week, on average, with another 14 weekly ER fatalities.

Factor: it contains 427 beds.

Factor: average admission duration is 1.9 days.

Circumstance: the dying don't get around much. Even so, many have a little flurry of activity, however brief—a day or two before succumbing.

I had figured out these things mainly through research on the internet computer in the family lounge, which sat down the hall near the nurse's station, and by asking a few discreet questions of the technicians when I waited or was getting prepped for tests or procedures.

Knowing the numbers, though, really didn't help that much. It made me feel more vulnerable, less secure, and a bit overwhelmed. It all meant that something like 70% of the people that I saw in a given day in the rooms, halls, units and centers, whether visiting, getting treated, or recuperating, would be gone two days later.

It meant the chances of my finding, acquaintancing, and then successfully following a dying, then dead, individual to a quiet and tranquil *post-mortem* rendezvous were frighteningly slim.

It's not working. Time to revise my approach.

Methods I'd developed in the nursing home took too long here, and despite some promising leads, none were bearing fruit yet. I needed mass-market methods. I needed reach and efficiency. I needed one-to-many communications.

Thus, I now sat ensconced in the Blodwynn tranquilitorium, engaged in phase two of my ingeniously haphazard two-step plan.

Phase one had been the souls survey. I had spent as much time as possible, from late morning until mid-afternoon, in the acute-care wings of the hospital, mostly in the family lounges and hallways, my butt stuck to my wheelchair, trying to look despairing and disinterested. I'd had a fair amount of practice at that, but now I was keenly interested in these people, listening, looking, feeling.

Telltale signs came to me through all three of those senses, and some unmentioned senses, too.

Listening is obvious—a brother and sister talking in low voices about their father, or a neice and her aunt whispering about her sister—

but many people don't talk that much when their lives are fraught with illness, morbidity, and impending finality. Some do, of course—the yackers, the ones that never shut up anyway, in any circumstance—but many people quiet down a lot in these circumstances. If they're with family, they communicate with single words, short sentences, body language, eye contact.

That's when *looking* becomes the more valuable tool, even at somebody alone. *Especially* when they're alone.

Earlier, during that loitering and reconnoitering phase, I had seen a man moving toward the family lounge, haggard and unkempt, holding his phone in front of him like a piece of food that had fallen on a dirty sidewalk, like a soiled burrito—unwanted, but you're stuck with it, when there's no convenient disposal for this inconvenient item.

I could tell where he was heading, so I moved on ahead, but with some strategic discretion passed the lounge entrance, and felt him enter behind me. I spun my chair and watched him through the safety glass— for some reason they constructed these little boxcar-sized spaces with half-walls, topped with transparent safety panels reaching to the ceiling, so there was really no privacy for anybody in or out.

He was texting, and his mouth quivered. Somewhere in there, he was crying, but being a man, he cried tearlessly. His eyes remained dull and dry, but his mouth betrayed his inner child.

When he headed back to the ward, I followed discreetly to where he waged the waning vigil. When I got the chance— when he left again for a few minutes—I went in and got acquainted with his relative.

Ralf wasn't especially glad, or mad, or sad, or feeling had, to see me. I didn't know him, and he didn't know me, but I reached for his hand, and held it. He briefly opened his eyes and looked at me, nodded, squeezed once, and then relaxed before closing his eyes again.

It was enough, but I stayed a few more minutes. It would have felt cheap to just go.

Nonetheless, I didn't want to overstay my welcome either. The phone fellow or another family member might return, and wonder. Tales of cats and lapdogs cultivated to comfort the dying in quaint nursing centers were one thing, but creepy human strangers visiting deathbeds unsolicited? Probably not welcome.

I patted Ralf's hand again four or five minutes later, and again he opened his eyes, this time looking a little puzzled. Then he moaned something and finally closed his eyes, as much, perhaps, to shut the interruptive me out as to return to his palliated stupor.

I repeated this circumstance, with minor variations, twice more that evening, with other candidates in varying stages of decline. I also received some good eye contact in the hallway near the dialysis suites on the critical care ward.

The next morning, having learned that people most commonly passed during the wee hours, I headed back to the tranquilitorium. I had some reasonable expectation that perhaps one of the four or five souls surveyed, perhaps even more than one, had moved on spiritually in the night, and physically to the morgue that occupied a space perhaps no more than forty feet or so beneath me at an oblique vector.

I was just settling into my induced reverie, when I had to cope with my own interruptive distraction.

It's different *in there* — in transient occupation of a recently vacated human shell — and familiar at the same time. Except for the very few ethereally adventurous, most people are born, live, and die having experienced only self-contained, and self-referenced, consciousness.

I couldn't really claim to possess any seriously cultivated insight in this area. I didn't start out trying to climb my comprehension into another universe, another era, a previous life or incarnation, or even into the abandoned husks of the departed. I merely tried a non-pharmacological, biorhythmic alternative for relieving pain and fatigue, and inadvertently thwocked my consciousness into a body recently left behind for the great beyond — and found the experience therapeutic.

I didn't study Grant and Kelsey or Fraser or Felkin, or Robert Monroe or Jane Roberts or the Maharishi or Deepak Chopra — at least not until after I had discovered the subjective usefulness of these unconventional, and completely unknown and undeveloped, therapies. Even then, such dabblings weren't because I wanted further development, greater insight, or enhancement of perception. I'd proceeded for baser reasons — for greater health, for relief of pain and interruption of further physical deterioration. Not to mention survival.

I was tired of feeling sick, and sick of feeling tired.

Sometimes, in sleep, when you're experiencing a detailed dream, the surroundings, the relationships, the setting and activities are so distinct, so different from your real waking world, it feels like you're somebody else.

Being *inside*... well, it's a little bit like that, but you're not asleep; you're aware.

I'd inhabited abandoned interiors only a handful of times, but already I felt that my knack was improving with practice, settling in a little deeper and better each time. This wasn't the case that last time, in the med transport, where I only had seconds, but during the previous visits, when I felt a little more secure and centered in the decedent each time, it had been true.

It wasn't like being in my own skin. It was temporary, and *felt* temporary. It was a borrowed being, and felt secondhand. My perceptions, my mind/body synchronicity, my coordination and senses... everything seemed significantly dulled and distant. In some ways, it had a drugged feel about it — not a heightening drug, more like a darkening or dimming drug, like anesthesia.

However, I still noticed things specific to each experience, and the things they had in common as well. One thing I noticed right away, and confirmed each time I inhabited another's shell: it wasn't completely empty in there.

That was sort of spooky.

The soul was gone. Otherwise, what I'd accomplished would have been simply impossible.

A human soul takes up all the volume in a body's spiritual vessel, leaving no spare space.

By this time, as I rolled around the halls of County seeking empty vessels, I knew this intuitively. Even so, some remnants held on. Perhaps it was simply the scientific reality, as the brain and central nervous system formed a chemical matrix, at some level pure physics. I found that I could actually perceive little bits and pieces of memory left behind by the departed soul.

I called these *inklings*.

Chapter 10

I wheeled into the Blodwyn Tranquilitorium, checked that it was truly empty, and tucked my wheelchair over with the other equipment so it looked like part of the collection. Then I stepped quietly back behind the last sofa on the opposite side of the room, where the light was a bit dim, farthest from the entrance. I actually moved the sofa a little, and repositioned one of the armchairs. Then I took one last good look around, and lowered myself to lie on my back on the floor. I could have sat on a sofa or in one of the chairs, and would even have been largely out of sight that way, but I wanted the room to truly look empty. For one thing, I couldn't be found, or traced, or in any way accounted for, if I remained *completely* out of sight. I also wanted as much privacy as possible. After all, I needed an hour, and would get more time in my purposeful reverie—more *duration*—if I were *incognito*. It was even possible that if some devoted individual came seeking quiet tranquility, they could come and go in peace without noticing me, and I could pursue my own tranquil ends uninterrupted.

Also, by staying hidden, I might learn something that I might not have had an opportunity to learn, when in plain sight.

It was relatively quiet and completely still, although a hospital is a bustling institution. The background hum of that bustle was still perceptible—muffled, muted, but still out there. Itwas funny though, how a muted bustle could be somehow lulling, even hypnotic. I could even feel faint vibrations, as if some pulsing equipment functioned not too distant from where I lay on the floor.

MRI? Dialysis?

I'd always found vibrations of a certain character, if fairly consistent, actually to be conducive to relaxation. Automobile motors, a ship's diesel, or the waterfall thrum of a 737—these mechanical throbs, when body is weary and mind still, rival artificial pharmaceuticals for soporificity.

I reached beta relatively quickly, and then, because of the distractions of throb fog, which kept resetting my attempts at further depth, it took another twenty minutes or so to reach delta. Upon reaching a delta wave and achieving separation, I didn't go straight down, then east. Nor did I go east, then down. It was as though the attracting body drew me right to itself, straight down on the oblique vector, down and east simultaneously. I slid right into the mortuary or morgue, and there lay Ralf.

I didn't even really notice if he was on a gurney or in a drawer, or some other situation. I merged right into his interstitial ethers, without hesitation. Indeed, it felt a lot like when you've been out too late and are happy to see your bed, and the next thing you know, you're in the bed and under the covers, without even seeming to have climbed into it.

I was ready for this.

I quickly reoriented myself to his shape and prone position. Oddly enough, I could actually remain upright while occupying a prone corpus, or, though it would be unusual, I could similarly remain spiritually longitudinal while in possession of a standing unit. Of course, it felt more natural to orient properly, and certainly, if I were to attempt any motion, I needed to fill out properly into the limbs and extremities.

I wasn't interested in motion, my sole objective this time being duration. Although I hadn't perused the surroundings at all, eager as I was to get the treatment initiated, I now became aware that living individuals were present.

One worked in the room with Ralf, and another very nearby, in an adjoining space. From time to time, they talked to each other room-to-room, but their voices sounded distant, watery.

I focused all of my awareness on remaining quiet, still, in full possession, yet peacefully fulfilled. I wasn't trying to feel, to explore, to move or hear or experience anything but healing. I flattened myself and let my spirit fill the space Ralf had vacated, and the nourishing replenishment of my ethereal substance proceeded, gradually, tricklingly, like a potted plant soaking cool liquid upward from the saucer.

Still, the *inklings* were there. I tried to ignore them. It seemed impolite, untoward, actually to focus on them—like looking in the medicine cabinet at a party. Yet these strong inklings were impossible to ignore.

Finally, I just let them flow through me. They were really quite meaningless, lacking as I was of their living context, so I didn't concern myself about them.

Then, something happened, not in the Ralf space, but in the Blodwyn space.

I tried to resist, tried to stay in possession, and actually succeeded for a reasonable stretch, but the interruption one floor up and a little to the west would not be resisted indefinitely.

There were people talking, arguing, in fact.

I didn't get my hour—maybe thirty, thirty-five minutes.

Then, I suddenly lay on the rug, behind the sofa, listening to an argument.

Chapter II

At first, their voices were watery too.

When people speak gently, or softly, or even in regular tones without excessive emotional curvature, human voices can backdrop near-sleep states and other relaxed conditions without disruption. Sometimes. Conversely, conversations laden with high emotion, forcefulness, stressings, firmness, and argumentation intrude upon the reverie. Furthermore, there's something about Germanic-origin, cursing-harsh sibilants, and midword, hard labial-palatal diphthongs sprinkled forcefully into dialog, which eventually causes them to infiltrate and upend any state of relaxed concentration.

I rapidly *unthwocked* from Ralf's skin, and as I reeled upward and spooled back into my own, the dueling voices gelled in my ears.

"You were here all along, while things got... while he weakened. You could have easily gotten the combination."

"And you come back too late to be helpful, too late for anything, really. And I didn't need to "get" the combination. It was right there, in a perfectly safe place — right where he put it, you *fucking* moron!"

"Now look, you had... what? Four years to write the fucking thing down somewhere safe? And I come back for his last two weeks, and it's my fucking fault he dies with the combination?"

"Yeah, it's your fucking fault, because you come back, and you've got nothing to do so you have to get all helpful. You fucking paint the closet where he had the safe propped up on a stack of 1970s yellow pages."

"How the fuck was I supposed to know he wrote the combo in there? It wasn't obvious. Why didn't you tell me? Why didn't *he* tell me?"

"He told me. I'm the one who's been here. You're the one who went to Denver, who barely wrote and rarely called. By the time you come back, he's on oxygen and falling over every time he gets up. He's not fucking responsible by this time, and he hasn't seen you for five years, and has only gotten a goofy birthday card twice."

"I sent at least three, and some funny emails."

"And he's going to trust you with this? He wrote it backwards, in mirror writing, on the back of one of the shelving boards, in pencil. Whenever he needed to get into the safe, he'd shift the shelf forward a bit, hold a mirror back there, and read off the numbers. Maybe he's a little more security conscious than to just tell you, funny-birthday-card-fuckoff-absentee-daughter, about something financially important."

"Right. Okay. Meanwhile, you're sponging off him, visiting when *you* need something, ignoring him when *he* needs something. Margo told me what you were up to. And you don't have the fucking wherewithal to take a mirror there yourself and write down the *fucking* numbers? I would think with your financial situation, and your exploitative fuckheadedness, you'd think of that first."

"Well, brainwave, I didn't really have to, did I? The fucking numbers were perfectly fucking safe right where they fucking were, *until you fucking painted them the fuck out!*"

On it went, the back and forth, the shitbrainings and fuckheadings and volleyed repetitions of two siblings, each guilty of his or her own unique stupidity, in that early pre-grief zone where it hadn't yet kicked in, really, that they'd lost a parent, and the realization that they only had two of the genuine article to lose. For these two, it sounded like they were down to zero on that count.

Of course, other little details were salted in among the cursed emphases and beratings.

Part of the problem here was that it remained unclear whether something very important resided in the mentioned safe, or if it was empty, or practically empty. The sister, who had apparently painted over the combination, held the opinion that it was probably empty, or had some inconsequential papers in it, like old birth certificates and genealogical records like 19th-century family bibles and diaries. The younger brother, who should have secured the combination when he could have, was sure the safe hid bundles of bonds, and possibly an updated will, and sheaves of weird foreign currencies—dinars and rupiyahs and riyals—and maybe even deeds to secret castles in the Hebrides.

Thus, their secondary debate raged over whether it was even worthwhile to: a) keep looking for the safe combination; b) try to contact the manufacturer to get assistance in opening it; c) contact a locksmith and try to get in legitimately, or; d) hire a criminal to break into their own property.

They ended up disagreeing to agree, and the sister stormed out and said she had to go pay her last respects.

When her brother finally left and the room fell still again, I sat up and thought about what to do. My first thought was to meet her there, without leaving the room of course.

I lay back down and slowed my breathing, relaxed all my muscles quickly, focused on non-focus, let my mind wander but then quickly harnessed it again, and once more moved through the floor and to the east.

Oddly, this time I didn't feel that pull, the attraction that had drawn me right to Ralf just a few minutes before. It felt more like a stumbling, blindly seeking and feeling my way, rather than an instant and attractive homing in. Still, after a few minutes of this, I did manage to relocate the body, and....

It wasn't working.

Like two north poles of an iron magnet pushing, repelling each other, I bounced off his body. At this moment, I learned more of the physics of—maybe *metaphysics* is a better word—this skill, this treatment, this therapy.

I could only do it once per customer.

As I tendrilled away from the body and back up and west, the watery voices came again, somehow, speaking in the room where the body lay. I recognized the female voice of the daughter among them, so I blinked rapidly, flexed a few times, and sat up, one floor above and a little ways west, in the Tranquilitorium.

What motivated me to do what I did next? Perhaps I felt just a little guilty about all this, and saw a way to use my weird talent, my gained knowledge, unselfishly. Perhaps I sided with her a little—after all, her brother seemed like a dick. Well, a little more of a dick than she was, at any rate.

There's more than one kind of lonely. A guy running a lighthouse on a breaker-beaten granite islet... he's lonely. A polar bear on a little chip-floe separated from the main berg, drifting south on a warming current... she's lonely. That long-distance runner chugging along a city sidewalk at 5 AM... lonely.

Another kind of lonely is the kind where you're surrounded by people, but they haven't any idea that you're there—because they don't know what you are, and you can't tell them. You can't exactly call a press conference or give a lecture about stuff like this. You see them, and they look at you, but you know things, feel things, are frightened of things, or perhaps do the frightening, and nobody recognizes the uniqueness. Maybe it's not even unique, just part of what you are—but not like a wooden leg or a glass eye. It's invisible to the passing glance. Maybe something changed you when you were eight years old, but you're the only one that knows about it, and nobody can see it.

Maybe that latter sort of loneliness motivated me.

I went to the other corner of the tranquilitorium, got my wheels, and pushed it out into the hallway. I had a bit more energy—not as much as I'd wanted, as I didn't get my full hour, but still, it felt good to walk again. So I walked my own chair out until I got to the elevator, and then sat in it.

The elevator chimed and the door slid open, exposing other people inside, so I backed in.

A little girl, maybe six years old, looked at me, then looked up at her mom.

"Down one floor," I said.

The little girl pushed the button for me.

Down one floor, I rolled out, and down the hall just a little ways to the east.

Chapter 12

I waited in the hall, between the morgue and the elevators, just a few yards away from the door I expected her to come out of.

I knew only her voice, and I didn't know much from hearing that, either. Well, she could curse like a Lycoming County roofing mechanic.

When she appeared, I looked at her only briefly — at her face, that is — as she came through the door. She stood about 5'4", with light brown hair the color of unfinished mahogany.

I didn't look harder because it didn't serve my purposes to have eye contact. I needed to give her information in a mysterious way, but a disarming way. In fact, I wanted actually to *repel* any curiosity or suspicion about the information, or at least about where it came from. Better yet, she should possibly *recoil* from considering its origin.

So I didn't look at her. I crossed my arms in a non-symmetrical way and lolled my head to one side a little, careful not to overdo it. Then, in a sort of groanish whisper, I repeated over and over my brief phrase:

"Eighty-two. Twelve. Thirty-three. Eighty-two. Twelve. Thirty-three. Eighty-two. Twelve. Thirty-three."

As she passed me, I raised my voice, actually sharpened it a bit: "*Eighty-Two.Twelve....*"

She hesitated. She'd never seen me before. She'd never heard me before, and had no idea that I'd heard her.

I kept my head tilted and my arms awkwardly crossed as I continued to drone my numbers.

"What did you say?" She stopped now, next to my wheelchair, and looked at me.

I repeated the numbers in my strange monotone.

She came around in front of me, and looked down at me. "Are you trying to tell me something?"

"Eighty-two. Twelve. Thirty-three."

I did glance up at her, but didn't shift my position or change my expression. I returned my gaze to my bent knees and chair footrests, and continued with the numbers.

She finally gave up trying to make a dialogue of it, took a pen and piece of scrap paper out of her purse, and wrote them down.

Eighty-Two. Twelve. Thirty-Three.

"Thank you," she whispered, and went on her way.

With that, the sequence of numbers, the *inkling* that had rattled around in Ralf's skull when I'd paid my visit, passed back to the woman who'd painted out the combination on the shelving in her father's safe closet.

Those three numbers were the only clear remnant in Ralf's skull, but they had been fairly strong. What else could they be but the lock's combination?

Old Ralf may have had to use a mirror every time he needed to open the safe when he was alive and winding down his last days, but in death, and afterward, it had remained firmly on his mind.

I wasn't very happy with the way that last session had gone, and not just because it had been cut short, or because I'd been interrupted and hadn't gotten the full hour I needed so badly.

Something else about it had been unsatisfying, unfulfilling, even considering its shortened duration. My treatments were becoming like a thirst, or a dependency, but this last session, the Ralf session, had left the thirst poorly slaked.

I had learned something important, though: perhaps I only had one shot, and couldn't use a body more than once. I would have to test that possibility again. Then again, maybe it was just Ralf, something particular about him, but I didn't think so. It had felt as if a membrane had hardened, toughened, when I withdrew the first time, and actually repelled or excluded me when I tried to re-enter.

I was already thinking about another hypothesis to test. I thought over all these experiences—just a handful, really—and began to wonder about other patterns, other consistencies, other commonalities, as well as uniquenesses from one session to another.

A strong feeling—an instinct—rose out of this. I remembered how great I felt after that very first, accidental possession into Mike back at the home. It had lasted about twenty minutes. With Ralf, I'd spent at least twenty minutes, maybe more like twenty-five. Despite the equal or even greater amount of time, I didn't feel nearly as good—as *revived*—afterward.

Was there something different?

Well, a lot of things *were* different, but I had a feeling about this, and was eager to test it out.

I've been in a handful of medical facilities, and a number of funeral homes and county morgues, and I've seen a lot of bodies.

Such institutions have... well, they have institutionalized modern society's recoil at the realities of death. Unless you're expecting to see a body — for instance, at a viewing, or when tasked to ID a friend or relative at a morgue — these institutions have devised clever routines for not offending sensitive eyes. They make sure people that have expired in inconvenient places — but really, is there such a thing as a *convenient* place to die? — don't *intrude* on their way to the morgue, hearse, or postmortem autopsy.

Some hospitals have special rolling carts, clean, seamless stainless-steel containers on wheels that look like they could be holding anything — equipment, supplies, roving imaging machinery, whatever — but look closely. They're just over seven feet long, about two feet wide, and they're much deeper than they need to be because, if they made them shallower, it would be obvious: this is a rolling cadaver conveyance.

My aunt once lived in a house that had a corpse window. The small home, several hundred years old, had a narrow, winding, enclosed stairway, at the top of which was a little window. My aunt explained that in the old days, if somebody died upstairs and stiffened up with rigor mortis, they couldn't easily bend the bodies around that twisty stairway. So, out the little corpse window they went.

That was probably around the same time as the death portraits. In the Victorian era, when photography was still young but no longer quite the novelty it had been around Civil War times, the fashion of mourning portraits arose. Families would dress their mourned ones in their Sunday finest and get a professional photograph taken. At one time, the average person's greatest likelihood of being photographed was arguably when they were dead. As personal cameras and photos of the living became more common, these death snaps gradually fell into history.

Perhaps I would soon come into a time, and a range of new activities, when having my subjects dressed in their Sunday finest would be far preferable to the modern hospital alternative of a papery gown with no back.

Many health facilities, as an alternative to the stainless "hot dog cart" of body conveyance, used the pup-tent variation.

Whereas the metal vehicle was a tank, heavy artillery, an armored vehicle, the tent was an adapted standard gurney with a light cuboid frame of PVC tubing or graphite composite struts, with a white muslin cover. When people see a pale oblong with square corners moving whitely through the hospital halls, and think "how ghostly," they're right on target.

The next chance I got to take a decent treatment, my subject lay parked in just such an oblong, at the end of the hall in the basement, waiting her turn to slide into a drawer in the mortuary. Things were a little crowded that day.

I'd decided that the most important thing, the factor missing from my treatments since that first one with Mike at the nursing home, hadn't been that I could see him and was lying right next to him. Nor was it that he was extremely... uh... recent in his abandonment, in his separation from his earthly husk—his *freshness*.

It was *activity*. Mike and I, when merged, had panicked and bounced off the walls and out the door, and caromed down the hall bleating unintelligibly.

In all these subsequent treatments, I'd been trying to remain as still, quiet, and unobtrusive as possible. Instinct dictated there was good reason for this: I didn't want any attention. Hey, if corpuses started wandering around the halls, people might take notice. I was beginning to think, however, that in order to get the *boost* I needed, I had to move, to really *possess* and interact with the abandoned tissues, bones, ligaments, and muscles.

Of course, I couldn't be sure; thus the need to test. I had to answer these new *research questions*, to evaluate each one, but this strong impression nagged at me: it would not be enough just to *occupy*; I had to *activate*.

Babby Oppfeloffigan lay in transit, but in way-station status. This wasn't one of the shiny brushed-steel *hot dog carts*. She occupied a *covered wagon*, the lighter pup tent-type covered gurney. That was fine— seemed less confining than all that dark, claustrophobic metal.

Because of the way the various wings and wards had formed organically, as the original little 'tween-rural-and-suburban hospital appendaged into a gigantic mednetwork complex in a growth spurt, I could actually sit in one of the lobbies. In this case, it was the original hospital's lobby, now more of an administrative waiting salon. It sat close enough to the basement hallways to make it easier for me to work my infiltration. Besides, in this setting, a guy nodding in a wheelchair rarely elicited a second thought.

I sank through the floor and the basement ceiling, and then slid down into Babby's covered wagon. As the cooling flesh encased my wandering spirit once more, it occurred to me that this was getting easier. I dropped the idea, however, needing to resume the relaxed concentration that made this all work. Experience had shown that if I dwelled on the mechanism itself, mused on its ease or difficulty, the *monumental* audacity of it, I was sure to cause a session to go haywire and crash out.

Objectivity is actually a *third-self* sort of mentation attitude, and as such is inherently anathema to smooth assimilation.

Later, I did think about it, and it *was* getting easier. The funny thing I realized was that all of this must have been impossible. Surely, nobody else could do it. Even *I* couldn't do it, or would have been completely unable to do this if I hadn't stumbled into the absolutely perfect combination of susceptibility and opportunity when my roommate Mike had dearly departed at just the right moment. That perfectly timed accident had turned a switch, or opened a pathway, or something, which then remained open. My subsequent practice, trial and error, had hardened the opening, had beaten the pathway a little more travelable for me. It had been impossible, but I'd found a loophole, and it gradually became merely difficult. Now, it was *getting easier*.

Babby had been the perfect example, not somebody I knew, or even someone I'd ever looked in the eye. I had *wanted* to visit her, to slip into her suite and spend some time, and I tried. But, poor girl—well, she was in her 40s, sort of a late-April pullet compared to some of my subjects— she was so surrounded by caregivers and family, and so wound up in the medical machinery, it hadn't worked out for me to get myself and my wheelchair edgewise into her waning physical presence.

So, knowing her room number, and therefore her phone extension, I called her—such a longshot, low odds, ricochet into the darkness, but at this point, I was reaching for ankle dankers.

We had a rather nice chat, actually. The morphine had her a bit freely associating, and I kept hearing a female relative in the background. *"Who is that? What are you telling that person? Why did they call?"*

"*Hello?*"

Her voice wasn't quite as weak as I would have expected, but its weakness signaled that it was her. I was a little surprised that she, at this point, would answer her own phone. I'd been expecting a gatekeeper to answer.

"Hello," I said. "How *are* you?"

"*Been* better," said Babby.

"Yes, I know."

"Wait. Who is this?"

"I'm a patient here too. My name wouldn't mean anything to you, especially now."

"*You know I'm dying.*" It was half statement, half question, and half confirmation. Yes, fully the sum of its *parts*, a statement over-full in and of all its meanings.

"I do," I said. "That's why I wanted to talk."

"May I know your name? Even if it's too late to matter?"

I hesitated. After a quick thought, I said, "Call me Sev."

"Sounds Iberian, or Jewish. You don't sound either."

"No, I made it up. From the curse of the seventh son of the seventh son. Though I don't actually know anything about my birth order. Not much, anyway."

"So you're an orphan."

"Something like that."

From the background now, the aunt/sis/mom voice said, "Who is that? What do they want? Why don't you hang up? You don't have the strength, dear. You have to let me answer when calls come in. It could be a stockbroker, or one of those awful fundraisers from Squirrel's Leap Theatre Company...."

All incoming sounds became muffled by a fragile palm thrust over the phone's receiver, but the muffled sounds were first familial, then mildly argumentative, and finally petered out and trailed off in a mixture of elderly resignation and maternal exasperation. Babby must have managed to convey her wishes non-verbally.

After half a minute, the muting palm withdrew and Babby's voice returned. "I'm so tired, but you interest me because of the circumstances. You call and introduce yourself to a dying woman, without really introducing yourself. I can't imagine your motives, or your interest in me, if without personal motive."

"I apologize for... agitating your relative," I said. "But my motive is a bit selfish, and I can't really explain that either. Just talking to you is of great benefit to me, I assure you. I'm not sure if I'm cursed, or blessed, or both, but talking to... people in circumstances like yours... seems to help somehow."

"Well, my mother got annoyed and went to get a cup of coffee in the cafeteria. Believe it or not, I think all this is more stressful on her than on me."

"When she gets back, just tell her that I was a secret admirer. It's true."

"How can that be? We've never met."

"We've been having a conversation for five minutes. That's how."

"I'm tired, Sev, but part of what I'm tired of is all the attention from familiar people. My family, I love them and they are very comforting, but something about hearing your voice, your strange voice...."

She couldn't finish the thought, but it didn't matter. I got it.

"I think you've always been a very outgoing person," I offered. "And now, while you're... um... *winding down*, you haven't had the opportunity to enjoy what has defined you for your whole life."

"Yes, for months now, I have been cocooned with my closest family and friends. No new faces, no new feelings, no new voices."

"I would think that suffering, and dying, brings many new feelings."

"You know what I mean. No new feelings, the vibrant kind, the kind that are... like opening a gift, rather than like closing up an old carton, for the last time."

"I do know what you mean."

"You're a patient too. Are you...."

"Dying? I thought I was. Well, yes, I was. Now, a new treatment.... Who knows."

"That's good, Sev. You're young, too, I can tell."

"Yes."

"Please, just tell me something. I have to close my eyes. I'm too tired to keep talking."

"Okay."

It *may* have been odd, but in this circumstance, *give* seemed as important as *take*. Even if I did most of the talking, I could feel the connection establishing. And, I knew *what* she meant. When a chronically ill person says *tired*, she means tired and sick and *exhausted* and overwhelmed and... other stuff.

I considered things to talk about. She didn't really seem to very much care what I had to say, specifically. She just wanted to hear words, preferably not about her aunts and nephews, or her mother's neighbors and prayer-group colleagues.

I thought about things I had top of mind—not having time to mull this over. I needed to launch right into something, but I didn't want to talk about my recent medical adventures and care experiences. That would be *bad form.* I thought about an old *Horizon* article I'd been reading in one of the waiting rooms, about modern musicians that evoked eerie owlcreeky occurrences by playing Civil War era songs in hallowed locations on period instruments. I thought about a silent film I'd seen at 3:00 AM on hospital cable—when I'd thrown my sleep/wake hours off by napping too much during daylight—a tragically ironic melodrama about a turn-of-the-century (20th) American serviceman who'd been rescued from big trouble in the orient by a local native woman, who had to marry him to save him from severe legal sanctions. The second half of the story was about how he lacked the class to return the favor when they got back to the USA. Kinda long, though. Then again, maybe something goofy about my own odd struggles....

But wait. I could give her *a choice...*

"Babby, would you like something mysterious, serious, or silly?"

"Delirious."

"That wasn't one of the choices though, Babby."

"You could say delirious instead of silly. It's sort of the same."

"Ah, I see. Okay, mysterious, serious, or delirious then?"

"Delirious, please."

I mused. It wasn't actually the *same* as silly, but I interpreted her answer as preferring something less mysterious, something non-serious. I decided to wing it, deliriously.

"Okay, once upon a time, as evening fell, a vole, waking from its afternoon nap, heard the sound of determined scurrying not far from its nest deep in the bramble. It went forth to investigate, and spotted the dormouse making its way alongside the bramble's edge. Curious about its slightly smaller cousin's intent progress, it emerged from its volehole and caught up.

"'Where you going this time of night, little dormouse,' said the vole.

"'Other side of the meadow,' said the dormouse.

"'A long journey for we shortleggers. What for?'

"'I'm supposed to find out when I get there, so I can't tell you.'

"'Whoa, now,' said the vole, stopping the dormouse. 'I'm bigger than you, so you have to tell me.'

"'There's no time for that, if I even really knew. In fact, I'm already late. Now you've stopped me and it's even worse.'

"The vole looked confused now, and a little ashamed.

"'I've got an idea, and it may work if we hurry,' said the dormouse. 'You're bigger, like you said, and that makes you faster. You can probably make it in time if you get started now.'

"'Okay,' said the vole, and thanked the dormouse and pointed its little shiny snout across the meadow and pulled away from the dormouse.

"Soon, the vole's path veered near a little copse of oaks, beloved turf of the ground squirrel. Ground squirrel poked its nose out of its burrow at the base of an acorn oak, saw the scurrying vole, popped out, and caught up.

"'You seem to be crossing the meadow with a purpose in mind," observed the ground squirrel.

"'Yes,' said the vole. 'No time to stop and chat, squirrel. I have to get there directly. I'm making up for lost time as it is,' said the vole.

"'Now hang on,' said the ground squirrel, stopping the vole. 'If it's that important, I want to hear more about it. All about it, in fact.'

"'There's no time for that, I'm afraid. Now that you've stopped me, you've made it worse. But maybe you can help.'

"'Help?' said the ground squirrel.

"'Yes,' said the vole. 'You're twice my size, and faster than me too. Hurry now, you can probably get across the meadow in time.'

"'Well, okay,' said the ground squirrel, an excitable little fellow, quickly catching the spirit of the thing. And he sprinted off ahead of the vole, soon out of sight.

"A small brook crossed the meadow, and ground squirrel darted across the stream on a fallen boxelder sapling. In his hurry, he didn't see the muskrat, who eyed him moving along briskly with obvious intention, and quickly went in pursuit.

"And so, on it went, with several more animals, each one a little bigger and faster than the—"

"No," said Babby.

"Eh?" I said.

"Tell it, please. I'd like to hear about each one. You do each one a little different, and I want to hear the whole story."

"Well, okay. The muskrat, his fur still sleeked with the creekwater that dripped and trailed behind as he ran along, caught up with the ground squirrel...."

And so I continued with the full-fledged story, with several more animals, mostly rodents, each one a little bigger and faster than the last, until finally the beaver reached the other end of the great meadow, the last of a cooperative chain that included all the mentioned forest dwellers, as well as the hare, the red squirrel, the weasel, the marmot, the raccoon, and the woodchuck.

"The beaver looked at the forest, and looked at the rough viney hedge that divided the open meadow from the taller trees, and then turned and looked back across the vast meadow, from where he had come, and where the earlier participants in this delirious relay were still making the crossing at their own individual rates. 'Now what?' he said.

"He was still pondering when the raccoon finally caught up. 'Good,' said the beaver. 'Now you can tell me what the big hurry was all about. Now that we're at the other side of the meadow, what is our purpose here?'

"Raccoon looked at beaver, and scratched at his chin with his dark spidery little hand. 'She didn't tell me,' he said.

"'*Who* didn't tell you *what?*' asked beaver.

"'Woodchuck... didn't tell me nothing. Just that I had to hurry.'

"Beaver slapped his tail on the ground, then looked like he was thinking about slapping raccoon, and sighed. 'Now what?'

"Raccoon threw up his hands. 'Well,' said beaver, 'We need to get cracking. You run back, catch up with woodchuck, and find out! I'll stay here and be ready to get started at... at whatever *it* is.'

"'Okay,' raccoon hollered, and he took off back across the meadow.

"When he met up with woodchuck, he sputtered out, 'Beaver wants to know... *now* what?'

"'Beaver?'

"'Yeah, he's bigger and faster, so he took over. He's all the way across the meadow. So what's the story?'

"'Don't know,' said woodchuck. 'Marmot wouldn't say. Just that it was urgent.'

"'Marmot?'

"'Yep, he started this thing. Didn't mention any details, though.'

Well, I was kind of wound up in this thing by now, so I had Woodchuck and Raccoon split up, with one going back to find out what Marmot had in mind, and the other heading on across the meadow to update Beaver, and although I was kind of on a roll, I actually had no idea, after I had a dozen or so small, warm-blooded creatures criss-crossing meadows with messages and inquiries, how this thing was going to end.

I stopped to get my breath and let the rest of it sort of mull around and well up, when I noticed how quiet the line was.

"Babby?"

Nothing, but no dial tone, either. No sounds of other activity, either — no family, no naggish mothering, no rushing around.

Just the faint beeping, distant, and regular, of a heart monitor or something similar.

"Goodnight, Babby." I hung up gently.

She hadn't died — yet — but I'm pretty sure she didn't regain consciousness, or if she did, it wasn't for long.

I felt sort of strange about the story, the fable of the Vole and the Beaver. I didn't finish it, even for my own satisfaction, wierd as that was. Although I'd made it up, it was never *for* me — never *mine*. I'd been improvising, and would have improvised an ending. At this point, I had a vague feeling that it was now Babby's story, and so I left it where I'd stopped.

The next afternoon, drifting down from my wheelchair parking spot in a quiet corner of the salon lobby, I found her. She lay in her pup tent covered wagon, stretched out on that long, thin gurney, so cold, so wan, so bare.

A pathology orderly must have parked her in the hallway temporarily, lined up with two more, one a second tent, and the third of the hot dog cart type.

So I dropped in, like butter melting through a hot pie crust — getting easier every time.

And there I was, in dim, but not darkness. This time, I needed to be active, to move, to flex, to energize and activate, but in that white fabric, box-shaped enclosure, I didn't have a lot of room.

I spent a few moments centering, then settling — getting comfortable, and listening. It was a quiet area. Staff wouldn't leave bodies, even covered ones, in busy spaces — good for staff, good for facility, good for public. Heap good for me.

I started by moving my legs. I just lifted, knees extended, flexing from the hips — leg lifts. Left, then right, scissor, scissor, but slowly, with deliberation. I didn't kick. I pointed Babby's toes, raised her leg to the tent's top, then slowly brought it back down. I then did the same with the other leg.

After a couple dozen repetitions of this, I stopped, and did similar exercises with the arms — raised them slowly, let them down. I did a few very slow, very shallow sit-ups.

As I did this, the mind became more engaged with the physicality of it, gradually. They felt a little more integrated, as though, if I had to move, or talk, or interact socially, it would be a little better, a little smoother.

It's working.

I remembered an exercise that a PT had suggested years ago, when I'd tried extensive therapy as part of an alternative regimen, which I'd hoped would improve my internal well-being by retuning my body's gross physical calibration. This exercise, developed by neurologists or neuroscientists, somehow used physical movement to rechannel neural pathways. It was called a "cross crawl."

In the cross crawl, lying on your back, you think about walking. You think about your legs moving alternately, as if you're strolling across an open space of floor, or down a hall, or along a woodland path. You imagine your arms swinging as you walk. You simulate the natural human motion, so as you imagine your left leg moving forward, your right arm swings in your mind, and then right leg with left arm.

Then you slowly, gradually begin to actualize the motions—the arms, the legs—until, lying on your back, you're walking in place. Your legs and arms deliberately and vigorously—but smoothly—move.

Then you think about turning your head, but only to the right. Finally, after a few little slight nods, you actually turn your head, swivel your neck to the right, but only when your left leg and your right arm are up. *Eyes right*, is how a military type would put it.

In that white tent, bathed in dim filtered light, I was just getting to that vigorous stage of the cross crawl. It was interesting, because in addition to feeling an improved mind/body connection, somehow this stimulation seemed to be priming the neurons themselves a little. I was just starting to get a significant *inkling* when....

Suddenly, startlingly, the sheet was whipped off. It was like the table cloth, dinner table trick, so swift and unexpected. One moment, I engaged in private ministrations, the next moment, I lay exposed.

There I was, a dead woman in an open graphite framework, wearing a hospital gown, doing an eyes-right goose step—like Snow White come to life in her little glass case, but doing a cross crawl.

My audience? No seven dwarfs here. It was just two kids, a boy and a girl.

I'd seen one of them before and, realizing it, now knew that he'd been lurking here and there on the periphery of some of my activities. I should have caught on earlier.

In a residential neighborhood, one expects children. Same in a mall, on a playground, on the sporadic sidewalks of the distinct villages beyond the outer suburbs, then the child-rich sidewalks of suburbia... then sidewalks stitching together an inner ring of contiguous communities, and children sprinkled here and there, when you're almost to the city itself....

But in a big hospital? Sure, you see children, but you expect to see any given individual child maybe once, or at the most, once a day when they visit. Or, of course, in the children's ward. They're always supervised, accompanied, or custodized in a treatment area or patient room.

This pair was none of those. They were roamers, nomads, itinerant juveniles gleaning amusement from institutional interstices.

The older kid, who looked to be about twelve years old, seemed to hang around here a lot. I'd seen him almost daily as I made my rounds, scouting for likely treatment candidates.

The other kid was a year younger, at least, and I'd never seen her before. The little one was there by my knees, and the boy was right in my face, just about, because they'd positioned themselves to pull the sheet as a team.

I looked at them, and took in their expressions. My eyes were a bit hazy, and the hallway glare after lying in the tent's dim light was uncomfortable for a few moments, but I could see their expressions. The boy backed away, and the two of them gravitated sideways toward each other, both of them unable to stop staring at me.

I froze in mid crawl, staring at the two of them with my head turned. I wasn't sure what to do, any more than they were.

They were terrified, but curious. Both emotions showed in their expressions, mingled into a startled confusion. Well, actually, the boy was both, but the girl was mainly terrified. I could see other emotions in there too, mixing around, trying to bust out, and because there were several, it was hard to tell what was what. Tears, a sudden sob or something like that, didn't seem out of the question, though.

I needed to lose these kids one way or the other. I knew that much pretty quickly. Nothing good could come of this, if it went on for long. I figured I could either scare them off, or bore them off. The latter seemed like the better idea under the circumstances, so I decided to just go limp. If I went back to being just dead, maybe they'd lose interest and go away.

I relaxed my frozen crawl and puddled back down to the limp skin and idle bones I was supposed to be. I lay still, dead, in a slightly awkward sort of piled-up attitude.

The kids were quiet for half a minute or so. I kept an eye open to keep an — well, an *eye* on them — but I had to stay dead, so to speak, and not blink. Since it wasn't my body, this was simple. In fact, I'd already learned, during my other sessions, that blinking was difficult. Blood wasn't circulating, tears weren't lubricating, joint fluid wasn't loose and luby, and involuntary reflexes weren't automatic like they were in the living. So once I got the eyes open, it was easier just to leave them that way. As the boy and girl stared, I didn't change focus or adjust my gaze, either — just a blank, dead stare.

The children, on the other hand, were indeed blinking — scowling, perhaps grimacing, and twitching a little. In fact, they both seemed about to lose it, but I couldn't be sure if they were about to laugh or scream. Sometimes, at that age, there's a fine line, a trigger/toggle that could go either way depending on what happens next.

"This is creeping me out!" The little one broke the silence, probably to ease her agitation — and avoid the toggle altogether. Laughter would be inappropriate, and a scream? Shameful!

"I told you, Henrietta," said the boy.

"What?"

"Zombies. I told you there were zombies in the hospital."

"Yeah." The little one's — Henrietta's — eyes widened and she backed away, and the toggle returned, but now she looked about to cry or *run*.

The older one saw it too, and grabbed her T-shirt and held on. "It's okay. Look, it's dormant or something. There's no way we can just *leave*. It's a *zombie!*"

"Yeah, I know, you and your zombies. My mom won't even let me read Harry Potter yet. C'mon, Myrt, let's go. Somebody's gonna come 'round the corner and see us."

This was going on too long, and I didn't want to stay and see how it turned out. I reasoned it was better at this point, perhaps, to cut my treatment visit short and leave poor Babby at the mercy of these two juvenile urchins.

Myrt took a step closer.

Yes, time to go.

I could do myself, and indeed these children, no good by hanging around. Much better to have this corpse return forthwith to its natural inanimate state, for them to quickly end up disappointed and just go away, and wonder if they'd really seen it trying to march toward the corridor ceiling.

So I snapped out. I retreated, unmerged, reeled myself out.

Uh-oh.

The rubber band wasn't snapping. The reel wasn't reeling. The essence wasn't channeling.

I tried again.

Hum-de-hum, la-de-dah, just zip right back, jo-jo, to where I once belonged....

Get back!

Nope. Nothing. And lying there in Babby's awkward dishevel, the first twinge of panic set in.

Why can't I get started?

I sort of twisted myself—my spirit self—around, and instead of looking out Babby's glazed eyes at the children, I looked instead back through the ether I had come from, looking for *the way.*

In the half-dozen or so transanimations I'd experienced, certain commonalities had emerged among the experiences. One of these was that, when crossing the ethereal space between my own living body and that of my non-living subject, a sort of tendril remained there—a little current or a vague remnant of my path, like Gretel's breadcrumbs, or a low hound's sniffing the ground trail home after a long track away. I'd always felt that tendril, sensed it, and followed it back.

It's not there. I can't see it. I can't feel it! Where is it!

The panic grew stronger. I didn't dare just go off looking for... for *it,* blindly wandering unbodied through the interstices, soul-sniffing, listening for wisps of tendril trail. I'd never passed through more than the briefest interval, knowing exactly where I was going, and going straight there—and back, of course.

Back. I need to go back.

But where *was* back. I felt completely lost, without bearings.

Something had happened, something different this time—perhaps a bad coupling of unexpected incidents, the distraction of these kids, and who knows what else. Something had destroyed my routine, and scattered, covered, or purloined my breadcrumbs.

A friend and I had scuba dived once, at night, off of a coral wall in Inagua, and we dove about forty feet down the submerged cliff at the coral's edge, fifty feet below the surface, and then drifted oceanward perhaps twenty feet from the face of the wall. Then, we turned off our underwater flashlights. We were suspended in pure liquid darkness. I turned a little submarine somersault, and another, and then stopped and looked around me. My buoyancy was neutralized by the tanks and belt weights. In the complete — and completely liquid — blackness, occasionally interrupted by tiny pinpoints of luminescence, enveloped by nothingness of warm ocean, I was completely de-egoed. I hung in aquatic zero-grav, and didn't know which way to the surface, or to the wall, or to the sea floor, or to the swirling Gulf stream and, beyond that, the endless Atlantic.

This felt something like that, but there, in the black ocean, I turned my light back on, turned slowly, and began to sense gravity again, and bouyancy. I remained relatively calm, and my bearings returned, one by one.

Where are my breadcrumbs? I don't.... Wait. Have I moved?

The panic seized hold now.

Somebody moved me!

I twisted back and looked out Babby's eyes again. Her knee and elbow joints jerked.

The children backed away.

I really didn't need the added complication they brought to this situation, so I twitched again, then half closed my eyes, and forced Babby's diaphragm to expand, very slowly. Then I extended her left index finger and, letting it wobble slightly, pointed it at the littler one, the girl.

I reversed the diaphragm, contracting instead of expanding, and forced air through Babby's vocal chords. The sound was something between a cicada mating call and baritone saxophone with a split reed. It was just noise. Perhaps that it was pure bleating noise added power — the sheer inarticulate rasp of it, void of all meaning excepting intention itself — because the intention was to scare, to warn, to terrify.

Toward the end of the croak, which went on for something over ten seconds, I tried shaping the sounds with Babby's tongue and lips, managing a rough approximation of the little girl's name.

"...ehchhennnrrchiieeetta..."

Very rough, but by then it didn't really matter much. They were forty feet away, running, already nearly to the double doors at the end of the hall. They probably didn't hear even that terminating, eeked-out attempt to personalize it.

They were out of my way, and it was time for me — well, for Babby — to move. *We* had to find *me*.

Since I couldn't find any remnant of an inter-ethereal tether back to my own tranced body, I needed to restore visual contact, or at least a verified near proximity, to put my consciousness back to normal status — *in me*.

At least, I *hoped* it could happen this way.

Chapter 13

Beyond inelegant, I slid Babby's legs off the gurney and tried to push to a sitting position. My panic rose in intensity, as it became clear that the exercise of *trying* this and *attempting* that wouldn't cut it. I needed to move, and fast.

Being stuck in a corpse could be dire. It certainly couldn't be good—not long term.

So I just stiffened everything, clumsily willed myself off the gurney, and started down the hall toward the double doors through which the pair of kids had retreated. The first step wasn't too bad, as I progressed the expected two and a half feet down the linoleum. The second step came harder, a little weakened, and I seemed to be a bit closer to the ground. By the third step... well, the third step was really more of a knee thing, about six inches of knee sliding, and my progressed screeched to a halt.

I lay on the floor—hadn't made it three steps before collapsing in a heap on my side.

Babby had been bedridden for some time—weeks, at least—and her body didn't have much left to give. Indeed, it had given out on her.

I struggled back to the gurney thing, and managed to pull myself— herself, *whatever*—back up so I could lean there and gather some strength. Then I pulled the tent-superstructure support rods completely off, laid them on the mattress, and bent over to grab the sheet cover off the floor where the children had abandoned it. I laid that on the mattress too, moved to the end of the thing, and started walking, half leaning on my arms for support while wheeling the gurney down the hall. This was good. I looked a lot less conspicuous pushing a gurney than reeling down the hall, legs buckling, arms a bit out of sync, in a hospital gown.

I still didn't quite look right, but I just needed to find myself. Then Babby—what remained of her—could rest in peace.

First, I had to head back to the administrative lobby a floor above me. I wasn't there, or at least didn't *think* I was there, but even so, that was the place to start.

It was a little weird, as I had to go down a hall to an elevator, up a floor, down some halls, turning corners, and heading generally away from patient and treatment areas toward more administrative populations. So I sort of hung back whenever clusters of people appeared up ahead. First, at the elevator, I waited until it cleared out, which took a while. No way to avoid people completely, but if I had to be close to people, limiting it to fellow patients or "civilians," and especially the oblivious ones, seemed preferable.

There's a fair amount of oblivion entrained into the population that wanders, strides, and meanders through health facility hallways, even among the staff. Some of it is due to busyness, perhaps some to stress, drugs, or nicotine withdrawal.

So on my way up, even some of the obliviates looked at me funny. I smiled and leaned on my gurney, and gave little waves with my stiff, gray fingers.

Nod, smile again. Gesture with canny embarrassment at my pink and white striped tie-in-back gown. Don't forget to breathe every once in a while.

They looked away, mostly, and I managed to get back to the salon lobby and walk through quickly, pushing my gurney in a businesslike plodding stroll. Several administrative gazes followed me, nonetheless.

Sure enough, my wheelchair was gone, along with me.

I wanted to stop and think, but with those gazes tracking on me, I really had to keep moving, just express-train my carcass right through the area. Fortunately, a loop corridor awaited at the building's west end past the lobby, and I could double back the way I had come.

Now I have to get my bad self to the next most logical destination for my sleeping self: Suite N222.

What if somebody recognizes Babby? This is insane!

"Do I have any choice?" I asked my bad self, and declined to answer.

Plunging onward, I headed for the old north halls, where they had a maintenance and service elevator, and managed to get to the 2nd floor uneventfully.

As I pushed through corridors, some busy, some quieter, I realized that if the nerves that enveloped my panicking consciousness were working better, this would all be quite wracking upon said nerves. I wondered if, wherever I was, my heart was beating at a hyperexcited clip.

Me! Where is me?

With some relief, I rounded the turn near the nurse station and zeroed in, on the home stretch now: 218, 219, 220....

The door to 222 was closed, perhaps a good thing. Doors tended to be open when the patient was out doing testing or therapies.

I shoved the gurney up along the wall next to the door, supported myself on the door while turning the knob, and looked around.

Clear. So far.

The feeling had now hit me, though—that slipping, dashed feeling—because I would have *felt* it if I were in there. I would have *felt*, and *known* that I was close. The breadcrumbs would be back, the scent.

I got *nothing*.

Little firings of faulty nerves made me twitch and stagger, a patchy panic, as I looked around the little cozy room, and verified what I already knew.

No one here — dead, alive, or asleep.

Still using the door frame and the knob to hold myself up, I staggered back out and grabbed the gurney.

A lost soul wandering the halls looking for his body.... It sounded like a back-woods ballad or an 18th-century ghost story, but what could I do? That was *exactly* what I had to do.

I hadn't gotten far when Dr. Jidalco came straight down the hall toward me, looking down at a clipboard as he moved briskly along. Suddenly, I needed to disappear.

He wouldn't see *me*, of course, hiding here in Babby's husk, but.... He'd been *Babby's* doctor too—vague inklings told me this—and it wouldn't do to have one of his deceased patients grin and nod and wave as they passed in the hospital hallway.

All the rooms I passed were occupied, so I couldn't duck in, and it was too late to reverse my direction. In fact, as the moments progressed, it was too late to do *anything*. With head down, I remained steady and passed by as quickly as possible.

His nose was still in his work, but he glanced up briefly before returning to it.

I nodded, looked away as we passed, made quick work of the criss-cross, and motored onward with just a quick glance back.

He slowed, the clipboard now down by the side of his leg. His head cocked over on an angle that screamed, *Curious! Curious!* He started to turn, and drew a breath as if to say something.

I could either stop and face him, run, or.... I chose a third alternative.

Before Dr. Jidalco fully turned back toward me, I stopped the gurney, hunched myself up onto it, laid myself out on my back, long and straight, and folded my hands over on my chest. Babby went back to being dead in about 1-1/2 seconds. Stupidly, I shut her eyes. I didn't have time to think, really, and instinctively closed them, so, relying on her ears for the next while, I listened.

His footsteps closed in, and now Dr. Jidalco was clearly looking at me. He walked up and down, no doubt gazing at the body.

"Ms. Oppfeloffigan...?" He sighed. "What the— I'll be a—" He half whispered, half grunted. "I don't know what I'll be. Who was push—" He paused for moment. "I thought...."

I counted on the fact that he'd been preoccupied as we passed, and hopefully wouldn't fully realize that he'd just seen a corpse walking down the ward's hallway wheeling an empty gurney. Of course, that made no sense, and here was a corpse on a gurney. That wasn't right either, but at least it wasn't ambulatory.

"Nurse!" he called.

I felt the gurney start to move, pushed by Jidalco.

A familiar voice responded, and steady, on-a-mission, nurse footsteps rose in volume as they neared.

"What is it, Doctor? I—" She stopped abruptly. It was Sinda, one of the nurses I was familiar with.

"Do *you* know what's going on?"

Sinda didn't answer.

Knowing her a little, I figured she was just at a loss for words. Some nurses were cheery and chatty. Others were businesslike and verged on dispassionate. Sinda was somewhere in between.

"Somebody was just wheeling Ms. Oppfeloffigan along this hallway. When I turned around, that person was gone, and here she was on this gurney. I needn't go into detail about why this is simply not... not... well, not correct, this circumstance we have here."

"I see what you mean," Sinda said. She straightened my gown and rearranged my legs a little bit, then went about efficiently reconstructing the lightweight superstructure around me.

"Did you see where the person went?" asked Dr. Jidalco.

"Are you sure you saw... um...?" Sinda now sighed too. "Nobody else is here in the hall, Dr."

They found the linen cover and together fit it over the frame.

Once again, I lay in a semi-dark translucence.

Chapter 14

A few minutes later, I rolled along the halls again, wondering what to do.

Nurse Sinda and Dr. Jidalco had fairly quickly pawned me off on an orderly or patient tech, and I was no doubt bound for the basement area where most of the cadaver processing began and ended. The nurse and the doctor, in all likelihood, were continuing, somewhere away from the public hallway, their discussion of the odd fact that Babby Oppfeloffigan's body made unauthorized and seemingly unaccompanied excursions to unexpected areas of the facility.

Through it all, I still had no idea where my own body was, and I felt increasingly insecure about this.

I tracked, in my borrowed mind, our location, feeling the motions and turns, hearing the orderly's footsteps. We worked our way down again toward the eastern end of the complex, waited a while, and then a chime signaled an arriving elevator. After being wheeled inside, my weight lessened slightly as the conveyance descended.

All this time, I was thinking, weighing options, and fighting against the surging panic. I was quite on the verge of simply sitting up, pushing the tent off the gurney, and running off down the corridors to continue my quest to get back into myself.

Several things held me back. One, I knew that with Jidalco and Sinda already puzzling and possibly suspicious of macabre doings, it could be perilous to push my luck. Thus far, I'd managed to keep my activities under the radar, and they needed to stay that way. Two, I wasn't sure if I could actually propel Babby's body down the hall, without the assistance of an empty gurney for support. Could Babby Oppfeloffigan's poor wasted *body* propel itself, along with my *mind*, anywhere without significant help? Unlikely. If I attempted it, Babby — and I — would likely begin by running down the corridor maybe three or four steps, then stumble for another yard or two, and end up crawling for maybe a few pathetic feet before collapsing completely.

The part of my mind that didn't dwell on this panicked state still used Babby's sensory inlets to process surroundings and nearby activity, and I became aware of something a little different than what I'd been knowing. It dawned on me gradually, and at first it didn't really have much significance other than curiosity.

I was in a service elevator. As we stopped on floors, the people entering and departing the elevator weren't so much patients, relatives, and caregivers, as they were techs, servicers, and other people doing the down-and-dirty that underpins the operations of a big facility. This workhorse elevator took more time, as these workers had to maneuver things in and out—carts, machinery, and other heavy-wheeled items.

I was bumming about the fact that a round trip back to where I'd started with Babby, down near the morgue, wouldn't do me much good. I needed to cover new ground to find myself, or some whiff or tendril of the breadcrumbs that I hoped still trailed away from my inert—but hopefully still viable—body. Like that low-down hound, I had to hope to cover some ground and cross my trail somehow, pick up the inkle-scent and follow it back to wholeness.

Then I felt something—no, *sensed* something. I had to fight my way back to considering and appreciating my surroundings, rather than keep perseverating on my lostness, my frustration.

I felt a wavering proximity thing. Suddenly it clarified, and I knew it: there was another body in the elevator.

I racked the dim, crackly short-term memory I was borrowing from Babby's flagging neurons, and reregistered the fact that the elevator had just been stopped for a long minute or two, and the ears had heard another large piece of equipment jockey into the roomy double-doored space of the freight elevator. Another cadaver cart had joined us.

As the elevator got under way, the drivers talked shop.

"Morgue?" said my driver.

"One of 'em. Got two in here. Other's going to the new scan path lab."

I'd heard of this. This hospital, about as up to date, high end and high tech as any, even had a relatively new service for families that wanted answers but didn't want traditional invasive forensics. Hence, non-surgical, noninvasive pathology—the no-cut autopsy.

"Goin' there first?" asked my guy.

"Yeah."

I probed, moving my energy and attention from the orderlies to the cargo. I didn't have much time.

Who was it? How had he or she died? Can I get in?

It didn't really matter. I knew this was a longshot, and a big one. Up to now, all my cadaver infiltrations had been with some preliminary, preparatory, or serendipitous familiarity, with that icebreaking I needed to facilitate assimilation. The one time I'd tried going in "blind," so to speak, it had been like a brick wall.

I got lucky. Because the proximity was so close, I didn't have to completely exit Babby's husk to move a section of my consciousness across a few feet of space and into the double-decker metal cart. This provided some reassurance. I really didn't relish ending up nowhere.

One body was unreachable. My probing bounced off as if I'd dropped onto the taut springy surface of a strong balloon.

With the other, I felt something permeable. No, permeable was what I normally felt when making an overture on someone I was acquainted with. This wasn't anybody I knew. Or, it might be, but... I didn't even know who it was.

I was intrigued and afraid at the same time, but figured I had nothing to lose at this point, so I flowed out of Babby and into this new body. Perhaps my desperation helped.

Not too hot, but stuffy. Pitch dark. Before I could even get my bearings, I heard the *ding* and the elevator door opening, then felt the jar of motion as we were rolling again—toward the path lab. This was new ground, and that was good.

Goodbye, and thank you, Babby.

As we rolled, I *sniffed*—not actually *sniffing*, or using any airborne or olfactory phenomena, but I spread pseudopodia of my awareness out around us, and into our direction of progress, seeing if I could deploy a sensory web across the nearby space. I sought, sniffing for a sign of my own trail, the tendril or remnant or whiff of my own body that was— had to be—still somewhere, in what must look like a catatonic trance to the....

I realized what must have happened. It had been stupid of me not to catch on earlier, but everything had happened so fast, and panic and lack of experience had layered bafflement onto the urgency of my predicament.

Whether a visitor or a health professional found me and called attention to this unconscious man in a wheelchair, the result would be the same, though the former might take longer. Somebody would undoubtedly think I—my body, anyway—needed medical attention. I'd assumed thus far that if something like this happened, they would think me asleep and roll me discreetly back to my assigned room unit, but I now realized, sweeping feet-first toward a pathology lab with my feelers out, that my coma-like body had probably been taken to one logical place: the ER.

The Path Lab, if I remembered correctly, was not too far away from the Emergency Room. Actually, the lab was directly on top of it.

I started to get excited, hopeful even.

Despair gives way to hope. Excitement becomes inevitable when the hope transcends possibility and approaches probability.

We weren't there quite yet.

We rolled along, and I needed to be ready to do almost anything. I might even have to somehow break secrecy, which I really, *really* didn't want to do, but with the precious connection between my spirit and my living body at stake, I might have no choice but to spring out when they slid the drawer out of this hot dog cart, and hopefully scare this technician out of my way and run through the corridors until I got that vital connection back. If that happened, if I played it right, maybe I could still somehow hope that it played out as a weird *One Step Beyond* sort of transcendent hospital phenomena, keep my distance, and hope suspicion didn't fall on me.

So, I was ready. I felt, thought, *sniffed*, and took stock of this body. As we rolled along, stopped, a door opened, and we rolled into a quiet room, I realized how I'd managed to enter this decedent, this body with whom I had no acquaintance — or *thought* I had none.

In fact, this wasn't quite a complete stranger; I knew this guy from reading the newspaper this morning. He'd been an equipment operator working the huge construction project widening the Route 30 bypass, and in a freak accident, he'd hit the high-voltage wires with his loader bucket. He'd died instantly, just yesterday.

My escort parked the cart. I heard and felt the clicks as he locked the little rubber wheels with the foot toggle.

I got ready to spring out, or lie still, or whatever I needed to do when he opened the drawer, but then I heard an intercom or a pager.

He didn't open the drawer. He was being called away. "Yes. Yes. *Yes.* I know they're all coming, but I can't push two of these things at once. Do I look like a freight train? Tell them to go ahead. I'll have the others here in a few minutes."

I heard the door open, then close and latch again.

I might be alone. This might be my chance, but how do I get out of this thing?

While feeling around in the dark, I remembered the stories about old-fashioned, abandoned refrigerators, and little kids dying trapped inside. It simply wasn't possible, these days, that equipment like this wouldn't have some sort of safety latch inside.

Sure enough, I found it, right where it should be, above my head on the left side, up in the corner — a polished metal lever, like a half pair of pliers or hole punch. I shoved it, then pulled it, heard a click, and saw a sliver of fluorescence above my head.

Tattoos on my forearms were the first thing I noticed as I thrust my hands out through that light sliver. I pulled against the stainless steel edge and rolled the drawer out into the light. My — well, his — big, tanned, hairy forearms each had a duck tattoed on it.

Daffy sat on my left, Donald on my right, both in their anger modes.

You really don't learn anything beyond the superficial about a person from an obituary, or a bit of reporting about an accidental death. I remembered his name, although it took the jarring reminder, seeing those tattoos to trigger it and get my mind to cough it back up. *Donald Daphleigh*, nicknamed Duck, lived in Ocean County, New Jersey, part of an out-of-state crew working on the huge construction project.

I wondered, with no small amount of hope, if remembering all that was a good sign. Perhaps digging something like that out of my own memory meant that I somehow remained, perhaps loosely, connected to my own resting nervous system — wherever it was.

I pushed myself up and flexed Duck's creaky joints and muscles, his body much more capable than poor Babby's spent husk — average size, but wiry, with big Popeye forearms and whiskers on chin and upper lip. I felt them with Duck's hands while looking around quickly, trying to see, in my surrounds, the elements of a plan. Nothing assembled, jigsawing together, which meant I might have to just be bold and wander.

I swung the legs out and skootched to standing, supporting myself against the cart. I wouldn't be alone for long, as there was the door we entered and, opposite it, another door to more workspace farther in — and voices in the corridor.

I quickly, but as quietly as possible, pushed the drawer back into the cart, and moved away from the outer door and toward the inner space. The voices grew louder, and had stopped moving along the corridor. It became clear they would enter the room, and soon.

In the second room sat gleaming steel tables with gutters, and a huge piece of machinery that looked at first glance like a clean, stainless, horizontal, streamlined cement mixer or asphalt drum. The room also contained assorted devices mounted on articulated arms, and instruments on rolling stands—the usual mix of familiar and unknown equipment one sees in a treatment department—or laboratory.

I heard the outer door opening behind me. Simultaneously, I closed the inner door and looked for my exit.

There was no exit. This was a *cul de sac*, a dead end.

Hide? Not a chance. Crawl into the CAT cave or MRI or whatever the big drum thing is? Foolish. Self entrapment.

Other than a couple undersized undersink cabinets, I spotted no other hideaways, And no place to run. I prepared to put on a ghoulish grin and get into bejesus mode, to see if I could macabre my way out, when I spotted another possibility. At this point, any possibility, even longshots, seemed better than *coming out.*

In the far wall, several good-sized, steel-framed panels with gleaming steel inserts interrupted the soup-green wall tiles. They had handles. At first, I thought they were installed bins, but then I focused on the block letters labeling them—had to squint because Duck's astigmatism was uncorrected by lens or spectacle. One was inscribed TRASH, the other LAUNDRY.

I was immediately reminded of my Aunt Gwen's old stone house with the winding stairway, and the corpse window. There had been no other way out for those bodies, either.

I hastily examined both of these gravity chutes, and made up my mind. With no time left for dither, the bigger of the two, LAUNDRY, would have to do.

I grabbed one of those rolling stands and wrenched the instrument off its clamp, about the size of a large portable radio. I thrust it down into the jaw of the hinge on one side of the laundry chute hatch, jamming it open.

Then I dove into the open chute.

I had to wiggle through the first section because it wasn't just a straight shot, and I managed to kick out the instrument I had wedged into the hinge as my flailing feet went by. Then, I hurtled head-first downward, through dark space, banging off the sides of the steel-lined shaftway.

A half-second after beginning the free fall, a lighted rectangle whizzed by. Rather, *I* whizzed by *it*—another chute access from the floor below me. I stiffened, readying for the impact or landing or whatever would come next.

But it never did. I never landed.

Somewhere between the 2nd and 1st floors of the building, I had a topsy-turvy moment, and suddenly, I stopped hurtling downward. I hovered in the darkness, and there it was—the diaphanous tendril of my own soul.

A whiff, a breadcrumb, an oh-so-faint gradient of the familiar mixed into the anonymous ether, and it literally brought me up short, stopped me in mid-fall, so that Duck's mortal coil continued hurtling downward while I momentarily spun in stasis. I then swam into the enriching side of the gradient, drinking in the increasingly familiar feel of it, hungry for the sensation of inhabiting my own skin, of surrounding my own bones, again.

And just like that, I sat in my wheelchair—*thwock*—and looked around. Next to me, on both sides, people waited in institutional maple chairs with maroon upholstered padding on the arms, seats, and backrests. The guy on my left had no shirt on. Instead, he wore wide areas and shredded stripes of road rash, scraped red and seepy, with a fat lip and blood-matted hair. I thought he was grinning at me, but then realized he was grimacing in pain.

On my right, a woman looked out the corner of her eye, her left eye, at me. Well, she likely looked at Road Rash more than focusing on me, while holding her white purse in her lap, knuckles tense and white.

I glanced left, right again, then settled my gaze midway, more or less straight ahead, to favor neither.

"How did I get here?" I asked, making it sound half rhetorical, but actually hoping one or the other of them might feel addressed and answer.

"Yeah. Right," said Road Rash.

"I'm next," said the woman.

"I'm not," said Road Rash.

"You can have my spot," I said, and released my levers and started rolling toward the ceiling-mounted TV, which displayed a courtroom show where two college girls argued with a female judge about which one bought all the liquor and which one drank all the liquor.

The way they'd designed the ER waiting room, there was no easy way out. It was sort of like one of those fish traps or lobster pots, whereas once you got your nose past the entrance, you couldn't really go back. You just had to proceed forward—in this case, into the digestive tract of the health care system. The triage/reception nurse's cubicle sat between me and the ER's double doors, and behind me, behind a secured vestibule, was the street entrance and the ambulance circle.

I rolled up to the nurse's counter and just started blabbing. "Listen please, Nurse, I already have a room. I'm an admitted patient. I just woke up here and don't really understand what I'm doing here."

"Who are you?" said the nurse, a nice-looking brunette in her late thirties or early forties. Nice looking, but businesslike, as many admin types were in these settings.

"Can you just buzz me through? I don't really need —"

A buzzer sounded, and the other set of double doors, the ones that led on into the hospital proper, swung open.

I said thanks and rolled on, just wanting to get back to my home base and assess. Oh yes, I had a lot of assessing to do.

Chapter 15

Two little kids had seen a zombie. A nurse and one of my doctors had been peripheral enough to some of my stranger accomplishments to have suspicions. I had to "leave" one body inexplicably three floors and two wings away from where I'd taken occupancy, uncomfortably close to my Sanctuary Suite, and had abandoned another in mid air where it—having lost my animating vitality—presumably returned to limp formlessness and finished its appointment with gravity as a puddled heap in a soiled laundry bin on the sub-sub-basement floor.

It felt sloppy, but I wasn't sure what I could have done any differently. I'd learned a few new things about both sides of these life-into-death equations—one side being where I was in another human being's assigned turret of flesh, the other side being what happened to my own turret when not occupied by me.

That last "thing" was something I actually *didn't* know about. It was more like a lapse, a blackout, a classic lost film rediscovered but missing one of its reels.

It might not be important, this reel. Then again, it might be.

I certainly didn't wheel *myself* to the ER. Maybe just a good Samaritan bystander had done so. One could hope.

Wasn't much I could do about that at this point. The memory thread of my own roving mentality had been otherwise occupied, so to speak, making little kids' hair stand on end, puzzling medical staff, giving last thrill rides to Daffy Donald heavy equipment operators, and annoying ER triage nurses.

As I rolled along toward good old N222, two things sorted themselves away from these other concerns, which I planned to get back to, but the two things rose to the top:

1. *I felt fantastic.*
2. *Babby's inklings.*

My hands, working the smooth steel push hoops of my chair wheels, gripped strongly, without spasm or ache. My arms felt tight and powerful, my joints loose and well oiled, and my bones throbbed with a centering strength instead of a sapping ache. It had been years—couldn't even be sure how many—since I'd moved any splicketier than a deliberate safety walk, and yet now I wanted to leave the chair and trot up to N222. I wanted to take the stairs and bound up them, two, three at a time.

I didn't, but I wanted to.

I'd already pushed things close to the edge of exposure, what with the kids and the doctor and my floor nurse and whoever had pushed me to the ER when I was literally pre-occupied—or pre-occupying—elsewhere. So I wheeled myself along deliberately, slowly, but with a controlled grin on my face for anybody I passed in the halls.

Instead of letting my body loose like it wanted, I let my mind run, because I had plenty of soaring to do there as well.

Babby's inklings were extraordinary, really. Left behind in her brain, almost as if she had willed it for me, or to me, was a story. Previous inklings I'd experienced—there was always *something* left behind—had been fragmentary, sometimes incoherent, often feeble, like a last few sparks from a dead battery. But Babby had a big, full, neatly trimmed and completed narrative in there.

When you read an article, or even a novel, or a true account, you have to consume it in the linear. Songs and movies are similar, but engage the brain in a subtly different way. Words on paper are like a bridge creating cooperation between an author and a reader, an active telepathy where the reader has to actually work to co-create, with the author's rendered imagination, the story, the characters, the textures of time and place, light and space.

Moving pictures with sound don't need the creative cooperation of the viewer like reading does. The brain need only process the linear delivery of sensory narrative, with a little imaginative leverage to fill in implied gaps and add spices and nuance.

Visiting somebody's brain, as I had with Babby, was not a linear consumption. The story resided there in full, waiting for me, and once I got her warmed up with the cross-crawl, I got it—*all* of it. It flashed into my mind in an instant.

Think about stories you know, novels you've read, movies and miniseries and dramas you've seen. Once you've seen them, they're there, complete in your mind.

I can think about *Casablanca, Bend in the River, Red Moon and Black Mountain,* or *Do It Again,* or any book, movie, or song that I've read, watched, or listened to—*lived through*—and I don't need to read, view, or hear it again to remember pretty much the whole gist of the story. Sure, details are shadowy, but I know these stories.

During the half-hour or so I spent cross-crawling and wandering the facility in Babby's bod, I didn't have to stop and think about this remnant inkling—I was a little too busy, anyway. It was there—*here*—and I knew about it. Fleetings of it crossed my mind, as I had moments here and there to consider it, but now, as I rolled on home to N222, I could really reflect upon it.

As she was expiring, Babby *finished the story*. Her mind, absorbed in *my* improvised story about little critters and a meadow between two woods, had kept it going.

Not only did she finish it, she finished it *her* way, not mine.

Chapter 16

When the mind is preoccupied, the body goes on autopilot, like when you arrive at work and realize that you don't actually remember seven of the nine miles you just drove. The body settles into a natural energy level when the mind spins its own threads.

My threads were about Babby and how the more this worked, and the better it got, the riskier the whole scenario became. The one good factor, the little escape clause, the deniability card, was that the better I got at it all, the better I could alibi to separate myself physically from the dead doing the deeds.

Me? I was in my room... in the chapel... in the lobby.

These were solid alibis. I could *literally* (or *spiritually?*) be in two places at the same time.

As I neared N222, thinking lots of things over, I'd lost track of myself. I was basically driving home from work, and not noticing my surroundings, or how I was driving, or exactly where I was. I should have been dawdling along at my usual chronically-ill pace, but with my mind whirling and my body in *hum-hum-hum* shape, I must have gotten a little carried away.

"Well, look at *Speed Racer*," said Sinda, my second shift floor nurse.

"Uuh," I said.

Sinda stood half behind one of those round pillar things they use to accentuate healing spaces in forward-edge facilities like *Sanctuary*. She stepped out into my path as I was thinking fast.

"Caught me," I said. "The lounge coffee is better than the dietician tea they serve in N222, which I think isn't really tea. But I think I may have overdone it," I said, holding out one hand and letting my fingers tremble with simulated overcaffeination stimulation.

She sighed. "It's probably interacting with your calcium channel blockers too."

I hadn't really pulled it off, I could tell, but she was too busy to pursue my long absence, and too pre-occupied to conceptually link it with the body she and Dr. Jidalco had found twenty minutes ago in the hall.

"Well, you missed your med round an hour and a half ago, but I can't get back to your room for another half hour at least. Dr. said to just double it this once to compensate. Stick around, it's supposed to work better if you stick to the schedule. Though it looks like it's working, doesn't it?"

She spun and rushed off to the other side of the wing with her tray of supplies and meds, but called back over her shoulder. "Oh yes, you have a visitor! Been waiting a few minutes."

A visitor?

Visitor is a word with multifaceted meanings in health-care environments. Those meanings can vary greatly depending on perspectives, such as subjectivity or objectivity, and also depending on conditional variables such as duration of stay and severity of suffering—also on depth, or *perceived* depth, of relationship.

In other words, there are times when visits from relatives or loved ones are strength-giving and spiritually enlivening, and times when another visit from an uncle or cross-department co-worker makes you wish it was time for your bone-marrow extraction. There are, criss-crossing the circumstances, times when some laughs with a bud are exactly what you need, or when the last thing on your mind is an hour of hand-holding from your significant other, mother, step-brother.

It all depends on where you're at, emotionally, where in the tidal cycle ebb and flow of hope and pain you are situated when the door opens and he/she/it walks in.

Sometimes it's welcome, and sometimes it ain't. And the kicker is, *usually you don't know, and can't predict, which is what and what is which.* Sometimes you may think, *oh Jesus, I can't see anybody right now,* and then you have one of the bestest visits you've had in weeks, and it's with your brother-in-law's wife who you've never really even had a meaningful conversation with at a family holiday party, for Christ's sake.

After a while, hospital inhabitants figure this out, and try to accept visitors in a spirit of guarded neutrality, neither overly cheerfully nor excessively droopily, even if they think they're gonna be faking an enema emergency, or think they're gonna happily gain hope and strength and both parties part refreshed and revived. You just never know.

At this moment, as I wheeled toward N222, I had more than the usual mixed feelings. In fact, so much whirled through my mind that I really didn't want a visitor, and it wasn't the usual depressed fatigue that made me that moody. I felt great! An unfamiliar feeling surged through my blood and tissues, an anxiousness that comes with well-being, an agitated energy that I hadn't felt, literally, in years. I wasn't sure what to do with it, but I was pretty sure I didn't want to have to get into visitor mode, updating status and progress and hopefullies with whatever friend/relative/acquaintance had just shown up.

I rolled up to my door and peered around the frame into my room.

She was sitting on the window seat.

I could only see her head and shoulders, because my elaborate bed with its attendant rails and trapezes and auxiliaries and undercarriage took up the center of the little Sanctuary suite, and her face was turned downward to something, likely a phone or tablet or book.

Recognition came quickly. I'd seen her oh-so-briefly, and only once, but it had been just yesterday. Although the thought wouldn't have even remotely entered my mind during that brief meeting, I now felt a little jolt of excitement as I considered a possible outlet for that unfamiliar, agitated energy I felt.

I rolled through the door. "Hello!" I swung the heavy wooden door closed, and maneuvered my wheelchair close in front of it before setting its brakes and pushing myself to my feet.

Although I had a lot of energy and vitality, compared to a normal day, I still wasn't accustomed to being agile and unselfconscious on my feet. I tried to be smooth and relatively nonchalant as I pulled the privacy curtain on its curved track to give a little more seclusion to the window half of the space.

"Hi." She pushed a couple buttons on the sides of her cell phone, and dropped it into her purse.

For a few moments, we looked at each other, she sitting with her purse in her lap, me standing by the bed with the curtain still in one hand. Actually, I leaned a slight amount of my weight on it to keep from having to maintain my balance.

"I'm surprised you don't look more surprised," she finally said. She shook her hair — dark brown with a red sheen — back and blinked as she laughed at her surprise and my lacking it. Her hair only looked medium length from the front, but in the back, it brushed her shoulders as it settled back down after its shaking.

"It's been a long day, already," I said.

She nodded. "From what I've seen, you've spent plenty of it resting."

I looked at her, trying to see the meaning that I knew was there, and her eyes sparkled with a challenge to fit the puzzle pieces to the patterns we already shared.

She sighed lightly. "I really came to say thank you, but I couldn't find you earlier."

"Ah," I said, beginning to see. "Then you did?"

"I did."

I nodded and let go the curtain, placed a hand on the corner of the bed, took the three steps to the settee, and sat on its edge next to her. I put my hand on her purse. "Resting... is more strenuous than you might think. Do you mind if I recline here for a moment?"

Without waiting for her answer, I lifted her purse, lay my head on her lap, and brought my legs up, lying on my back and using her lap as my pillow. I placed her purse in my own lap.

"Okay," she said.

I looked up at her, into her face, settling my eyes into hers. I enjoyed this first relaxed, close contact with a woman—an attractive woman—I'd experienced in a very long time. Her soft, yet firm, thigh under my neck, the way the back of my head nestled into the little dip between her thighs where her skirt stretched across, comforted me.

"So," I said, "those numbers were... useful, I take it."

"Yes, very. I don't know how you did it, or how you knew, but it was crucial information that... well, let's just say it helped sort things out, and leave it at that."

"It's a gift." I saw no reason to share thorough details. "But it can be exhausting."

"You seem much stronger today, although I was very worried about you earlier. And frankly, I'm a bit surprised...."

"That I'm lucid, and articulate, and not autistic or neurologically impaired or—"

"Something like that. When you had the numbers, you weren't exactly, you know... you weren't...."

"I was babbling and my eyes were rolling back in my head? My face was ticcing and my limbs were shaking? At the time—and looking back on it, I think it was a wise judgement—I thought it best to dissemble that way to keep the mystery obscure. Wouldn't do to look too... methodical or... scientific."

"And yet I found you unresponsive and incoherent—catatonic really—this afternoon in the lobby there. Was that an act too?" She rested her hand on my head, her fingers lightly touching my hair.

I idly looked through her purse, taking items out and putting them back, and she didn't seem to mind.

"No," I said. "I was busy. I get that way when I get... busy. It was a shock waking later in the ER though."

"I was worried." Now she combed her fingers through my hair, smoothing it. "I didn't know what else to do."

It felt very peaceful, my head cradled in her lap and the caresses of her fingers, but I had energy that I hadn't felt for ages, and I needed to use it.

I stretched my neck and relaxed my head backwards, under her gently moving fingers. Then I slowly turned my head this way and that, un-kinking my neck, and she kneaded the base of my neck and the top of my spine. I looked up into her face, half closed my eyes, then turned onto my side, so that I was looking at her knees.

Her skirt hem stopped just a few inches above her knees. She had lovely knees. She continued to softly touch and stroke my neck. I reached with my left hand, and cupped my palm over her left knee, her flesh soft and firm and oddly cool. When I reached up her skirt, though, her skin was warmer there.

And when my lips met hers, warmer still.

She untied my gown, and I unbuttoned a few buttons of her blouse. Other than that, preparations were relatively simple. The only other thing we needed spilled out of her purse when it fell off the settee to the floor.

"Sinda is bringing my meds in 15 minutes," I whispered.

She drew her knees up and whispered back, "You better get my panties off now then."

As it turned out, we had about two minutes to spare. She tied my gown for me, and I went and moved the wheelchair and got back into my bed.

Sinda knocked when she came in, and we were having a typical visitor-patient chat by then, about how much more pleasant these new suites were than the old cubically sterile green-walled hospital rooms.

It appeared we weren't fooling Sinda, who wore that flat cynic's grin that hinted she had her suspicions. Was there still a slight sheen on our foreheads, a faint mist of fulfilled desire in the air?

Even though I would not go back and change that opportunistic pleasure, I knew my actions were closing in on me, that it would only be a matter of time before one thing or another gave me away.

Then again, furtive sex might have been a good decoy. In other words, which sounds like the lesser of two evils?

I think that patient is sneaking around the hospital, cultivating friendships with hospice palliatives and deathbed accident victims, and then performing Vulcan mind-melds with their deceased remains.

Or....

I know we're supposed to have a healing atmosphere of relaxed tranquility here, but I think this patient is snorkeling pre-cougars on his guest settee at the peak time of family visiting hours.

Either way, I'd begun to feel the hospital closing in on me, but I still needed it. I still desperately needed the unique and convenient availability to the dead — and near dead — that a hospital delivered, but it wasn't exactly an atmosphere of freedom. Indeed, a hospital — military service might have been mixed in there too — was the average experience that, for the majority of people, felt the most like a prison.

Perhaps that explained why, one week later, I was out of the hospital, gainfully employed, and living with her at her apartment. As it turned out, ours wasn't just a quickie anonymous afternoon delight.

But what *was* it then? What had happened? What had come over me? Her? Us?

Speaking only for myself, something actually *did* come over me. I'd never felt quite that way before, but I was getting used to it.

Following my recent treatment, harrowing as the surrounding events had been, I'd felt better than I had for many months, perhaps years. As I rolled my wheelchair back to N222, I felt something like a drug high, but there was more to it than that, something else at work. It had been coming over me in waves, regularly, ever since. It had become familiar.

But that first time, it was new.

In the past few years, I'd read a lot of caution leaflets, those little wads of thin white paper crammed into the boxes that prescription medications come in. I unfolded them accordion style, like little road maps, because like road maps, refolding them was akin to putting the toothpaste back in the tube.

My suspicion is that people generally don't bother reading these leaflets, unless they suddenly find themselves randomly falling asleep at intersections, calling their male relatives "Dolores," or noticing suddenly that one or both of their big toes are falling off. The bulk of these caution leaflets is devoted to listings of side effects—sometimes dozens, even hundreds of them.

I began to think *I* was suffering—or benefiting from—a strange new side effect, though not from some externally ingested substance. This side effect, similar to the leaflets' vague winner, *impulsive behavior*, had developed through my own discoveries. I didn't *get* a side effect. It wasn't *inflicted* like the furry black tongue of Pepto, or the half-day erection of Cialis. It came from within, from my own mind, my unique ability, my self-discovered treatment protocol. My life-saving, vitality-renewing, death-exploiting treatments had a halcion effect on my natural inhibitions.

It made me fearless, and to a degree, perhaps, conscienceless.

And why not? I had discovered something powerful, certainly more powerful than Xanax, Cialis, Wellbutrin, or Halcion.

And this had been a *big* dose, my biggest dose to date, my first real megadose. After serially possessing two ex-people, staggering the first one through the hallways of several floors of the complex barrowing on her own gurney, then pulling my first straight double-husk transfer, deflecting a post-mortem in a pathology lab by descending head first into a soiled-linens chute, and resuming my own corporealus on a different floor in a different wing by sniffing out and following some osmotic ethersense, I was well-charged—revived and ready. My internally developed side effect was so compelling, I realistically thought I had no real choice. If I'd walked into my suite at N222 and found a foursome of firemen and welders playing high-stakes PaiGow, I would have sat in and played with inscrutable bristo. I had become utterly risk aloof.

Thank you, Duck and Babby.

I really felt the need to acknowledge those whose passing had assisted in my treatments, honoring them by name.

Do their names matter more than mine? Yes.

Anyway, it wasn't poker. It was her.

I was energized, and horny, and uninhibited, like my old self but with guts.

I liked it.

Chapter 17

She lived in the borough, up on the ridge above the hospital, and although, out in the suburbs, nothing seemed to be designed for foot traffic anymore, it was really a walking-distance kind of stretch. Still, when she visited me in the ward the next day, my side effects were wearing off just a bit, so she came in and wheeled me down to the breezeway above the atrium that connected the second floor to the parking garage. We stashed the chair in a stairwell, and took the five-minute drive to her little apartment.

After that, without exactly discharging myself from County, I started taking that walk pretty frequently. I still needed the hospital, and they continued to "treat" me, and I treated myself, and spent time with her when I could get away.

It was, at least for a while, surprisingly easy to be a part-time inpatient.

The *her* in all this was Lorethe. When she first told me her name, in the breezeway that next morning, I said to myself, *Oh, Loretta, nice name.* Because it's spelled with the terminal *-ethe*, but sounds like *-etta*.

Problem was, I had a full time job. Not a *job*, not employment per se, but I was just as busy. I loved spending time with Lorethe, and truly *living* again, but in order to keep being the *good* me, who could enjoy and be enjoyed as a lover and companion, I had to keep my treatments up. Doing so consisted of a labor-intensive round of duties: terminal case detection; cultivating new friendships with likely dies; and by luck, pluck, and cunning, getting proximate access to do my *Lazarus* impressions.

Of course, at the time, Lorethe knew little or nothing of this... detail. Although aware of what she called my "talent," to her it was a mysterious insight, a sixth sense, a telepathic clairvoyance with the drifting mentalities of dead or dying souls. I left it at that, because she didn't need to know, at least not yet, that the deeper truth was much more crucial to me than a parapsychological parlor trick.

Getting out of the hospital — moreso getting away from the medical culture those few hours and minutes those couple of days — had inspired a new yearning in me. For so many months, I had gyrated between those other yearnings: the desire to feel well, to have energy, and the *other* other one, which was simply to have some kind of peace. Yes, *that* yearning.

Now, such yearnings of desperation seemed like faint memories, and their departing left some room.

When desperation leaves a void, what better to fill it than hope?

This new yearning initially came over me, and came on strong, when I first went on foot. We had driven the afternoon before, so I knew the way. I was observant. I noticed things. This didn't come naturally, at least not to me; I had to cultivate it. It took some discipline to look, and look again, and to keep looking. Eventually, it became habit, and I finally began to really *see.*

So I knew where to find what I required, but I needed to look a little different—just a little. Not quite a disguise, but a... a *diverted identity.* On a rack by the lockers in the imaging area, where they do all the MRIs and X-rays, I'd seen a light jacket. A week later, I noticed it again, in the same place. Now, a few days later, it still lay there, a khaki, canvassy thing with a dark collar, suitably neutral. A patient had undoubtedly left it, either absent-minded or so discouraged by ill health that he or she had been apathetic about being cold. I'd known the feeling myself.

I swung by there on my wheels, snagged the coat, and swiped a pair of green scrubs from a cart on my way to the lobby. In the big handicapped stall of the men's ground-floor public rest room, I tucked my gown into the scrubs. On foot now, I wheeled out my own chair and escorted it out across the breezeway, pretending to be Clint Eastwood with one of his invisible chairbound companions. I folded it and parked it in an under-stair well. With some luck, it would remain there until I returned for it.

Then, wearing my borrowed jacket, I walked.

I strolled past the heliport, across the tended empty lawn, down to the traffic light with no pedestrian buttons or lanes because nobody ever walked there. I jaywalked across to Central, which was anything but, because once I passed the last string of medical buildings with their colorectal outpatient centers and dermatology and psychiatry offices, I quickly entered a residential neighborhood. It seemed neither upscale, nor rundown, nor even in between, really. It was just a neighborhood, not a planned neighborhood, but not quite postwar veteran's starter homes either. It was an organic neighborhood with cape cods, split-levels, a few ranch homes, and an old stone farm dwelling every quarter mile or so.

I wasn't jaded or cynical. In fact, I was yearning. When I saw a sailboat on a trailer, with its mast stepped and its blue canvas cover faded and torn, in a driveway where it had obviously been dry-docked for a dozen years, I yearned.

I strolled slowly, regarding the great variety of aging suburban cheeses — those chainsaw sculptures that suddenly dotted the county a decade ago, now slumping with age and weather. The skillfully carved, artlessly posed, fat, haunched bears and generic prey birds that came across more as caricatures of ugly Italian football coaches than as fierce symbols of vulpine vigilance. On a pencil-neck galvanized post sat a brick and metal-fortified end-of-driveway mailbox, with a domed roof to rival any brick pizza oven, but perfectly sized for one of those Pepperidge Farm French Bread pizzas. I could almost hear, "Let those rotten kids try to smash my mailbox now," still echoing from its brick-muffled interior.

I relished my first taste of society, of reality, in many months. I didn't count the other reality that hospital habitants know all too well, the reality between channels 38 and 94 on the basic cable menu in the hospital entertainment contract, no DVR, no VCR — just real pawn shops, real toddler white trash beauty queens, real hillbillies living in controlled communities, real competitions where real losers watch their $10,000 prize pushed out a ten-story window, real brides paid to be unreal in their unreasonablenesses, real housewives, real parasites, real cops, real criminals, real New Jersey, real song singers, real life and death struggles for survival, and real myth busters. And who could forget the real investigations of mythical creatures, where the investigators had these two-foot poles attached to their hats with flashlights and infravid cameras so the viewers could see their green faces at weird angles as they panted around in the dark, shibboleth seeking.

Television was better when there weren't so many channels, and when it was less real.

As I walked through the neighborhood, I yearned, and because I seemed to be improving while pacing through an odd, tepid July wind, looking at homes and cars and trees and neglected boats, listening to the trees' leaves whisper and the dogs bark, the yearned-for seemed almost possible.

I needed to get out of the hospital... for good. But how?

How is how I ended up living with Lorethe a week later. In the meantime, I still needed my treatments.

By that Wednesday, when I'd been four days without a Lazarus fix, partly because I was enjoying Lorethe's company, partly because the last dose had been strong enough to spoil me a bit, it became clear that I would have to return to the grind, and soon. The dark curtain of fatigue had started closing in on my mind, and the returning morbidity stiffened my joints and queased my innards.

I needed to take some shortcuts because of my neglect for the prep work: the hospital reconnoitering, the ID and acquaintencing phases. With my growing skill, or improving knack, I hoped to truncate some of that prep.

I hoped something else, and actually planned it: This time, I would *try* to double shift, not just stumble into it. The extra boost would be worth the extra planning.

Not easy though.

When I got back to the hospital after my little visit to Lorethe, I again rolled through the corridors a few times, simply soaking up the vibe. This, like all hospitals, was a community, but a transient one — lots of turnover. Yet many of the community's people — elderly and chronic cases, mostly — made return trips and recognized staff, and were in turn recognized. The staff themselves were increasingly itinerant, as some equipment specialists roved all over the county, or several counties, doing dialyses or positive airway training or phlebotomies. So the vibe, the texture, the taste and feel of the community varied from day to day, and even more from week to week, month to month, year to year.

The planning required litte prep, as I couldn't really organize the steps beyond this: get the vibe, figure out who's who, then get ready, and go find two.

Perhaps I had become reckless, as a gnawing fear grew. During that last treatment, I'd felt the bottomless panic of actually losing my self, my *me*, that helpless feeling of having uprooted my consciousness and then slipping up. I feared the ultimate slip-up of either being stuck in a stiffening stiff, or getting lost between bodies, somehow losing track of my own near-and-dear, warm, living, and breathing home. I needed to avoid, in future plans, misplacing my soul somewhere in the interstitial nowhere between the precious quick and the desolate dead.

First, while I still had the energy, I walked to Lorethe's. I hadn't noticed it while riding in her car, perhaps because we were involved in conversation. It's just as well.

What hadn't I noticed?

The *it* loomed up slowly on the left. I didn't want it looming any faster, grateful to be walking at a modest pedestrian pace, because as I gradually became aware and more sharply focused on *it*, I needed time to cope with the idea.

It was a cemetery.

The homes had thinned out, on this little lonelyish stretch of the avenue between the busier ends of Central, the end behind me being busy with medical satellites, then those slightly run-down homes with fortified mailboxes and bohemian yuppy statuary, with the end ahead feathering out into the borough proper with its fencing manufacturers and boutiques. This little stretch was part fallow, part brownfield, and... part graveyard.

The headstones peeked their curved gray crowns above the cement-capped fieldstone fencewall that framed the old yard, fighting their way through sprays of seeding grasses.

I slowed further, not sure how I felt about this — not sure how it would *feel*, period.

My death sense had unquestionably developed, so this felt familiar, and I realized that I *had* felt it during our drive-by yesterday; I simply hadn't recognized it. I'd been chatting with Lorethe, and I felt it but dismissed it, and it passed.

Now, putting two and two together while staring at the graveyard, I *felt* the graveyard. This time, I couldn't zoom past at a vehicular speed. On foot, the feeling hit me strongly, and it confused me.

I kept going, desperate to understand this, at once both repelled and attracted. Impelled rather than attracted, really, because this external influence had become an inner force driving me.

I walked right up to the iron gate, stared in briefly, then turned my back on the dead and closed my eyes.

It was probably a good thing, for me in this circumstance anyway, that these days people *didn't* walk around much anymore, or really notice things when they drove from place to place. Because perhaps the sight of a man in green scrubs and an Elmer Fudd coat, standing centered in front of a derelict graveyard with his eyes closed, on a weekday in July, at 10:28 AM, would cause a few eyebrows to arch, if people were still inclined to slow down and notice things.

I felt it, but only as a faintly palpable energy, a minimal residual vibration. It was old, creaky, spent death. There were no concrete inklings, just thin streams of low-level non-informational nuance. Like faint, oxygen-starved wind through ruined, cracked boards of a high-altitude ghost town, they made no sound, left no impression — save a not-quite-haunting vagueness.

I turned in place, a complete 360 degrees, and I understood.

There were many places like this, in these eastern states, in the Midwest, the South — the orphaned remainders of lost cultures. Like those ghost towns in the mountains and prairies out west, they gradually decayed in these urban and suburban landscapes, surrounded not by encroaching overgrowth, but by suburban sprawl and unplanned neglect. As I turned through that circle, I saw no church, just the walled space, half an acre or so, the crumbling monument stones, the granite specimens weathering a little better, and the limestone markers weeping away their engravings over time, losing their identities.

I opened the gate and went in.

Something stopped me from just plunging straight into the center of the space. Nor did I wander aimlessly, or zero-in on a big stone or a broken monument. I stopped, then turned, and followed the wall to my right until I reached the first corner. It happened to be the northwest corner of the square enclosure. I stopped there and again looked over the whole. Part of the wall had deteriorated here, a few yards along from that corner. With the grass overgrown, and many of the grave markers tilted by long standing through wet and dry, through cold and heat, and many others chipped or outright broken, it was hard to see the patterns, to see rows and columns in the plan of this old churchyard.

Interred here were families, couples, generations, and loners. They dated back as far, on the legible stones, to the 1700s, perhaps further, because some rounded and weathered white limestone tablets were simply blank, any engraving they may have once had long, long gone.

Something odd, too, was that a large central section of the plot lay completely stoneless. This didn't really make sense, unless there'd been a long stretch of control-freak sextons, or some other anti-random factor, keeping the prime burial sites reserved. I paced the area carefully, parting the grass here and there, and satisfied my curiosity. Oblong depressions appeared hither and thither, along with other slot-shaped cavities, hard to discern through the evening of time and weather. Yet it became clear: the central clearing was stoneless, but not graveless.

So why were stones removed, and why aren't they piled up, in the corner perhaps, where the perimeter walls meet?

I returned to the gate and leaned against the wall there, closing my eyes and letting my breathing slow. I wanted to feel the rhythm, the peace and history of this place. I wanted to know more than I could see.

First, I thought.

I thought about the names I had just read: Bloomhart, Detwiler, Wagaman, Wismer.... I thought about the dates: none past the early 20th century, and even those just a few compared to the majority of this population—half a dozen markers dated 1904, 1906, 1908 the very latest one. I thought about those years, a hundred years ago and more, and what it must have been like. People still visited then, I was sure. Jump ahead a decade. Then, 1918. Visitors? Yes.

1928, 1938, 1948? There were no World War One dead in this yard, nor any victims of that 1914 pandemic flu. No World War Two casualties, either. When had the church ceased to be? Presumably when the graves had stopped arriving, around 1908 or so, perhaps earlier.

And where are those lost stones?

I thought of some of the people lying here, dead a century, others dead for 200, 300 years. I thought of a man coming here, perhaps in the late 1800s, visiting a parent, himself a brother, someone's child grown up. I thought of him taking some comfort in knowing that, in a few years, he would lie in this place too, and that he would, in turn, have visitors who would remember him. I thought further into the future, of others who would remember those that had remembered him, with those now lying nearby.

Then it stopped. Some time twenty, thirty years after his visit, some fifteen or twenty years after the church itself had vanished, the visits too, evaporated.

That line—the line of community, of family, of descending relations—would have dwindled, migrated, and forgotten, until it finally stopped completely.

Then I stopped thinking. I wanted only to *feel*.

That's when answers came.

I was wrong. Yes, the regular small visits stopped, the single widows and pairs of adult siblings. They died off, moved on, forgot, and were in turn forgotten, but.... I could see, in my mind's eye, a tour bus pulling up, slowing down as it swept past the old walls. Feeling it, I knew that it made this scheduled trip twice a year, spring and fall.

The community wasn't gone. It had just moved, farther west where open land remained, with room for vegetables, where draft horses still yoked hay rakes, and families still had a milk cow or two even when they weren't really dairy people by trade.

I turned to move on, to resume my walk to Lorethe's, but couldn't help wondering about the lost stones, even though I knew concentrating would just push the knowledge further away.

I looked back over my shoulder, and saw one tall hank of grass that seemed to wave counter to the pulsing sway of the wind. I didn't want to look too hard, because I thought there was bone, weathered white and chalky, with darker streaks like etchings on scrimshaw, and maybe carpals, in there with the dry brown stalks and blades, and seed-head tufts.

Ten minutes later, I sat on a tall stool at the kitchen counter in Lorethe's apartment, while she made egg-salad sandwiches and poured jasmine tea into big, blue, crudely glazed, hand-thrown mugs.

Chapter 18

After months of institutional feedings, I watched fascinated as food and drink actually took form before my eyes, rather than arriving on a tray under plastic wrap and stainless domes.

In the small apartment, where one of the post-Victorian family homes had been quartered, Lorethe had half a second floor and half an attic. Her neighbor below her, I presumed, had half a basement in addition to a similar main layout. Her apartment had a kitchen/dining area, a living room, and a bedroom, which I hadn't seen yet but felt somewhat confident that I would—if not today, then perhaps soon.

We perched across from each other, seated on stools on opposite sides of the counter, and seemed to be taking turns being alternately absorbed in the food and feeding, then in each other, the former in a sort of obligatory way, the latter, curiously. As we ate our sandwiches and sipped our tea, me sitting in the living room and she in the kitchen, I could tell by her slightly ironic smile that she knew as well as I did that this was a moment, or perhaps a stretch of moments, when two people figure something out.

Intimate relationships start in an endless variety of ways, but when minds meet before physical intimacy, a stretch of moments like this one might never occur.

When such a relationship begins with physical interplay, or that interplay comes early, as it did in our case, there does come a time when you both know you're going to find out—when you're actually *about to find out* if you *like* each other, beyond just... well, *lusting* each other.

"Was it cold?" she asked. She'd stopped between sandwich halves, and concentrated on her tea, cupping it in her hands rather than holding the cup by the loop.

"It?"

"The walk over."

"Actually, it got my circulation going. My feet are warmer than they've been in months."

"You've been there a while?"

"Just a week, but before that it was the nursing home for a month plus, and before that in and out of labs and diagnostics."

Her eyes brightened, and I could feel her empathy, her assumption of my pain and frustration. "I'm glad it's improving."

"It's more than a breakthrough. I really think I could discharge immediately, and even... well, even stay out."

For some reason, I thought my words might perpetuate the flow of conversation on this topic, stimulate a response and some give and take, but instead the thread seemed to die off in spite of what I thought would have been a floating loose end waiting to be seized. She sipped her tea as I munched another sandwich half, and the silence grew awkward.

I warded that off with a new thought. "The other day... um... well, thank you."

She stopped sipping, moved the tea half an inch from her lips, and looked at me over it. "You're thanking me for...?"

"That? No, no. No, I meant what you did earlier, before... um... *that*. Taking me to the ER."

She seemed relieved, but only momentarily. She was about to sip, then stopped after her lips made a brief reedy whistle over the rim. "What?"

"The other day. You said you found me in the lobby, asleep in my wheelchair."

"Yes."

"So you took me to the ER."

"I said that?"

"You did, right?"

She continued to regard me over her tea, and hadn't moved.

I could already tell that, no, she hadn't. "No, you didn't. Oh... okay... you didn't say it, and you didn't do it. How did I get there?"

She looked at me, and put her tea down. "You're messing with me."

I thought about agreeing with her, but I needed to figure this out. I still wasn't sure how much of my issues, my talents, my treatments, my thoughts and theories—my *world*, bizarre as it was becoming—I wanted to share. Perhaps *wanted* didn't fit. I *wanted* to tell her things, to unburden myself, to have another mind involved in my puzzles, to have help, to have a partner, a friend, a co-conspirator. But could I? Was it safe? Would she understand, or would this scare her?

No, I might *want* these things, but it was too soon.

Still, I couldn't just be *messing with her*. I needed to figure out what had happened. How I had gotten to the ER, and why?

I shook my head. "You did see me in the lobby." I stated it, but looked at her and my eyebrows made it a question, a little bit.

She nodded and toyed with her sandwich, turning it over. Then she looked back at me. "I found you asleep, or passed out. I thought, passed out, which was worrisome. It was, after all, a medical facility and you were a patient in a wheelchair. I didn't want to wake you, but as I stood there, you startled. Your eyes opened, and you smiled at me, there in the lobby, but...."

Her shrug told me what she was wondering: *I shouldn't have to tell him this.* After all, I was there too.

"You're going to have to help me... *remember*," I said. "It's sort of sketchy. Parts are missing."

"This has something to do with your... your *talent*, doesn't it?"

"Yeah," I said, and sipped. "It's like a side effect."

She reached across the counter and placed her hand over mine. "Don't worry, I'm on your side."

She picked up the half sandwich, corner-cut in a triangle shape, with thumb and finger and, opening wide, just ate it—the whole thing. At first, it looked like she was just going to give a dainty bite, and then, she snarfed it and chewed half her lunch with fat cheeks.

I just looked at her—the twinkling eye, her trembling lip. She probably expected me to chuckle, at least, but once known as a sharp at the poker table, I held my expression and lifted my chin about an eighth of an inch.

Her eyes crinkled as she raised one hand and sort of waved it, like a white flag surrendering, and when I still didn't crack a smile, she lost it.

Had to give her credit, though. I expected an egg-salad spit-take, but, eyes tearing up and her temples sort of throbbing, she managed to gag it down *before* she started laughing. And that—the fact that she pulled it off, that she kept it together enough to maintain some dignity—finally broke through to me, and I laughed.

Laughter must have been an aphrodisiac. She came around the counter and sat on my lap, as best she could on the high stool, and together we laughed. We tried to fit some sips of tea between the breaks in the giggles, and then her mouth was on mine, and my hands were in her full dark hair, and then under her shirt, and then her skirt, and then my scrubs were untied and she was leaning on the counter, with me close behind.

Afterwards, we lay on the couch together, still zipless but fully clothed, cozily spooned, and she continued.

"I was coming to see you. In the lobby — the other lobby, the main one — the receptionist looked you up for me and wrote the number, 222N, on a sticky note. You weren't there, though, in your suite, so I asked the nurse. She seems to have an attitude, doesn't she?"

"She's really very good. I like to think of it as personality."

"Well, she's all *oh, that one, our little wanderer,* but she said you come back pretty often. I decided to go get a cup of tea, and the coffee shop is next to that far lobby, so that's when I found you."

She explained how she got her tea at the shop, then came back out and saw me in my chair in the old lobby. She had come to see me, to thank me, to tell me that that number sequence had been so helpful, and to ask about how I did it. She was curious, and the way she now tilted her head and shifted her eyes, I knew we'd at some point be circling back around to it. Anyway, she said I was asleep or passed out, but I startled, and then awoke and smiled at her.

Then, I was asleep again. After waiting a few minutes, without any further sign of stirring from me, not wanting to wake me, she decided to wheel me to my room. As she pushed the wheelchair along, I would startle now and then, mumbling.

As we neared my room, she said, we passed one of the lounges they tended to put near elevators and at hallway corners, where family members could go wait while bedpans or phlebotomies made company uncomfortable. It was a long narrow room with warm tones in the furnishings, and institutional touches in the room design itself. Transparent glass walls bordered the hallway, and some kind of medical pinkish germicide tile enclosed the rest of the space. A cathode-ray television sat mounted on a retrofuturistic stalk, like those machine necks in War of the Worlds.

I didn't remember any of this, but Lorethe said I startled, seemed to awake and look at the television. She kept pushing, and I kept looking, my eyes tracking on the screen as we moved past. I almost fell out of the chair craning my neck, and made some moaning noises that finally got her attention. She stopped and pushed the chair back under me, gathered me back in, and turned it toward the television.

Then, she said, something changed. She said it was almost like, in a sense, a filling, an arrival. Whereas up to now I'd been weakly in and out of presence and consciousness, it was as if I *inflated* before her eyes. Gone was the faltering, blundering, drifting, aceless deck.

First of all, she said, I focused, riveted to the screen. Second, I strengthened. Rather than awkwardly flopping and lolling, I steadied and tensed and unwavered. My hands gripped the chair, my legs stiffened and pushed against the leg-rests, and I attended to the images moving on, and voices coming from, the television.

And then, Lorethe said, I slowly turned my head to look at her, and said, "I'll be back in a few minutes." My voice had been steady and even, and rather cold and chilling, in a way. I'd turned the chair, with my hands gripping the wheels and now capably propelling and steering it, and wheeled myself briskly down the hall the way we had come.

She said there was really no question of her following or attending me, that my intention and preference to remain alone had been quite clear.

Although Lorethe had been placing just about all her attention on me as I came back to life, as I reanimated, quickly gathered information from the television, and then took my leave, now, left standing there in the hallway holding her bag while watching me roll away, she had to assemble herself and try to understand. She hadn't really been listening to or watching the report on the video screen, but now, she looked and listened. She just caught the tail end of it, she said, something about "...and the cause of the accident, and the circumstances, are still under investigation. This is Nera Zilpajic reporting from County Hospital."

She forced her mind back, she said, and gathered back a few words and images that had washed over her as she watched the change in my presence that had taken place before her eyes. She remembered images of heavy equipment, the yellow road machinery, strips of orange flags and orange-vested men, bared and mounded earth, red brown, heaps of gray gravel.

As she told me these things, remembered from her hospital visit several days ago, I remembered, too. I remembered returning to my body, in my wheelchair, in the emergency room, and the corner of a woman's left eye, a small woman in her thirties with a white purse in her lap—nervous, terrified even.

Poor Duck's widow.

I'd thought she was reacting to the road rash, but now, I thought it was something else. It was me, or rather, my body.

This was the first inkling I had that this wasn't a one-way street, that while my consciousness temporarily vacated my own body, a restless and wandering consciousness could take residence.

My treatments, which reinvigorated and restored me, might have side effects, might have costs or consequences, of which I'd been completely unaware.

I became aware that I was not alone. For several minutes, I'd been virtually alone in my thoughts, realizing the meaning, the *meanings*, of this new information that Lorethe had just shared. But she was still here, in my arms, and she must have been aware that she'd just delivered a revelation.

I thought about her, and knew that I had to teeter one way or the other. I'd been keeping facts, theories, ideas to myself, wondering about her, wondering about me, wondering about... well, all the things one wonders about when starting a relationship, when intimacy opens large gaps in the curiosity of both partners. The vacuum forms, and then each decides how to fill it, fast or slow, honestly or slyly, strategically or without caution. I could either start that process now, somehow, some way, or get up and leave.

"We have so much to talk about," I whispered.

"Oh, you're back," she said.

Then and there, I told her all.

After that, we came up with a plan, but first, I had to go back. I needed a recharge.

Chapter 19

The good thing about mystery illnesses is they can become *conveniently* mysterious when circumstances require. Like so many bad things, that which makes them bad can become an advantage. Just like so many good things, that which makes them good can eventually backfire.

Not only that, but in outpatient medical settings, much of the population is serially involved in receiving or delivering procedures of one sort or another, either waiting for them, enduring them, or getting over them. This constant cycling of people getting sick, getting treated, and getting well or getting worse, or perhaps dying, and maybe gyrating from well to sick and back, this churn makes for short attention spans among the professionals themselves.

I'd never been *chased* by a specialist or diagnostician. These physicians rarely became interested enough in individual patients like me, no matter how challenging or unusual our symptoms and pathologies, to develop any obsessive persistence, or to grow attached in any deep or emotional way.

At least, this had been my experience up to that point. I'd migrated from doctor to doctor, from therapy to therapy, from diagnosis to diagnosis, from syndrome to syndrome, from protocol to protocol. Always, when I called and cancelled that last follow-up appointment, I got little or no argument. I never actually spoke with the doctor, and rarely to a nurse or P.A. Usually, I just spoke with a receptionist, and she'd say, *"Well, all right, you call us if you need the doctor to have another look, okay?"*

It was a little trickier in an institutional setting, because in a hospital like this, doctors had to discharge me. The finance office needed to clear my account with whatever insurance plans, research objectives, and special deals may have come into play.

Maybe this is why so many of these institutions have the policy where patients aren't actually allowed to depart under their own power, but must be rolled out in a wheelchair, with escorts. They want to slow you down, supervise your disconnection with their systems, and make sure they've crossed their T's and dotted their I's. Legal concerns play a role too. They need to make sure somebody won't collapse in the parking lot and transform into a malpractice lawsuit. Or, behind the wheel half a mile from the hospital, in heavy traffic, that they'll lose consciousness, start a chain collision, and initiate seven *simultaneous* lawsuits while concurrently creating a crowded triage situation in their ER.

I was ready to leave, yet nervous about leaving. Lorethe and I had figured out some ideas for continuing to recharge my vitality outside the institutional setting, but these were untested. At any rate, it would take me a few days, at the least, to work out all the details of my discharge. This time, too, a few doctors had a greater interest in my case than all those other outpatient dischargings, when the receptionists had been so ready to move on to their next chart, their next insurance card, their next set of lab results, the next intake questionnaire and progress checklist.

The nurses and other floor staff, on the other hand, may have been more than ready to see the last of me. Not that they actively disliked me or developed personal feelings one way or the other, but they likely saw me as an inconvenience, troublesome, puzzling, and in some ways mysterious.

Professional staffers *understand* patients who self-advocate, who are proactive in their care, who ask lots of questions, who read the leaflets and the fine print and the disclaimers. These pros understand, yes, but they also get irritated, because these advocacy behaviors slow down the works and disengage the intermeshed gears that keep all the processes efficiently moving. I was like these patients, but different—worse. I would completely disappear, reappear, wane and wax, ebb and flow worse than any of them. I wasn't belligerent, or sour, or uncooperative, but I was a PITA—*Pain In The Ass*—due to my independence and wandering tendencies.

PART TWO

THE DEAD AMONG THE LIVING

Chapter 20

If zombies were truly real, I would, perhaps, have been the only human being on Earth capable of describing their existential reality. Having reanimated numerous corpses, I could explain what it felt like to arise, to awaken, *to come to* inside another soul's corporeal host—to transition, to achieve a transferred sentience, to feel somebody else's flesh surrounding my spirit, to inhabit somebody else's worldview, their vantage, their perspective, *their* soft-centered selfness in *their* hard physical sphere.

I'd done it enough times by then that it no longer surprised me or jarred me. I would simply shrug my way in, and it really wasn't at all like awakening—more like parking *one* car, engaging the parking brake, and then getting into and starting up *another* car.

After Lorethe and I had made our plans, I went back to the hospital for some last preparations, and for one last clinical recharge—a real doozy I'd scoped out. It had only taken me a day or so, and I'd lined up two likely terminal friendships, and one decent alternate in case one of the better likelies fell through. I was even reasonably confident that I could possibly, even probably, get the double-treatment boost by accomplishing another host-host spirit transfer, hopefully with extra *juice* from a bit of physical activity with *both*.

Ambitious? Sure, but Lorethe and I had ambitious plans, and we couldn't be sure how long it would take to get them started. I might need a really strong recharge, because if it didn't go well at first, and our plans for new treatment sources took longer to materialize than expected, my condition could deteriorate rapidly.

This time, however, I awoke confused. My first thought, as soon as I could move or feel, was that something was missing.

Where am I?

I quite simply was not ready, not in a planned reanimation, an expected treatment. Things didn't feel right. I didn't know what had happened.

What's happening? Where's my turban?

Those were my first thoughts, before I even opened my eyes or flexed a muscle.

Turban?

I heard a voice, grunting, and then another voice, also grunting. These weren't inchoate gruntings, sleep grunts, pain grunts, or other types of unfocused or unpurposed gruntulations. These were *evaluative* grunts.

Then, a word: "Look!"

The other voice: "Yes!"

The first vioice: "Eyelids too."

It started to come back to me. I'd been rolling down the North Wing of the old section of the hospital, mid-morning, just about ready to make my first leap, if my target was available and the timing ideal. If the time wasn't ripe, I'd back off and wait for availability.

Then, something happened. In a way, it was more like an *absence* of happen, because in the middle of the proverbial minding my own business, I suddenly wasn't *minding* at all. The next thing I knew, here I lay on a gurney with a pair of observers making cryptic comments and qualitative grunts about my facial tics.

I didn't know what was going on, but I knew enough to proceed — or not — carefully.

I was suspicious that somehow, maybe, my cat had been unbagged, that my little deal, my skill, my special rejuvenating *friendships*, had been hijacked.

Is my secret out?

Although I'd only heard grunts and brief commentary, I sensed these weren't a couple of kids messing with me — no *undead-cinema* fanboys.

Somehow I'd briefly lost control of my own trickage, perhaps due to drugs. If I ventured back into my own husk, wherever it was, I might find myself unconscious, or sedated and twilighted to grogginess at best. I needed to think, which wasn't easy using this fellow's brain, and....

...Without my turban.

These not being ten-year-olds, whom I could startle and freak, left that psychological weapon out of my arsenal. My coming to life — in this body — could be exactly what these whitecoats wanted.

Luckily, enough of my deathsense remained intact that I could tell that I was right where I wanted to be. Treatment candidates resided, shiftable and ready, nearby. So I remained still, and thought.

Lying there, still as death, aware but unmoving, I struggled with the urge to look. I wanted to open these eyes to see whom I was dealing with, to look around and figure out where I was, to gather information to use, to influence my next actions. I seriously considered the possibility of playing along, of waking up, leaning up on one elbow, and talking it all over with these chaps, but....

I had an uncomfortable feeling. Something about the voices I'd heard, even though all I'd heard were some grunts and isolated words; something about the quality and tone of those voices, of the *breathing* of those observing me... gave the atmosphere an air of intention, of scientific purpose, of leverage and ambition.

There was *want* in it.

Well, *I* wanted to keep pursuing my own agenda, not some guinea-pig plan, but as I lay there, my lips and eyelids gaining a little color, the gruntings became more appreciative.

Then I remembered a waiting room, and waiting there for treatment, comfort, and answers that never came. On the wall of the waiting room hung the usual diplomas and certificates and specialty group qualifications, and... among them, an aircraft carrier.

One of my specialists had been a Navy medical corpsman, a military neurologist. Something about his breathing, those grunts, felt familiar.

I became, quite suddenly, angry—unusual for me. Anger usually seethed its way to a head for me, starting as frustration or annoyance, and transitioning through irritant pique to true itching, scratching anger. The anger, coming on suddenly as it had, almost became a reflex, and almost blew my cover.

Dr. Scutcheon. His aircraft carrier breathing. And those Jidalco grunts.

These two hovered over me like medical jackals or vultures. They'd trapped me here somehow, carefully preserving my gamma-alpha-delta-wave flow. They needed my spirit-tapping intact in order to manipulate it.

Propofol? Maybe. More likely a twilight cocktail, sodium oxybate gin with thorazinic vermouth.

What were they up to? Just curiosity? Research? Or something else?

As the anger scalded my emerging mind in that motionless, lifeless, turbanless body, threatening to lash forth in physical reaction, I finally got it tamed and under control. With any unwanted reflex now safely stowed, I felt around for more and clearer information about which other bodies lay nearby.

Then it hit me! My sweet little plan to enjoy a little feast of energy-giving jumps, my good fortune in having several nice subjects all serendipitously available to me, conveniently in useful proximity, wasn't really *my* plan at all. It had been *their* plan all along.

We were in the forensic lab, next door to the morgue. I'd become quite familiar with this place, having seen most of the connecting spaces, many of the vault drawers, the insides of the rooms, the analytical machinery and forensic instrumentation, the gurneys and tables and troughs and trays—I'd seen all this with several sets of eyes. I'd even seen the insides of the laundry chute here, accelerating at roughly 11 feet per second.

I knew my way around here, and in this room at the moment were four people: two alive, two on tables.

In the next room, behind a closed door, two more lay: one dead, and me.

I really had it quite under control, doing quite well, considering.

Then Scutcheon had to open up his mouth. Maybe he got impatient, not good with the deceased—they have eternity on their side.

"I think you overestimated him," he said, and chuckled. This wasn't a chortle of amusement, or a chuff of dismissiveness. This chuckle was a *p-phhh* of disparagement and disrespect.

The anger, which had been simmering beneath the surface, surged, and I almost jumped up and beaned the eminent asshole with a stainless organ receptacle. Instead, I twitched just a little.

Then I jumped.

Chapter 21

I didn't jump in the sense that the body I occupied made any movement other than that slight twitch. Rather, I jumped out, leaving that body to go back to my own home body.

Too bad I didn't learn more about that missing turban.

I didn't really have a plan, but I needed to get away from these guys.

In truth, I was continuing to get better at this. In moments like this, I realized that I would *continue* to improve. For that, I was thankful, because the timing was fortunate. When I needed confidence, this awareness that my growing knack could run circles around Scutcheon's arrogance gave me a certain... strength, or boldness, or power, or....

Glee. It gave me glee—and maybe some strength, boldness, and power, too.

I immediately hovered in the next room, temporarily unconnected to any pair of ears, which made me nervous. I really, really wanted—needed—some sense of what was going on in the room I'd just left. I wanted to keep tabs on Jidalco and Scutcheon. In fact, part of me wished I'd stayed for just that purpose—I needed to know their plans. I would have to gain information in other ways, but first, I needed to regain control.

Right now, *they* were in control. This would not do.

Without even really thinking it over, I followed my first instinct and started to reassimilate into my own body. It was suddenly so comfortable, so easy, so smooth and enveloping, that I grew wary. At least, I wanted to, but it was a dark, heavy blanket in there—slow, dense, cool, and still. I almost just fell in and went to sleep, because there were, indeed, strong drugs in there. My body had been sedated, but not anesthetized.

It seemed these medicos, my manipulators, my guinea kings, knew what they were doing. At that moment, though, I didn't have time to think about it. I could only react and follow my instincts.

If they'd used general anesthesia, they would have damped down my consciousness, quelled my brain activity, and prevented my movable mind from the migration they wished to observe. They knew they needed an active, but detachable, mind. These guys were good — arrogant, ulterior, mercenary, but good.

I got about a quarter of the way back into my husk, and noticed pretty quickly that this would not serve my purposes. I would simply melt into the sludge of twilight consciousness, and either remain inactive until I woke up physically, or end up just like I'd been a few minutes ago, waking up groggy and under the observation of the doctors, with them grunting and sighing about a different pair of lips and eyelids — this time my own — gaining color as my energizing presence came awake.

I needed to stay out of my own, drugged body, so I could stay alert, so I could either find out what was going on, or get away. The third alternative, staying for their unknown ministrations, was the option I wasn't willing to experience just now.

I reversed, and stretched back out. This was hard, because I was nervous and shaky, unclear about where I was going and what dangers awaited me. The easy thing would have been just to continue, to go the rest of the way home and just take a nap in there with one arm around the Propofol and the other around the oxybate.

I couldn't go back into the body I'd just exited, and I risked my consciousness going instantly dormant if I went back into my own body. So I couldn't go home, and I couldn't go back with the doctors. Only one real choice remained: this other body, next to my own in the adjoining room.

Well, I had another choice, but it scared me: remaining disembodied. I'd not yet experimented with this. Up to now, I'd always spent the minimum of time in the between spaces, going straight from my body to my host, or from host to another host — no lingering in that neither-here-nor-there. And when in transit, I didn't look left or right, up or down. I had my blinders on, and concentrated on my corporeal destination.

I didn't want to examine the ether, the interstitial, the third realm. Just thinking about it gave me the heebie-jeebies. I knew all too well what I was playing with here. I'd seen things there out of the corners of my eyes — glowing things, arcs of gravity, strangely buzzing darknesses that silently echoed into endless distances. I knew one thing with absolute certainty: should I choose to explore that realm, possibly even just to *look*, that would be it. I would not return.

Remaining disembodied for a fairly brief time remained theoretically possible, but it would require a level of concentration, or paradoxically, mindlessness, which I hadn't yet developed. I was simply not ready to attempt it.

So, I went for the other body, an old one, as usual. I couldn't *see* this, being temporarily bodyless and therefore without vision, but the disembodied mind projects a visual sense. Rather, it projects part of the entirety of what it senses as a visual element, because that's a convenient way to divide and delimit the whole stream, among the five senses that we have practiced with our whole lives.

Thus, I could feel-see-smell-taste that this guy was old. Then, I was in.

I went quickly, because I needed to activate his ears, and I heard activity from the next room. Maybe I was projecting, or streaming their thoughts. Maybe I was just paranoid, but I could have sworn they were on to me. The lips and eyelids of turban guy had undoubtedly gone cold and pale, after the twitch, but the twitch might have been a good thing. It might have bought me time.

Now, whether I heard it, imagined it, or simply sensed it somehow, I knew they were starting to panic.

Once I got the ears going, I confirmed this.

"He's gone!" one said.

"Wait," the other said. "He can't go back. If he does, he's so buzzed we'll have to wait hours."

"No, no, you fool, he'll move on."

Soon, very soon, they'd figure out what I'd done, where I'd gone, and would come barging in from the next room.

I couldn't figure out what to do. They had my sedated body, and I couldn't *leave* with this old body and leave my flesh with them. I'd have to come back to myself at some point, but right now, I wanted to get away from them. I didn't know what they were capable of, but it seemed foolish to risk underestimating them. If I were to overestimate them, I would think them capable of keeping me unconscious and immobile, or even inducing some low-level coma, indefinitely.

Panic filled me, and I proceeded to do the only logical thing left to me.

I flicked on the old guy's shiver switch, trying to get the old dead flesh and bones limbered up.

Then a commotion came from the next room. They were coming.

I wanted to run, but they were about to come in, and I may not have time to slide back out. Then they'd have me. I couldn't move fast in a cold body, but maybe I could buy some time.

I saw that the electrodes and wiring on this guy, the body I now occupied, were hooked up to a single pole-mounted monitor. EEG, I figured. I looked at the monitor, and then over at the monitor they'd hooked up to my own body. They'd attached more instruments and wires to my body, but they also had instrumentation corresponding to this body over there, and it showed activity. Now that I resided in this body, it showed a moving wave too, a yellow line moving across a green screen with gridlines. The one on my body was smooth and largely consistent, probably mainly delta waves.

This one showed a fairly quiet activity—erratic, but indicating life. I needed it to go back to dead, so I reached up and pulled one of the wiring jacks out. The machine beeped, so I quickly shoved it back in. I tried another one, and the wave went still, but again the beeping started. I started to pull out a third, and when I had it only halfway out, the warning beep hadn't sounded, but the wave had gone flat. I did the same with the others, then heard the door opening, and had to quickly lie flat myself.

I listened, quietly, perfectly still.

The door opened, and a new layer of white noise invaded from the other lab environment, sounds of instruments and people. Footsteps came a few feet into the room.

"No, it's quiet in here," said Jidalco. "His own status is still showing pseudo coma. And nothing showing on the other specimen. I think he's still in there, but deep. Maybe we overanesthetized?"

"Come back, then. We can try the stimulus again," said Scutcheon.

"Yeah."

Footsteps again, and the door closed audibly.

I jiggled the guy's biothermostat again and, shivering and with joints popping, I rolled off the gurney to the floor, pulled himself up on the edge of the gurney, and looked over at my body, lying inert and respiring shallowly on the other gurney. I hit all the resets and unplugged all the monitoring equipment for both gurneys, to avoid beepings and warnings, and removed all the sensors from our temples and fingers. Then, I wheeled me—my body on the gurney—to the door, and stopped to look around.

A green lab coat hung on a hook by a little bank of lockers. I grabbed it, put it on this borrowed body, and found my wheelchair stashed behind a radiation shield.

Better.

A minute later, after transferring my sleeping body to the wheelchair, I banged the door switch.

We took off.

Chapter 22

My first instinct was to flee. More than that, I really wanted to get started right away upon the plans we'd made. So, pushing myself, my head lolling and my body slumped in the wheelchair, I headed across the medical campus as directly as possible toward the south end of the complex, where the parking garages were. Lorethe and I had passed by there several times, and I'd also made my way from there alone, when I'd left the complex for her place.

That was the plan, at first: find Lorethe, get away from these manipulators, seekers, and experimenters, whatever their motives. I thought I could find a courtesy phone or borrow a mobile, and actually try to get hold of her to come assist my getaway, but the farther I got away from forensics and the morgue, the slower I went.

It occurred the me that perhaps I was being a bit too hasty, because I might not get such an opportunity so easily again. I needed to know more. As unlikely as it might be, perhaps knowing more, I would fear less. Maybe their motives weren't so awful.

If they were indeed, awful, I needed to know that too, and if I played it right, I could gain information without great risk.

When they had my body, they had control. When I kept charge of my body, even if I wasn't in it, I kept control.

So... I had to figure out a place to stash me. Then, I was going back.

My room would not do because, if they came looking, they'd look there first. There wasn't time to involve Lorethe because I wanted to find out what the pair of doctors were saying, planning, panicking over with me missing, so I had to go now. *Now*. Besides, I was nervous about creating too much distance between my body and my traveling mind, whether traveling ethereally or in the physical realm by co-opted decedent. The memory of a few days ago remained fresh, of the panic I felt at not knowing where I was—a cold, lonely, and trapped sensation. I needed a secure place, but perhaps not an obscure one.

Plain sight might be better than stashing a rollerchair with an unconscious occupant in a supply closet or an empty patient suite. I didn't want any surprises, didn't want to return in half an hour to find that once again a misguided Samaritan had taken me to dermatology or the psych ward or — *eek!* — the morgue.

I hung a left and headed for the meetings zone, an atrium-like area between the hospital proper and the interconnected medical office and research buildings. Some conference spaces over there might suit my purposes.

After poking the footrests into a couple of unsuitable collectives — a Friends of Bill W. meeting for facility employees — *I'm dead, and I'm an alcoholic? Nah.* — a tea and Entenmanns reception for the Ladies Auxiliary, where I mumbled something about looking for a Candy Striper — I finally found an in-progress session on The History and Future of Wart Reduction, Removal, and Preservation. So read the placard on the wall by the entrance. Surprisingly, it was well attended, and diversely so. Between two and three dozen rapt wartsters made up the audience, representing a wide range of ages, ethnicities, and functionalities, including a small cluster of Candy Stripers.

After a preliminary look, I pulled back out again, and manipulated my sleeping form just a little, adjusting my limp limbs, propping my elbow on one of my knees, and placing my chin in the palm to give me a pensive, attentive air, with my eyes closed in contemplation of the presenter waxing plantar, viral, cruciate, and substengular. As I left, the declempt young Dermatology resident was droning on about the mid-century formalin soak, so I figured we had decades of history to go, and then there was the *future* yet to come. I figured to have plenty of time.

I *would* have had plenty of time, if I could have simply headed straight back down to forensics, which I did attempt, but there were complications, interruptions.

I felt a little exposed plodding down the halls without a wheelchair to hold onto. And this body's neurology, now that I had it warmed up, was changing, devolving, becoming ever weirder, which combined to make that plodding a little more gyrating than desired, and also affected the quality of the vision with which I had to navigate. It wasn't just that the vision had deteriorated or weakened. This man's name, which I'd never heard before, came to me as Westnorthwest, which may have been corrupted by neuron damage. He saw a different world with his left eye as compared to his right. In fact, while his left eye saw pretty much the world as it was, his right eye saw things that didn't mesh with this world, or the other eye, at all. Whether this distortion had happened sporadically while he was alive or while his mortality waned was unclear, and the inklings offered no help. Perhaps this hallucinatory neurology had occurred as a by-product of the normal deterioration of nervous tissue after death.

So I stumbled, trying to keep one eye closed, but I really couldn't because the left eye was weak and dim and blurry, while the right eye saw... well, indescribable distortions. So I stumbled down the halls blinking first one eye and then the other, trying to get back to the morgue to eavesdrop on Drs. Scutcheon and Jidalco. But it seemed that Mr. Westnorthwest had been — still *was*, under the circumstances — well known, popular, familiar. He wasn't simply *recognized* in this itinerant, unhealthy community; for some reason, people noticed him, wanted to be seen by him, wanted to wave to and talk to and tell things to him.

Bad combination.

It was excruciating, in many ways. An attractive woman, seen from my left eye, would approach me, and I could see how pleased and proud she was, so dignified swinging her Burberry pocketbook. So I couldn't help closing that eye and looking with the other, and *then* her left half remained *veddy* nice, but her symmetry vanished now that her right half sparkled like an interrupted signal, jagged. That purse swinging from the shoulder on the *good* side was now an Irish wolfhound's head, swinging on its Burberry straps. It kept raising its chin at me and rolling its eyes, as if trying to tell me something.

Had I not been so intent on getting to my destination, I might have found it quite interesting — the interactions, the reactions to my slurred walk, and the inchoate replies to my fans, Westnorthwest's fans. Whenever one approached, in one of the atriums or a hub snack area, clearly recognizing my borrowed body, I got a *balloon* sensation. It was like when a clown had made a balloon animal, and a couple days later a kid found it, no longer resembling the poodle or dachshund it once was. Yet the kid had almost as much fun with it because when he squeezed its leg, the deflated little head came back to life as if by magic, three twists and half an animal away.

I thought security had been called a couple times, and were probably looking for me, but I had — not altogether intentionally — made several loops and doublebacks, and they didn't know where I was going. Besides, I was going to the last place anybody would to think to look, in normal circumstances.

In the end, I got there without anybody tailing me.

Except the kid.

Entr' Acte

Now, my unique experiences have inspired a new perspective on the ebbs and flows of mind/body locus.

It's been said that, truly, everything is subjective — that objectivity is by definition impossible due to the ruthless individuality of human consciousness. When you think about it, how could it be otherwise? Nobody — until me, as far as I know — has ever had a chance to directly experience any viewpoint other than the subjective one. We can talk about objectivity until we're blue in the face, or red or... very, very pale, which I've done now a few times — even beyond the pale, I guess. So while objectivity may be an illusion, it's a necessary one, and an instructive and useful one.

An interesting way to think about this subject is... what's the opposite of anthropomorphic? In school I learned that anthropomorphic means to ascribe uniquely human capabilities to animals. Even intelligent animals, canines and primates and cetaceans, are presumably incapable of self examination, self consciousness, or human projections such as objectivity, or, for that matter, subjectivity.

So ask yourself, can a dog be objective? Can a dog assume or imagine the viewpoint and mindset of another dog, or a cat? Animals, with the possible exception of social collectives like bees and ants and termites, are stuck in their own selves.

Humans are not, but we're limited to the imagination of objectivity. Because we are conscious of our consciousness, our minds, unlike the minds of other higher orders of the animal kingdom, can project our imaginations into circumstances outside our own realities. Even the cave man could put himself, imaginatively, in the moccasins of his captive, his enemy, his prey. This was a great advantage in warfare and the hunt.

Humans can get outside ourselves, and enough of us have done so. Through our gift of communication, first via spoken and then via written language, we have shared these experiences enough that we can generalize about these abilities, including the ability to be objective, to try to disregard the influence of our own experience and personally evolved psychology. We can examine experiences, feelings, and emotions as if through someone else's eyes, brain, and perspective.

So, knowing what I now know, I think back to before, to when I was like everybody else. There were days, and then there were **days** – *every day wasn't like every other day. Some days, we feel great, some days not so great. Some days we're smarter than others. Some days we're more musical, or creative, or angrier, or happier.*

Some days, we feel more connected to ourselves, and other days, not so much.

I remember this. I still experience this, but I experience it differently now, of course, because some days I have been literally, completely disconnected.

Objective. Subjective. Connected. Disconnected.

If objectivity is the ability to imagine the viewpoint and experience of another consciousness, could objectivity be a primitive form of clairvoyance or whatever you would call the ability to project your mind?

Have I discovered the next evolutionary step in human talent? In some circumstances, I can move my consciousness into another vessel of consciousness, as long as it's empty. Is this related to self-consciousness, self-awareness, and objectivity/subjectivity somehow?

Chapter 23

I stood, and the kid stood. When I'd first noticed him tailing me—using the good left eye—I'd purposely taken a little detour to a dead-end backwater hallway, and I turned the corner into the *cul de sac* that led to a utility stairway. Before he could catch up, I pushed through the door and closed it as quietly as I could.

My first thought had been to lose the kid, but he was a bright kid so I wasn't really counting on it. I crouched behind the door as it slowly opened, and remained still. It was a little-used stairway that led down to boiler rooms and workshop areas, so I thought he might chicken out or think he lost me.

No such luck.

I rose from my crouch and looked at him, and he looked at me. The door closer finished its automatic elbow bend with an industrial click-bump as the heavy steel door swung into its institutional gray frame.

I was wavering in my locus/focus, perhaps understandably. After all, I was occupying this flesh suit *here* in this stairwell, but I was thinking as well about the two eccentric doctors and their unknown objectives, and my wheelchair-bound, chin-in-hand body with consciousness set on pause pretending to ponder all things warts, as well as Lorethe and our plans and schemes that had seemed incipient so recently, but now... not so much. On top of it all, this flesh suit had—or *had* had—a personality of its own, which continued to burble its odd and wonderful inklings at me. Its shifting, folding neurology had just created some urgency for me in all these aspects, as I had just blazed the popular Westnorthwest's final trail through the halls, stirring up staff, patients, and security alike while blinking one eye then the other.

When the locus/focus wavered, it was sort of like being whirly dizzy, or badly hungover, or almost asleep, or distracted while driving.

Time slowed down as I looked at the kid.

He looked at me, and seemed a little lost, a little surprised, like a kid who'd been trying to catch a zombie, and finally caught one, and now didn't know quite what to do.

I didn't help him. I just stood there, and wavered.

Enough stayed there in the stairwell to keep WNW upright, but....

The filiform papilloma played the high-hat, the rhythm shifty and hot. The kid's left arm's left arm left, and it kept going in a sparkly migraine sway, but had plenty of room to grow. Two walls over and one floor down, Scutcheon and Jidalco peeked. Still, still, still from way, way up high, I could see her, oh yes, yes, tamales from scratch, chin chin chin palm palm palm, but not for long, as chin wants knee. Then what, wart people? WNW drooped, and the kid opened his mouth, but a quick blink and wolfhound closed it.

Got to get down there. Can't stay here. But the wart-whistlers are going to be a problem.

Wavering, I was actually being very objective; better yet, I was *multisubjective*. I had no full focus in any single locus, and I wasn't sure how accurate the tamale stuff was, but everything was going to fall apart if I couldn't pull something together and get control. Amazingly, I realized as the kid was opening his mouth that I *needed* to fall apart this way in order to find the order, to see everything at once, see the separate pieces, pick them up and put them back together, to know what to do next.

The only problem was communication.

"You're a big disappointment," the kid said.

I'd never resided outside my own fleshvelope this long, and instinct told me that *for that reason alone*, I occupied unpredictable territory. I didn't know whether duration affected the strength of focus, or if other factors came into play, or if duration might affect mobility of spirit. In other words, I didn't know if staying too long might force me out before I was ready, or on the other hand make it difficult or impossible to transfer back out at all. This made me nervous on top of everything else happening—the simultaneous streams of thought and vision, the wavering, and the deteriorating physicality and neurology of WNW's once-human apparatus. I would need to work fast.

I nodded and said, "Ah eeh oor ell," and then shrugged. I had no idea what my expression looked like, but I had one eye closed—the usual culprit. Because the labial consonants and aspirants weren't working at all—no *n*, no *d*, a silent *y*, no *h* or *p*—the 34 facial muscles that controlled empathy-inducing expression—now called the Degeneres Muscles—were out of action. Still, even if he didn't understand the words, I was hoping the boy recognized my entreaty as a plea rather than a desperate threat or a simple complaint.

He sighed. "So, the brain eating thing, just bullshit then?"

Again I nodded and shrugged. "ur ool ih."

He sighed. "What kind of help? I'm just a little kid." He gave back my shrug as an exaggerated impression that would have made me shudder, if I'd still had those nerves intact.

I used a nonverbal expression that I'd never used with my own hand, or with my own body, and which I hoped never to need to use again. It wasn't easy to bend WNW's three inside fingers down to his palm, but I did, and raised his hand to the side of his head and pointed his little finger at his mouth, his thumb to his ear. The hand shook.

Somehow, I needed to get a message to Lorethe.

With that tight-lipped, closed-mouth smile that kids and women use to indicate their habitual frustration with their fathers and spouses, he dug into his pocket and produced his little cellular phone. He held it for a moment, considering, then widened the grin.

It may have been clairvoyance or just common sense, but I thought I knew what crossed his mind — *a zombie used my phone!*

He handed it to me, and I tapped in Lorethe's portable number, typed in the seven-word message, though my fingers felt like refrigerated pork loins. Then I hit send, typed three more words, sent it again, and gave the boy back his phone.

He looked at the screen and read it, then looked up at me. We nodded at each other, and I took hold of the handrail and headed down the stairwell toward the morgue. The boy went back through the door we both had come in.

When I got back down to the morgue level, I'd been thinking about all the other distractions — the unwanted attention and curiosity I'd aroused wandering through the hospital, dead, inarticulate, in the body of somebody well-known in this half-transient community for reasons his inklings hadn't yet revealed to me. Would Lorethe get my message? Would she understand it? Would the kid keep his mouth shut?

Many other questions persisted, but all the musing came to a halt, as I had to focus quickly when I got to the door of the forensics lab and found it locked. Of course, it was locked; they locked by default, and I hadn't rigged the door to get this body back in when I'd left hurriedly 20 minutes earlier.

I considered how to proceed. Knock? No. I really needed to be stealthy, at least as long as possible. I wanted to eavesdrop, to hear what these doctors said to one another while being completely candid.

I couldn't go in, but I couldn't just stand here either. So, not having time to fart around, I had to act. A gurney sat down the hall, past the last door, where it wouldn't be in the way. I really wanted to put WNW back where I'd found him, but this would have to do.

I went and lay on the stretcher, and closed WestNorthWest's eyes for the last time.

Turban guy was already used up, of course, but I drifted there anyway just to see if that "rule" remained in effect. Again, it was like fighting an elasticity, a tough but stretchy limning circumferent membrane that would not yield, one I could impinge but not penetrate. Some things, it seemed, were susceptible to improved skills, experience, practice, and gained knack, while others were perhaps more immutable. Too bad, because it might have been nice—fun even—to switch around and sew some of that confusion in the minds of the duplicitous doctors.

So I slipped into the other, and last available, decedent, the one lying on a gurney a few feet away from the docs. I went in quietly, being as stealthy and unphysical as possible. I kept a low physiological profile, so to speak, wanting to escape detection. I stayed mainly in the most elemental and primitive parts of the mind, what would probably correspond with what the anatomists called the reptilian brain, hoping my presence wouldn't show up on the instrumentation. I needed ears, though, so I did establish rudimentary channels to the inner ears and hearing nerve regions.

Now, neither moving nor breathing, I concentrated on listening.

Chapter 24

"How long has it been?" said Jidalco. He sounded a little anxious.

"I'm not ready to give up yet," Scutcheon said. "Twenty-four minutes since steady activity, but that blip a minute ago, and the first one 8 minutes ago... he's got to be in here."

The *blip* must have been when I'd tried to re-enter and banged up against the membrane. And 8 minutes... what was 8 minutes? That was when I'd been having locus/focus confusion, and had swirled my soul back through this area momentarily. Luckily, these little tantalizings had kept them interested, and quite obviously, they must not have checked the other room since I'd left as WNW, wheeling my own sedated form in my wheelchair.

"Look," said Jidalco. "We don't actually know when he's fully... uh... activated... or assimilated. We don't actually know what we're looking for, do we? Maybe we're expecting all kinds of brain activity when there's actually very little."

Good point, I thought. I didn't know either.

"Or none?" said Scutcheon. "Maybe there's none, but he's in here now, lying here listening to us."

As he spoke, I heard a little *slapping* sound. He probably tapped his hand or a medical instrument against the skin of the dead turban guy.

Invisible chuckle.

"All the reports, though...." Jidalco trailed off. "And I saw it myself. I saw... well, I told you. While I didn't actually see *possession*, or any *actual* animation, I'm quite convinced that somebody was somehow... *influencing* path specimens and morgue bodies, and all the evidence seemed to suggest that it was *my* patient—maybe even somehow *more than* influencing, *inhabiting* or assuming control in some way."

So they'd not only been discussing me and my stealthy actions, but they'd been more aware of my activities than I'd thought.

Scutcheon took up the thread. "I heard some of the rumors myself, and not just from you—but then why doesn't he say something, or jump up, or move or breathe or something? I'm starting to wonder if all this social disturbia is just what it sounds like logically, just collective hysteria or some other mass psychological phenomena. Why, Jidalco, doesn't he *move* like you say he can."

"Two possibilities: one, he can't. We may have over-drugged him. Or two: he won't."

"Or three, this is all bullshit."

"You know it isn't. You saw the EEG, and you saw the informal... let's call it a *tally*: the body found in a linens cart under a laundry chute, another two floors and a building away from where she should have been; and the other little whispers about deceased patients in the nursing home moving around under their own power. They all had one thing in common: *my patient, Mr. R.* He's the common denominator."

"Wait a minute," said the Scutcheon voice. "Back up to that last part. What you said...."

"Two floors and a building away? What—"

"No, before that—one, he *can't*, or two, he *won't*. Why *won't*?" He didn't wait for Jidalco's answer. "And before that, what if he's been listening to us? Here, *now*?"

"I wonder what he thought of that part about the patent."

Patent? These guys were worse than I thought. I was sorry I'd missed that part, but they were edging into territory that made me nervous.

"That was just a silly thought. I don't think Apple really got a patent on the letter *i*, by the way. And even if we could get such legal protection, patents are public, and the last thing we, or *they*, for that matter, would want this to be is public."

"If you really think he might be listening, then don't you think you should shut...."

He trailed off.

Then, I felt a strange energy for a few moments, or maybe a *lack* of energy—a vacuum in the conversation, a lull that felt like a break in rhythm.

A lull, such as those lulls in a quiet forest, when the hunted senses danger not in an increase in the accustomed tapestry of backgrounds sounds, but in their sudden absence—as an unseen signal silences all raspings and twitterings and stills all movement. Suddenly, every creature, large and small, would hold, wait, and listen to determine the target, and which creature would flinch first.

Here, this lull of silence meant no chatter or motion, no cushion sounds, no little chair casters against tiled floor—and suddenly I knew: they were *eyeing* instead of talking. Maybe their lips were moving, or maybe they were making little hand signals, but somehow I felt it was time to bring their interest back to the body. So I did the one thing that would both be of clinical interest to them, and also, perhaps, give *me* more sensory input.

I opened one eye.

I picked the right eye, relieved to see normal geometry and undistorted shadows with a right eye, a change from WNW's. That eye faced the doctors, and the door, of course, and I had been right. While Scutcheon was still sitting by the body, Jidalco had moved toward the door, on the other side of which WNW's body, and my own, had been waiting, but were now gone. The discovery awaited these guys that their other two corpus quantities had somehow left their care.

I *didn't* want them to realize that fact yet. I wanted to drag that out as long as possible, but Scutcheon hadn't seen me open my eye, as his attention was on Jidalco.

Dang!

Maybe this was actually better. I shut the eye again, and moaned.

"*Hey,*" whispered Scutcheon.

Moments later, I heard shoe leather on institutional flooring, and the squeak of a vinyl lab stool cushion taking weight. I fluttered both eyes.

"*Look,*" whispered Jidalco.

Through the cold film on these corneas, and the veil of half-lashed lids, I could see that they were watching the instrument screens. My increased activity must have been registering as sensed electrical signals.

I waited ten seconds, a long time when you're being acutely observed, then twitched my legs and set off a little shivering palsy in my hands.

I waited another five seconds, then started inhaling very, very slowly. I stopped the twitchy stuff, and tried to completely relax every muscle in this body, continuing the steady respiration.

I tried to switch among different physiological states, to show some variety. I wanted them to see their instruments coming alive, to puzzle over their incoming data, to think about what was happening here in this body, rather than about their subject — their other subject. *Me.*

I employed distraction, decoy, dissemination, and had two objectives now: in addition to gathering information about motive, I needed to keep them busy, and keep them in this room as long as possible.

I really, really hope Lorethe received, and understood, my message.

I was trying to stall these guys because the longer I had them in this room, the more I might learn. More importantly, I needed Lorethe to save me, and that could take time.

My body was anesthetized, so I wasn't sure what would happen if I reinhabited my own husk — many uncertainties remained about that state of consciousness and how it interrelated with my abilities to come and go. Right now, I needed flexibility and maneuverability. Could I get stuck there, bottled up in my unconscious selfbody? I had felt the sludginess of my mentality when I'd briefly tried to "go home."

One way or the other, I needed both my consciousness and my physical form, to be out of reach, out of control, of these men who had motives, *plans, prerogatives* that didn't match mine, and might well be dangerous to me and my own P&Ps.

So, when I'd borrowed the boy's cellular phone, I sent Lorethe a message, a cry for help.

In our planning at her place, we'd discussed dangerous possibilities. We both thought it likely that people were beginning to catch on to my activities. We'd made our plans and begun executing them precisely because we needed to act soon, before complications arose.

Now it was painfully obvious that we'd miscalculated the urgency.

Fortunately, we'd discussed the possibility of unforeseen trouble, and made a contingency plan. For that possibility, she'd given me her cellular number, and made me memorize it.

When I texted her from the boy's phone, I'd sent just seven words.

I at wart talk. Take me home.

These medicals obviously meant business, having administered anesthesia, and procedures, without consent—a pretty serious liability and risk for professionals. While I didn't know precisely what their *serious business* was, I had ideas of possibilities, some unpleasant, some dastardly, and some downright perilous. None of those I could think of were savory in the least. Indeed, if these gents were willing to risk their careers violating my self and my rights, simply to perform their investigations, benevolence could not be involved, leastwise as regarded *my* future and *my* preferences.

So, as I continued to surge the primitive lamellae of my nervous system, and palsy, and neurostimulate various skeletal and muscle systems, I was buying time, both for Lorethe to respond, and to figure out how I could get more information out of these conspirators.

Finally, when I'd pretty much settled on a strategy, I waited until just the right moment.

I'd been rigidizing the whole body, but alternatively flexing/stiffening each elbow and each ankle, without moving them, which must have looked adequately bizarre, appearing, as it did, involuntary but rhythmic and regular at the same time. I also rolled the eyes back, showing the whites, and vocalized a steady, papery, throaty whisper, again rhythmic, albeit only on the exhales, but very short and utterly inchoate.

This display had the two of them alternatively staring at the body, and then trying to see what their instrumentation made of it. I picked the exact moment, when both of them were looking not at me but at the displays, to speak.

"Think you've got enough?" I said, in a steady clinical sort of voice.

Because they weren't attending me at that moment, and were concentrating on data, each of them, for the necessary fraction of a second, thought the other had spoken.

"Enough for what?" said Scutcheon.

"No," said Jidalco. "It's too random. We need conscious status for...."

They both froze for a half second, then turned their faces as one to look at me—err... at the face of the body I was in.

I'd been doing this long enough, and had done it enough times to recognize some limits. While my skills were still developing, I knew something about my limitations too. One limit that worried me was duration. I wasn't quite sure how long I'd been outside my own body, because I wasn't quite sure whether I'd actually been *conscious* when I made my last exit, when I'd been ambushed with anesthesia. That whole sequence remained a little fuzzy, but I was pretty sure that now, in my third carcass and after all these doings, more time had passed than any previous excursion. I already felt further distanced, mind-to-body, from my physical self than I'd ever felt before. What kept my body alive while the essential *me* was missing? How fragile and perilous might that status be? What effect might deep anesthesia have on that whole teetering mechanism.

I felt an uneasy, itchy, edgy kind of sensation. There was a *noticeable* pull. I was scared. I had to move this along.

At the same time, I felt the conflict of trying to give Lorethe time to get my body out of the hospital, but those two urges were coming into balance.

I looked back into their faces—first Scutcheon's, then Jidalco's—and raised up on one elbow.

To Scutcheon, I said, "You believe it now?"

To Jidalco, who'd started to look a little smug, I said nothing. I just looked at him, moving these eyes from Scutcheon to him. I didn't smile, or frown.

He started to look uneasy, and might have wanted to say something, but he seemed to be waiting for me. At first, he might have thought I was supporting him, but now, the way I stared clearly made him squirmy.

Good. I did a little lunge fake.

Scutcheon and I started laughing, because Jidalco was halfway across the room tripping over himself, so startled that he stumbled backwards and knocked over a rolling tray carriage.

The voice in this body was much better, though I had no idea why. These sessions were really the only ones where I'd needed a voice, and I'd attempted very little vocalization in previous inhabitings. I could speak, and laugh.

Still, I didn't like laughing, because I was laughing with Scutcheon. I didn't like Scutcheon. I sort of liked Jidalco.

I was angry with both of them, and needed them both to know this.

Anger is sometimes best expressed with a quiet menace, an understated seething, a barely contained and poorly concealed buildup of latent explosivity.

I wasn't in my own body, though, and wasn't familiar with this fellow's nostril-twitch/lip-curling sneer, or, for that matter, his forehead-furrow/eyebrow-muscle matrix. So, in a single sweeping motion, I rose from the gurney and flatfoot-kicked over the three nearest instrument carriages. Then, with broad windmilling arms, I swept the EEG wiring from my head and chest and toppled the electronic readout screens on their stands.

Then, I lay back down without having touched either of my attendant physicians.

Jidalco had retreated to near one of the exits, and Scutcheon held a bone saw in one hand and a large loaded hypo in the other.

"Tell me what it is you're up to," I said.

"We could ask you the same thing," said Scutcheon.

I let some moments pass; if I didn't, I might have to pick everything up, because I wanted to knock it over again.

"There's no *same thing* about it. There is no *up to* for me. This is not a choice *for me.* I'm not trying to learn anything, or patent anything, or *use* anybody, *any person,* to develop some amazing new capability. This is something I'm stuck with. I'm just trying to get better and get out of here."

"We're just trying to find out about your extraordinary... ability," said Jidalco.

I paused again.

"Yes, I believe that," I said. "The part about *finding out,* I believe, but the *just...* no, that doesn't ring true." I looked at Scutcheon and wobbled my head. I was trying to shake it in an expression of negativity, but couldn't quite manage the fine motor control for that subtle gesture. "And put those down, you smurt. What are you going to do, kill me again?"

That was when I realized something: I hadn't yet consciously studied this body's inklings, but they were there, and a hint of one had just popped out. I wasn't even sure about it. It was a subconscious thing, but *boom*, there it was.

They looked at each other, and finally Scutcheon acted. First, he leaned over and righted one of the rolling steel trays. Then he picked up the saw and syringe where he'd temporarily placed them on the floor. He put down the saw and the syringe on the surface he'd uprighted, and then sorted through the stray debris on the floor to pick up a piece of cotton waste and wipe his hands.

"We've had some complaints from families," he said, "about their... their loved ones being abused post-mortem. We've been quietly looking for answers—"

"Don't lie to me," I said. "I can wander at will in and out of the minds of these loved ones you're talking about. You think I can't tell when you're lying?" I was bluffing. While emoting with my own body, I'd never been much good at inscrutable, but my poker face was excellent when the face I was pokering with wasn't my own—again, mainly because the *fine* motor control was anything but.

Jidalco edged toward the door again, and Scutcheon moved his eyes in a weird way.

"All right, I'm leaving," I said, and was about to do so.

"Wait," said Scutcheon. "Why should we tell you?" His voice carried a push of *nervous* behind it, not *curious*, not *power*.

Nerves. Fear.

"I think you know why," I said. "This junkie body wasn't that wasted. I'll tell you this: in general when I arrive, they're dead, of course, but there's always still something there—little memories." I closed the junkie's eyes and concentrated on the fragments of what had been a shattered, wasted existence when it was still intact and alive. After eight seconds, I opened the lids and looked again at my medical team. "This self-administered overdose was toxic, but it wasn't fatal. I'd guess there was another bump that bumped him over that last edge."

"Okay, okay, leave it at that," said Scutcheon. "We needed several specimens, and didn't know much about how you actually manage it— your consciousness transfer, whether any and all cadavers were compatible with your... talent, or how fresh they needed to be."

"Well," I said, stalling. Suddenly, I needed to be as far from here as possible, as quickly as possible, but I felt like I hadn't really gained anything. I hadn't heard the one nugget of information, of motivation, of intelligence that would make this worthwhile. I had to keep going, maybe just a little longer. "That's all irrelevant, actually. I'm going to tell you the truth, the only thing you really need to know about me. Here it is: I am doing this because it lets me survive. Dr. J., your IVs and immunity enhancers and centrifuged cells and irradiated tracers and all that... for me, that's all just going through the motions. That's right. This is why I've improved. *This.*" I waved a shaky hand at this heroin-ravaged body, at the cold corpse on the next gurney that I'd briefly worn half an hour ago without its essential turban, and at the next room where these guys thought two more bodies waited.

The expressions of Jidalco and Scutcheon while I explained this puzzled me. Jidalco looked like a man hearing that his home had just fallen off one of those mudslid cliffs, in one of those west coast communities where building officials should have never let people build. Scutcheon looked like an executive listening to a phone call, telling him that the parent company had been secretly sold to Bernie Madoff or Enron seven years ago, and the SEC has finally untangled all the financial instrumentation, and his employer didn't technically, legally exist, and all back salaries had to be repaid within fourteen days.

They both developed these looks of disbelief, confusion, fear, loss, and suspicion. One was more of a bureaucratic look, *sort of*, the other more mercenary, *sort of*. But Jidalco had something else, something I couldn't quite tally up.

He spoke first. "What?"

Now I knew what the *something else* was: curiosity.

Scutcheon looked itchy now, like he wanted his improvised weaponry back handy. He also got another layer going: denial, or possibly disgust.

"I do it to live," I said.

My doctors fell silent, and very still. They looked at each other, and at me, and at each other again.

Finally, Jidalco blurted out, "Um, we can help you! Look, we got three bodies together, see? We have access, we have privileges, facilities. It must be difficult, working solo."

I looked at him. I didn't really want to look at Scutcheon too, but I did. It was clear that he was trying to outthink me, and possibly outthink Jidalco too.

"Your country needs this," Scutcheon said. "This is bigger than you, you know. There's a need."

"That's what I thought," I said. "So what need is that?"

The two doctors looked at each other, clearly with some conflict there. Jidalco was about to speak up, and Scutcheon saw this, and I could see his decision. I could see the race on his face, because he beat Jidalco to it, and it wasn't a competitive thing. It was pre-emptive.

"Space program," he said, looking hard at Jidalco.

Again, I knew they were lying, not because I could read their minds, but because of their faces. I was about to say something like, '*Stop the bullshit. The space program is as dead as I am,*' but held my tongue, wanting to see how deep they would dig.

"I knew it," I said, but of course I *knew* when I was being *lied* to. I played along anyway. "When the good and honest Dr. Wade suddenly wasn't my case manager anymore, I knew something was—"

"Dr. Jidalco, are you there?" said a female voice over the intercom.

All three of us looked over at the speaker by the door.

It was only a step away for Jidalco, so he took that step and pushed a button. "Yes."

"Doctor, I have a message for you. It's happening again. Incident sightings just fifteen minutes ago, in the north building, main floor, and ten minutes ago near the main lobby."

Again, Jidalco looked confused, but Scutcheon jumped up. He ran the few steps to the door, threw it open, and looked for his other two bodies, including mine.

"Jesus Christ! Oh, Jesus, they're gone," he said.

It was time for me to go, but I stayed, in spirit so to speak, long enough to watch them scurry—maybe another minute or so.

Scutcheon pushed Jidalco out of the way, glanced over at me, then jabbed the intercom button and shouted, "Tell security to seal all the exits if they can. Get maintenance to help. We've got to keep all patients in the facility. Right away!"

Then he ran to the trays, and again grabbed his big hypo full of some knockout dosage, and came toward me.

It was funny, but I felt a nice warmth, looking at that needle, feeling an inkling of its power and what it once symbolized for this man's body, and mind, and soul.

"Too late for that, Scutcheon," I said. "For both of us."

Then, I left.

Chapter 25

Straight up.

We must have instincts. When the mind/spirit is bodybound, we instinctively move in certain ways, within the restrictions that our physics and our human physiology permit. Marine and aquatic creatures, unbound by gravity, and birds as well to some extent, have three-dimensional instincts to match their environments. We also have vague impressions, from dreams, of what this might be like. As wonderful and freeing as it must be to fly in air or water, there's also some comfort, perhaps, for the earthbound creature in not having to worry about predators rising from beneath you.

So perhaps it had been, up to that point, my human/mammalian/terrestrial instincts that had kept me down. In any case, when I departed rapidly from pathology that afternoon, not quite sure about where I needed to go, I moved vaguely south at first, then quite suddenly — instantly, really — I was very, very high.

I hovered there, taking it in. Simultaneously, I *sensed*. Without specific receptors, borrowed or my own, vision, hearing, and spacial awareness were altogether a mixture I'd call, for convenience, *feeling*.

At the moment I'd detached from the last body, the one with the drug hollowness, an immediate swirl of information had relieved me of my recent worries about my own physical body. I'd known already that it was safe, that I was already outside the trap that Scutcheon was trying to seal around me.

So hovering up here, I took my bearings. First, a new rhythm played underneath everything else, a repetitive, whisperish ringing sensation that propelled my being in a light, swingy-swishy sort of way that I'd never felt before. I sort of liked it. I knew also that I needed to reunite with my own body — a compelling feeling, if not quite urgent. I drifted south, gradually descending. It felt like the right direction, like a homing. A crow flew right by me with French fries dangling from his beak.

Reason told me that Lorethe had taken me to her place, but the homing sensations rather conflicted this, suggesting I descend to ground rather than keep bearing south toward her apartment.

I followed the instinct down. A second crow flanked me, and cawed twice in approval of my navigation.

Thwock.

I watched a crow coming in for a landing atop a weathered, white grave marker. I had my own eyeballs back, and everything else, but I wasn't looking out the window of Lorethe's car, as expected. I wasn't looking through glass at all.

I looked around, and got the picture: I sat in my wheelchair, pushed by Lorethe, and we were about halfway home to her place from the hospital, right by that old, abandoned, congregationless cemetery.

"Oh, there you are," Lorethe said from behind me.

"Um," I said, "We might need the car."

"Yeah," she said. "You try transferring 180 pounds of dead weight all by yourself from a wheelchair to a Toyota bucket seat."

I used the brakes to slow, then stop the chair. I stretched briefly, then stood and took her — all 110 pounds of her — in my arms. "I've been maneuvering quite a few pounds of dead weight all day, by myself, you know."

"Your message was brief, so I figured I'd better take it literally," she said.

"Well done." She deserved a kiss too, and got one.

She went back to get the car, while I pushed the chair the rest of the way back to her place.

First, however, I gave a little James-Frain nodfuck salute to the crows, the stones, and the French fries. I didn't look too hard, though. I felt extremely rejuvenated from my successful treatment, which carried vague tendrils of guilt, layered upon my deathsense in such proximity to so many long-gone souls resting. Also, though extremely rejuvenated, simultaneously I still felt somewhat groggy from the mickey the doctors had used to subdue me. It had been short-acting, but packed a real wallop. It made me feel a little susceptible to miscarriages of my own abilities, so I wanted to put distance between myself and the cemetery, as well as the hospital — and especially those doctors.

I'd just spent an active hour and a half outside myself, moving psychically between three bodies, performing vigorous physical expression with two of them. I'd gained much in the way of knowledge, practice, and further development of my abilities, and a great boost in wellness and energy. I'd also learned a little about an effort to exploit me.

Up to now, I'd thought secrecy would be my major challenge regarding the interface between my treatments—my interactions with the deceased—and the general public, including the medical establishment. With good reason, I'd been trying to keep my rather distasteful, macabre doings as quiet as possible. Of course, that secrecy needed to continue.

But now I had another problem. Something official was going on. Or unofficial. I wasn't sure how they classified these things, *authoritatively unofficial* or *officially non-authoritative,* but one way or the other, they wanted me. They wanted to study me, or use me, or develop me, or all of the above.

Space program? SWAT team? Crisis first response? Human bathysphere? Oil well fires?

How many dire and dicey jobs wouldn't benefit from getting a dead guy to do it?

I'd certainly spent some time speculating about the possibilities. In an institutional setting, in hospitals and nursing facilities, one has ample time to think, to ponder, to muse on one's life and circumstances. There are many fraught chores in our modern world that the living might love having the luxury of assigning to the dead.

Now, I'd become acutely aware that someone else was also speculating about the possibilities. Scary, because while I was speculating and pondering, somebody else was *planning.*

Chapter 26

We didn't linger long at Lorethe's. She grabbed a few things, including a bag she hadn't unpacked yet from her recent move, and we headed back out for her car.

All I had was my wheelchair, but it had been so long since I'd seen more than a handful of my personal belongings that, other than my toothbrush and my notebook — things I saw and used every day — the rest of the stuff, which I hadn't seen in months, seemed abstract now, unreal or surreal. My rugs, my furniture, my books, my file cabinet of important papers — I really didn't miss them.

Your car is like your house, your home, when you're a suburban American. It's a rolling distillation of your life, with essential elements from your various roles — your work role, your home role. In the trunk, in that little compartment between the front seats, in the glovebox, under the seat, in the door pockets — you have the stuff that defines you, or that you find divine.

When you're a sick suburban American, your wheelchair becomes a double-distillation of your life. There's a little pouch that hangs from the back of the chair. If you're lucky, or you need a little more accessorizing, you add a saddlebag or two.

Fortunately, most of what I held dear at that point was in my backpouch and my saddlebags. For that reason, because Lorethe rescued both my body and my chair, I left very little that I valued at the hospital.

We folded and stowed the chair in her trunk, but I had my stuff in the front seat with me: the pocket notebook I used to keep treatment notes; my copy of Lydia Fraser's *The Fourth Monkey*, with a hospital bracelet bookmarking page 118; a sack of pistachios; a bag of Corn Nuts; and the one little blue glass insulator from my collection, which was part good luck charm, part talisman, part life maguffin, and in a concrete and non-abstract way, the only thing I still had close to me that represented the life I'd once had. Small, blue, but simple of form, matched to simple function.

I'd once had a cellphone too, and it was, I remembered vaguely, sort of important in an annoying way, at the time—like a politician, or an intellectual-property lawyer, other things that were important and annoying.

Three or four months ago, as I sunk deeper and deeper into that wall-less tunnel of pain and exhaustion, I'd begun to forget to charge it. Days would go by, and it would sit uncharged on the coffee table, or on the hospital night stand, or in the rehab center dresser drawer. Then I would charge it, or a visiting chum would chide me about never answering it and plug it in, and it would come to life, but then it would ring. And buzz. It would want me to pick it up, to open it, to listen and talk and read and tap messages, and I just didn't feel like it, so the battery would die again. Finally, one move too many from or to or between facilities or home, the charger went missing. Then the phone itself vanished, useless after all, anyway.

Now, I felt better, and I felt better of *it*, maybe. After all, a cellphone had proved quite useful.

Now, as Lorethe drove on the Lancashire County Bypass, heading west into the heart of rural eastern Pennsylvania, I had the little pocket notebook on one knee and was updating my recent treatment notes. I had wanted to drive, but Lorethe hadn't let me because of the groggydrugs.

Her phone, sitting on the console between us, chimed. "That's a text," she said.

I picked up the phone and looked at her. When she nodded, I opened it and read the message. "'Did he make it?' it says."

Lorethe chuckled, but kept looking ahead at the road. I must have looked puzzled, because she added, "Read a message or two above it, and you'll probably understand."

"Oh, I see," I said. "Your messages are in a greenish window, and the other person's are bathed in a yellow glow."

"Right," she said.

"'On my way,' in green. That's you coming to get me."

She nodded.

"And above that in the yellow, 'I at wart talk. Take me home.'"

We rode in silence for a few miles while I thought about it.

Finally, she broke the silence. "Me so horny."

"He grin and fart," I quoted.

When we finished laughing, I felt it necessary to defend my caveman text. "I wasn't using my own fingers, the left half of my nervous system was an ant war, and my visual cortex was on its last neuron. I needed to be efficient, to say the least."

"I guess you're—we're—lucky you got hold of a phone at all."

"It's a kid," I said, in a by-the-way manner.

"You stole a phone from a kid?"

"Would a kid I stole from be asking you how I'm doing?"

"He's not, he's asking if you made it. Maybe he hopes you didn't."

"I don't really *get* kids these days, do you? But... I don't know. It seemed like the kid was... like he was *rooting* for me."

"This was one of the kids that's been following you around, snooping?"

"Well, not following *me* so much, just a zombie nut, I think. I feel uneasy about it, just the same. I don't want to encourage him. He either thinks I'm a zombie, or he's catching on to what I really am, whatever that is. He could get into trouble. I think the doctors, whoever is behind all this and what they're doing, whoever was trying to capture me, may have some powerful... may be dangerous."

"But you don't want the kid resenting you either, or feeling brushed off, do you?"

"Look, it's your phone he's connecting with. That could put you in their sights too."

"Maybe the best way to keep him quiet is to make friends."

"Can pre-teen kids keep secrets?"

"Some of the best secret keepers I've ever known were pre-teens."

I thought about that for a moment, and she had a point. For instance, without pre-teens keeping secrets, the lid would have blown off the whole priesthood sex scandals thing two decades ago, instead of two years.

She seemed to be holding her next utterance back, so I looked at her with a nod to get on with it.

"Yeah, yeah, and some of the worst, too," she said.

Finally, I figured that a kid pissed off was as likely to be self-endangering as a kid playing along, and the latter might be better for our purposes. I tried touch-typing but pinching the fingers in like that was carpally painful, so I switched to an index-stabbing finger style. Since I knew his name now that he'd included it in his text, I could better address him. I read the strings aloud for Lorethe.

Me: *It's me, Myrt. Yes, I made it.*

Myrt: *The cops were even here. A lot of cops. But they looked really annoyed, because there was nothing for them to do when*

they got here. Somebody called them, and security was running
around trying to contain you, but it was kind of funny because
there was no crime, and no criminal.

Me: *So Scutcheon and Jidalco were left holding the bag, and*
had to act dumb?

Myrt: *They acted like their usual arrogant selves, but they*
had to play dumb, yeah.

"You've got to respect this Myrt," she said. "He's a kid, but he's sharp."

She was right. I thought about it for a minute, but didn't want to take too long.

Me: *What do you know about dr scutcheon?*

I typed with my thumbs, then held it up to Lorethe's face.

She glanced at it, then back at the road. "I like it. You're not asking him to do anything proactive, but you're including him, confiding with him. Try it."

I tapped *send.*

After a minute of waiting and no answer came, I put the phone down. We resumed our caveman chat again, but wore that out in five minutes. I counted the horsebuggies for a few miles—it worked out to one every 3.4 miles—and then the phone chimed again.

I picked it up, and read it aloud for Lorethe:

Myrt: *He's divorced, has two grown kids, both boys, that*
hate his guts. He skydives one weekend a month, and collects pre-
1905 antique motorcycles. He and the tall redhead from
admissions fool around.

I laughed. "I wonder how he knows this stuff. It'll be interesting to find out."

Chapter 27

We arrived in Adolfstown, the flea market capital of the Middle Atlantic region, at just around noon. Neither of us had ever been in Adolfstown, so we were halfway through it before we knew it.

"Where's the town?" I said.

We cut through, on the 2-lane winding road, a forest of dark hickories and silvery beech, gleaming poplars and occasional sorethumb baldly leprous sycamores, hilly terrain, winding streams, and emerged on the valley bottom alongside a few old mills. We passed long, blocky, vaguely Tudor masonry streamside structures, lone stone chimneys nearby, their surrounding rubble ruins flattened and overgrown, leaving only these—stark, and too tall without surrounding structure, necks with wings. We then encountered some modern strip buildings, then a modern diner, into which we swung the car for lunch.

Small towns in Pennsylvania meant diners.

This one was called Mortenton's Station. Lorethe ordered a chef's salad, and I had the lunch special. In an old fashioned one-car diner with the deco stainless shell, neon, and jukebox remotes at each booth, the lunch special was typically $5.99. In the enhanced diners, you could figure an extra dollar for each enhancement. At Mortenton's, it was 7.99, and the chicken croquets, mashed potatoes, green beans, pickled cauliflower, hot puffy rolls, and choice of ice cream, pie, or cheesecake, was worth every penny.

People looked at us, probably just because we were travelers, not natives.

I wasn't used to being among healthy people.

When you live in a *real* home—as in, not a *nursing* home—and go to work, and go grocery shopping, or go to *clubs*, whether church clubs or book clubs or health clubs or night clubs, you get into a rhythm where you interact with little whirlpools of people in each setting. It's sort of the same in each place, each time, with minor variations when a person or two swirls out and somebody else swirls in, but the experience itself doesn't change much. Some call it a rut, some call it a routine, some call it a schedule, and some commercials call it *your beach.*

When you don't have that anymore, but "live" in a health facility — maybe *unhealth* facility would be a better fit, but network PR departments might not find such gritty accuracy splendid — if there's a rhythm at all, it's a little too grim and businesslike. You don't have coworkers, but you can grouse with fellow patients much like colleagues at dysfunctional companies do.

In the comfy vortex of this diner, we must have stuck out. I smiled at our onlookers, nodding as I forked the tender crusts of my little conical croquets, and tore warm shreds of yeasty bread to swab in the pale khaki chicken gravy. I wondered why we seemed like minor celebrities here in a village diner.

Then Lorethe looked at me and said, "Stop it."

"Stop what?"

She continued to look at me — just look — letting the period at the end of both our sentence-ending *t's* echo in silence, because it was the same period.

"Stop what?" I repeated.

"Encouraging them." She was rather deadpan in her countenance as she clipped her answers to me.

"We seem to be interesting intruders or something, like when Africans visit Madrid. See, I've heard — "

"We? Look again. It's all you."

I finished up my plate and shook my head. "Nonsense." I wiped my lips and eased my torso out of the booth. "Be right back," I said, and headed to the gents.

"Watch out," she said quietly to my back.

When I came back out, three women were waiting for me — a little, round, middle-aged blonde; and a pair that might have been a mother and daughter, early twenties and fortyish, both with gerbil-colored hair. All three looked at me. A fourth came up, and a sweeping glance over their heads showed other gleaming eyes in faces looming out of the diner stir. Yet more were on their way, and I lost track of distinctions that would let me describe them.

I paused, because I had to. There was something transfixing in this surreality, as all their gazes, all trained upon me, combined in a criss-crossing, converging stasis array.

"Well," I said, wondering how to rupture stasis.

They grew still, quiet, and became an audience, but not just an audience. I'd seen this before, and it quickly came to me: in newsreel footage, crowds rapt, emotional, each individual singularly focused, yet coalesced in their uniting obsession. Sinatra in the 40s, with that cool smile, had females melting by rows and columns under their rolled bangs and wavy tresses, trembling to their padded shoulders. Presley in the 50s, with his smirky sneer, ponytails and poodle hems, and a flip of male hip, fainted them seven rows back. More recently, we've had the Beatles, the Backstreet Boys, Bieber....

Me? What?

Yet here they were, with those newsreel looks, the slack jaws, the fingers intertwined, the humid suggestion of pheromone, the beaming rosy faces, some still, some bouncing girlishly.

What?

I looked around and behind me, expecting to see a Donny Osmond or a Rick Springfield, with an entourage in leather tour jackets and some big, black bodyguards.

Nothing. Just me.

I shook my head, and was about to try to backtrack, to ease backwards into the gent's room to seek a back exit, when a voice spoke out of the gathering mob.

"Get over here." Lorethe was talking to me, but she was looking at them. Suddenly, and as if no one had taken any discernible steps, space cleared around her. She stood in a buffer, a halo of her own.

I walked to her, entered her silent cone, and together we bubbled our way out of Mortenson's, women and girls somehow antimagnetically repelled, bouncing off the force field's outer perimeter as we moved within it.

Safely back in the car, she seemed to be waiting for me to say something first, but I was busy processing. All those faces, the slack-eyed look they each had, vacant stares, stumbling half obsessed, half mindless. In my dreams, I kept seeing them, closing in on me.

What was that?

Maybe I said it out loud, because Lorethe accommodated my request by explaining.

"Emotion," she said. "It took two switches, and both had to be flicked — yours, and theirs. In the hospital, you would charge up, but this element was suppressed. Out here, your switch is flicked. You're north, they're... *we're* south.

Creepy. She's my biggest fan.

Chapter 28

For three days, we stayed out in the green counties, in hexland, in German Pennsylvania, in the misnomered Dutch country. That first afternoon, we had a fine time, with a little pink map and Lorethe's credit card. We thought we were just laying low and enjoying ourselves out in the countryside, but really, we were gathering supplies and formulating a plan, in the ideal place for both.

We went to the flea markets. Since we arrived toward the end of the week, we got to nearly all those in the area. It was like a cascading of scheduling, of operating hours. Some were open Thursday to Sunday, some were just Sunday, one or two Sunday and Monday, and one outlier didn't open until Tuesday. We started with Abramsburg, of course, with its pink map and 34 emporia, each a loose clustering of dozens of independent dealers, as consortia members or simply renting space from a building, barn, field, or parking lot owner. Some of them set up in long, low buildings, like old swine barns with decent roofs and paved or tiled floors, while others simply occupied open air lanes painted on paved asphalt, or even strips mowed to delineate rows across a roadside hayfield.

We bought some odd things, stayed in motels, picked up a copy of the Reading Eagle, read the obituaries, and went to a funeral. We ate at diners with 2, 3, and even 4 tourist-bait enhancements, but we shifted our meals to odd hours, eating when the places were empty, or nearly so.

It all started to come together as we moved among the working public, the shopping, dining, and doing public — when we were back among the living again. I realized that the odd behavior of those women in the first diner hadn't been random, nor simply a reactive phenomenon. It happened not simply due to some social amplification of an observed or word-of-mouth excitement.

The Beatles and Herman's Hermits and Bieber and Sinatra and Elvis, too, I realized, were more than simply an explainable hysteria.

There seemed to be a *heightened space* around us, everywhere we went. People looked, perked up, gravitated, forgot their surroundings, and stepped into traffic. Horns honked and women screamed.

Dogs barked, cats pilated, horses flickered or nickered or whatever horses do, cows came to fences and stood in evenly spaced rows.

I remembered a book from college, maybe part of a sociology curriculum: *Rumor, Fear and the Madness of Crowds.* I didn't really remember reading it, not in any detail, but it had a memorable title. I did remember vague implications sprinkled among the accounts of riots, hoaxes, rallies, plagues, and schemes. Implications that something unexplainable went to work, some intangible communication channel, when people gathered, not for something planned, but for reasons unexpected — a *mob* mentality.

I now stood at the end of a narrow aisle, where the space opened up a bit because of the arrangement of the shelving. On one side, the shelving went all the way to the wall, but the opposite side came up short, and a variety of items that didn't shelve well stood in odd fellowship on the floor: a 2-quart cider press; a black iron, very heavy, but so very small, really, looking almost like a model or a pilot plant, with its wood-handled crank and swing-out plunger, the whole mounted on an old plank long enough for two people to stand on to weigh it down; next to a worm-gear jack of rusted steel and built on a folding A-frame, possibly of Model-T vintage. The thing that really drew my attention, though, for me the centerpiece of the odd assortment of presses and jacks and pumps and easels, was mechanical like the others, but also playful and potentially kinetic. Although old and dusty and showing rust like the others, it somehow still held something of its youth and vitality.

And it slipped right into place, as I stood looking at it, knowing it, completing my little puzzle, because it gave a physical and visual form to that swishing rhythm I'd been riding, back of my mind, ever since I'd left that third brief enfleshment back at the hospital.

It was a pair of cymbals, tarnished brass, each just 8 or 9 inches in diameter, paired like clamshells atop a once-chromed, now-oxidized-to-a-hazed-gleam metal stand, with a linkaged foot pedal below.

When I carried the hi-hat stand up toward the cashier, and Lorethe raised her eyebrows at me and said, "Are you serious?" I felt my left half smiling at her, while the right side of my face felt as puzzled as she looked.

I set the instrument down with a little metallic rattle and splash, and though I hadn't tried it out back there by myself, and indeed had never played a drum set or banged a bongo in my life, I set my foot on the pedal and my right index finger on the top clam, and that swishing rhythm that had been playing in my head came to life in a very swingy, 1920s way.

Lorethe cocked her head like a curious fox hound should.

I paid $40, plus $2.50 for a book of mathematical puzzles for Lorethe, by the guy who took over for Martin Gardner at Scientific American.

Once again, a rapt audience had suddenly formed, 80% female, for my 25-second hi-hat concert. They clapped ridiculously and shrilled for an encore.

Chapter 29

After three mornings of shopping adventures, three lunches in enhanced diners, and three nights at long low motels, I had begin to flag, wane, and sputter. I needed to wave, wax, and glow again. At one of the few emporia with old hats and apparel, we bought Lorethe a vintage 50s gray pencil skirt, seafoam blouse, midnight green blazer, and a pinned black linen pillow hat with a little lace veil. We also grabbed what I thought were old Austrian Mennonite shoes, like maryjanes but with a two inch leather chunk heel. For me, we picked up a 70s charcoal gray suit, double breasted, and a The Hill School tie, gray and maroon.

There's a lot of the English out there in Pennsylvania country, too — not all Amish and Mennonites, not even mostly. The funeral we ended up attending was for one of the English, just as well since we wouldn't have looked right at a German service, us being English, and strangers to boot.

We were among the first to arrive at Sperle's Funeral Home, having no real home base and without other daily routines to occupy us, other than our flea marketing and episodic planning. We waited in the parking lot, sitting in Lorethe's car, until several dozen of the early arrivals had filtered in.

Isn't there always, at a well-attended funeral or viewing or memorial service, what we might call a "mystery guest?" Somebody, or more likely a couple, comes in and sits a little apart, and the family starts thinking, "Oh, that must be a work person," and the coworkers think, "Oh, that must be a wayward cousin." Then the work people see the family checking out the mystery guest, and the family sees the work people wondering, so they all start to wonder *together*. Generally, it's likely the mystery simply remains a mystery. There's that built-in discretion — the death social-slack, funeral leeway, one last benefit of the doubt — because probably 90% of the time, there's some good reason for the mystery guest. Maybe it's a long lost high school teammate, a short-term roomie after college but before the decedent met the spouse, the real estate agent that sold his parents their first home, or their shore home, or their mobile home, or their Martin Condo. Maybe it's the distant—and long-distance—relative found late in life, during that genealogical spree, who supplied that ancestral bridge to solve the broken generation quandary that had puzzled all seven known present-day lateral extensions of the family.

We went in, nodding and giving the flat grin of sympathetic courtesy without much eye contact. We elicited the criss-crossing glances from the family, the friends, the coworkers—we were today's mystery guests, for sure.

While we were tempted to just sit and be mysterious, I needed to connect. So, as the folding seats continued to fill, and after getting the feel of the space, with the collage of pictures and the guest book and the casket up front and the line of his adult children standing with their mom up by the grand piano, I picked my moment. A short line had formed up front, and a little group milled up where the widow and other family stood looking tired, a little relieved in a sad way, and ready to get on with it.

It gave me a chance to observe the children, adult children, in their dark suits and subdued dresses, their in-law spouses with them and hanging a little behind. They received the condolences in that distracted way, half autopilot keeping it together, and half pre-occupied with other aspects as bits of denial and disbelief swirled around. Half-ready eulogical phrases joggled among the remembrances brought back by this revolving line of old friends of the family, or by the uncle-cousin-aunt-boss-assistant-lodgemember lawnmower borrowers.

I needed to study them, look at their eyes, try to see into their lives. His sons, I picked out quickly, paired on the front lines; the two women back alongside the piano their spouses. Over by the piano bench stood his daughter, still single....

I was getting better at this, but remained unsure if I could do a cold connect. *This* cold, I rather doubted it, but if I could find my way into this man's lost pattern, his vibe, the present void that so recently had been his life, perhaps I could pry open a wee flap and gain some standby strength.

It happened when I shook the boys' hands. Having read the obit in the Eagle, and having looked over the easled snapshot collages out in the vestibule, I was ready with my little ivory lies *'I was a fellow member of the local chapter of the Pigments, Paint & Coatings Council. Your dad was the best event chair we ever had, you know.'*

This was not at all like the hospital, nor the nursing and rehab center. In those settings, I could discreetly pick my times and spaces, find quiet moments to commune with the recently departed. Here, my target subject was the focus of all attention, his freshly closed life on center stage, his absence foremost in the thoughts of his circles of loved ones and colleagues.

Yet even as I felt that focus, and appreciated it—because it helped me, along with the living connection I could discern from the blood relatives, the branching tendrils of his soul pulsing within the living—I could yet feel attention diverting, like light bending through a fresnel, to me. It didn't happen right away, but I gradually began to again feel eyes flashing at me, women noticing, mens' postures veering into guard status.

This wasn't going to be easy.

The newly bereaved were the most confused. Sleep deprivation, grief, sibling rivalry, denial—these all worked to unsettle the solidarity and organization that any family maintained under normal circumstances—and which many families failed to maintain in the best circumstances. So I met them all, and my acceptance by the first exhausted greeter transferred without explanation, by approval osmosis, making it possible for me to sympathize candidly all the way through the line, the boys' wives, the widow, the brother and stepsister, and finally, the unmarried daughter. From each I got a little sliver of understanding, insight, and intangible pointiles adding up to outlines, or synclines, or shapenotes, or soundings, of the lostwax casting of a man's soul.

Finally, I went back and sat with Lorethe, placed my hands together in my lap, closed my eyes, and listened to the ceremonial presentation. To some, it may have looked like I prayed. Maybe I did.

The voices dwindled away, and I was drifting, drifting....

Then I was in the closed casket. It was dark, and I didn't stay long, not because it was uninviting, or uncomfortable, or unenlightening. I was unnerved by the reflection of a feeling, an emotion, a longing, an experience I would likely never myself have but could in a way understand. Realizing that made me shudder, as I felt its temporary embodiment.

His family thought he had a stroke or some sort of cognitive lapse at the wheel, and ploughed into the back end of a string of cars jammed on US 422. He didn't—at least not the sort of lapse they thought.

He'd had the sort of lapse you have when that aggressive asshole in the silver BMW cuts you off at the entrance ramp and speeds away, while you curse and try to get the circulation back in your toes after having to swerve and jam on the brakes; the kind where you know your kidneys are only going to last six months at the most anyway, so when you see that same A-Rod Bobblehead in the same rear window framed by the same pale silver BMW looming up ahead, last in line for the northbound exit, with a swell of amused anger you figure: *Hey, this is as good a time as any.*

That kind of lapse.

With the vague, lukewarm indirect introduction, I wasn't that firmly enfleshed anyway, so for enervation energization exercise, I really had to concentrate, until I could roll over on one side then the other, rocking the casket a little. If anybody had really looked, they might have seen it shaking like that, actually boogying a little when the two bagpipers walked in playing Amazing Grace, and circled the room to signal the final farewell.

When I slipped back into myself at Lorethe's side, I noticed one grandchild, a young girl in the front row, maybe 10 or 11 years of age, who looked a little puzzled. This *puzzled* wasn't exactly a fearful *puzzled*. A *little bit*, of course, but the way she looked at the casket, then around at her aunts and uncles and cousins—who didn't really notice her much—then settled down in her seat nodding, I wondered if she'd been close to her granddad. Maybe she figured that, in rocking the casket to the bagpipes, he was making a last gesture, acknowledging his favorite just for her.

That the mind chooses to rationalize the mysterious is comforting, sometimes. After all, wouldn't the alternative be simply terrifying?

Chapter 30

I forgot to mention *the device* — more important than the high-hat, or the vintage clothes, or the two-and-a-half additions to my glass and ceramic high-voltage insulator collection.

The device was an important part of the plan, not because of what it could do, but because it *looked like* it really could *do*... something impressively technical.

It had old-fashioned analog meters and dials, and leads with heavy-gauge, gray rubberized wires, grommeted into a dark brown, slightly reddish Bakelite housing. It all nestled into a black, leather-clad portable travel case about the size of a sofa seat cushion, but a little fatter.

One of the antique markets, the kind with separate booths for different specialized sellers, featured a collection of vintage medical equipment. Assortments from those past eras tended to be mixtures of the familiar with the unfathomable, the tried-and-true alongside failed or quack fads. Fifty-year-old dental chests with 60-70 little compartments and drawers full of stainless steel instruments, powders, adhesives, amalgam components, and additives. There were binocular microscopes, pickled cow fetuses, those little pink rubber-headed tomahawks that all general practitioners had until they suddenly weren't called GPs anymore, and suddenly you never saw the little tomahawks used to test knee reflexes anymore either. We saw a framed polio humerus mounted on faded mauve velvet, a stim-u-belt, an electric hammock that you're supposed to fall asleep in while it kneads and pummels your gluteus until, weeks later, it transforms magically from maximus to, if not minimus, manipulated maximus. We found elbow traction, and a 1920s formulary with recipes for over 1245 patent medicines, salves, ointments, tinctures, liniments, poultices, pessaries and astringents.

And of course, *the device*, which we bought for $125.

Self-sufficiency, access to medical care, entrepreneurship — great American ideals, and somehow we needed to combine them to stay together, stay free, and keep me healthy.

Lorethe helped figure it out. I told her I really wanted to stay away from dense population centers and major medical facilities. Jidalco and Scutcheon were probably still looking for me, and might even have had more reach, more of a network, than we thought. In rural communities and small towns, we'd have less access to the dead and their institutions, due to sparser populations.

So how could I get the treatments I needed without going back?

She was brilliant. "We bring the dead to us."

She was a computer whiz, but not like the nerdy guys who took them apart and combined the chips and souped them up like information hotrods. She was more the female or feminine angle on computer wizardry, more of a sorceress, knowing the ins and outs of the communities interacting, the mappings and minings and data centers and community networks, and their underlying personalities and subsurface societies.

She'd learned it all by pursuing her entrepreneurial bent, not content to sit around real estate offices waiting for listings, or sitting on open houses to make sales. She created her own personal website, social pages, and stunt videos. She showed me one that had nearly half a million views, a quirky thing about a house that eerily preps itself to perfect readiness for showing. Of course, it was a simple matter of a camera, a tripod, and clever time-lapse settings, but first the home appeared messy and lived in, and then, item by item, the rug vacuumed itself, scattered toys vanished, magazines stacked, windows squeegeed, and a batch of chocolate chip cookies plopped onto a cookie sheet and baked themselves. At the end, Lorethe walked in, her eye twinkling, and she began greeting home hunters. She did all this to build a following, a buzz, and a sort of free advertising based on niche celebrity.

Crashing funerals wasn't going to cut it; she was right about that. We needed circumstances where the subjects, or at least their relatives and loved ones, were actually asking for something, needing something, which I—we—could provide. It quickly became apparent that we were a team, she the marketing and sales arm, me the technical service itself.

So she pulled out her laptop and did the same sort of thing she'd done before, but lower key, to design a way to continue my treatments, and to provide a service at the same time.

The other benefit? When you provide a service, you get paid, and we needed that too. Lorethe's credit card was creaking under the weight of our living and traveling expenses, and we weren't comfortable with the trail it left, either. Cash income would be useful now.

Lorethe put a listing on the internet, in a place called Craig's List. She'd said we had to be discreet, but people still needed to be able to figure it out, or at least be curious enough to respond. So it went like this:

> Lost a Loved One? Still have questions? We can help.
> Scientific, not occult or psychic methods, explore the unanswered,
> revealing missing details, or last thoughts and feelings. Recent
> departures only.

We figured to charge $200 as sort of an access fee. Lorethe explained all this to prospective customers, at first via email, and later on the phone when they got serious. If I succeeded in finding any information, that's when the success charge would kick in: $500.

Then, if the customer was satisfied—if the information answered the questions that prompted the commission—additional fees could add up to $1,000 or more. Of course, we assured complete discretion with the information found.

Lorethe handled the account management, not only running the behind-the-scenes booking and organizational work, but scheduling all the setting up, greeting, talking, and reassuring. She would sometimes refer to me as "The Technician," and I would play that role—quiet, businesslike, polite and pleasant, responsive but unvolunteering. We were still working out our professional workflow at that point, but generally it had gone pretty smoothly.

Within a few days after that last funeral, we'd had a couple of stabs at it, including an old lady whose children wanted something more from her, postmortem, because she'd been suffering from Alzheimer's, and they felt letdown when it was over and they'd had no final exchanges. We told them her last thought had been about bowling, which, although true, wasn't especially interesting or exciting. Another inquiry concerned a painkiller overdose, a young woman. I found nothing for her, and his haunted eyes told me he'd held the prescription. I gave him his $200 back and told him she slipped away without leaving any thoughts one way or the other—also true.

Then a lady named Helen contacted us and... well, initially Lorethe wasn't sure about this one, because, if Helen's husband had been alive, this would have been a private detective's job. It was beyond what we'd discussed as related to fees, but Helen wanted to know if her husband had been cheating on her.

I listened, in the motel room, as Lorethe told her how it worked over the phone.

"Yes," she said. "That's right. No, no tea, no cards. No, no scattering of knuckle bones. It's more a scientific procedure.... Yes, we use a specialized device, and receive indications of the imprints left by the... the departed's last brainwaves. My partner, the technician, is very — no, *uniquely* — talented in translating those.... What's that? No, Helen, it's not like a medium or a psychic. Don't worry, we're not in that business. So, that's right — there's no communication, and we can't tell him anything. And no, you can't ask anything. It doesn't work like that, but you can tell us what you're interested in learning. It can't hurt. The technician will see what's there, and might be able to find what you want. Believe me, I really don't know if, well, if psychics can really do that. We've been doing this for a while, and we haven't seen any evidence like that. When they're gone, they're gone, and that door closes.... That's right. If there's a bit of this and that left on this side of the door, we record it, and interpret it... Okay, okay. You're welcome. We'll see you there.... Yes, 10:00 AM. That's confirmed then, Helen. See you tomorrow morning."

The funeral had been held the day before, and Helen had his remains held for our visit.

"Highly unusual," the home director said.

We assured him we would be fast and efficient, and that he could resume his normal routine shortly.

Lorethe sat with Helen as I took the device into the parlor. Daniel, the director, led me through a curtain, to a door, down a hallway, and to a working space where the body rested in a casket of golden-blond polished wood with brass trim. I set up my little folding stand, like the kind waiters use, settled the mahogany chest upon it, unfastened the clasps, and carefully opened the box. Then I laid out the leads on the chest of the decedent.

"Excuse me, sir, but I need privacy for this procedure. I assure you that there is no invasive or destructive aspect to my methods or the equipment. But... well, trade secrets, you understand."

He nodded. "Since you're sanctioned by the relations, I must allow it, but please ring when you're finished." He indicated a maroon velvet sash, presumably attached to a bell, and went through a door to the next area.

I went through the motions of attaching the leads to the thumbs and left earlobe of the dead man, and turned the crank. The machine made soft grinding sounds as I sat in a nearby pink stuffed armchair, and I closed my eyes and went in.

Chapter 31

It was a new experience for me, to have a purpose in these... visits. Purpose, that is, other than survival and revival. For the first twenty or so treatments, starting with Mike in the nursing home, I had my schemeless therapeutic objective, and got better and better at inducing the experience, and experiencing the experience, and in turn got better — *healthier*. When complications arose, I had to improvise, pushing gurneys and diving down laundry chutes. Even then, the purpose was always health itself.

The purpose remained wellness maintenance, of course, but now I had seeking to do, and it was a good thing I'd had a lot of practice. Up to now, the inklings of the departed life — short, medium, or long — were little remnant flashes that I stumbled upon, or crumbling pillars that I ended up mentally standing next to, or shuddering dark shadows that I backed into, briefly glanced over my shoulder at, and then turned away from. In any given case, I could choose to embrace or disregard. Now, I had to become an active seeker, to examine and assimilate whatever I found — bright, dark, or unfathomable.

Sometimes, though, in aspects mental, intellectual, cerebral, I think it's more effective to approach a thing sideways than head on. It's like trying to remember something that's right on the tip of your tongue, something that, moments ago, verged to top of mind and suddenly slipped away. The law of reverse effect makes it harder to seize, if you try too much.

So, being an active seeker didn't mean charging into this fellow's brain and scooping up whatever remnants lingered there. It meant finding a quiet place and stopping, waiting, letting whatever remained drift over. I need to catch a tendril, a waft of something meaningful.

Don't grab, let it linger. Nonchalant now.

At this point, I couldn't grasp anything solid or obvious. It was like symbols, or poetry — something that looked woven... a basket weave; a magazine folded open; a coffee cup.

Like a brown trout nibbling; whether you're standing on a creekbank, or by the slanted seadrifted surf when the stripers are running, it's the same. Those meditative stretches when nothing is happening, and then, the nibbles. Tension accelerates, but you don't want to set the hook too early. You must let tension induce tranquility. Not easy, but the harder you try, the harder it becomes.

I let the impressions form, starting as gray patterns, gradually swimming into firmer relief: a woman's leg, a black hem across a soft thigh....

Just as the brown trout was about to siphon in the worm, the faux mayfly; just as that juvenile striper was about to seriously mouth that squidbaited treblehook, a Golden Retriever appeared out of nowhere and plunged into the stream, the surf... my womanleg reverie.

Something was going on, like being called back. I could hear a little bit of it with Mr. McGuilder's dead ears: doors opening and closing, sharp voices. I resisted the elastic snapback, the nearly overpowering urge to return home and feel safe while seeing what was up. I still hadn't managed a single re-entry, and believed it to be somehow impossible, some law of death and consciousness at work—immutable, intransient. I had a hunch, though.

How the hell does a hunch work when my soul substance isn't even connected to my own neural network? Who knows? Actually, it stands to reason, when you think about it, that as long as one is alive, or perhaps capable of a return to life, one is always somehow, by the tiniest, thinnest, most insubstantial thread, still connected to one's own brain/mind/neurons.

So I got up, did a little vitusoid shake to get McGuilder's joints as limber as they'd go, walked over to the door, and opened it.

Helen McGuilder stood alone, Lorethe no longer in the room.

Sometimes, when you see somebody familiar, even before you look at them, when it's still the corner of your eye, you already know. Before she even fully looked at me, Mrs. McGuilder started to scream.

"No, don't be alarmed. I'm still dead. Please, I'll be gone for good in a few minutes. This is temporary. By the way, I *did* cheat on you, but it wasn't an affair, just a single tryst, thirteen years ago."

This seemed to calm her down, perhaps because she'd been focused on this, because she'd hired these post mortal investigations for precisely this.

"Yes," I said through her deceased husband. "I'm the technician, temporarily in here for your answers, but please, help me. Where is Lorethe? What's going on?"

Her voice barely registered, as if 2/3 of her vocal chords had fallen inactive, or like the whole apparatus had migrated several inches down her esophagus. "Lorethe? Lorethe... Oh, some men came. Didn't you hear? She called for you. They took her."

"Who?"

"I don't know. Lorethe didn't seem to know them, but they left this." She held out a card and I took it.

It had a red and blue hot air balloon illustration on it, a card for a real estate franchise, but this didn't make any sense. I turned it over, and saw two words written all the way across the card: *Come Home.*

Home?

I knew in an instant. It was the doctors. Rather than deal with me jumping in and out of corpses, they'd been pretty clever. They knew I would follow Lorethe back.

They were right, but I preferred to do this on my own terms.

I told Mrs. McGuilder thank you, that her husband loved her. Then, because I'd seen them say it on television — the reality TV psychics — I told her he wanted her to know he was fine, and safe. I didn't really know that, but I figured it wouldn't hurt to tell her what she wanted to hear. Come to think of it, maybe that's what these professionals were doing anyway. It seemed to be one of the Best Practices of the profession or something. I didn't tell her his last thought before he died, which wasn't a verbal thought at all, but more of an image — a moving image with some metadata and a little bit of descriptive context.

Late 1980s episode, one of the Soul Train dancers, the smiling one with the wavy brown hair, in the shiny gold mini dress. Dancing, of course.

Chapter 32

With his croaker vocal chords, I told Mrs. McGuilder that the next time she saw her husband, he'd be pale, still and wan again. Then I stiffed back into the mortician space where my own inert body sat in suspension.

I had to figure out what to do. I knew *what* I wanted to do, but just didn't know how.

Footsteps.

Somebody was coming from the other direction, likely the funeral director, having heard Mrs. McGuilder's distress.

I still wasn't sure I was ready to uncouple from McGuilder, so I hurriedly gave the crank a spin, lay back down on the stainless steel workbench, and reattached the leads connecting me to my present earlobe and thumbs. I had positioned my present head with a slight angle, and kept the glassy eyes open to glimpse whoever came in.

The funeral director came in with a hurried attitude, looked at my meditative form, then looked at the prone McGuilder, and seemed about to go through to Mrs. McGuilder. Then he saw the eyes, and couldn't help himself; he came over, and I felt his fingers, pushing the eyelids down for the properly composed countenance of the peacefully dead.

"I'll be back shortly to get you properly arranged," he muttered. He then departed to see what was going on in his parlor.

This had given me time to consider. I really needed a vehicle, but one made of metal and glass and other durable materials, rather than the bone and flesh and fluids type. And I needed to get on with it.

Lorethe's Toyota came to mind, but she had the keys.

This funeral home surely had vehicles, though. Most had several hearses, and one or two cadaver transport vans.

The keys must be around somewhere.

I thought about scouting around first, and thought about zipping back into my own body and just getting on with it, but I had two reasons to keep using McGuilder. *One,* the longer I used him, the more treatment vitality I gained. *Two...* well, I wasn't sure what *two* was, exactly, but something of a hunch. I was keeping my options open, and still needed to figure out how to get my plan underway. Giving up a body prematurely might be a tactical mistake.

I sort of wished they'd just taken *me*. It would have been a lot easier. At the very least, they could have left me the keys to the Toyota. Now, I had to get creative.

Instead of scouting around or returning immediately to my own form, I sat up, took the machine leads off, swung my legs out, got off the table, and stiffed over to where my own body sat.

This would be delicate, and it might not work. I didn't want to get too far away from my own body, or to shift out of McGuilder yet.

I didn't have a big body, but wasn't small either—pretty average, really. It was good that I wasn't stocky, or portly. I was pretty lean, and McGuilder had been a good sized man, with decent strength....

The iffy part was not knowing whether I would awaken, startle, somehow jar myself back to consciousness. If I did, I'd be done with Mr. McG, and would have one less body to use in clever and unexpected ways as I tried to get Lorethe back, and get the situation back under *our* control rather than *theirs*.

So, as gently as I could with McGuilder's rigored joints and pale-fleshed hands, I leaned over, gathered my limp and inert self into McGuilder's arms, and lifted me out of the chair. We stiffed our way over to the door that led into the further workings of the funeral operation. While concentrating on gentleness and deliberate intention, I also focused on keeping my consciousness centered in its borrowed location.

Fortunately, this set of double doors had push-bar hardware, and I was able to open one side with a slight McG knee-bend, to align the hip of my unconscious form with the latch bar, then an awkward push. The door released and we were on our way toward, I hoped, the loading and unloading areas where the hearses must be.

As we emerged into a hallway, I used McG's eyes to look around. There wasn't much to the right, just a short passage ending with one door opening to the right, probably leading to a second parlor, or possibly storage or an office. To the left, the hall stretched farther, with single doors—with knobs, not bars—on both sides. At the end, the hall made a right. That's where we headed, because carrying a body—my body—it was just easier to follow the passage rather than try any knobs. We could always come back if we got nowhere good.

I hadn't been observant of the layout and surroundings when we'd arrived in Lorethe's car, an omission I'd have to improve upon in the future, given the opportunity. My general sense of direction and orientation helped me filter through McGuilder's mushy brain, and I felt we were on the right track.

Then, a texture of sound arose, but within the texture, something distinct stood out, below the conscious threshold, below recognizable, so faint. Faint sounds, muffled through walls and corridors, contaminated by other white noises like the background-audible texture of air circulation, plumbing, rubber on pavement, faraway radios, and elevators.... It was hard to source a direction for a faint sound, and this one came so faint that I almost couldn't hear it. I had to stop, stand there quietly, turning this borrowed head this way and that, but had a sense that if I didn't get on with it, I'd lose my chance. It would stop.

What is it?

Somehow, I knew it was important, even though it was so faint that I couldn't identify it. I had to follow it.

I kept walking, carrying, as it became louder. I took the right, followed the hall around, and saw double doors.

Beep. Beep. Beep. Beep.

It was the clear sound of a vehicle backing up, not far away—the reverse alarm.

I kept going. Even when the beeping stopped, I kept going.

As I grew closer, I heard better—an engine running, then not; a vehicle door opening, then crunching closed—all still muffled, but clear.

A door stood next to the double doors at the termination of the hallway, a room to the side. On the wall opposite the side room hung one of those buttons to open the double doors.

Somebody was coming, and I became sensitive to the fact that I didn't look quite... well, perhaps what I did look like, which was out of place—a dead man carrying a sleeping man... in the halls of a funeral parlor.

I shifted my burden, which was me, and freed McG's dead right hand to turn the knob. When the door opened, I went in, backed into the door, and got it closed just as I heard the double doors open.

"What the fuck?" somebody said.

Then another said, "Geez, we got the custom backup beeps now, and still nobody's ready!"

Footsteps dwindled away into the interior of the building, where we'd just come from.

I didn't dare wait any longer than just long enough. During that brief wait, I looked. This room was dark, but I didn't bother looking for a light switch. The space felt small and crowded, but tension made it hard to wait that long. I almost dropped me, but managed to fumble with McG's stiff dead hand, grabbed the doorknob, got it opened, across the hall, and used my sleeping foot to bang the door button.

The doors flew open, and we stepped into a loading zone, a roofed, paved utility area with several long, gurney-type wheeled carts staged in an orderly way along the sides, some tall gray metal cabinets, and shelving with groundskeeping and property upkeep items.

Backed right up six feet from the double doors, still ticking as its engine cooled, sat a first call vehicle.

I looked it over, then got close enough to peer through the tinted windows, all the while holding my unoccupied form cradled in McG's arms.

It was an older model, a Buick Roadmaster Estate, probably a '92 or '93, customized for the funeral trade with the gurney rails and channels, and exterior paint and adornment. The keys still dangled from the steering column, and a body lay in the back.

I didn't want to wake up yet. Well, I wanted to, but it wasn't time. I had lots to do, and needed to get going, so I sent out a little pseudoplasm probe to this new body. When I realized something familiar resided here, I almost startled myself awake, then and there. Fortunately, I was getting better and better at this, and managed to keep my cool.

I stiffed over to the side of the garage and carefully parked my sleeping self on one of the gurneys there. Then I stiffed back over to the Buick and opened the front door, went back and got me, and put me in the passenger seat—riding shotgun. I even had enough forethought to open up one of the rear side doors, lean in, and unzip the body bag.

Then, unburdened and gaining awareness of what I had for the moment at my disposal, I simply stood there thinking for nearly a minute. I just needed to think a few things through, unwise as it may have been to use that much time.

I made up my mind.

As quietly as possible, I closed the car door, and went back into the funeral home, down the hall, and returned to the room with the technician apparatus. I put the wire clamp back on, and lay down on the table. This time, I closed McG's eyes.

Chapter 33

At times like that, when busy outside my own frame, reacting to circumstances not of my own making and moving from body to body — decedents as well as my own dormant form — I couldn't quite think and feel like a normal person. I suffered what might be called deferred feelings, or postponed emotions. After all, I was quite literally *detached*. My mind was not only busy and distracted, but also, being temporarily disconnected from my own brain, my own neurons and synapses and the whole neural network of connections and memories and sentiments and references.... Perhaps I couldn't quite process information the same way as I would when sitting, in a lawn chair by a gurgling river, or driving from Mannheim to Quakertown, or at a dispatch desk in a freight hub in Royersford.

Maybe the left brain, controlling the rational mind, traveled and projected better than the emotional right brain.

So, in that brief lull, as I left McG lifeless once again there in the mortician lab, I had applied logic, and considered how I would feel. I needed to base my actions on what might feel right, once back in home flesh with all my brain informing my whole mind, body, and soul.

When I'd made up my mind — and it only took microseconds to figure out — I detached from McG and went straight up.

My body sat nodded off in the shotgun seat out in the loading dock area, but I didn't go right back there, choosing to do a little remote sensing first, a little aerial recon.

When I'd gone up high back at the hospital, it had been because I'd lost track, lost the thread, because I needed desperately to seek and find my own body. It had been instinctive. Now, Lorethe occupied my desperate thoughts. They'd taken her nearly five minutes ago, and I had no clear idea where they'd gone. I needed to pursue, but had no idea where to go.

A naked spirit, a consciousness unencumbered, is free to explore unaccustomed influences. With no body to direct, no physics to consider, no senses to consult, and unbound from the constraints of physical existence, it can travel freely and quickly, nearly instantaneously. Yet without recourse to any physical or palpable influence, it can only observe.

I shot straight up, then rotated for the panoramic view, and "saw" the rolling wooded hills dotted with homes, the parallel ridges, meandering waters, and roads feeding major highways. I looked back across the county Lorethe and I had been gradually exploring, east toward where we'd started. I didn't know if it was just a reasonable guess, good intuition, or if she was sitting in the car, captive, concentrating on sending me a message, but I felt certain they'd taken her in that direction.

I descended and hovered low enough to fly along the roads east from the funeral home, taking maybe a second to follow one route all the way back to the hospital, then retracting all the way, another part of one second, and start over. This time, I found her.

She sat in the back seat, with one of two goons. Goon was just my label, as they were no more goonlike than any other operations specialists hired by a private company with a government contract, as I figured these to be. If there'd been a familiar dead person nearby, I could have taken residence, and been there that much quicker.

She was frightened, by the look on her face, which I could almost feel.

I retracted again and zipped backwards, like a videotape with the triple reverse button held down, to the loading zone, and saw myself still comatose, strapped into the front passenger seat of the Buick wagon. Maybe a minute had passed since I'd left the other body back in the parlor.

I encountered and reabsorbed into the dead man lying in the back of the vehicle.

Knowing I had to work fast—because funeral workers, perhaps even the director, would be back soon for this body—I'd prepared myself in advance, pulling together a quick plan of action. Sometimes, upon arrival and initializing a new inhabiting, I suffered a brief period of confusion, cobwebs, cold brain. This time, I wanted—*needed*—to power through that, so I landed in there already prepared to move.

Also, I already knew something about this one, because I'd had a quick "peek" before, and while I hadn't exactly known this person, there was a connection. It wasn't even somebody, really, who knew somebody I'd previously inhabited. Nor was it somebody *known to* somebody I'd previously inhabited. Still, some connection existed.

Right away, as I opened the eyes, I knew for sure this one would be different. It was somebody *killed* by somebody I'd previously inhabited. Somehow, I just *knew*.

The muscle memory was... impressive. As this body emerged from the black body bag, sloughing it off like a cocoon, I felt a twitchy eagerness to get behind the wheel. There'd been no need, after all, to prepare. This body was already primed, somehow, to drive, so I looked over at me, seat belt fastened, shoulder harness in Miss America diagonal, sitting inertly with chin on chest. Suddenly a longing came over me, and I wanted to return, to be myself again — *right now* — not just to be myself, but because there was something chilling about this one.

I almost succumbed, but then a flicker of motion in the rearview mirror caught my attention.

I reached for the key in the column and cranked up the engine, then the same hand slid right to the gearshift, with that frequent-driver's muscle memory. One hand fell right there where it belonged on one of Detroit's last full-size wagons, and the other on the steering column too. I yanked it down to D, stopped there, and smoothly pressed my right foot firmly down.

With the exodus initiated, I took another glance in the rearview mirror. The body pickup man, a low level employee, stood a few feet outside the door, frozen, just staring. He wore a black polo shirt and blue uniform pants, close-cropped hair, and appeared to be twenty-something. He'd been swearing earlier, and if the engine weren't roaring I'd hear it now too. Based on his moving mouth, and the way his head and shoulders bobbed, he was swearing a stream.

The funeral director came up behind him, bumped past, and came fully into view as I'd already moved 30, 40, 50, 60 feet away. Unlike pickup man, the director made a feeble attempt to chase, but he stopped running, continuing to walk dissolutely as I made the turn and the end of the building.

That took away the line of site for him, and for my borrowed eyes. They probably hadn't even seen who was driving. Just as well.

Chapter 34

If zombies really existed, they probably wouldn't all have that homogenized zombie personality so often depicted on TV. You see the fat ones and the emaciated ones, the ones with clothes and the ones in rags, the hollow-eyed female ones and the bug-eyed male ones, but generally, they all engage in that same grunting, moaning, sub-mental, instinct-driven, base-level behavior.

Considering the purposes for which they were created, this is understandable, of course. To be fearsome, shudder-inducing, ghastly, undead fiends, they must display a relentless, clueless, oblivious, single-minded menace.

Real zombies, however, would be just a little smarter, and have a little more uniqueness in their outlook and deportment. There would be a little more residue of the body's longtime inhabitant. This I know from first-hand experience with second-hand physiques. There would be more palpable and recognizable remnants of the personality left behind to color the preferences and predilections, as this slightly more discerning, more unpredictable zombiedom wreaked an incrementally more creative mayhem.

There's much talk of continua these days. The blendings of learning styles, left and right brains, spectra of genetic disorders, maleness, femaleness, sexuality, and asexuality—as in sexual preference, or lack thereof. We're all at least a little stupid, at least a little intuitive, and all men are at least a little girly, women at least a little manly, and we're all a little gay, or a little straight—at least a little.

I would propose another continuum: *The Assholeness Spectrum.* Didn't someone write a whole book about how Mother Theresa was actually an asshole? The point is, probably even the best and sweetest of us have a twitch of bitch, a pinch of grinch.

The concept of personality spectra, though, is sort of like a sliding scale, an allocation, a vessel of a measured capacity. For example, a keyboard interface device used to write has a little scale utility somewhere, which one can slide to allocate between program memory and storage memory. All the bytes in there have to be one or the other. A serviceable vinaigrette, as another example, is always 100% salad dressing, whether it's 80% oil and 20% vinegar, or 75/25.

On the Assholeness scale, it's similar. If you're 35% asshole, you've got 65% left for empathy, altruism, bonhomie, and such things as paying random acts of overly forward kindness. Maybe the slider itself is broad or fuzzy, to accommodate attitudinal grays like indifference, sarcasm, ennui, apathy and disinterest.

From what I could see of the inklings here, Reginald had, either from birth, or at best from a very early age, slid his scale all the way to the right, and then broke off the little holder.

Pure vinegar.

For the moment, this served my purposes well. It might or might not do so in the longer term, but I'd cross that bridge when the time came.

I knew where to drive, and the muscle memory at my disposal knew how to drive fast. At first, while just getting situated, I remembered the geography—both from the driving here with Lorethe, and then the high remote overview, which wasn't really vision-based, even though the mind reinterpreted it that way—as spacial information functioning as a two-dimensional representation. In other words, I formed a mental map.

On these neighborhood back streets, however, it was just me, really, overriding the muscle memory's hotrod mentality, being somewhat careful on the side streets, the intersections, at the stop signs and traffic lights. I headed toward US 30, a main road with four lanes, strip malls, and turn lanes, but even on these little streets, every now and then, an urge struck. I had an impulse to jerk the wheel, to pass on the shoulder to get around a slow Fiat or a dawdling housewife, to ice a stop sign—muscle memory with a life of its own.

When I got on the highway, the open road called US 30, that muscle memory really kicked in, And it grew stronger. I felt antsy, wanting to catch up to Lorethe and the scum that had taken her. I *needed* to, and that need inched toward the muscle memory, itching to interface with it, to fan it aflame.

The Buick had a decent engine, and an automatic transmission. For its time, pre-SUV, or at least before they were monstrous, it was a big car.

I smiled a cadaverous smile across the front seat, past my comalike drooping head, through the passenger window at the neighboring driver who looked back at me with some curiosity, and I pushed this total asshole's vinegral foot down smoothly on the gas, pulled that big cruiser out into a surging acceleration, and left it there—the foot.

Ta-ta, curious driver.

I got it up to seventy, and must have had the traffic lights' timing doubled, because for about four miles, I didn't hit a single red light. When I finally did, nobody entered the intersection from left or right— well, they weren't coming very fast—so I goosed it a little more.

Honking ensued, but I left that behind me right quick. I just needed a little swerve—a left swerve, a little right swerve, and some tastefully short *Bap-Bap* fist taps on my own horn bar—and I was back in the groove. I enjoyed another three to four miles of mostly green, with a yellow or two mixed in here and there.

Then I could feel it. I—we—were getting close. When the speed limit is 40 at the most, and then where denser stretches of businesses and offices drop it down to 25, it takes a certain knack to do 70 for any extended period. That knack involves timing and vision, intuition, and careful control of all the available tools and variables an automobile provides. It might have been easier in a little Saab or 'Stang, than in a big Buick Wagon, but I just plowed heedlessly forward. I steered into whatever moving and shifting vacancies appeared, plummeting our way eastward Jerome Bettis-style. It may have picked us up a little dent, or a scratch or two, but I didn't care. Sometimes I would *see* ahead, *feel* the tide and ebb of the traffic, the different sorts of cars and trucks and two-wheeled things, the different styles of drivers, with different ages and temperaments. In that moment, I'd know—I'd *feel*—that the texture would momentarily open, loosen, unchink, and create a perfect flow of holes to weave in and out of. Maybe I just needed to hang back a little, and wait until just the right time, then take off and accelerate, knitting my Buick Roadmaster Body Wagon needle in and out of those holes Barry Sanders-style.

Using Mr. Liveridge's body muscle memory, we made very good time.

As we gyrated through traffic, despite not having driven much other than a wheelchair for many months, my own inherent habit and training kept trying to assert itself. Yet the muscle memory of Liveridge, assholeness dialed up to eleven, proved predominant. If there were a place and time for enhanced sphincterhood, this would have been it.

Sometimes it bothered me—the me inside, my own instincts inside Liveridge's asshole husk. For instance, I kept wanting to use the turn signal, early on back in the neighborhood, for turns, and later on the highway for lane changes, as we careened our way through eastern Kerbs County. I would twitch that cold gray hand toward the lever, but muscle memory said the hell with turn signals. Besides, when you're trying to steer in and out of those moving vacancies at 70, sometimes turn signals are a bit of an extravagance. They distract from the mechanics of steering, and might really be lost on fellow drivers watching as you swing in and out of their lanes, missing their front and/or rear fender by an inch or two.

In other circumstances, muscle memory won by initiating an action, rather than preventing one, perhaps even something I would *never* do. as when we whipped past a pair of those little county transit vans. We then squeezed in front of a large truck, so we could wait for the space to open up in the right lane, in order to pass a lavender Jeep, which was probably just looking for the local TJ Maxx outlet, anyway. The jeep honked and did a little wiggle and slow-down-speed-up thing, indicating outrage. I even caught a glimpse of feminine hands and shoulders shrugging *what the...* as we flashed past.

That's when muscle memory, with no input from me, bent the left elbow and framed a dead hand solidly in the window. Then, after a quick beep to assure Lavender's attention, and before I could stop it, muscle memory bent down fingers one, three, and four, tucking one and three under the thumb, and....

We had pressing matters, however, so it was time I suppressed muscle memory.

Chapter 35

The last mile or so had to be handled more delicately. We had to get the timing right, had to spot the target vehicle, had to maneuver, needed a *just so* arrangement of vehicles. All the while, we didn't want to tip our hand, to call attention to ourselves, or to let on we were coming.

The maneuvers took several traffic lights to get set just right. Then we had it in our sights.

At a red light, two lanes of stopped traffic either way, we were in the right lane, next to a dark green Nissan Murano SUV, mid-sized with darkened windows. We weren't first in line, but side-by-side near the front of the paired lines of cars.

The previous mile or two, I'd been thinking about how to proceed once I found Lorethe and her captors. I didn't have a lot of tools—no *obvious* tools, at any rate. I had a couple of advantages, though, not the least of which was surprise. They wouldn't be expecting me—well, not *this* me.

Muscle memory... *MM*, of course, wanted to do it *his* way, the asshole way. MM wanted to bash them, cut them off, drive them off the highway, use the car's long, sleek, retrolix station wagonism, with its purring Buick V6, to... well, to muscle them.

I fought MM, though, because we had a more subtle idea. It wouldn't be enough just to catch up to them. The best scenario would have me and Lorethe leaving together, healthy and free to pursue our own interests, and under our own power. That last part would be optional, as we had none of our own power in the near vicinity.

This was a long red-light, so I rolled down the driver side window and gave the inscrutable car right next to me, with its black reflective privacy windows, a long, dead, asshole stare.

Nothing.

I opened the driver door as the light change was coming ripe. The crossing traffic was speeding up—no yellow light to warn the stream yet, but soon.

I got out and stumbled over to the SUV, leaving my own door open. Muffled voices came from inside the dark SUV. Maybe Lorethe could see into the Buick, could see my inert body leaning into my shoulder belt, unconscious, waiting for her.

Then I heard her muffled voice.

I banged once, dead fist against the front window, but didn't persist. I walked on around to the front of the SUV. I heard the click and hum that meant the traffic light had come to its cycle. Crossing in front of us, vehicles were speeding through the long yellow warning.

I stood right in front of the SUV and stared into the tinted windshield, sun shining on my dead face. I let the muscle memory and asinine inklings have their one last fling. The tinting wasn't as strong on the front, so I could vaguely see the driver shaking his head, as somebody else shouted. Then came the middle fingers, two of them, for our one last gesture.

Then, asshole died... for the last time. He slumped across the hood, in that rumpled gray suit he'd been wearing on his last drive.

The light turned green, and the pair of cars in front of our two vehicles pulled away, leaving our cars blocking the traffic behind us.

In the right lane, the Buick meatwagon stood, driver door open, not moving. I was strapped into the passenger seat, and started to wake up.

In the left lane, the SUV had a corpse draped over the hood, its feet on the street.

A horn honked.

For your average driver, as horrific as this situation might be, it certainly wouldn't create rash, undisciplined, reactive actions. For these shady hirelings, however, or agents, or whatever they were, this probably presented something of a dilemma. They'd kidnapped a woman, and had instructions. They certainly weren't prepared to deal with authorities, or even first responders.

Cops? Ambulances? No.

They really just need to get away, as fast as possible, but a person lay draped over the hood of their vehicle... dead.

They could just drive on, and Reginald might simply fall under, for the next vehicle to have to deal with, or he might snag there, riding on the front of the Murano for a few yards, or more, dragging his feet. He might even fall off in the middle of this busy intersection.

Either way, driving with a body, or driving over a body, draws attention. Hardly mattered whether it was living or dead at the time of said driving over, nor whether it was an asshole or a sister of the order of Loreto.

So, this was my... err... plan — to distract and occupy these guys with this problem, and then somehow Lorethe and I would sayonara. It wasn't really a *plan* — more like a string of connected hopefulnesses, speculations in series, or thinkings wishful of serendipidous cascadings tumbling toward success.

The traffic light turned red.

Another horn beeped, then a shout, and car doors opened and closed. It seemed odd, now that the light was *red*, that the little minds in the idling machinery got really irritated.

What the fuck. We missed a whole fucking light cycle. Now we're pissed.

I was back and centered now, not just perceiving, but capable of action. Something wasn't quite right, though. I felt sludgy, disconnected, and had a headache. All my nerves felt soft and inflamed, connected to a ball of nushed-out moths in my center, sort of a full-being, sepsic nausea.

The Murano's door opened, and one of the agents stepped out. I registered the sunglasses first. The big guy was clean shaven, with hair, and a personal version of the privacy windshield over his eyes. The opposite door opened, and big guy number two steppedout, bald, also wearing sunglasses. They both stared back, four black lenses shimmering in the light, at the cars idling, the people getting out and grumbling.

I looked back and saw two, maybe three men standing beside their cars, one of them even moving forward. Bald guy and hair guy sunglassed them back, and they all stopped. I could hear only the quiet atmospheric sound of metal cooling in the sun, and the quiet rumble of rotating machinery at idle.

Then the two of them went to the front of the car, and looked at each other. Bald looked at Hair, and nodded. Hair grabbed Reginald under his armpits, and pulled him up and off the car hood. Bald grabbed his feet, and together he and Hair carried Reginald, calmly but briskly, toward the side of the road.

Although they might have been quite intelligent individually, it seemed intelligent individuals could sometimes combine to become stupid as a team.

Still blinking myself awake in the passenger seat of the first-call Buick, I unfastened my seatbelt, and forced myself to move faster than my well-being — which at the moment was unwell-being — actually supported. I slid across the Buick's old bench seat, grabbed the keys and, keeping them in my hand, slipped out the other door. I took the two steps straight across the asphalt to the open door of the Nissan—*their car*—climbed over the center console somehow, twisted myself around to sit, pulled the console shifter back, and hit the gas.

The traffic light facing us had just turned red. From right and left, with a fresh green light, cars had started into the intersection.

I dodged around a little, but this was plain-old me, no special muscle memory. Also, I inexplicably felt terrible. Something had gone wrong. I'd just done a double treatment, and should have felt great.

As soon as I cleared the cross traffic and smoothed out into even acceleration, I looked up, into the rear view mirror, and saw three things—a foreground thing, and some background things.

Big, in the foreground, looking back at me from right there in the back seat, was Lorethe. Dwindling, in the background, were the background things—those two agents, one of them standing, shading his eyes with his hand and staring after me, the other leaning into the front seat of the first-call Buick. Behind him, other motorists milled about, the ones I'd heard beeping and shouting, angry at missing a single cycle of a red light. It seemed the irritable itch of urban and suburban impatience had already infected the bucolic rolling hectares of the exurban hinterlands—too soon, alas.

I also thought I saw, dwindling there in the rearview mirror, a long dark glint in somebody's hand. It could have been a shotgun, or a lacquered pool cue, or... something else.

PART THREE

LORETHE:
THE LIVING AMONG THE DEAD

Chapter 36

You pretty much winked out at that traffic intersection, out there in Dutch country, in the middle of Lancaster Pike, in the middle of Kerbs County, in the middle of that long pursuit by those hoodlum doctors who had their utilitarian obsession with your metanormal talents. Well, by those bastards they'd hired, at any rate. Not to mention the weirdoes, because by then the weirdoes were already starting to sniff around.

From Linville to Gwyddtomen, you weren't really there. You drifted, flagged, barely conscious while curled up against the door. If you could have coiled up like a dog in the footwell, you probably would have.

As we left that intersection scene, you were still at the wheel, but you'd turned off of Route 30 as quickly as possible, meaning as soon as we'd left those Borises behind and of out of sight. You didn't cough, wheeze, or gasp, and you hadn't said a word. You barely looked at me in the rearview mirror, where I sat in the back seat. You just said "You drive," in a weak voice, and sort of squirmed your way over to the passenger side, where I had to buckle you in because you were so exhausted.

Back at that insane road-warrior occurrence, I'd sat in the backseat next to one of the Borises, with the other one in the driver seat in front of me. I'd been watching the whole sequence unfold, including the reactions of other drivers and passengers in the cars behind us. Some people became so ridiculous, not only when they had to wait an extra second or three, but also when they faced things or situations they couldn't understand.

When I wanted to be subtle about actively observing, I used the mirrors. I could get a little glimpse behind us using either of the side mirrors, but not much, because they weren't close enough. With Boris One right next to me, I didn't want to just turn and gawk out the back window, or flip around onto my knees and lean on the back seat like a thirteen-year-old girl. Normally, I wouldn't care, but these Borises seemed sensitive to sudden movements. I'd abruptly sneezed a few minutes after we zoomed out of the funeral parlor parking lot, and the jagged startle from both of them, followed by their grim faces turned upon me, had me wanting to remain in a little slow-motion cone of stillness for as long as I remained in their custody.

I also used my own mirror – my makeup mirror – which I could use without violating the cone of stillness, to see some of what was going on around us. Somebody had been carrying a shotgun, and someone else carried what looked like a broom handle, but it might have been a pool stick.

So, once clear of the mayhem, with you securely buckled up against the passenger door, I took over driving. Actually, I took over everything, my amazing boyfriend being in no shape to be amazing. You could barely remain in that seat, and the remaining *was more the seatbelt/shoulder harness's doing than yours.*

"Are you injured?" I asked. "What's wrong?"

"No... not." Your words alternated between gasped and inhaled. Your breaths were so short, your center so weak, that in order to string out a sentence, you had to sputter one word and inhale the next. "Back.. to.. your.. car," you ratcheted.

It took less than fifteen minutes to get back to the funeral parlor. I could tell, the way you looked at the building, that you

really wanted to linger, to visit a body and somehow gain some strength back, but we couldn't risk it. Fortunately, we encountered no police there.

Presumably, when funeral directors lose bodies, they prefer to first make some low-key efforts to retrieve them quietly, before they involve the authorities, and their inevitable questions.

We prepared to make the swap, to leave the SUV there and drive quietly off in my Corolla – taking the Borises' keys with us. We faced our own challenges, tasks, and housekeepings – no need to facilitate their pursuit. It was almost as hard to transfer you over to the passenger seat in my car, in your current state, as it might have been in one of your treatment unconsciousnesses. I spooned the cars in the parking lot to make it easier, but still, during one touchy moment when you were between cars, barely supporting yourself, you swayed and leaned like a benevolent drunk between a pair of bouncers.

You said you didn't want your name known to anyone, but names are important.

Like the Borises.... A few minutes after those two Borises escorted me out of the funeral parlor and whisked me away in their SUV, I asked the one next to me — unaware that anybody other than state troopers still wore mirror sunglasses, until this experience — who looked like a pair of giant stuffed sausages loosely linked to an angular meatloaf, what his name was.

"Boris," he said in a clean, middle-atlantic accent. He could have been from a suburb of Baltimore, or somewhere in southern New Jersey, or any of a dozen other places that didn't sound southern, didn't sound New York, Boston, Jersey, or Midwestern. As he spoke, my own face — doubled in the reflection — stared roundly back at me from his eyepatch mirrors.

"And you?" I said, addressing the driver and shifting my eyes to the rearview mirror.

This one, who looked like two pairs of sausages tightly wound into one of those long, punchy pork-loin roasts, tipped the brim of his cap up slightly with an index finger and, on the downstroke, pushed his dark glasses, wire framed but not mirrored, down far enough to show me his eyes. "Boris," he said.

"You guys ought to write for network television," I said.

They looked at each other as if exchanging a mutual realization of great irony.

As if.

Anyway, if this is my part of the story, I want you to have a name, even if it's just a placeholder. I'm thinking ahead to some parts where I'm uneasy writing you, addressing you. Let's pick a name with boldness and jolt in its very sound: Craig Morton, Mort Krim, George C. Scott, Frederick Funston.

Funston is too much like fun. *Scott went and talked to dolphins and sort of trashed the whole Patton thing. The other two... there's something there.*

Morton Grumm *then. Syllabically, too, it echoes reality. Close enough, anyway.*

Chapter 37

We pulled up to a diner, and Morton was delirious.

The last time we'd been in a diner like this, I'd noticed Morton's odd magnetism. Everyone, especially women, had been drawn to look at him, even to gravitate toward him. Now, in his present condition, that wasn't a problem. If anything, people stared because he simply looked ghastly. It probably didn't help that I'd almost had to carry him in, and hold him up once I got him into a booth. Fortunately, the booth had a corner, where I could prop him snugly and securely, so it didn't look too dire once we got situated. It was clear, however, that whatever spark he'd been swagging when Elvising in that earlier diner had departed. His poor condition lacked that spark, and was devastating his health, so it seemed likely that whatever had made him vibrant and lively had also made him magnetic.

"What are we doing here?" Morton hasped.

"You just rest," I said. "We're here to get your strength back."

This classic diner served breakfast anytime, so I ordered a big double classic German/American breakfast for both of us, and fed some of his to him, between bites for myself.

"That's good," he said.

"Feel better?"

"No," he said, and he didn't look it.

"I guess it was a longshot."

"What?"

"The scrapple."

"Scrapple?"

"Yes, it has brains in it. You know, it's made out of all kinds of unusual pork parts, including brains."

What followed wasn't so much a long pause as it was time standing still... for over a minute. He didn't move, didn't nod his head, didn't roll his eyes.

Finally, without looking up or looking at me, he said, "You thought I would be satisfied with pork brains?" Without moving his head, he moved his eyes then, very slowly, to meet mine.

I didn't say anything, just looked away. I might have shrugged a little. Well, maybe it was more a shiver than a shrug.

"Swine brain? Pig brain?"

I knew he was still looking at me, but I was still shrugging, and looking at a little green crenellated border on the paper placemat.

He picked up a fork.

Now I couldn't help myself, and looked up at him.

He dug back into the plate with the fork, helping himself to a mouthful of eggs and a crispy enhancement of scrapple, cutting it off the fried slice with the side of the fork. "I like it, though. Still gotta eat."

"Of course."

He looked at me, and managed to force a little smile, but he was so weary, weak, and sick, that I felt a little ill myself, and felt a twist inside—in my heart too. So little remained of the Morton I'd grown to know, and grown fond of, but still, I could see a little here. After all, we'd actually met on one of his highs and... well, we'd sort of launched our relationship on another peak of his revivifying energy, and with treatment bursts, we'd managed to ride along at a decent level ever since.

After a couple more little bites, he handed me the fork and leaned back against the booth cushions.

I ate some more, but he was nodding off, drifting on the edge of sleep or some other lapse of consciousness.

"Let's go," I said, and helped him out to the car. This time, no groupies stared, followed, or grouped. I hurried back and bought a local paper from one of the machines outside the diner.

Once we got going again, I asked him, "Did the food help at all?"

His eyes were closed, and his head leaned against the window, leaving a little spot where his hair, limp and a little too slick with fatigue, smudged the glass. "Yes, just a little, though it—just eating— wouldn't have occurred to me. No appetite. But like you say, still gotta eat."

"So what happened? I expected you to wake up in the car after all that *treatment* with snap, with mojo, with exaggerated *Mortonistics*."

He took a breath, then another. "Turns out there are some bad ones."

"Bad bodies?"

"Not the bodies."

He explained how it was, what he'd figured out. When a person left the mortal coil behind, Morton Grumm could park his own flagging spirit there, and somehow it recharged the vitality that drained away when he'd been too long deteriorating in his own flawed coil. It cleaned up his vital *kime* like the big humming cyclone filters removed the curds from the blood in those merry rows of overstuffed recliners in an outpatient dialysis center.

Bad treatments.

He'd learned some good lessons, and hard ones too. *Good*, he needed an introduction of some sort—and as he got more practice, these needed less and less personal connection—to make his entry. He needed to find the little weak point, the holiday in the exterior of the invisible capsule, the spirit envelope that held one living being's personality in and kept others out—and presumably kept other evil things out, and which occasionally failed, and when those other invaders got through, shamans and exorcists were called in. *But* once he was *in*, he *didn't* need any introduction to transfer directly to another coil; he could simply *go*. So, difficult to get in, but once in, easy to slide from coil to coil, *as long as he didn't go home in between.*

Hard, there was *danger* in a direct coil-to-coil transfer. He couldn't see, really, where he was going, or what he was getting into. And, as he'd just learned, some remnant beings were so vile, so negative, that they did *not* revitalize, and in fact, rather than improving his health with duration and exertion, would *undo* any gains and leave him weakened, sickened, and in as bad shape as I'd seen him—actually worse, much worse, indeed.

I had many things to tell him too, but after he'd explained how that Reginald prick had affected him, how his negative remnant life-force had drained him, like an infecting poison, and then how this revised his theories of how it all worked.... By this time, what little energy he still had was utterly spent, and he fell asleep—or unconscious—with his head lolling against the car window.

Just before he dozed off, though, he said not to be too hard on the Reginald prick, for after all, his muscle memory had enabled my rescue from the Borises.

He had a point.

Chapter 38

We headed east.

When going west, and just breaking into Amish country—or Pennsylvania Dutch country—there's a transition where the land opens up, the valleys stretch out and you can see much more countryside, including the ridgetops farther away. Sometimes you see a horse and buggy a mile or two away, very tiny on a narrow gravel lane, between hayfields and plowed furrows.

Going east, it's the opposite. The rolling hills start to close in on you. You see less, and what you do see is more and more cul de sacs, planned communities, malls, assisted living, corporate parks and business zoning. You might still see a horse, but now it's alongside a mini-stripmall on one side, and a fenced cattle grazelot on the other.

As we crossed those transitional miles, I was on the cellphone. I couldn't very well text the kid and drive, so I called him.

I couldn't help but wonder about how things were these days, for a kid. It was all just way, way different from when I was ten. For instance, what would his mom think about him having these complicated, convoluted phone conversations with a woman decades older than him? About things that would likely make a med-school instructor blanch?

You could go back in time in thirty-year generational chunks, and see that life—and especially childhood—had changed drastically. Over the past century or so, sweeping changes occurred with the car, and the phone, and then the movies and television (when it had 3 channels), and then computers and the television again (when it had 300 channels), and then the phone again when you could put it in your pocket, and *then* computers again when they become the phone in your purse, the little screen connected to the world. That might have been the biggest gamechanger of all, at least thus far, especially considering it contained all the knowledge of mankind for all time.

Myrt had been keeping tabs on those doctors. We'd asked him to, of course, but from the way he sounded—talking about their changed routines, their additional assistants and techs, the activity in their offices and research labs, his eagerness and thoroughness about observing and reporting all this—it was pretty obvious he'd have done it anyway. He knew something was up, and he was, after all, the institutional nomad, self-appointed to know the obscured knowledge, bag the unbagged baggage, and stow the unstowed stowledge.

Still, now I was worried. He was just a little boy, and clearly this was a dangerous game. Maybe that was the problem: he saw it as a game.

I told him it wasn't a game, and that I didn't want him catching anybody's eye, *especially* Jidalco and Scutcheon. "Don't take any risks."

"I need to keep busy, and there's something else... I got an idea," he said. "I'll call you back." And he was gone.

I wondered what *something else* was, and I would have asked Morton if he knew anything, but it wasn't the time to interrupt his rest.

We drove on, headed the right way. There wasn't any point in fooling around with the local paper, looking for regional morgues or crematoria or memorial services—too much speculation, uncertainty, rolling of the dice. As sick as Morton was, we needed to go back to where we knew the surroundings, where we could access the spent coils of mortality. From what Myrt had told me, we had plenty to choose from.

We'd agreed that we had to—well, Morton had to, really—face the uncomfortable fact that this institutional or political interest in his condition/talent wouldn't just go away. He would have to take steps to make it go away, steps that everyone would take seriously.

Then, there was that *other*, other interest.

When Morton stirred after twenty minutes or so of dozing, I turned the radio on and tuned it to the all-news-all-the-time station. I didn't want to hit him over the head with it, but we needed to heighten his awareness a level or two.

The news included something about a hockey player with a concussion, then something about slow bridge traffic getting across the Delaware River somewhere up north a ways, and then....

> *"New reports have come in, this time from Kerbs County, about unusual activity involving human remains. This on the heels of last week's...."*

I turned it up a little and glanced over at him, awake and listening. Traffic was tightening up now in mid-afternoon, so I had to keep my mind on the road.

When the announcer had moved on to a story about a broken water main in Hatfield, I looked over at Morton, wide awake now but clearly still at a low, low ebb, energywise.

I touched his arm and nodded, indicating the radio. He nodded back, and I started to talk.

"Yes, it's not just a quiet little thing anymore. Back there, when you were doing your Chinese fire drill at the traffic light in Linville, men were coming — men holding things. One thinks of men with grim faces in circumstances like this, maybe from movies and such, but this was real, and these men, with bats and pool cues and a tire iron, didn't have grim theatrical faces. They were *excited*.

"Maybe that's what the announcer was hinting at. It sounds like, maybe, just because you... *departed* and that *sick* fellow went limp over the hood of their SUV... well, unless the Borises could stop them, those excited men wanted to waste a zombie."

"I never wanted this," Morton said. He gestured with his hand, but it was weak and trembly.

"This is the *teeter* point," I said. "I've seen it before, when I was newsediting. Little stories would teeter locally, before they tipped and exploded regionally. Now, with the web and new media, there is no *regionally* anymore. One more spill, maybe two, and you're a national — even *world* — item. And... I think I know *how* it's been spilling."

"How?"

"I think, at first, the doctors were keeping all this quiet. We even saw signs of that, back at the health center. But they might now have some reason to let it go frenzy a little."

"Can there be a *little* frenzy?"

"Frenzy can sometimes amplify and obscure, distract and obfuscate. That must be what they're thinking. While fanatic people and wishing-it-real types are jumping at shadows, flinching at farting cadavers, and chasing *each other* around county parks and bike trails, and descending on graveyards.... While the authorities are dealing with these decoys, the doctors are quietly rounding you up, and tending some other mysterious *needs*, and doing the *real* work, whatever that is."

"And that's where we're going?"

"You're very sick. That last husk was so malevolent, so venomous, that it drained away much of the progress you've had. It set you back. You need good remains, healthful exertions, and fast. That's why we're going back, but with foreknowledge. Myrt is helping us."

He took a breath, a hard one, and rasped. "Lorethe, I'm tired. I don't know if I can keep going."

"Look, Morton." I took my hands off the wheel, and nodded, and put my hands back, steering. "*You* don't have to. *We'll* keep going. You've got *me*. I'm driving." I picked up the phone. "I've been on the phone with Myrt. We'll get things started. We'll get you back to *okay*."

He sighed. The way the sighing air moved in him was a lot like when he breathed, because it also rasped, but this rasp held resignation rather than argument, a sigh in a minor key rather than a drum-swish breath.

In barely more than a whisper, he said, "When I'm in somebody else's remnant memory, I'm lost. I don't know the passageways, the hidden lost secrets, the well-worn remembrances, the guilty repressions, the red-faced faux pas's. Everybody's seems to be different, and not just the unique experiences — of course, they're different — but also differently tucked in, differently scarred over, differently coiled spring-like, ready to pop out and be felt, avoided, relished, or simply tolerated."

Another rasp, and, "But with all that... all that difference... all that uniqueness, something... something almost consistent has... has puzzled me. Lorethe...."

There's a moment, in a meaningful conversation, or even in an ordinary conversation, when you realize what's coming, when the person talking is about to say something that *you* know, but didn't realize *they* knew. This was that moment, and it was no ordinary conversation.

"We're all, each one of us, utterly alone in one respect. Your mind is a place, whether you consider it such in an abstract or real sense, where only you go. That's why this thing puzzles me. My unique ability... well, I guess it has given me unique insight."

He took several ragged breaths, a long pause of thirty or forty seconds, and I thought he might have gone back to sleep. Then, with a shallow ragged breath that he looked like he wished he could make deeper, he resumed.

"Not every time, Lorethe, but many times. Well, several times, I've noticed something. Visiting the dead, the way only I can, and these amazing places I've been, where only *one other person has ever* been to — these mental spaces, vacated by people that were *in there* for 80 or 70 or 52 or 47 years before... *poof*, they left.... Several times, I got in there, in a little spot not far from the surface — not deep, not far rooted, not very hidden, but there just the same."

He paused again.

I drove, but felt his gaze on me.

"You, Lorethe... what were you doing there?"

I kept driving, looking at the road, still feeling his eyes on me, and I didn't answer.

He went on. "I didn't recognize you at first, of course, because I hadn't met you. Then, later, it could have been coincidence, even when I did begin to notice. That's what I thought. It's what I *wanted* to believe, but.... You know how I'm a hi-hat player now? Well, I can also run a backhoe, cascade a running cable stitch over a double knit half purl, fit square virtuals into round hashes, replace nested tables with cascading styles, play the simple-system seven-valve flute in the key of D, hot-wire any GM vehicle produced between 1949 and 1991, and launch a bowling ball at a 2-8 split with a very unusual wrist-first release and what's called the Watusi follow-through."

"You're tired. You're sick," I said, but my denial was weak, not even much of a denial, really.

"Okay, forget about the Watusi thing. I was exaggerating. But really, certain things stick with me. I'm not sure why one thing does while another doesn't. Weird, isn't it, that I really only assimilated what the left foot and leg, and right wrist, of that old Brit drummer could do? I can play the hi-hat now, and quite well. What good is that? Where's the rest of it?"

He drifted off on a tangent, and I was content to let him stay on it, at first. Then I wasn't. "Morton—"

"No, it's hard to get momentum," he interrupted. "Let me keep going."

I'd wanted to say, *I wanted to say something, to tell you....*

Just then, he lost his momentum. Perhaps I'd ruined it. He coughed, and looked for a moment as if he'd passed out, but it was only extreme pain that just about paralyzed him. He was locked into an exhaled gasp, immobile, eyes closed, so wracked with his unique agony that he literally couldn't move. It lasted about ten seconds.

I wasn't sure if he could hear me through the pain, but I took my edgewise when I could get it. "No matter what I was, or what I was doing then, I promise you that *now* I'm taking you to where you can get what you need, and I promise I'm using what I know, and everything I have access to, to get it—for you to get it *your* way, not their way."

He offered a little nod, so little that I could only really see it because I wasn't looking at him, that way you see certain things better with the corner of your eye.

Another ten seconds ran by while, from the corner of my eye, I could see him thaw. The pain, like a skeleton of internal ice that had paralyzed him, warmed, and some of it passed, and he came back.

He sighed and continued. "I went back and revisited some of those earlier remnants, *inklings*, from way back at the hospital, before I ever saw you, even back in the rehab center. Some of the inklings—remnants that stick around—are not all weird skills and unusual experiences. Some are just mixtures of odd and ordinary memories, things that seem mundane, lacking significance. Some of these have a unique stamp, and I found you there. And there. And *there*. In a way, it was a good feeling, and in a way, it was... not frightening, more like puzzling."

I almost interrupted him again, but he looked at me and I knew not to. I really wanted to, because I knew what was coming, but the momentum, weak as he was, was unstoppable.

"Well, yeah," he said, "a little frightening too, I guess."

He stopped, and seemed to be gathering energy, so again I couldn't stop him. He was poising a hand out in mid gesture, to hold his spot, to keep the floor, to pause his momentum but not interrupt it.

"You know how cool it is when you're talking to a newer friend, and you figure out that you were at the same beach the same summer when you were a kid, or you were at the same Harry Connick Jr. concert twenty years ago, or whatever? There was something... somehow ephemeral that you both experienced, and even though you didn't know each other, and didn't even probably see each other on the beach or in the arena center, it still somehow feels like a better friendship, a more in-common friendship."

I nodded.

"Well, the good-feeling part was like that, with a couple of those souls back at the convalescent rehab, and some early ones at the hospital. I couldn't go back in time, but I remembered. I experienced brief little memories... of you, of Lorethe. Retrospectively, I recognized you. Because of what I can do, of what I've *had* to do, I've actually experienced Lorethe with more than one mind. The memories, though not mine, had become a part of me, and the instinct was, 'Oh, this is nice.' Because I love her. I love Lorethe now. I didn't love her then, when I didn't know her."

His gaze almost bored into me.

"But I love you now, Lorethe."

I cried. He was gasping, rasping, and talking, while I was driving, and crying.

"So," he continued, "I figured it was something that, if we both know it, but one of us doesn't know the other knows... well, that person should tell the other. So, I'm telling you: *I know*." He closed his eyes and inhaled very slowly, regathering some strength.

My turn had come. "My brother was... *is*... a military contractor. He was Navy, eight years, still in the reserve, but his day job is with a connected civilian contractor. He takes care of unusual needs, liaison issues, public relations stuff, as a third party, a civilian entity — those odd little items that don't really fit within a military job description. He hired me to visit dying people. I didn't even know why — at first, anyway."

"It's okay, Lorethe. Now we both know I know."

He closed his eyes, and seemed to drift off. After a few minutes, though, he spoke up again.

"The safe," he said. "What was in the safe?"

This seemed to come out of nowhere. For a moment, I didn't realize what he was talking about. It had been so long since he'd muttered those numbers in the hospital hallway... at any rate, it *seemed* long ago, though it had only been a matter of weeks, less than a month.

"Maybe that was part of it," I laughed a little. "I was right about that! Dad's safe was pretty empty — some insurance papers, old automobile titles, a thousand in cash, an old will that wasn't much different than his last one, marriage license, things of sentimental value. I think my brother had hoped for some sort of motherlode, because when the safe was a dud, his attitude about the... the experiments intensified. He has a stake in the outcome. And that's when I began getting cold feet about the whole thing."

Again, I thought he had fallen asleep. But no. "I'm listening," he said, without opening his eyes.

I could tell he was so very, very tired. It worried me. "When we left the hospital, you in the wheelchair, unconscious, I was done. Finished. I even texted my brother, because by then, of course, I knew they were looking for the zombie. Zombie maker? They were looking for you."

"Lorethe?"

"Oh," I said. "I love you too, Morton."

"Lorethe," he repeated. "Can we drive to a quiet place, out there somewhere, in the trees, away from, from, from...."

"What?"

"I can't do it anymore. Please? I think if we got to a quiet place, with wind through trees, and sky through branches, but a quiet place alive with quiet life, I could just... let go."

Somehow, it just didn't seem proper to persist, to insist on disrespecting this yearning, not so much to die but to cease the struggle to live, from a man with a relationship to death unlike anybody else's... ever. I tried — a little — but I could see on his face that he had just enough struggle left in him to fight for this... last peace.

I saw a sign for a small state-numbered route up ahead, which looked like it headed up into the hills, and when we got to it, we took it.

Chapter 39

It must have been just what Morton wanted—a winding road, uphill for a while, then down, then following a streambed that seemed too big for the trickle that surfaced here and there. We saw trees, trees, and more trees, occasionally parting for a trail head or dirt road, the first few with sagging cables and rusting padlocks restricting access. We resolved to take the first open trail, or look for one with a rusty enough lock to just knock it off.

I said, "Don't think I've given up. I couldn't argue with you. I wouldn't. You just told me you loved me, and I know you're smart. You did that to disarm me, so I'd let you die, but it's going to backfire—"

Even in great pain, he managed a smile, and was either spasming a weak cough, or chuckling, but what interrupted my impassioned plea was a truck.

It came up behind us, a blue pickup—not dark blue, or light blue, but that metallic aluminumy in-between blue that always looks like a really old truck. Suddenly, this roaring old blue closed the gap behind us, swung into the wrong lane, and came up alongside.

I slammed on the brakes, because the young man riding shotgun, in a rough coal-pile beard and a feed-store cap, was indeed pointing two barrels of shotgun out *his* window, at *my* window.

"Die zombie fiends!" he yelled out the window from behind the double barrels.

These must have been some of the zombie hunters who'd spotted Morton's Chinese fire drill for the Borises back there, the ones who had the cues and bats and handles—and smoothbore guns. It seemed likely they'd been tailing us all along, just waiting for us to get into relative seclusion, or traffic thin enough, to make their move.

We screeched, skidded, and fishtailed, and as they scooted ahead of us, a double blast rang out. The two loads of buckshot went across our hood.

What happened next came quick but oh-so-logical, if not sensible. They must not have been ready for me to decelerate so fast, or the driver and gunman hadn't coordinated their actions. Or something. For whatever reason, coal-pile had slipped a bit, and the gun hadn't been shouldered properly when he let both barrels go. Perhaps he wasn't accustomed to shooting left-handed.

When the shotgun rider pulled the triggers, we saw the gun fly across the cab, propelled by the kick, the recoil. The stock smacked the driver on the side of the head, and his head jerked violently and banged on the side window.

The truck instantly sped up, left the road, bounded over a few berms and boulders, sideswiped a large tree bole, turned sideways, rolled over and righted as a door flew off and something large flew out. Then the truck rolled over two more times, clearing the stream bank and ending up in the stream proper, upright but crumpled, twisted, with all the glass shattered.

I pulled over and got out, and stood holding the door for support. Two things came to mind: we'd just been shot at, and we'd just witnessed a possibly fatal accident. The altruistic instinct one might normally feel due to the latter was compromised a bit by the fact that the former had been perpetrated by the victims.

I just stood there for probably longer than your average accident witness might—long enough that another car eventually pulled up behind me.

"Morton?" I said.

An older, silver-haired gentleman stepped out of the driver's side of the maroon sedan, then leaned back in to say something to his companion.

When Morton didn't answer, I made much the same motion, leaning down, and saw that he was out, not conscious, hunched over and leaning into his shoulder belt. Was he hurt? Had he expired? Was this adequate enough breeze/trees/sky for him already? The scene and situation didn't seem especially peaceful to me.

I leaned in and lifted Morton's chin, checking. He was okay, just back in his dozing, hospitalized mode. Or...?

"Hey. Hey! What happened here?" The silver-haired motorist was insistent.

I rose again, so that now we both were in door-open, half-out-of-car mode, observing the accident scene.

I'd already taken in the settled details, and in my indecision I'd had plenty of time to absorb the tableau. The wreck was sixty yards down the slope, in the gut bottom of the little ravine. Twenty-five or thirty yards down, on the edge of a small spinney of straight saplings, lay the ejected passenger, our gunman, in a truly awkward, tossed-and-left attitude, sort of hunched over but not at all upright, sort of laid out but not at all prone, one knee bent and the other likely dislocated, and with one arm apparently missing.

"Not sure," I said. "We just came up. Must have just happened."

Then came a little rumbling sound, and flames and black smoke started rolling out of the front end of the truck.

And then, most unexpectedly, the ejected passenger rolled over and sat up.

With his remaining arm, he reached up and all the way over the top of his head, sort of hugging his own cranium, gave a twist, and appeared to partially straighten his bent neck. Again, with that sole remaining arm, he pushed off and rolled, manipulating his body to a transition position on one knee.

Silverhair and I both stared. I heard him say to his passenger, "No, dear, best you stay where you are, I think."

I looked back at him, but he didn't even return my glance. He continued to watch as the accident victim struggled to his feet, then pushed and pulled on the bad leg. There was an audible crackling pop from his knee joint, and then, he began limping toward the truck.

"I thought that man was dead," said the other bystander, his tone a mixture of *am I dreaming* and *and I'm still not sure he isn't not dead.*

"Might be, um, reflexes," I said, just to keep the patter up.

The cab of the truck had filled with black smoke, and the flames writhing thirty feet up from the burning engine compartment were visually dampened to a deep, hellish orange by the same black billows. The one-armed man, his one leg crackling as he half dragged it, half relied on it, limped without hesitation around the front end of the truck, heading for the driver's door. Flames licked at his clothes, and one of his sleeves caught fire.

"Shouldn't we...?" The silver-haired bystander didn't seem to know what to do.

I turned my head slightly in his direction, to indicate that I heard him, but we both had our eyes riveted on the rescue scene.

"No." I shook my head, then nodded at the flames licking around all those car hoses and fluid pumps and reservoirs. "Not safe."

"But—"

"Look!"

Little tongues of smoke now tasted at new places, finding its way out of the engine and cab from a dozen seams and cracks. It ran, strangely channeled, like little gray and black rivers alongside the vehicle's quarterpanels, as if honoring an odd and sinister form of gravity — scouting parties for the following hungry tongues of flame, leading them to new things to burn. We could no longer see the one-armed man, but could hear that he was still doing something — the crunch of an opening door mechanism, the creak and moan of damaged hinges.

He returned the way he had come, around the front of the burning vehicle. He was slow, for, using his one remaining arm, he dragged the body of his Zombie-hunting companion, the driver, by *his* limp, sweatshirted arm.

They weren't more than twenty feet from the burning wreck when there was a *whoosh* — a *whoosh* that was both a sound and a sight. Then the gas tank exploded, and the one-armed man dropped the arm of the driver and collapsed next to his companion. Unsteady as he was, the blast had blown him over.

Leaning on our cars, the other bystander and I both felt the concussion and the heat from the exploding gasoline, but we were far enough away to escape anything painful or terribly dangerous. Nothing large flew off the wreck, so perhaps the fuel tank was relatively empty.

The one-armed man, after a few seconds on the ground, rolled onto his back, flexed, and hunched in place, seeming to test his compromised core and battered limbs. He engaged in a combination of shaking and writhing gestures, insect-larventine in character. It seemed they didn't pass the function test, because he remained on his back for a moment, then reached around feeling all his pockets. He seemed to feel what he was looking for in his shirt pocket. With a motion that looked practiced and habitual, his fingers found the pocket opening and drew a small rectangular item out. I thought he was going to flip up a hard box of Viceroy's and light one up.

It was a cellphone. He rubbed it against his chin whiskers to open it to the button face and flip screen. Then he rested it against his thigh and, craning his head forward, used his one good hand to dial something.

Then he collapsed.

Five seconds later, a voice from inside the car spoke. "Let's go," Morton said.

Chapter 40

I didn't think much about it, not until later, at least, after a bunch of other stuff happened. What do you say to a fellow bystander when the stuff you're bystanding is still percolating along, and you're just going to drive away? "Bye for now?" "BRB?" "I just, um, remembered I need to turn the slow cooker off, bye!"

So I gave a little wave, got into the car, started it up and put it in gear, then straightened the wheel and made to continue on up the valley.

"No," said Morton.

I stopped and idled and looked at him. "Feeling better?"

"Yes."

"Back to plan A?"

He wasn't quite so fast to answer, but he didn't say no, so I turned the car around and started back down toward the strings of villages and towns in the bowl of the long valley.

He seemed a little moody, perhaps natural for somebody who'd been so ready for, even yearning for, peace, now back amidst a variety of dilemmas.

I figured perhaps an open-ended question might be best. "What happened?"

"Tell me more about Plan A." He wasn't *quite* looking at me—a sideways vaguely peripheral thing, more an *attitude* of attention than actual looking or glancing my way. Maybe he was still... tired.

"Okay, plan A: well, we go back to where you have all kinds of options. Jidalco and Scutcheon are setting up a special lab somewhere near, but not in, the facility. They've been gathering... specimens. You can get strong, and find out what they want. Maybe it's not so bad. Or, you could, when you're stronger, sabotage their evil and sinister plans. You could stop them, expose them, or somehow publicize their objectives as... as fundamentally evil and sinister. That shouldn't be hard. You have the advantage. You can move in mysterious ways."

"Your brother... he's not deeply involved, then?"

It was my turn to not answer.

This had become easily the weirdest conversation so far in our relationship. It felt goosey, but his eyes had been slowly working their way around, and now he was actually looking at me. Almost. Sort of.

I gave up this much: "Plausible deniability. He was given specific instructions, but they were strictly tactical. He didn't know, or want to know, what was actually happening. No whys or wherefores. I knew even less. It was only when I got to... know you that I realized how... astounding their work must be. I began to feel that I was maybe on the wrong side of things."

Morton nodded.

I reaffixed my attention to driving, but a question did occur to me. I needed, and I hoped *we* needed, some bantery quippage to get us feeling comradely again.

"So, what odd new skill did you just pick up this time?" I shook my hair back, the nod that means the just-now recent past, and smiled.

He gave the slow chin-raise that means irony, eyelids tracking slowly up, eyes a little to the side, then lids halfway down again. No smile. "Pretty good with a shotgun."

He must not have liked the answering look I gave him.

Do we all—we women—have a look, or looks, that men always misinterpret as disapproval, when what we're really going for is unamused understanding?

He added, "I can brew small batches of fully krausened mild ale, too."

I laughed.

Chapter 41

I could see the hurt in him, in the eyes and the mouth — actually, the way his eyes and mouth rearranged themselves in relation to the less-mobile centerpiece, the nose.

When a man — your usual naturally stoic man — is emotional in certain ways, you can tell because he looks non-emotional, or attempts to hold emotion off. His eyes sort of freeze and the mouth goes flat. And there's the nose, the only thing that's acting normal, because there isn't much you can do about it, one way or the other.

He liked making me laugh, but he didn't really laugh along the way he had before. He still wasn't sure about trusting me. Maybe I had to show him, somehow, that I trusted him.

"What made you change your mind?" I said. This was what I'd been trying for before, but couldn't seem to quite find the direct question.

He looked at me, still with the hurt behind his flat eyes and flat mouth,but I could tell from his nose, roiling in its unnatural stillness, that he did want to answer. Or, maybe something inside him wanted him to want to answer — wanted to come out.

"C'mon," I said, and was about to do what women do. I could feel it coming on — what women do, at times like these, is encourage self-expression and emotion, *not* suppress it. The cry. But I held it off. "C'mon. Please, Morton, I'm sorry. I just want us to feel right again."

I looked right at him, because now his eyes were on my face. Then I took my hands off the wheel and put them behind my head, then around my face.

His eyes met mine, and it didn't take long. The car drifted, and it seemed as if he did think about it for a part of a second — about just leaving it. Then, he took the wheel and kept us in the proper lane.

Our eyes had not unlocked, but I had to look at the road. I did, and took the wheel back.

I'd lost the staring contest, but he'd lost the chicken contest.

He started laughing, I laughed too.

"Yeah," he said, and smiled.

PART FOUR

NAUGHTY SWEETY'S BLUES

Chapter 42

Yes, I smiled. Half an hour ago, I'd been figuring I'd be dead by now, in some sort of peaceful or surgeful flowing current of energy that all transitions seem to need. I was so far gone that I was actually ready to go. Yet now, I laughed and rolled down the road playing chicken.

And now, thirty seconds later, Lorethe held back her tears and laughed with me.

I guess she got to me though, because I answered her.

I told her I was lying there, in the front seat of the car, half gone already, so exhausted, my head so full of pain, pressure, and desperate thoughts.... This strange last few days of my life, my waning, and then my lying there in her car right after the gun blasted and the truck crashed, and she'd pulled over, as I half-sat in the seat while lying half-crumpled on the floor, I thought: *What now!*

In a few brief flashes of partial seconds, change crept across my intentions.

I looked across the seats, across the car, at Lorethe standing in the open car door, her leg bent with one foot up on the car doorwell, her arms holding the driver door in front of her like a shield. As I did this, at the very end of my juice, my mojo, my depleting life-will, I couldn't help but think of her. It occurred to me in those micro partial seconds flashing by, that although we'd made love on a hospital-room settee soon after we'd met, and again found ourselves a bit of horizontal accommodation in her kitchen when I was AWOL from the hospital, and yet again enjoyed some measure of comfort in Kerbs County motel rooms, *we'd never had a chance to sleep all night together in her bed or my bed.* We hadn't yet been able to wander, say, from the porch to the kitchen with a cooling cup of coffee, then linger there and eat something, and then drift back to the living room with the big bed back there down a hall somewhere, or up some stairs, *and sleep skin-on-skin in the dark through the hours – mindless... comfort... unloosed.*

For that matter, we'd never been able to stay in the bed, even the motels' beds, just idling there, dozing some, sleeping some, a little of this and a little of that, until 11:00, 11:30, or noon. No, we always had 10:00 AM checkout the last few mornings—or left even earlier for appointments or errands—or worse, a noise would alert us in the night and we'd wake to adrenaline and wonder, never quite getting past stage three half-sleep, if we were lucky.

I loved her, and yet.... Did I—*could I*—trust her?

So I told her all of that—well, not the part about trusting/not trusting.

And I said, "Lorethe, see? When I saw you, like a picture framed in that car doorway, I wanted that. I wanted, just once, to be able to sleep a night with you in a... in that big bed, like in a *cocoon*—no stress, no threats, just us together. Like a picture in a frame, composed, with clean edges and it's own place on it's own wall."

She had to drive, and we'd now gotten back down the valley and onto real maintained roads, but she nodded and sort of wiped one of her eyes with her knuckles, then leaned back and readjusted her hands on the wheel.

"And so," I said, "when I sensed it, when that truck wrecked, I was almost gone myself. But when I got that feeling, that *pull*, I thought, *okay*."

Death was there, and I sensed it. It pulled, so I went.

A silhouette in a cotton dress, in a car door. With Death *standing witness.*

Chapter 43

Myrt's single mom was a sleep physician who on occasion handled some care matters for patients involved in sleep studies or clinical research, so Myrt sometimes ended up hanging around the hospital in the evenings. Technicians normally handled sleep-lab admissions, but occasionally, for special electrode hookups or unusual programming needs, or complicated cases with multiple sleep disorders, the doctor herself would be involved.

This was how Myrt came to be in the hospital complex at 9:00 PM, walking down the quiet corridors of the Medical Office Building Annex C.

Those were all the details we got, really, or derived, or extrapolated, about how and why he managed to gather that crucial bit of the important information we needed.

I scolded him, because he'd promised me he wouldn't do anything foolish or dangerous on our behalf.

He said, "Sure, I promised. That's why I hid my cellphone, with the vidcam running, on a center shelf of the housekeeping cart, taped just right to shoot and record wherever the cart went."

So using little tricks like that, he'd found out things, maybe just little hints. Some things he could pursue through his other information outlets, while other little sparks he could fan and nurture to figure out what and where the real flame was hiding.

Then, having uncovered such intriguing details, he wanted to come with us... to the Limelands.

That was impossible, of course. He'd done his little cellphone/workcart espionage the night before, and now hung out with his mom in the hospital sleep center. We could hardly risk his in-person involvement for a whole slew of reaons—his mom, his age, his safety, the danger we'd already put him near by involving him in the first place.

Still, we owed him *something*. So we decided that, instead of thanking him and saying *this is too dangerous, you need to stay out of it now*, we thanked him and told him that he couldn't come with us because we still needed him to keep his eyes open. We thought that little white fib — *sure, you're still on the team* — would do the trick.

Not so much. Turns out that when things get weird, kids keep secrets.

The Limelands were very, very close to the hospital, which was simply inexplicable.

This modern, major medical facility had a 20-acre footprint and another 15 in parking, and a network of dozens of satellite medical clinics, office complexes, and therapy centers that fanned out in every direction on the hillsides surrounding the hospital hub. A town center sat a quarter mile away, up Manchester Pike, home to fast food, fine dining, entertainment clubs, ice cream parlors, historical landmarks, autobody shops, garages, and counseling centers.

In other words, it was a busy, thriving, developed node of the suburban string — professional medicine mixed with and supported by, and supporting, everything else.

And yet... exit the big parking complex by the northeast corner where the employee lots are, hang a left, head down the hill — straight slope at first — and you'll hit a wide boulevard with office and medical buildings moated by their own parking lots, then a warehouse or two. Then you wind down a couple pretty short switchbacks that already seem a little odd embedded in this dense sub-urbanity. But the change in elevation is steep, and the switch hairpins are well laid out with wide round loops and perfectly engineered, inward-angled, physics-compensating pavement.

Another quarter mile down into the valley, after the wide underpass where the richly orange clay is exposed and dust swirls from the machinery accomplishing the bypass expansion, surroundings become just a bit more rural — no longer agricultural, just unimproved, and the land levels out. So, less than a five-minute drive from the hospital, it's not really so unusual that there's less development, less impermeables plating the rich but porous ground.

Then, continuing onward, a steep, dark hill looms at the roadside, behind a tangle of angled trunks, sprawling vines, low bushes, and upspraying brush. It looms because it's so sudden, so tall and steep, so suddenly blocking against the western side of the sky, it doesn't seem quite natural—because it's not.

Or it wasn't. If earthmovers push up a geologically instant plateau, eighteen acres in area and in parts elevated nearly two hundred feet above the surround, and sixty years later the whole construction has been largely reclaimed by sumac, sassafras, spicebush, ironwood, ryegrass, jimson, catnip, and jewelweed, and is home to deer, opossum, gray squirrel, woodpecker, grouse, catbird, wren, and finch... is it now back to natural?

A turn-in appeared, but the opening path, just wide enough for a vehicle and on a grassy surface with overhanging tree branches, was blocked. Whoever blocked it used some boulders and stumps, the latter beginning to rot now in the fecund northeastern shadows, rather than construct posts and chains. It looked like the kind of trail that ten years ago, maybe even five, was just open, and anybody that wanted to could drive in and look around. Legal liability, attractive nuisance, did away with those freedoms borne of unintended neglect.

Anyone who did wander in back in the 1990s didn't explore long, because in the Limelands, there wasn't much to see, even less to do, and nearly nothing to remember.

One-hundred-twenty-three yards farther on, there was a break in the regularity of the tree trunks alongside the western shoulder of St. John's Road, barely visible under tangles of honeysuckle and poison oak left and right of the break, and piles of field stone, dozens of tons of it, resting in rubble status. This was once a home, a farmhouse, a barn, a carriage house—homestead. You could just feel from the layout of the stonepiles and older larger trees, that this had been part of a microsettlement—big foundations and smaller outbuildings. Which rubble was which structure would probably take an archaeologist a week, or a local historian digging out an old county map, to determine. Even now, though, I could feel some remnant of the life, the lives, that had once spun here, not so long ago.

Anybody could, really. The overgrowth of natural vegetation, together with deterioration of whatever structures by the elements, had worn down and rounded all the straight and curved lines of former structures, but they were still discernable under the averaging of time. The moisture and microbes of those fecund northeastern shadows worked quickly. A few decades later, a few visible traces remained. Undisturbed for another forty years, maybe it would take an archaeologist to discern.

We turned in slowly, tires crunching rocks and dried vegetation, picking our way between the trees and stonepiles. As we got past the old settlement and into some grassland, it became clear that this had once been a trail or wagon-rutted lane, and that it wasn't entirely abandoned. The grass was parted and tamped, not enough to be a trail again, but enough to see that others were occasionally, discreetly, passing this way. A single trail could be deer or fox, but this was a double trail.

"Myrt gives good directions," I said.

"He sent a little sketch." She tossed me the phone. "I had a glance earlier, when you were dy— uh, resting."

She had to keep her focus on the road, or non-road. It wasn't easy to stay with it, like a real paved road, or even rural, worn wheel tracks. It was more like following traces, like Tonto tracking bent stems for his ranger pal—well, not quite that bad, but it wasn't like mindlessly driving to work either. Still, although she had her mind on her driving, I could see something else distracted her. Something about the way she tossed the phone to me also was a clue, as if that was also reminding her.

"You're worried about him," I said.

She looked at me, then back at the green and yellow stems bending under our front bumper as we rolled over them.

In southeastern Pennsylvania, where the climate is humid and the land rich, unattended—or untended—land can go wild so quickly. In this case, as we wound through sections where quarry pit tailings had upraised the level of the landscape, then descended to areas where the original elevation prevailed, we alternated between barren, rutted, weedy, stony stretches, and wildly overgrown jungle hummocks, brambles, briars, and fringelands where tall thick grass bordered high shady stands of hardwoods like black locust, black walnut, beech, and sycamore. We saw no oak at all, but little bits of evergreen popped here and there, on particular slopes where the light wasn't *too* good, and the water flowed just right, and the drainage was better than average.

In some places, the vines were so prolific, so invasively woven in and out of this scramble of mature and emerging growth, that the actual vines themselves, some of them thicker than your shins, made some of the trees, some of the forest canopy itself even, appear pulled down, as if descending into the earth rather than growing upward. The trees hunched, and bent, and the fat vines had spread and opened like long-fingered hands, pulling at the canopies, the branches, even the trunks. Deep inside the weave, individual trees were succumbing, or had already succumbed—sad, vanquished lumps and bulges, overgrown and digested inside somewhere.

At the other end of one of these stretches, with slick but hard mud under our wheels, a thin film of green moss over the mud, we emerged through what was almost a tunnel of those fingered vines and succumbing humps, into a shaded clearing. We stopped, because we didn't want to drive into this clearing. In fact, we stopped well before we cleared the vine jungle, well before our engine could be heard—if there was someone in there to hear it—but we could see into the clearing.

Some odd shapes had been vaguely organized around the edges, decrepit little utility-looking, vine- and weed-crusted cubes. In the middle, an oblong, weathered, thirty-foot long, twelve-foot wide, aluminum-siding clad structure sat up on blocks. Even before I'd seen what purpose it served, I wouldn't have used the word *home* in any designation describing it. It certainly wasn't mobile—not anymore—though it must have gotten there by mobile means at one time, perhaps twenty or thirty years previous, or more.

Next to it, pulled around in a faintly delinquent pose, handlebars cockily angled off to one side, sat a heavy duty, antique-looking motorcycle, mounted with a little bullet-shaped sidecar.

We stood idling for a minute, just looking, just feeling, just sensing.

We both knew quiet was called for—no car door opening and closing, no jarring noises to cut into the Limeland's stillness, no shutting the engine off, only to have to noisily start it back up. We just idled in place and... felt. *Listened.*

I stared at that building, at the other lumps or vaults cubed around the fringe of the clearing, and appreciated the motorcycle.

Lorethe looked too, and periodically—every forty seconds or so—she did a status check by looking at me.

I was busy, but I finally returned the status check and looked back at her.

"Back out," I said, calmly, nodding at her.

"I can probably turn around. There was a little patch of flat limestone gravel back there."

"Fine, but just don't drive any farther in."

"Okay."

I could tell by her look what she wanted to know.

"Yes, they're here. You were right: dead, but not too long. Five, maybe six... I'm not sure."

"And?"

"No, not now. Something's not right. That's the five or six part. I'm not quite sure whether there's five dead and one live person here, or six dead. That's why we just leave."

Lorethe put the car in reverse, goosed the gas a little, and we slowly began to move. We inched backwards along the tangled tunnel of vines and downpulled locusts. When we got past the jungly area, Lorethe swung the back end over the limestone gravel, which crunched under our tires. She stopped, with her foot on the brakes, and reached out for my hand.

"It has to be dark," I said.

Chapter 44

Killing two hours and forty-five minutes....

We drove back up out of the valley. Of course, we couldn't go to her place, and we didn't really have time to hole up, to hunker down, anyway. With five hours, we might have considered some sort of hunker, but with two, it was time-killing time.

We waited for something to happen, or to figure out what to do. We ended up, as people trying-to-stay-out-of-view-but-not-having-any-convenient-roof-to-get-under might, in a public park.

There were big parks around, and this was one of them, but not a big national park, nor a state park. It wasn't county, either. The township had turned its last remaining farm, two or three decades ago, into a sprawling spread of open land, dotted with patches of trees and threaded with jogging trails, ballfields, park benches, bandshells, and parking lots.

As the sun moved ever closer to those scrawly, gnarled trees a mile west of us, where the Limelands waited, we sat together in Lorethe's Toyota. We'd picked a small lot, a 16-car double-wide, white-lined strip tucked in where a bike path terminated, but in a part of the park where the hilly, honeysuckle-hump terrain created isolation.

A thumping noise ensued.

I heard it, steady, certainly not musical at that distance, and twirled. Muffled by the hill, the honeysuckle, the vines and the rhythmic enticement, I got out and wandered up the hill to look.

"Where you going?" asked Lorethe lazily, without really insisting. She'd been reclined in her seat with her eyes resting, closed.

I saw him, sitting and looking quiet, with a bouncy strum as just his right arm moved, really. Very subtle movements of the left hand appeared on the strings, the fingerboard, slight sequential adjustments to the chords — chords evolving rather than changing.

My right hand twitched, my left foot itched, and I went back and got the cymbal kit.

Lorethe had heard too, and knew this song, though I had no idea how. *Tonight, I Feel The Sky is About to Cry* was a slower number, but possessed that unstoppable, thumping rhythm of chord, bass, and thick-strung texture — bluesier, sadder. She joined me as I joined him.

He just played chords. Sometimes he leaned on the low end of it, sometimes the middle, sometimes the trebles pretty far up the fretted fingerboard. He didn't play any plain melody lines, though somehow the song's melody suggested itself through his variations, those evolutions of the chords creeping up and down the neck of the instrument. When a chorus would come around, or a repeated line — the third, fourth, fifth time — I sang too, left foot chunking, right hand sweeping and brushing on the clapping cymbals. I held it down for the verses, letting it open and ring and clamp on the choruses. The guitarist sang too, a verse here and there, scat while we rested and listened, and the choruses.

Half an hour later, we three sat on a walled bank fifty yards from one of the bandshells, out of sight of the car, belting a trio version of *Blues My Naughty Sweetie Gives To Me*. Yes, just an hour after emerging from the forebodement of gnarled decaying trees, struggling to aeonically escape from grasping, tendrilling vines, I played the hi-hat, accompanying a near-retired man-kid named Darl with an acoustic Black-Sox era guitar, very plain, finish unrestored, scraped and sanded by time, and by the nails and claws and ale spills of... how many guitarists in a century? Eight? Fifteen?

We didn't talk much. We played, and sang. Lorethe sang verses on two or three more songs, trading with Darl. Some of her lyrics sounded sure and right, some sounded spontaneously imagined, and others were clearly thieved.

I played. Or rather, my left foot and right hand had access to the ability. It was mostly me singing along on the choruses and responses — though at times I felt a little like that gyrating drummer you see in a concert video, face sweaty, eyes half lidded, lips moving with silent words.

Darl worked, maintaining digital security and network connections at an office building in one of the business campuses that rimmed the park. He was on a late lunch break.

"One more, please," we both said.

He strummed as I *tick-tick-ticked* with my one brush. He took it through, and turned an ending phrase around again, and Lorethe started to sing.

She knew this one too: *Baby Won't You Please Come Home.*

> *I have tried tried in vain*
> *I have tried to make it plain*
> *When I made to call your name*

Thought I heard an answer there
Turned around but could not see
Anything in front of me
Baby won't you please come home.

Like I said: half remembered, half stolen, half made up. Too many halves, too. So be it.

Later, we sat in the car after Darl had said his farewells and wandered up the bike trail toward the big, wide buildings with all the windows—still thumping.

I turned to Lorethe. "How did you know all those songs? It was like you and he were in a big band or a blues band or something."

"I only really knew three of them," she said. "One was from a movie I saw when I was little, on Television—an old movie. It was the kind of old movie that has songs in it, but not quite what you'd call a musical—not a Broadway-type musical, anyway. I don't really remember the movie itself, at least for years and years, but I loved that song, and I saw it again many years later, and the song came right back, like it just did now.

"Then, the other... it wasn't a movie thing, but a record thing. That song about the sky crying... I heard that song a lot when I was young. My parents—my father, really—had a record, an album, which he played a lot. I remember the needle crackling on the record as that song came first, or maybe it was first on side two. A song about seven bridges followed it, and my daddy...." She trailed off, and looked as if a tear might roll from her eye.

"The third song... I have no idea. It just came to me. I heard Darl playing it, and when he came around to that first line, *Baby I Feel So Lonely*, it just came to me. Maybe it wasn't even what he thought he was playing, but if not... by this time, *he* was following *me*. What do *you* think?"

"Either way, you were in the same place. You and Darl locked in musically."

"Have you ever felt like... right when you meet somebody for the first time, even if it's in a group or a really non-social situation, work or election day or jury duty or whatever... sometimes you meet somebody and... it's not a love thing—it might or might not be opposite sex, even—but something clicks and it's as if you're long lost friends almost right away?"

"Well, I suppose you'd believe me if I said yes. I've had a few eerie feelings, times where I feel I'm getting more of my share of rattling karma from the cosmic interstices. Yes, I get the feel, and I know what you mean. So this was...?"

"Yes, I felt that way—something like that, anyway."

"About Darl?" I wasn't looking at her, but knew she was looking at me, wanting me to look back. I did glance, and... oh, that smile.

She started the car, looked over her shoulder, backed out, turned, and we were underway again, our little musical idyll over.

"No," she said. "That old scratched-up guitar."

Chapter 45

Killing forty-seven minutes in half a second....

Then, something a little weird happened. I sort of remembered things *right after* we left the guitar park, driving toward the town, the hospital, and then, next thing I knew, I was walking down the hospital halls again.

Only, I wasn't me. I couldn't remember where me was, but I knew whom I was inside of.

It was Hazel... Hazel Rathlay. Last time I'd seen her had been at the nursing home, at Chester Valley. She must have finally raided her last young man's closet. But how, what...? How had I gotten here? What had happened?

It was especially odd because I actually knew why I was walking in this medical hallway and in this direction. I knew the motive, the plan, *the result* of the just-past period of time; it just wasn't quite lined up in the continuity of my mind. A big chunk had gone missing.

I figured out later that it was around three-quarters of an hour or so that I'd lost, somehow. It was long enough to get to the hospital— Lorethe filled some of it in for me later, where I had the angles twisted or the conjecture warped—and figure out that things were already in motion. Maybe the boy, Myrt, was in trouble of some sort, or maybe he was just laying low. I needed to get sheathed and get to work on one element, while Lorethe's element of the mission was to locate Myrt. If he was secure, that would mean it was something else, and a following element awaited her and/or both of us.

So that's what had just gone down when I suddenly surfaced, strolling decrepitly down the hall of MedicalOffice Building 3, wisps of wavy white hair half covering my rather ashen face.

I did have a theory, which I called the *countersap seepage.*

If you can break it down far enough, of course, it's all physics. Information flows. We've figured out how to clumsily send information screaming through optic fibers and wires and airwaves of various lengths, but it flows *very* efficiently in living brains, and living systems, and metasystems too, like ecosystems and microclimates, and maybe even that big red spot over on Jupiter.

With my odd new talent, I'd managed, or stumbled, or wandered into a way to short-circuit some living information network or networks, but I didn't really know what I was doing. I learned as I went, as I *stumbled* really, so maybe there *was* more than one network. Or maybe not.

As they say, as we live our lives, we rely on the relationships we develop and deepen, but in the end, we all face death alone. Each brain, in that sense — each mind — is an island. We bridge the gap, the channel, the intervening seas, and connect our minds through the miracles of speech, conversation, written narrative, but that's not a direct conduit. The speech itself must leave the lips, cross the air, catch the ear. The written word must be first written and then read, and reinterpreted through the filters of the receiver. Broadcasts, whether visible or audible, are simply collections of written concepts rehearsed, produced, and put on the air.

There were other channels, though, and in my awkward way, I found one. I thought there were others too, that we weren't really islands, not really alone. I *felt* this — some swift river, unseen, untapped, unridden.

Normally, all these flows moved in a single direction: forward — my mind, your mind, Hazel's mind while she lived, moving forward.

And that's where the forty-seven minutes went.

The single direction points forward from the now, to the future. Time is the axis of information. Information doesn't exist without it. *Without time.* The transfer of information, whether the invisible substance of a soul in migration, or the thoughts that assemble as an adventure story, becomes a manuscript, and eventually is downloaded and read on small wireless devices or large crystalline screens in 3D theaters. It consumes time, actually *trades itself* for time.

Some of Hazel's special elixir had managed to slip backwards up the information stream, into my own mentality and bank of historical memory, and pushed forty-seven minutes up, back, and beyond the curve, into some side stream.

Perhaps. Why not? People have mind lapses from four-too-many martinis, or as a side effect of *Restoril*.

This was nothing.

In a dream, people might experience a whole and complete set of memories that have nothing to do with their waking life, as if from another life? Where do things like that come from?

It made sense, in the hospital environment, that Lorethe and I split up, not just for our individual yet complementary tasks, but because we *were* more conspicuous together; *they* knew we'd joined up—*teamed up*—in this struggle.

Of course, my mind was all over the place, in more ways than one—elements of panic. Part of my thoughts were trying to sense, to feel where I'd left my dozing body, because I couldn't quite use memory to just track back to where I'd left it. The memories in this husk were just remnants. Under it all, or over, lay a nervous feeling of unconnectedness. There was no anchor line leading back to the living sphere, like at any moment I'd just drift off and... *I'd be gone.*

Part of it was casting back over a last remnant of available memory, that clearing amidst dark and twisted hummocks of vines and half unfoliaged trees hunching into the ground rather than reaching for the sky, and the paneled trailer centered in the clearing. More death had resided there, the sort of death that to me so paradoxically meant life, and was somehow key in whatever loose and incoherent plan we were making up as we went along.

Part of my wandering mind, of course, surrounded Lorethe, not remembering where she'd gone, but knowing she was busy. She was somewhere, doing something—something I needed her to do so I could do what she needed *me* to do.

Part of me focused on the present as we walked down the hall, me and Hazel—well, not much left of Hazel, really: her shape, her face, her bones, her gait, her grayness.

As I passed, I overheard a radio or television from a patient room in the North wing, second floor—reports of zombies, or more likely, masqueraders or cosplay fanboys, custumed enthusiasts, on the loose in Garregh County. At worst, this might be some unfortunate, delirious, sick patients, disoriented and alone.

Finally I realized: as Hazel, I didn't have a mission. Hazel *was* the mission, the doorway we needed. It wasn't something that I so much *remembered* as it was a dawning, as a logical conclusion. I had no idea why I was walking down the hall at all, but it really didn't matter.

Then, I'm pulled into a stairwell, yanked sort of backwards-sideways and to the right, firmly gripped by the right elbow.

Chapter 46

We'd managed to kill two hours and forty-five minutes, yet somehow only the last forty-seven minutes of it were truly dead, gone and irretrievable.

Still holding firmly to my arm, Lorethe spun me around in the dim stairwell and thrust a bundle, oblong and with just a bit of heft, into my hands. It was the size and weight of one of those family-sized seasoned pork loins, packaged and ready to roast. It was wrapped, wound into a light blue cotton T-shirt. The part of me that remained of Hazel wondered if it was a menswear T-shirt.

"I realized that you need a prop, something to complete the look, enhance the impact," Lorethe whispered.

I, in turn, realized that she was talking about the Lemon-Tarragon Swift-Premium she handed me, so I peeled back the blue cotton enough to see knuckles, grayish skin.

"Walk around with that," she whispered.

It hit me that she was leaving me to it, or leaving *it* to me. "Where did you get this?"

"They've got a whole room of them set up for the forensics seminar — cadavers, parts, heads. Interesting timing. Go!" She then left.

She was right. Whereas, walking the halls as Hazel, dead, I'd seen a few raised eyebrows, this would make a wholly different socio-statement. It elevated a *walk* to a *chant*.

A dead human walking the halls of a hospital facility wasn't all that different from the many mortally ill and near-dead being escorted and wheeled through the premises, from testing to imaging to treatment, and back to TVs and crosswords and family. Gray or jaundiced, bleary, perception-dimmed, sleep-deprived, hypothermic — all were superficial physical characteristics shared by both categories.

Then again, have one of either category walk those same halls carrying a severed human hand and forearm — or even an unwrapped three-pound pork loin, for that matter — and the eyebrows would keep going, and become the immediate preludes to screeches, screams, and the slapping, shoed feet echoing the way only hospital corridors echo.

Also, a loose patient, even a patient thought to be... expired, would likely be quietly rounded up and quickly secured out of view by experienced security professionals that would have certainly, in a large health facility, seen a few odd and macabre occurrences. They could handle it.

Perhaps it helped that poor Hazel had suffered a mild reputation as a character with a unique mentality, when alive, because I made the rounds of most of the facility, North, West, and East wings — avoiding the South for the obvious reasons that pathology and the nemeses were headquartered there. We wanted to milk it, so I did the turn two and a half times, with all that shrieking and screaming, and a lot of those echoing running footsteps. Now and then I put the wrist between Hazel's teeth and carried it Tango-style for a few steps. What the heck, it wasn't my mouth; it was Hazel's, and she was dead anyway. A more ordinary decedent — say, one missing an arm, with a bloody stump instead of carrying an extra one — might have been apprehended during the second circuit anyway, if not sooner.

It all came to a halt when I entered the lobby that last time. By then, two types of reactions had manifested to Hazel's March, both moving through the halls organically with her progress — the running screamers that preceded her, and the curious but timid entourage that followed.

Of course, all the while, security geared up, gathered their forces, and summoned the response contingent of local law enforcement always on call for big hospitals. All this was likely a bit unprecedented, and a bit disarrayed in a distant suburb that simply didn't get such *all-hands up and at 'em* calls very often. Perhaps some of those hands responded with the inevitable *"Really?"* when told that the target was a shriveled old lady, possibly deceased, walking around with three arms. Except that by now, those radio and television reports had upraised awareness that something surreal and abominable had become *all too real*, and perhaps even irresistible. The throngs were responding to the irresistible part.

The lobby at the *Sanctuary* wasn't like an old-fashioned, low-ceilinged hospital, institutional-variety reception area. It was more like a shopping mall entrance, or the atrium of a Fortune 500 corporate headquarters, with its polished floor, big open space, the roof, checkerboarded with big domed skylights, eighty feet up there, with arching beams, curved glass above and high vertical glass out front, and lots and lots of airy light, a pair of alcoved escalators, and an inclined spiral walkway around the perimeter.

Hazel came down the walkway, carrying her extra arm. Facility security and law enforcement had cleared the lobby, but there was still an audience—several audiences, really. The entourage still followed behind, twenty yards back. A mob had also formed behind the front glass, those tall glass panels across the front of the lobby space, which ran all the way up to give the lobby skywalks open views of the heliport, the parking garages, the green summer valley beyond the nearby medical and office buildings. Out there on the sidewalks, on the walkway skybridges to the storied parking, even along the abutments of the garages themselves, people had gathered. They mostly kept quite still, and watched. It had all the elements of a grand entrance, really, except for the reality of dissipated Hazel... and the bloodless arm.

Through her corneas, I looked down and around as I wound along that spiral skywalk, slowly descending, seeing the people out there, feeling those behind me. Way in front were the ones *really* waiting, those who had to *do something* when I arrived, and they looked nervous about it. I sized them up. I needed to make an impact.

Near a dozen local or state cops stood ready in riot gear, the familiar curved plexi shields and visored helmets. They tried to look like dutiful *Robocops*, but I couldn't blame them for their self-consciousness, facing a gray nonegenarianette with an extra arm. I looked up to see that they were thorough indeed, with glinting, burnished, blued cylindrical steel up at the edge of one of the high dome skylights.

Gunbarrel.

Down by the robocops, several specialists tended their special gear: tasers, stun guns, wheeled remote robotics with dollied laptop magic screens for remote viewing. What sounded like a large metal insect whizzed past my ear, then swooped an arc upward to hover below the skylights. A phalanx of ten yellow biohazard suits stood, too, presumably with invisible people inside.

An appropriate setting, perhaps, when so much was up in the air at once—plenty of air for proper buoyancy. Myriad questions floated there, from all the different factions present.

"*How did all these bystanders get here so fast?*" from the cops and security.

"*What good is a rubber bullet on a walking cadaver?*" from the guardsmen in riot gear.

"*Externalized fluids?*" from the biohazard suits.

"*Really, there's no such thing as a zombie. Right?*" From all of them.

And so on.

With those and similar questions in the air, nobody was as aware of them as me, slowing my steps as I reached the bottom of the spiral and set foot on the polished gray stone of the atrium floor, bringing the answers — some of them.

"Stop," barked an invisible megaphone.

This is interesting.

Nobody carried a megaphone, that I could see. Nobody looked at me with a megaphone. I scanned the crowd, seeking the squawking polycarbonate blunderbuss in some gay pastel like aqua or mauve, probably obscuring most of a face under a flat-topped, black-brimmed, blue captain's cap, but....

Nothing here, at least not visible.

Still, it spoke: "Stand where you are. Put up your... uh, put *down* the... uh, that... uh, hand. Put it down, please, and put your *own* hands up in the air."

I figured this was some new psychological tactic, the unnerving, disembodied voice of authority: *I am the great and powerful spokesman for the Bleddwyn Township Fireworks and Peacekeeping Corps.*

Disembodied voice speaks to disembodied hand.

Just then, the drone robobug came a little too close, stupidly hovering in place. On a whim, I heaved the loose arm at it, and caught the joystick jockey off guard, apparently. The arm spun through the air and palmed the chassis of the little dual-rotor drone, upending it, and slewing it straight at the biohazard stack, sending them in turn careening and scattering like so many pointy-headed yellow bowling pins.

Then I feinted at the taser/stun gun group. Hazel wasn't much of a runner, but just by leaning toward them, and avoiding falling over forward by keeping her legs moving just enough, I'd initiated the terror.

The snap and crackle of ozone filled the air, fine wires criss-crossed, and I felt the little probes and darts in Hazel's midsection and upper legs. I was a little surprised, because I didn't think they would have any effect at all, which was stupid of me. Fortunately — *very* fortunately — I'd been about to topple forward, a final falling tumble into the wall of responders when they all fired. All this current flowing through me set every muscle in Hazel's body into a fibrillizing tension that immediately acted to offset that inexorable feeling that her legs couldn't possibly catch up with the rest of me, and....

The result was that I almost didn't topple. Almost.

Hazel's body went into arrested motion, an electrically induced *rigor* that had the effect of prolonging her exposure as a target. Her nerves themselves were largely inactive, as clinical death had been declared some six hours previous, but I felt the rubber bullets as impacts, little poundings that drove *us* yet further upright against the tendency to topple. All the while, the little robotics scurried with whirring treads up to our ankles, and banged their articulators on our shins, these treaded utility tenders the awkward height of wastebaskets, with mechanical pincers and 12-megapixel tentacular eyes.

To clarify, the objective here—in front of these public-safety professionals with their shining polycarbonate and Pillsbury kevlar, their invisible megaphones and remote-controlled surrogates; in front of incidental bystanders, hospital patients and staff, and citizen social-media journalists—was to display a scene from the worst of their nightmares, or at least something like they routinely saw in hi-def after 10:00 on a weeknight on cable.

Except... this would be real. Well, it would look real. In fact, it would *be* real. If they interpreted it in terms of nightmares and/or all that Romero-inspired visionry... well, so be it. We remained unclear about what Jidalco and Scutcheon were actually aiming for, but Lorethe and I were about to do a bit of branding work on their behalf.

With a silly-string-esque spaghetti of stun wires sprouting from her midsection, and black rubber items varying from BB to dildo-size/shape bouncing off her ribs, Hazel fell. I had hoped to have her pull off a zombie impervious sort of performance, twitching and jerking and remaining upright through it all, but mechanically, what remained of her just wasn't up to the task.

Suddenly, all was quiet, until....

A voice, moving above us all, shrieked through the sickening silence of overkill aftermath. "My patient! What are you doing to my patient?"

Descending the arrested escalator, scolding the entire assembled response force of one large health-system branch, half a county, and three municipal entities, was my girl, Lorethe. All ears and eyes shifted to her, so at that moment, it didn't matter if I snuck a peek, so I did. She stomped down the last few metal escalalons, white lab coattails snapping round her striding hips, stethoscope flying over a shoulder like the Red Baron's *escréppe*, and she stopped and glared around at them before kneeling by Hazel's head.

She spoke quietly now. "This poor woman has been deceased since she was pronounced...." She looked at her watch, and pulled her stetho down off her shoulder with a move that looked *beyond* practiced—natural, like a sportswriter pulling a pencil stub from behind one ear, or like a doctor bringing a stethoscope into action. "...six hours and twenty-seven minutes ago."

She spoke quietly, but the atrium remained so pregnantly tranquil, and so acoustically responsive, that her voice seemed to hang in the air, buoyed by the light, helping itself to every ear available, in every part of the dimensional space, at any range and every distance—and in circumstances in which every ear was tuned to her voice, her tone, her every word.

She stood again, looked around, and selected a target. Halfway between her and the reception desk stood an odd little cluster of people and equipment that didn't quite fit with the action-burnished types up front. I hadn't seen it before, but Lorethe later mentioned that she spotted it as the nerve center of the operation—and somewhere in there was the heart and soul behind the disembodied megaphone.

Driven by this recognition, she moved with such deliberation and authority that everybody just watched. Nobody thought to stop her, or preempt her, or say, "Hey, wait a minute."

When she arrived, she simply snatched the mic right out of the Queeg's hand and handed him her stethoscope. A clever piece of sleight-of-mind, it was, because he stood holding it like a divining rod, thoroughly distracted, while she thumbed the switch and told the world, very efficiently, what was up: "Somebody around here—I think it's one or more of my fellow physicians—have apparently succumbed to some ridiculous Frankenstein impulse, and it's ghastly and absurd. This isn't the only deceased patient to be—"

I figured she'd gotten her point across, and chose my moment to mobilize *The Hazel*. She sat up, tumbled forward to a crawl, rose to her feet, and charged.

I did it as fast as I could, because the surprise element really was crucial, and I didn't know how long I could avoid the troops, eager with their non-lethal interventions or, at this point, worse.

I managed to charge right after Dr. Lorethe—right behind her, in fact. The crowd of professionals parted for my progress. Was that any surprise?

Lorethe quickly became aware, by the faces before her reflecting the approach of something unbelievably ghastly, that I was coming. She looked over her shoulder, locked eyes briefly with Hazel/me, allowed a microsecond of nostril flare as our invisible handshake of conspiracy, and then screamed.

Of course, by then, others were already screaming, but Lorethe's scream outflanked, outcurdled, and outlasted all the others, and she ran throughout its duration.

Before she ran, she tossed the mic. It probably looked like she just threw it up randomly, but I was conveniently arriving at the space she was fleeing, and me and Hazel managed to snag the trailing coily cord and reel it back in.

The screams trailed off.

The zombie has a megaphone.

The room went quiet. Through the corner of Hazel's eye, I saw Lorethe disappear through the crowd toward one of the halls that led into the facility's interior wards and departments. I also glimpsed a pair of muscular men dressed in dark clothes quietly following — the Borises.

I had no time dwell on Lorethe and her pursuers. I was about to learn how electrical shock and neurological deterioration affected speech and thought centers even more than they compromised gross motor functions. Yes, I could move, I could walk, and I could even do the medium motor feat of catching a microphone and thumbing the talk button.

Speech, however, was messed up.

"Ah wan...." I was trying for *I want.*

"Ah, Ah...."

I didn't have a lot of time, as they seemed to be recovering from flabbergasty, these responders. They didn't know what to do, and had no clue how to handle rising, walking, attempting-to-talk cadavers, but they knew they had to do *something* when one was rising, walking, and mumbling in a publicly spectacular way. Multiple *somethings* were coming.

"Ah want, I want... buh... buh... *s-s-scrapple*," Hazel finally blurted into the mic.

"*Bwains*," I corrected quickly. "Brains," I said again, nodding.

Then, while compressed air puffed and hissed, the ropes and nets descended, and again, the crackling red wires and rubber missiles converged, criss-crossing.

Chapter 47

It was time to leave Hazel to her sanctic vitusian watusi, pummeled and electrified, enmeshed and mini-tank harassed. *I* didn't need to be there. These peace-and-order interventions provided their own motilities, stimulating nervous tissue, pushing and pulling skeletals and musculature, and keeping her going as well as I could have. As I unfleshed, the last thing I saw through Hazel's eyes were the big outer doors to the breezeway buckling and swaying, and honestly I couldn't tell whether the stresses upon them were inward or outward directed. Both?

I wisped out, and straight up, and immediately found my next stage.

A rolling stage.

Scanning downward, I sensed a pair of cadaver carts slowly descending — almost meandering — unmanned, near the top of the long curving skywalk from floor one down to the lobby floor. As Hazel, I had plodded the same course just minutes before. This certainly held potential for greater, more vibrant death-drama.

In the lead rolled one of the portable, makeshift stretcher models, basically a white box-tent on a wheeled cot. Behind it rolled one of the stainless-steel hot-dog carts.

One of my allies — the kid? Lorethe? — had staged these wheeled carriers, had given them their initial push just as my first act with good 'ol Hazel was taking its curtain call under the nets and wires and non-lethal projectiles. I could sense that these carts weren't empty.

I was about to make the leap into one when I realized that I might be able to *inject a wee extra ampoule of drama* into this macabre tragedy, so instead of simply decanting myself into one of the cart corpses, I improvised. Lorethe had mentioned '*a whole room full of cadavers prepped and waiting for Scutcheon's advanced pathology workshop,*' so....

There I was, with four rows of decedents, three files deep. I didn't stop to look these candidates over, or to pick and choose. I sheathed into the first body I sensed that seemed receptive. Actually, I just up and ensouled the thing, sat up, pushed off the table, and popped out the door hurrying for the atrium.

Completely naked, of course.

I didn't feel bashful about it. It wasn't my body, so what did I care? Well, no. I always tried for more respect than *that*, but expediency breeds necessity, and its little baby is convenience. I was in a hurry. It seemed that most of the patients, visitors, and pros that normally would be moving through the halls were either already down below where the action was, or lying low with a mind to avoid the action. It took less than half a minute to hustle *Jamisten's* naked ass—I had already inkled his name—to the top curl of the skywalk.

Nobody down below had yet noticed the box tent and the hot-dog cart, and they'd actually rolled a few yards along the curving incline and stalled.

I took a plodding, head down, momentum-gathering, running start, and belly-flopped onto the hot-dog cart, which held the caboose position in our little funeral train, and the slow roll began.

I pushed up with Jamisten's arms, then lifted his torso to a kneeling position, reached up and pulled on my beard.

I had a *beard*.

I inkled right away that yanking on it pensively was a frequent gesture, a natural touchstone, a getting-bearings-and-beginning-ritual move for the former occupant. This beard, gray and forked, was long enough that I could see the tip of the left fork with Jamisten's left eye, and the tip of the right fork with his right eye.

From the beard, hand groping farther up across this wrinkled face, I found hair, wiry and stringy, long enough to pull strands down and see, also gray—gray and white—tangled and matted, but plentiful. I pushed it back, raised one knee, and planted Jamisten's right foot.

The carts were rolling pretty good now. The incline, though the slope looked consistent, must steepen slightly—enough—in the middle.

Pushing knuckles down, I rose, wobbly on Jamisten's feet, and took in the scene below me as I rolled, gliding silently above the mayhem. Medical and public-safety professionals swirl like rival swarms of social insects, wasps and hornets banging and dodging, tripping over their tools and their weaponry and each other, holding back the public and fighting over the spoil that was Hazel, and none of them paying the slightest attention to anything above their eye level.

Just as I thought I'd have to do something extra to get attention— getting itchy that this dramatic entrance would go to waste—a shriek rose quickly, thickly above the general noisiness. The shriek, saturated with that involuntary abandon, quickly turned alarmed heads, raised hackles, made coronary rhythms pause and restart, and perhaps curdled plasma in living circulatory systems — and possibly also in those clear vinyl bags hanging on high stainless wheeled stands by bedsides.

That kind of scream conveys more than simple horror. It has furry edges and liquid texture. It carries ponderous depths of wordless meaning. Most of all, a potent and full-throated scream like this one thrusts forth an indication of directionality. *It points.*

This thrusting wail pointed its ragged acoustic finger at me, and hundreds of heads turned.

Of course, anything with as much attention mojo, as much directionality, as that scream was in itself a spectacle. Most of the heads turned to me, balanced as I was atop the hotdog cart, shredding my way down the spiral skyway, beard splitting the air for my upheld chin, hair trying to fly and stream from my head, but really just laying there like a deconstructed Brillo pad. I held the shoulders back, arms at my sides, loose-limbed, like any good posably geriatric Quixotic surfer. Genitalia in their gray nest led the charge, a proudly forked beard close behind.

Some — me included — did not look at me, focusing instead on the screamer.

She was a nurse or tech, in her parti-colored scrubs, and she was running out of breath, and turning to run, period. When others, compelled by the gestureless pointing of her scream, saw what had caused it, the scream triggered more screaming, some with throat-hollowing tones, others gasping, fractured yodels. Unlike with socially contagious merriment, or chain-vomiting, there was in this instance none of the usual incidental awkward laughter. Most of the echoing screams came as wordless, gurgling, warbling yodels from hell. In a strange way, some of the screams even seemed *noiseless*. Women and children gaped with open mouths, trembling lips, and wobbling throats, but no sound came forth to contribute to the decibelia that was a rough and vile texture of noise.

"There's another one!" came through, though. These words emerged through the weave of multiple scream threads — more like cords or cables, or jib sheets or hawsers of sound. I was seen, I was screamed, and I was tagged.

Good.

So I let it all hang out.

Across the atrium, the glass doors and panels holding the assembled outdoor public at bay imploded and explunketed simultaneously, if that's possible, yielding to this transient local manifestation of mass hysteria. Some people left, fled actually, while those suffering the opposite obsession ached to replace those trying to escape. Some faces showed terror, while others sought it.

Like the random molecules in the headspace of a heated boiling flask, everybody else—everybody that didn't have either of those specific intentions or stimuli—also moved, but they did so vigorously, in every and all directions, bouncing off each other, sprawling, falling, rising.

Toward this cacophonous human entropy, we rolled, me and Jamisten, together in one person—his body and my soul.

Chapter 48

Jamisten was long gone, of course. All that remained of him was a faint inkling of a sleeping bag, a grassy hillside, pine trees, and something about pink pouting lips and a half-gallon glass jug of purple home-made mulberry wine.

I ignored the inkling and planned my flourishing entrance, when the front cart somehow caught abruptly on an obstruction. It either stopped the wheel on the floor, or possibly caught an upper corner of the cart frame on one of the walkway rail posts.

Either way, Jamisten hurtled forward, and all I could do was try to guide the impetus with some strategy to make his entrance and arrival impactful. So, he planted the ball of one bare foot upon the handrail and altered trajectory to descend with arms and legs outspread — cold gray flesh, surface area maximized to fall upon the upgazing heads of the crowd below.

I had by then already transitioned again, shifted into the prone occupant of the tented cot, so what fell upon those screaming fans was no longer a reanimated Sam Jamisten but simply his stiffening husk. That would be enough.

I thus crept into yet another body, a recently forsaken and abandoned physical form, and continued my campaign to impress, to win friends and influence people.

The inoculation of the mass hysteria kicked into high gear, with Hazel underfoot, hypnotic zombie mayhem enthusiasts breaking through the joints in the glass atrium walls, others streaming out and away in horror, Jamisten riding the crowd like a naked-mole mosh jumper — in this case, the crowd fending him off rather than protecting him from hitting the floor — and the hidden inhabitants of the tent cot and the hot dog cart inhabitant sailing forward. At this point, it all started to blend confusingly. I didn't know much about this one, except that it was a he, and his name was Herb or Derwood or something. I didn't capture his personal inklings, if he had any. I just manipulated him to bust out of the flimsy white tent, and then sort of surfboard that heavy gurney into the crowd, rowing it with one knee on, the other leg off and extended for propulsion kicks, its white canvas awkwardly draped and trailing.

As soon as I'd set all this in motion, and each element had set off on its own little sequential eddy of panic, I left them to run on their own accord, and moved on to phase two.

I shot straight up and observed those roof skylight snipers, and my friends the darkling crows perched on the parapets, cackling at them. I paused there, a little pulsing fountain of energy hovering above the sprawling medical complex. Nerves, if they can be called such when referring to a disembodied spirit, tingled my ethereal envelope with anxiety about my own body, which was still down there *somewhere*. I was tempted to go back, to seek it, to wander the familiar and unfamiliar wards and hallways, or to track down Lorethe and ask her. I wanted to find reassurance and strength in both her and my own reassembled self, but that thirsted solace was risky in itself. I hadn't been cultivating any dying acquaintances lately, and if I broke the chain of enfleshments, it might be difficult to resume. Indeed, it would require a total restart with a viable body, and I—we—had no time to spare. So with a supernotional shrug, I continued straight up, and then descended in a slow swooping arc to hover over the Limelands, until I saw that clearing with the little sheds, that vintage motorcycle and sidecar, the mobile-home trailer, and an old silver Ford Bronco SUV parked next to it.

I proceeded, with no great relish or personal volition, to take my mission outward, out into the public spaces.

Scutcheon and Jidalco had left some lackey in charge here, the type that might have been a video store clerk back when, or before that a soda jerk, or before that maybe a shovel salesman or buttonhook vendor, or some other lost profession that ends in -erk and that nobody even *really old* remembers anymore. In this case, he wasn't even somewhat capable, not like the efficient but sporadically clumsy Borises. So when I abruptly sat up on one of the gurneys in the morgue trailer, this fellow, who apparently had been sitting in front of a laptop with one hand in his khakis, turned in his chair. It squeaked because of unoiled springs down in the swivelworks somewhere.

A dead woman sitting up, a squeaky chair, masturbatus interruptus—all that would be enough to unnerve just about anybody.

I slid off the gurney and gyrated over to the counter, where a bunch of keys perched next to a black flip phone. I slowly covered the ring of keys with the dead woman's right palm, and nodded at the man's laptop screen, which displayed a rhythmically vigorous scene in the specialty known as doggie style. Reaching down with my left hand, and tugging upward on the front hem of her gray hospital gown, I turned my neck far enough to gaze the only eye that would open, as seductively as possible, into his wide-open, panicked countenance.

"C'mon," we croaked, hem slowly rising. "Have some of this!"

The moaning, projectile scream that came out of his mouth bellowed forth continually from the time he jumped up and began to stumble, running somehow backwardsish, across the room, then out of the door. He crossed the clearing still loud enough that I could clearly hear it with this dead woman's ears, hoarse and dwindling, until—still on foot—he'd run down the dirt road and into the darkness of crawling trees and hulking vines. He seemed so thoroughly and irretrievably unnerved, he might have reached Ohio before managing to stop. Or beyond.

Now it was time to load up the bodies!

Efficiency is important. Inhabiting and manipulating one cadaver at a time might seem limiting, but with some thought, planning, and... arrangement of the props and provisional players in our little showpiece, the resulting effect and impression could become quite vibrant, dynamic, riveting even.

For that, an injection of some doubt and mystery was needed. Without it, others might have thought it was all a sick high school prank. Was there something abominably horrorful going on, or did the seniors take too much Oxycontin and get carried away again?

The little old gray lady in the gray hospital gown got busy, oblivious to the popping and tearing of some of her ligaments, the fraying of a few tendon tissues—pain threshold is an element of physical strength; dead and dying nerves remove that item from the capability equation. She dragged most of the bodies out of the trailer and into the back seats and cargo bay of the silver Bronco, and then fired it up and headed for the back roads. She emerged into the edgelands where the parks and stripmalls almost touched upon business campuses and residential zones, where rusted and overgrown railroad rights-of-way and powerline corridors crisscrossed well-traveled commuter bottlenecks.

There, she stashed her ripening cargo inside honeysuckle hummocks, under dumpsters, alongside transformer sheds, behind ballfields, beside a grader on a construction site, and beneath a forest-green grommetted tarp holding down three tons of shredded black licorice root aside a newly landscaped corporate entrance.

Finally, her work done, she took a seat in the empty gatehouse of the nearest corporate campus, and her cold-filmed eyes looked upon the awakening world for their unexpected extra last time.

Then I swirled back for the motorcycle.

Now I tried to bend the stiff out of the two days dead, 210 pounds of a Lenape County concrete laborer, *female,* because night waned and dawn — the bonafide *dawn of the dead* — beckoned.

Chapter 49

I probably could have left it at that, but I really wanted to ride the motorcycle, to haul one more load out. I wanted the overkill, and to achieve it on the motorcycle, because it was an old BSA, and because it was Jidalco's. And the sidecar... hasn't every dude, everywhere, had a secret dream to ride at least once with an old-fashioned sidecar?

Before hauling out the first load, I'd already stashed the BSA behind one of the abattoir sheds, pre-loaded with the obese 245-pounder in the sidecar and the dead poodle from the freezer. I took another five minutes to wire the frozen poodle atop the sidecar cowl, in that wind-in-your-jowls dog pose, and then got behind the handlebars and headed out onto the highway.

Dawn came, and after settling the sidecar trio out there by the pavilion in Caledonia Park, my spirit then made the rounds, re-animating little groups and solos to crawl forth from those honeysuckly hummocks, from beneath and behind those dumpsters and tarps and dugouts.

As the world came awake on that dewy summer morning, screams sliced through the haze as a pair of schoolgirls waited for their bus on St. Gerard's Lane in Gwyddtomen Township. A car, it's driver distracted by a scene from a nightmare, overran the barriers at the edge of the remote parking lot between the County Hospital and the Hospice in West Garregh. Seconds later, several frenzied citizens called 911 to report suspicious and morbid activity by a trio on a Harley with a sidecar, out on Route 340. Of course, more screaming ensued as students arrived to salute their flag at Grand Valley High.

A Harley? Really.

I could *feel* the growing buzz of the county as my spirit flew through these setups, these little humanistic—yet so inhuman—dioramas. It notched up the level of undead hysteria, the non-zombie mayhem that, I hoped, would permanently sidetrack whatever coalition of dark agencies and military intelligence had aligned to trap me, to use me, to turn a therapy that I needed to survive into some sort of test pilot, foolproof, kamikaze, behind-enemy-lines wounded retrieval, corpse-manned space program they had in mind.

I planed rapidfire through the variety of enfleshments I'd strategically sprinkled around the northern county, my spirit swooping in vast barnswallow arcs, dipping into brain after brain, each of differing freshness—differing in its waning personality, the remnants there being not so much inklings as flashes. The acts seemed much more random than when I'd had better time and patience, for more leisurely reflection and perusal of the remainders of the previous inhabitants.

The term *flashed* might not have been the best way to describe it, as I wasn't just seeing images. The information came in many varieties—yes, images, but also phrases, inarticulate thoughts and concepts, sounds, sensations, even proustian odors. It came as emotions, yearnings, regrets, reflections, aspirations, love, hate, resentment, envy, cravings, loathings, terrors, appetites, revulsions, and lusts. I experienced sins revealed, virtues reviewed. Some felt like experiences remembered, even scorched upon the surface of the soul, whereas others seemed more fleeting in nature, perhaps second-hand or vicarious, yet still indelible.

Kezar Falls 1973. A saxophone like a Clemons turnaround somehow evolves into the scream of a woman, and then the murmuring burbling of water flowing over rocks. A small blue box on a gray pavement in a mist of cold drizzle bass notes floating featherlike. Women, in dresses, walking dogs in the dawn. The rain on bare goosebump forearms, not cold but blue, light, effervescent. Fleeting images. An elephant... an elephant smoking. An elephant smoking a Camel. The smoke has that vanilla sulfur, as when a person lights up in a fresh room. I hate my neck. *Was he painting what he saw or what he remembered?*

MD7066F. A camel. A camel drinking. A camel drinking an Elephant. 548. Four *Kitchen Range* meatballs on a toasted-onion bun. The irreversible film vault. *If it was by McFee, I would have read it, but it wasn't, so I didn't.* 5325. A sunny morning, a swarm of ants on a flat surface, a magnifying glass. *Why would I want to prolong my life?* The smell of burning nitro at Maple Grove on a Friday evening in late September. Striding toward the boss's office like Robert Ryan on the set of *The Underwater City.* Effingham hellgrammites. *Captain, look at my legs.*

Suppository of wisdom. The night has five hundred noses, the gun has a dozen roses. *Well, I come from Hampton Wick myself, so I'm used to innuendo.*

I'll remember this night until I get to my car; a face that will never change; making music by hacking into outmoded video-game systems; *what is the opposite of suicidal thoughts or actions?*; the puck-pause-puck sound of tennis in a misty fog; *Il va s'aggraver avant qu'il ne s'aggrave*; all this from killing innocent animals; his and her bathtubs; inadequate kinesthetic empathy; Radio Flyer Deluxe; *was that my intestine?*; the Bermuda grass was my biggest mistake; koala of solace; *but does it work does it really really work?*; sometimes you face the wave and sometimes the wave lurks behind you; sometimes you get to turn and sometimes you do not; pants and pants and pants and pants and pants....

Thinking with somebody else's brain, but treating it as your own. *The one about how you and Van wrote Northwest Passage, just one more time, please, Uncle Les.* Reaching for familiar faces, habitual memory, and finding something else there, something else entirely, *something else not entirely there.* Something not mine.

If a flaming ostrich is flying south for the winter, which direction does the smoke go? Relative to what? The Truth. The silhouette of a dog in a deerstalker smoking a pipe. Wherever we go, we'll take ourselves with us, making contamination inevitable.

My own mind continued to work somehow, directing all the undead action and flashing through, simultaneously, all the disparate inklings of other lives, dissipating, seeping away. All this happened even as the bodies contributing the thoughts slipped further and further from the hearts and minds of their loved ones, already getting started with getting on with the moving-on, which is inevitable for some and impossible for others, and which proceeds at its own pace, varied pacings, in every circumstance. *The getting on.*

My own mind, centered somewhere, yet now flitting across and back through the night and into the breaking dawn, tasted these little lashings of other visited minds. Yet it remained centered, *wherever* my brain might have been, *yearning.* That *wherever* also shared mindspace in a little corner of worry, somewhere next to and underneath the directing and inkling and flitting.

I must get back, but where?

How long, how many hours, had it been since I'd been myself, since I'd been whole?

Must find it. Or find Lorethe. Or...?

The county buzzed below as I flew my comet-shaped spirit overhead, a french-fry fortified black crow on either flank—my black-eyed wingmen. I slowed down because, unless I matched their flapping pace, there *was* no flanking. Once slowed, I could feel the waking land below me, sun about to rise, normally a quiet hour but with sirens howling. I felt in good company.

Flashing colored lights. Highways blocked strategically. Checkpoints, roadblocks.

An electrified mayhem blanketed the whole county. I'd spread my dead friends widely, yet close enough to seem interconnected.

A county in confusion, in dread, denial, and disbelief.

Still, it all remained centered there.

My crows look down. We descend, together.

The medical complex sat like it always did, seen from above—sprawling geometric swastikoid edificial wings separated by lined and slotted bollarded blacktop, pine-bark carpeted designated smoker courtyards, rows of cars, cavernous parking garages, heliports with red and white painted targets, and bits of tailored green mounds and little landscaped groves around and between, sun just now lighting the leaves golden orange green.

Those sirens bleated, and those blue beacons blinked atop the squad sedans and ambulances parked crossways here and cattybalanced there, with engines running, ready to pounce.

Good thing I could just slip in. I didn't have to walk, or drive, or face these bewildered uniforms trying mightily to squeeze the world back into some sort of routine, some recognizable pattern.

Chapter 50

Where to go? A plan.

I did have a plan, a very loose, unfocused idea of how to finish this. I wanted to get in front of Jidalco or Scutcheon, or both, not necessarily to confront them, or even exchange any significant conversation. I didn't feel such was necessary.

A glance. A wave. A wink? Then, go. Go!

I wanted to leave them to themselves to find answers, give answers, ask for answers, *grope* for answers.

Let them grope like I have.

That was why I didn't just spirit through half the cemeteries in Garregh County, waking the dead and making them writhe for my selfish purposes. I needed the bodies found wandering the dewy dawn that day to be those special people, the ones gathered, or registered, or paperworked, or donated, or otherwise selected and connected to the "project." My legions of death needed to be Scutcheon's legions.

Also, in a practical sense, the nonliving in those graveyards, under four or five feet of dirt and encased in a hinged, latched, metal-framed, quilt-lined casket, just lacked mobility. Realistically, I would have had to start with either my own living husk, or an able-bodied, borrowed dead one, and use its labor to dig up every further candidate, to be a serially habitated decedent one by one. I could have chained a few labors, perhaps, but still, this needed to be a quick strike, not a month-long series of nights digging my way through the departed population of the community.

The b-movies and graphic novels mak e it look so easy, but *I tried it,* in person — well, in spirit.

When you wake up in a coffin, you either — eventually — go back to some sort of eternal sleep in the same coffin, or you slip out of there in some other nonphysical way, like I did. There is no "push up the lid, push the dirt around, swim your way to the surface, push up the daisies," and emerge tired, dirt under your fingernails, and angry. Or hungry.

Push up the lid?

That's where it ends. The lid is half a hundred pounds, easy, and if it's six feet under, that's a ton or more of earth holding it down.

Still, as I narrowed in on the hospital for the last time, I remembered the abandoned cemetery across the pike and up the lane on the way to Lorethe's little Victorian apartment building. It was where I'd first seen crows carrying fried potatoes among the chainsawn lawn sculptures. So I swept across the pike one more time, which only took an instant, and found the graves where I'd felt those weird distortions in the light waves, where I'd seen something waving in the corner of my eye but, when I tried to look straight on, nothing.

I did manage to push and part the dirt, and to briefly... influence the arrangement of a few bones. These old coffins had long since rotted, caved in and down, now just dust and splinters—and bones.

Some bits had migrated upward some on their own. How? Who knows? Near the surface lay a bit of hand, of foot. I managed to rattle them upward, up to the surface where they shone whitely, a few carpals or tarsals still connected, a few loose extremities scattered like dice. My crow friends might have pitched in, influenced by my intentions, with their black beaks and scratching yellow talons. Maybe they were just following their own scavenging instincts, for bones white and brown, stark against the overgrown grass and pushed-up soil. The buzzards that nested in the limelands would, I knew, begin to circle within minutes. People would wonder—people always wonder. But especially on this day, people would wonder, and even remember.

Then, I moved onward to the hospital, and in through the east wall.

I thought I'd have a choice, a plethora, an assortment of stilled hosts to select from, including of course my own resident corporeality, which had to be around *somewhere*. I still couldn't *feel* it, though, couldn't get the thread, so I gulped around the empty ether for other possibilities.

First thought was the cadavers, of course, the room that Scutcheon had set up for his medical education class seminar. I had dipped into this cast of characters once already for the finale of the Atrium mayhem, but they were gone.

All of them. Empty steel tables.

Down through the floor and a few walls to the morgue, the hospital mortuary... nothing there either.

What?

I began to feel some twinges of panic.

I flitted now, nearly instantaneously from spot to spot, wing over wing in the hospital and across the wider medical complex. I visited familiar places, where I'd parked my own flesh in the past, now a soul on the move, sliding through walls and bouncing off those cold, springy zones I had no name for, but where I couldn't easily go, if at all. I dropped by N222, and the Blodwyn Tranquilitorium—those and the other little stairwells and alcoves that I associated with Lorethe, with Myrt and Henri, with idle time seeking a body session. I found nothing, and realizing with each *nothing found* that I had nowhere to go—nowhere new, nowhere familiar, no soulhome to occupy—I realized also, with a mentation that seemed increasingly light in weight and felt increasingly unanchored, that I may not have a lot of time. I knew by instinct—had known all along—that I had a shelf life for my out-of-body wanderings, just as there was an expiration on time in a borrowed body.

How long? How long could I go bodyless? How long could I borrow a given—taken, actually—body? I didn't know, but as in a car with a broken gas gauge, I just knew it was a matter of time, and felt a growing tension the farther I drove. Unlike in the car, I realized that with practice I'd expanded that envelope, but wandering between corporeal anchors felt so tentative, so perilous. I'd never, ever dared to free-fly for a wide-open period of time without a target body—until now.

And yet, as I swirled around the facility like Gaspar's omnicient camera, I felt a subtle pull, and it was small as well. Part of me—whatever roving-spirit *me* was at that point, hours removed from my own home flesh and lengthening minutes separated from *any* enfleshment, with physical existence feeling increasingly tenuous—even so, part of me denied that small, still pull, that call of a ready host.

There was one—*just one*—and I was avoiding it. I looked away.

Perhaps it was easier to deny because it *was* small. I wasn't sure what *small* meant, but instinctively, I didn't look there, didn't feel it, didn't *go* there. Something about it, about the *feel* of it.... It was a vacuum, flesh without spirit, but somehow I didn't feel that it would *fit*.

I continued to wander, pushing back against the small, still voice, trying to be thorough first.

Ah, here's one! Recently departed, a lifeless body, here for the taking.

No, that was Fremont Bengleby, eight months in a coma, but tentatively still in possession and still struggling, deep in there somewhere, with that age-old musical question: *should I stay or should I go?*

I had to admit that briefly, *very briefly*, I did consider checking in with Fremont. After eight months of coma, a shriveled soul rattling around the echoed corridors, there might have been room for me to slide in and ask around.

Mr. Bengleby, uh, I was just wondering... do you think you could make up your mind? Sooner rather than later?

Or....

Fremmy old boy, could I just take 'er for a little spin? You won't miss this old heap for fifteen minutes or so, will you? In the perspective of all eternity, it's really just an utterly insignificant blip.

Or....

Fremont Bengleby. Fremont. FREEMONT! Do not fear. Do you see it? Yes, Fremont, the light... er, rather, the Light."

But even just *thinking* about it, I *couldn't* continue that thought. My soul shuddered and I shrugged it away, and the overhead fluorescents in that part of the hospital corridor dimmed a little, there outside Bengleby's hospital room — a manifestation I hadn't seen before.

No, no, no! I will not influence... outcomes.

Then and there, I drew the line. In fact, I wasn't sure whether or not I could even exact such influence, whether I could even manage to push my way into an occupied enfleshment, no matter how tentatively claimed.

County was a big hospital. There were, of course, other borderline cases, some I knew about, others of which I undoubtedly had no inkling — a suspected brain death in the North Wing ICU, the next code-black down in trauma, an incoming recreational OD, the next vehicular accident victim, accidental benzo opioid antidepressant combo, or sexual asphyxiation gone wrong.

I didn't have time to wait for the *next* anything. It had been almost *seventeen hours* since I'd been incarnate, and my previous record was something like one-and-a-half! I was way, way, *way* overdue.

Through it all, I couldn't shake the sense that all this was some sort of setup.

Chapter 51

The chair felt big.

First, because I *didn't want to sit in it*, I made the rounds again, weakly now, wispily, checking pointless corners I hadn't checked, and meaningful places that I'd checked twice—the corners where only dusty wheelchairs with bad bearings or faulty brakes waited for disposal; the checked places where checking a third time was repetitively futile, like looking again in your pockets for the inexplicably missing keys or wallet, for which you'd already turned them inside out again and again and again and again. Of course, denial denies undeniably. In that round, I looked, futilely, for *me*. The empty pockets I checked undeniably didn't contain my substantial self, or any other useable non-self.

Then, I spent another round looking for any port in a storm, expanding the perimeter... again... and this time....

What is this?

In a ditch among the trees, down the slope from the corner of the medical complex's farthest parking lot, where a disused grounds equipment shed sat dark and damp, spread a small no-man's land neither medical nor residential, but bordered by both. And here, beside an unbabbling ditch, lay a dog's carcass—a week dead.

But no. No!

The idea seemed somehow bestial, to say nothing of the likelihood that interspecies ensoulment might be simply... unmixable.

Just say no to the ditchside bitch. Keep moving, keep swirling.

I spotted those knucklebones again, teased to the cemetery surface and eyed by the buzzards. It was silly, because not enough corporeality existed there to become physically capable. This wasn't a freakin' Harryhausen film... or Corman.

I swirled back, outward, then back in, back to the center where the chair sat, in front of the big desk in the big office.

A big chair. This is where I am wanted. *So be it.*

I decanted into the soulless guppy, opened these eyes, and I was sitting across from him.

"Dr. Jidalco," I said, my voice that of a child.

"You've been busy," said the doctor.

"This is on you," I said in that high, soft voice. "All of it. But *this*...."
I raised the little girl's hands, turned the palms up, lifted feet from their
dangling, and pointed toes to the ceiling. "This is *especially* on *you*. How
could you?"

"Children die. Men die. Women die. You were—she was—going to
die. *You* are going to die. I am *going* to die. I'm a doctor, and I see a lot
of dying. I'm familiar with death, but I never say that I'm accustomed to
it."

"I don't get *it* though. What's the point? You've cleared out the
morgue and transferred all the eminently terminal patients out of here,
and.... Hey, where's *my* body?"

"What leverage I have to get you here, and keep you long enough
to communicate—something, by the way, that I think we *both* need at
the moment—well, your unoccupied body *is* that leverage, or at the
very least a large part of it. So don't be concerned about your body. It
will be... available."

I nodded the girl's head. "Okay. Communicate."

"We needed—*need*—you to come in. We want to help you. You're
out there crashing funerals and loitering in mausoleums and mortuary
parking garages, hijacking hearses.... Can't you see that we have what
you need? Not only that, we have equipment, and we need to learn
and—"

"And study, and poke and prod, and biopsy and vivisect, or see
how much sleep I can go without, or how long I can occupy a corpse, or
if I can operate underwater, or in a vacuum, or without a heart, or how
long I'll last in a burning building? Three legs? Four? Six? Can I fly a
suicide mission? If the pilot's already dead—"

"We've thought of all that," he said, and nodded. "Of course, we
have." He paused, standing behind his desk, then went to the window,
and came back. "We brought you back into a child's form."

"You bastard."

"Okay, we'll come back to that. I want to do something for you
first. Do you want to know what we've learned so far?"

"Go ahead. I'll let you know whether it's remotely believable."

"One of the trial medicines, the experimental autoimmune
antibody, Arkanestaline, has an unusual pathway for an MC/AB-type
chemical. It crosses the blood/brain barrier, but—and this part we don't
understand yet—it only crosses under very specific circumstances. It's

as if only certain brain states permit the transfer, and some people seem more susceptible — or capable — than others."

A remnant inkling lingered in this immature brain, a physical, habitual one, so I started — without thinking — impatiently kicking these spindly legs, alternating left and right, because they dangled short of the floor. The shiny black patent-leather mary-janes — left and right, rising and falling, like a neurostimulation cross-crawl — became almost hypnotic as the Doctor droned on. Having been out of body for so long, I was hypnotically sensitive, technically already in a trance — had been for over thirteen hours now — and lucid in that trance, and now falling into a trance within a trance....

He continued. "It turns out there's a side effect when this susceptibility exists, this exceptional blood/brain condition, and that side effect creates a tendency to OBEs, or out-of-body experiences. But we are scientists. We don't jump to conclusions, and we try to analyze and understand before we take drastic action, and.... Well, it took us too long to figure out, and begin to understand this unforeseen result, because the unexpected efficacy of the medicine was indirect. It wasn't directly observable. That's why we couldn't tell you — because we didn't know. When we finally began to suspect, to zero-in on what we thought might be happening, you became... elusive."

I made the legs stop and looked up at Jidalco. "What? Medicine? This was from your *medicine*?"

He ignored me and continued. "We also didn't know because we were looking at it wrong. We didn't know what was happening, the *entire* cycle, because you weren't showing us — understandably, under the circumstances.

"It was a side effect of a side effect. Your improvement has something to do with your... ability to rest your soul or your... psyche, or both, when you migrate your sentience outside your own body. Some kind of healing takes place. That was the secondary side effect — no, the *once removed* side effect — we didn't know about. The intermediate stage of the cycle, rather, which we didn't know about *at first*. While we knew you were getting better — miraculously so — we *didn't* know that you had the unexpected ability to turn the OBE into a healing side effect. We had no idea you could actually displace your spirit, and send it — *take it* — to places vacated by departed spirits, and park it there while your body recharges or rebuilds some inner defense network we haven't yet identified."

I held up the girl's little hands. "Wait a minute! When you started the protocol, you didn't say anything about side effects."

It took him half a minute to get going on that question. A thoughtful look took him while he paused and made several false starts. If Jidalco had been at all the sparkly type, this was where we'd say his eyes showed a little twinkle.

Finally, he settled on a researcher's convenient excuse – the small print. "Well, actually we did. There was a whole long list of things, and a useful phrase at the end of the long list to the effect of, 'These are symptoms reported by significant minorities of subjects, and may not represent all possible side effects. Individuals may experience singular or unique side effects, as with all medications, as all patients experience differing treatment efficacy.' You saw it. You signed it."

He sighed. "Other pseudopsychic, perceptual effects had been rarely reported in the earlier trials, and nothing like your... reaction."

"Jeez, I had no idea. So I'm supposed to say to my busy and overworked nurse when she comes on at noon, 'Uh, Sheila? I repossessed the dead corpse of my roommate last night, which I think you better let the doctors know about.' Like that?"

This time, after a twenty second pause, Dr. Jidalco's face froze for another five, then it collapsed as his eyes fell and his hands shook, and he started to cry.

"We understand, yes," he said, getting back some control. "We understand that you could have... that you had good reasons for *your* side of the poor communication, and *we* should have communicated better, but we didn't. There had been some... um... *debate* among the... uh... the team. I thought we should look into it, but I was overruled. We weren't aware that time was... that you were aware of your circumstances, and likely to... to self-discharge. Then, when we *did* understand your mindset and concerns, and we wanted to make up for not communicating... by then, you were gone."

"Are you telling me I was out there, wandering the hinterlands, with a paranoid persecution fantasy?" Now I started to cry.

I blamed emotional contagion, that and the reflex inklings of the poor girl. As I wept, I scrutinized those inklings, the girl cry, and the girl, and realized where I was – whom I was borrowing – and the crying became grievous.

She was Henrietta, Myrt's little friend, but she wasn't just his *friend*. She'd been a hospital regular, like him, some doctor's or administrator's kid. That's what I'd thought – seeing them palling around, a couple of kids on mischief runs around the facility—but she'd actually been a *patient*, and a dying one at that.

I cried for her, I cried for him, I cried for me.... Then I stopped crying and looked at Dr. Jidalco.

There must have been something in my look, something arresting, perhaps, or incongruous or uncharacteristic, because *his* look became reactive. His eyes sort of dilated and his fleshy face tightened as he paid close attention.

That was exactly what I needed. "When did she die? *I*... when did *I* die?"

After another of those wandering pauses, he said, "Henrietta? She... uh... well, today."

"Today? When today?"

Then the door flew open behind me, and by the time I'd half turned in that chair, and half risen, it was too late.

He was a step away and already reaching for me—for Henrietta. It was Scutcheon.

Chapter 52

"You fool," Scutcheon said.

He wasn't talking to me, but his hands were on my shoulders—Henrietta's, actually.

Those hands on my shoulders were firm and strong, but not in a good way. I tried to shrug them off—just instinct—as even with Henrietta's dwindling senses, I smelled the animal of him, a beastly rage. My half rise was slowly, evenly reversed by the force of Scutcheon's hands on my shoulders as he pushed down and held me in the chair.

"What's wrong with you," he said, in that condescending, berating tone an asshole uses to talk down to a child. But he *still* wasn't talking to me, and it wasn't a question. "You should have given her the... the treatment... right away, before reviving, even. We have to keep going. This is something that we need to try, something.... It's a perfect opportunity."

Across the desk, Jidalco's face seemed to physically widen, and darken, unable to resist the emotion in there, and though he hadn't really *stopped* crying, clearly he was about to jag again. His whole body slumped.

I felt Scutcheon let go of me, and he moved again, fast.

"But, no," Jidalco said. "But Cliff, we're... we're *scientists*." He seemed to have more to say, but something about Scutcheon's face or movement stopped him.

The pressure on my shoulders lightened, and was gone. "Where is it?" Scutcheon strode around my chair and toward Jidalco's desk. "Where is it?" he said again, now with urgency and the condescension doubled.

"I just wanted to talk to her," Jidalco said. "One more time, her."

"It's not her, you fool." Scutcheon reached Jidalco behind the desk, but didn't stop the usual interpersonal distance away. Then, with a flash of white-coated arm, he suddenly slapped Dr. Jidalco and spoke the inevitably bitter, bilious, "Get ahold of yourself, man."

I jumped up onto Henrietta's feet, and realized a bunch of things at once, Including that Jidalco had started to sob again, and as a result, whatever he said next was unintelligible. I turned, ready to run.

Scutcheon slapped through the papers and items on Jidalco's desk now, looking for it. "There it is!" He reached for a hypodermic.

Then I remembered — hidden among the bundle of competing thoughts, with my mind working nimbly inside a young girl's remnant nerve tissues, somehow relaying back to my own reel of experiences — the sludgy mentation, the heavy blanket, the anesthetic entrapment. *The Mickey.*

Something about how her flesh felt, and something about a twist in the edge of expression on Scutcheon's face when he first came in and saw life in this little body, and the feel of his hands on little shoulders....

Now an adrenalinelike surge jolted through this little feminine body, coming with the realization that this man had also tried his serum, *was also trying* his method, his sloppy science, on at least one other terminal case.

This girl.

He now came with the syringe, only paces away.

I was already heading for the door, the distance between Scutcheon and me suddenly the most important thing in existence. It wouldn't be enough, though. I was little, and too slow, and he was big and fast.

I felt the needle, a jab of ice, then fire. It pierced right through the thin, deep green fabric of the dress, between ribs and hip. I cried out in her voice.

He probably could have grabbed me instead, and held me there, but the needle seemed to be the first priority in his mind. I heard it clatter empty to the office floor as his hands clutched for me, and I thought he would have me, but I kept striving for the door, still hoping to get clear.

Then shouts came, and I looked over my shoulder as Jidalco collapsed on him from behind. I doubled my running.

Scutcheon's hoarse yelling accompanied me as I reached the door.

Jidalco now hung upon his medical research partner like a grimy wet cloth, wrapped around him in a sobbing hug. He also made noises vocally — regrets and sorrows and apologies — but the effect was restriction rather than submission.

I wasn't sure whether he was intending to help me, or simply continuing his earlier purpose of sympathy and jagged emotion. Either way, I got the door open and got out of there while Scutcheon continued to struggle his way free.

Speed was my best option at this point. I thought about trying to block the door or lock it somehow, but there was no blockage object nearby, or even not-so-near, that an eleven-year-old could manage, so I ran, and I turned, and I ran some more, and turned again. I wasn't really watching which corridors, which wings and sections of the facility, I was zigging and zagging into and out of. I just wanted distance, and mazeance, between him — *them* – and me.

Finally, I felt it – a *drawn* sensation, very faint. I followed it, but couldn't exactly ID it. I wasn't even sure I could fully trust it at this point, but I had nothing else to go on. I simply relied, for better or worse, on instinct. There was a faintness of idea in there, though, along with a faintness of purpose, and those faintnesses contained reciprocating affinities. Somewhere inside, a workable plan amorphously shaped and poked around within it all, and following that pull was the beginning of it.

I followed it, turned a corner into hallways of light-amber tile, ran to a familiar doorway, and.... It opened, so in I went.

Across the room, a technician looked up as if about to speak. Then he was speaking, but by then, I'd crossed the room, dodging around the stainless-steel gutter table that made a centerpiece work island of the room's main space, grabbed and swung down the stainless steel portway, and pushed my head into the laundry chute. By the time whatever he was saying had become a word, I'd pushed Henrietta's whole little body in, and was hurtling downward toward the linens facility, formerly known as the laundry room.

I'd been in that laundry room once before, when I dove down the chute, but I never reached bottom — not that time, in that body.

Henrietta now proved an altogether easier linen-duct passenger, small as she was — easier to load, smoother in the barrel, easier at the discharge. Thus, she/we/I/*it* landed quickly, after a fast *whoosh,* deposited into a jaunty gray polypropylene linen cart, atop a bed of stained linen, terry, and jersey from beds and gurneys and treatment wards. Even though this body was dead, we didn't want to linger among those multi-use medical items in their post-use, pre-laundering heap. So, with a lurch and a leap, Henrietta had popped up and out, and now stood on the smooth clean concrete, looking around.

The feeling was strong. It was that *most familiar* of feelings: of self.

People sometimes use an expression: "I'm just not myself today." For a whole evening, all night, and a good part of the morning, I'd just *not been myself.* When *not myself* for that long, and then sensing my self nearby, it was not unlike hearing my own voice on a tape recorder for the first time.

Even though there's nothing quite so familiar as one's self, having been inside one's self for thirty or forty years or more, being *outside* one's self is not familiar at all. "Do I really sound like that?" becomes, "Is that *self* really *me?*"

In this case, "most familiar" still felt strange, other, new, and yet also familiar — *so* familiar, in ways unlike anything else that had *ever* felt familiar. I had to hold onto myself, hold my spirit in check just a bit, because I needed to think clearly and not be too hasty.

Careful.

I'd been out of my own body for so long that a criss-cross muddling had overlaid my own solid selfsense — so many inklings, so many different brief residences in distinct bodies with distinct remnants, all the smoky elephants and sloshed camels, the wriggly hellgrammites and cold drizzles, the lost yearnings and indelible soulmates, random numbers and rosebuds, so long away from my own *familiar* foibular channels and quirkus distinguishments....

I'd found my way back. I could feel it — *it* was here, and *it* was *me* — and this hunger in my ethereal soul to return home, to reunite spirit to body, to re-*thwock* and be complete again, and then get on with whatever next business I would need to enroll my weary soul upon....

But not so fast.

As I looked around with Henri's eyes, standing among the laundry tubs and folding tables, amidst humid air and churning rotational sloshings of industrial latherings and launderings, I remembered.... No, I wasn't *remembering* this. It was *like* a memory, probably because my perceptions were routed through Henrietta's nerve and emotion system, but this wasn't memory — not *chemical, elemental* like memory. It was more of a... a self — another self, a presence. Though not near, it wasn't too far either, and it was interested. It wanted presence. It craved inclusion.

And it gave me pause.

Although it wasn't a memory, it was like a memory in that it contained concepts, recurrence, elements of an idea, an objective — back in Jidalco's office.

Henrietta died an hour ago.

The feeling of eyes struck me. Even with deadened — dead, actually — nerves, that intuition survived. There were eyes on me.

I turned, and saw, with Henrietta's cooling eyes, Myrt.

And I remembered, back in the car, when I was half delirious as Myrt and Lorethe talked on the phone, when Myrt had seemed distracted.

"I need to keep busy. There's something else."

That *something else* had been Henrietta.

Now he stood, his own eyes gleaming with a sheen of tears, leaning against the corner of a huge, polished, high-volume industrial launderer drum, the side of his face reflected and magnified in the smudged stainless curvature. He leaned not in an *I'm cool* way, but in an *I need support* way.

"You took her," he said. He didn't sound accusatory, exactly, although his voice dripped with emotion, as well as fatigue. His voice was spent, its expressive capital not drained by overuse or misuse, but by exhaustion or sleep deprivation or stress, or all three. Here stood a kid in crisis.

"Yes," I said, stepping toward him. "They had it all planned out somehow, and left me no other... place to go."

"I... know." His body slumped against the polished stainless steel. His face slumped too.

"She was your friend," I said.

It was mostly me talking, my recollection, remembering two kids wide-eyed, peeking under a gurney shroud, in a collaboration of discovery and investigation, into the reality of death, and the unreality of it coming back to life on a hospital gurney.

It was partly her too, though, at least an inkling of her, something perhaps unspoken while she lived. Many kids that age left things unspoken—unsure, both of themselves, and especially that pre-teen fear that emotions expressed might be rebuffed or, even worse, ridiculed.

The moment was in danger of diving somewhere deep and dark, but the boy abruptly pushed away from the metal and shook the glooming moment off, regaining his poise and groping for a new momentum. He found it in a return to a subject of shared interest.

He took a few steps to where a half-dozen wheeled linen bins sat parked in two rows of three each. "In there." He nodded to indicate the one in the middle.

He pulled and pushed at the carts, to get to the one that counted. With his attention firmly on this activity, he didn't see me backing away at first, but then he sensed it, and turned around.

He'd lain his hands on the gray formed handle of the cart, the one that counted, and again he gestured. "It's you."

"Don't show me," I said, remembering. I'd been too long out of my body, and longed to let it pull me back in. I felt strands of reality spreading and dissipating, and the reception—*the signal*—had grown weak. It felt tenuous. Sound was going white and airy, and vision was going snowy.

I remembered, in spite of the fog and fade, that we must hurry. We had to try, but I worried that if I saw my own form, that if I reestablished any sort of contact, even visual, that I wouldn't be capable of helping myself. It would be over.

Suddenly, I realized what *the opposite of suicidal thoughts* meant.

Suicidal thoughts are when you're too alive, and wish for, or wonder about, death. The *opposite* of *suicidal thoughts* are when you're dying, or dead, and wish for, or wonder about, living.

This isn't what most people would instinctively think. Why would they?

Chapter 53

It was still very early in the morning, and the laundry staff's first shift hadn't even shown up yet, but they probably would any minute. So we set off.

Two kids pushing a cart through the hospital's halls at dawn would probably seem odd in any circumstance, but it didn't matter that much because there was almost nobody else around. The more I thought of it, the more it occurred to me that we should have been at least a little alarmed by it. Not so much the stillness and quiet at 6:38 AM in the colonic lower-level corridors of a vast health complex—that was no surprise. What perhaps should have arched our eyebrows was that it was so completely still and quiet just a few minutes after Henri had bolted out of Jidalco's office, leaving big old enraged Scutcheon clenching his empty, frustrated fists.

Corridor to utility elevator to second floor, east wing, and we encountered no one. This area of the facility had once been the ER, but was being repurposed, so gypsum dust, brown paper, and scraps of upripped carpet lay strewn about the paint-stained floors. Myrt knew all the angles, and picked the ideal route. Still, as we worked our way up and toward the center of the network of wings and hallways, and closed in on the patient habitations, we heard, saw, and smelled more and more signs of activity. At crosshalls, we glanced quickly left and right, often seeing brisk movement at other distant crossings, as the pros arrived and the orderlies pushed carts and equipment around.

At one point, we had to get small. We were approaching a busy zone, and heard the *whump* of group feet approaching around the corner on the tight pile commercial carpet.

Myrt carefully parked the cart tight against the wall and jumped in. "C'mon!" he urged, whispering but not daring to carry on about it.

I couldn't do it, and shook my head.

He understood immediately, and ducked under a pile of linens, sharing space with my inert body.

I walked back the way we had come, not fast, but fast enough to stay ahead of the party of docs and administrators that made the turn. As expected, they walked right on by Myrt and the cart.

In order to stay ahead of the coterie, I kept going, and took the first right turn. By the time I was down that stretch far enough to shake loose the paranoia of pursuit, I realized I might as well just keep going, and make rights turns until I'd returned to Myrt and the cart.

So I took a right, and another right.

Pale little girl, keep your head down, and keep walking.

I took two more rights, and should have been back, but when I got there—at least, I thought I was there—he was gone.

I was there. Yes, this was the right place. Of that, I was sure, really.

Several times I walked by the spot, first one way and then the other. Maybe I was just pacing, or indecisive about what to do and where to go, or going one way then changing my mind, then changing it again, or all of it at once.

Finally, I turned and started to run. I ran *hard*, because in that instant, something had just happened. An awareness occurred: there was another. I sensed it, and it was connected to me in some way, and in that instant, I knew how to run, homing on that connection, knowing that I would understand clearly all that I didn't yet know... once I got there.

Once I'd started running, I didn't slow, or look around, or puzzle over where I was or where I was bound. I didn't feel the pairs of eyes following behind me, nor hear any of the voices calling out as I ran by.

I didn't notice if I turned or mounted steps or went down ramps or scaled escalators. I *blurred* my way to where I needed to be.

When I got there, it all slowed down again. The blur settled and things cleared once more.

Myrt stood there, as did Lorethe, in this room.

Colored patterns had been painted on the walls in pastel tones. They were symbols—punctuations, commas, and umlauts. Muscle memory recognized the place, institutional, of course, but with juvenile overtones superimposed, overdone in that gauche institutional interior-decorator way. There were personal touches too: a poster for a boy band, with B2ST in jumbly letters slashing across the bottom.

The linen cart sat empty now, and there stood, with Myrt and Lorethe, my body.

The look on my body's face was simply lost, an expression of little-girl confusion on a just-woke-from-a-long-nap manface—*my* face, my weary, not-quite-middle-aged, three-days-unshaved face.

The body swap was complete. Through the twist of circumstances, jumbling together and reassembling, somehow Henrietta had lodged her little eleven-year-old spirit in *my* receptive and recumbent male form.

And it stood—*she* stood— with Lorethe and Myrt in the pediatric suite where *this* little body of *hers*, the one I now occupied, had dwindled and enfeebled and finally gone still. It had remained still, *moved* perhaps by others, but *still*... until I'd taken it and made it move again.

"You did it," I said.

Myrt nodded.

I rubbed my ribs, remembering Scutcheon's hypo. "I thought he was sedating me, but it was... *it was the experimental stuff.* I was in their offices, and Scutcheon injected me! And now Henri...." I couldn't finish the thought, because the rest was obvious, though Henri, in my body, still looked totally lost.

Lorethe looked as though about to cry, but as if she didn't know what kind of cry it would be.

I started jumping up and down, trying to think, trying to make something happen, because, think or not, something had to happen. Forces were converging.

This was all fine and good. It was, after all, an acceptable variation of what we'd been trying for. At the same time, because it *was* happening, it also had to be, quite likely, exactly what *somebody else* wanted to happen, somebody like Scutcheon or Jidalco—or whoever pulled their strings.

"Don't cry, Lorethe," I said, and went to her.

"Can you switch back?" She seemed ready to take a step back, but managed to hold her ground.

I pulled up short because I didn't want her to take that step. "I could, maybe. Oh, but how much practice have I had? Dozens of sessions, hours and hours in and out of different.... But she...." I nodded toward her, toward my body. "She's just a beginner."

Little Henri spoke up, having somehow found the lever that tuned up my vocal cords, which had been inactive for about fourteen hours now. It came out a rasping honk. "I know all you people."

Very strange, seeing my body moving and talking without me in it.

One by one, she looked at the others, Myrt and Lorethe. "It wasn't a dream. You and you and...."

She finally looked at me, and then looked at her hands. *My* hands. Man hands. She looked around the room, found what she was looking for, and ran to the wall mirror. She looked at the glass, and my face stared back at her.

"...and you," she said, touching my face with my hand. My face... now her face. She turned and looked at Myrt. "It's him! I'm him. The zombie man!"

"He is not a zombie," said Myrt.

"Why did you leave without me?" I said to him.

"I had to. The Borises went by."

A chill ran up my — Henri's — spine.

She spoke again. "The zombie man. I'm the zombie man."

"No," said Myrt. "There is no zombie. He isn't, and you're not...." He turned and looked at me. "Tell her."

I shrugged Henrietta's shoulders, and looked at my body, still not quite looking *owned* by the little soul inside. I didn't think Henri, in there, was ready to listen.

"No," said Lorethe, seeing my expression, seeming to agree. "She's a bright girl, but being told wild things about body swaps and secret experimental abilities, by you, inhabiting her own former form.... It's too much too soon, and we have to move. We have to go. She'll catch on."

Myrt looked confused, and seemed about to cry again. "Put her back. Can't you put her back?"

I shook my head, thinking it through. Lorethe and I looked at each other.

Trying to be his friend, as he remembered and respected her, I went to Myrt, took his hand, led him to the long settee, and sat him down.

"It's not that easy," I said. "For one thing, she'll need some time in... in there, or the treatment won't do her any good, and she needs practice before we try another transfer. And I can't just *exit*, just go out, to let her in. It's been so long.... Human bodies aren't just boxes, or bottles, where you can just pour out the plain milk and fill it up with chocolate. I can't be sure what might happen. I might just push her out into the cold. It's been so long since I've been in there, I might not be able to help myself. It could *just happen* that way."

I was pretty sure I wouldn't do that, but I also didn't want to just slip away, myself. After all this, I wasn't quite ready to die. Well, maybe I wasn't completely unready either, but I had some stuff to do yet, and some scores to settle.

Something was wrong, though — something else.

Myrt wasn't telling us something. As a child, when he held something in, and wanted to be unburdened, but was conflicted, and also didn't want to say it.... He had that squirmy, unmistakable, visible agony of immature indecision about him.

"C'mon now," I said, without staring him down, but with gentleness.

"I think it's my fault," he said finally. "I wanted her to... oh, I don't know. Maybe I did an awful thing. I wanted her to be like you. When you had me snoop their offices, I figured it out, and took some of the medicine. You... she... Henri was already in a coma, and I gave it to her. I took a syringe and...." He hung his head.

I went up to Henri, from within her body, and looked up into her eyes, within my body — the window, I could see clearly, into her soul. I reached out for her hand, my man hand, and I pulled on it. She bent over, then crouched down, and I looked into her eyes, and she looked into mine. She was looking into her own eyes, and I was looking into my own. For each of us, it wasn't really any different from the thousand and more times we'd looked into a mirror, yet, with the window reversed, so very, very different.

I went back to Myrt. "No, kid, it's not your fault. Maybe it's good what you did." I lifted her dress and showed him the puncture where Scutcheon had just given her another dose — a posthumous boost. "You might have started it, but the dastardly doctor doubled it. Heck, I had — my body, that is — had eight or nine doses. At this point, I think we need to see where all this takes us."

I looked over at Henri, in my body, and she looked back at me, in mine.

"You okay?" I said, and then looked at Lorethe.

Henri nodded, and Lorethe nodded, murmuring something that sounded like a quiet yes. One by one, they both nodded at me, and at Myrt too.

"We can fix this," I said. "C'mon."

We moved, all four of us, at once toward the middle of the room. Then, holding hands, we headed for the door.

"No, wait," said Lorethe. She moved between us and the door.

"You can come too," I said.

"It's not that. Where are you going to go?"

"Yes, what do we do now?" said Myrt.

"All we need is a third body," I said. "We can't shift back where we belong without a place to park for at least one of us on the way."

"You know they're coming for you," Lorethe said. "They want to supervise."

She went to the door, and motioned the rest of us back. She opened it, stuck her head out, looked left and right, then pulled her head in and swiftly pulled the door shut. She pushed the lock button, then turned and leaned back against the door, looking at me and shaking her head.

I sighed with Henrietta's lungs. "Who?" I said.

"Nobody."

"Then why—"

"*That's* why. *Nothing.* It's too quiet. *Nobody!* There's something going on. There should be meds, techs, nurses getting the day started, meal trays, OTs and PTs, dieticians, dialysis carts...."

"Nothing?"

She shook her head.

"Maybe we should let them," I said.

"Let them?"

"Supervise."

"Ah."

After a moment, she said, "I know that look, but on a little girl's face, it's not right."

"Exactly," I said.

Chapter 54

A better idea might have been to sneak out, or bust out. We did think about hurling a chair through the window of Henri's pediatric Sanctuary suite, or the four of us hoisting up the sectional as a battering ram for a more controlled defenestration, but in the end, we chose to just go at them with the advantages that our—mine and Henri's—special talents might provide.

We split up, girls together and boys together—but it only *looked* that way. Actually, my body went with Myrt, occupied by Henri, and I went with Lorethe this time, occupying Henri's body.

We unbolted and opened the door, and we stepped out and turned right, just Lorethe and Henrietta, looking like a mom and her little girl, or maybe more of an *aunt and niece* in this case.

A minute later, according to plan, Myrt took Henri, minding my body, walked out and took a left.

We didn't know how much *they*—the medical military, or whatever they were—knew, but we were pretty sure they wouldn't know, *couldn't* know, that we'd managed to somehow animate my body with Henri's spirit. This could have been an advantage—should have been. However, maintaining this advantage required that Henrietta and I not be seen together.

When we got to the first cross hall, we were of course tempted to creep, but we had agreed to be confident. We did look around, though.

Boris was there, standing in a white coat and wearing a stethoscope, holding a thin white electronic tablet. He might have even been using the thing's camera, because he didn't even look up. He may even have been recording video. And that's all he did, if that's what he was doing. He didn't visibly register our presence, didn't follow.

That's how it remained, for a while. We "girls" circled, and Myrt, with his friend Henri stuck in my body, circled ahead of us. We just, for the time being, wanted to see what would happen while the cats watched us.

Cat and mouse? In those old classic cartoons, Pixie and Dixie or Tom and Jerry, it was like that. Smart mice circled round the suburban home, passing the same little rounded mouse holes over and over, the same familiar corner with the light switch by the kitchen door, then scampered past Jemima's thick ankle socks. All the while, the dumb cat repeatedly ran into swinging brooms, waffle irons, or conveniently materialized anvils.

With real cats, and real mice, furry little felines and rodents, it didn't really work that way—no anvils, and certainly no circling frenzy. The metaphor didn't stand up, sadly.

Then, as I spaced out in this childhood, childish nostalgia, Henri, from a hundred yards away on the opposite side of the loop, spoke in my ear.

"Hey you," she said. "Zombie man."

One might have expected that I would jump out of my temporary skin, or react with some sort of surprise, but I just replied, "I am not a zombie," because it wasn't a surprise at all.

I hadn't exactly been expecting this, but somehow it seemed quite natural to have this ethereal communication channel between us. I'd felt it too, beginning especially a few minutes before, in my solo panic, when I'd felt so lost *a building and a half* away, but then felt something, some connection, pulling me, and I'd run blindly on Henri's spindly little legs to make those ends meet.

She was the one smart enough, or clever enough—*both*—to try using this conduit for communication. Verbalization.

"Huh," I said out loud. "How did you figure that out?"

Walking next to me, Lorethe said, "What? What are you talking about?"

"I'm talking to Henrietta," I said. Then I realized that I didn't have to actually speak—to Henri, at least.

"Talking to yourself?" Lorethe said as we walked, but I ignored her and continued the pathic chat with my little soulmate.

Just as we were figuring this all out, this little walkie-talkie, mind-mind thing we could do, our pairs had been walking for ten minutes. We'd covered a circuit and a half around the outer edges of the whole cluster, and the whole hospital community really came to life now. Whatever control or restriction they'd placed on the west wing, where the children's ward resided, had been dropped. Now, we noticed something we should have anticipated.

We were being followed—not watched, *followed*.

We were being watched too, of course, by Boris One, certainly, and probably Boris Two, and undoubtedly by other peering eyes. Now, however, I noticed, with a glance over my shoulder, that whenever we turned a corner to start down another stretch of corridor, a collective murmuring rose back there somewhere, back at our *last* corner turning—thudding scudding feet and subdued crowd murmuring. I knew right away what it was.

Timid now, I thought, *but still drawn, curious, attracted.*

That unexplainable charisma had surfaced, the BeatleElvisBieber thing, which I'd noticed when wandering out in the rural center of the county. Now, it was partially tamed by the fears and rumors, the collision of myth and imagination with living, breathing—or at least walking—beings that defied logic, if not reason and science.

"Henri," I beamed silently. "Is there a... do you have a... well...."

"*A retinue?*" she said. It came straight into my head, but I chose to recognize this channel that connected us, her in my body and me in hers, as coming into my right ear. "*A posse, a throng, a mob?*"

Little Henrietta is probably smarter than I am, and certainly has that quick and bright clarity of youth. Or had, anyway, until she....

"*It gets a little bigger every time we circle,*" she said.

I was in her body, and her voice was in my head. It gave me a little vertigo, and I began to wonder, worry even, about *me.*

Is she so strong that I'm in danger of... of getting lost, of fading? Will I ever get my body back?

"*No, don't,*" she said into my right ear, cutting short my string of thought. "*That's not productive. Stay focused. We can see and feel each other's thoughts, but that's all. There's no stupid getting lost or fading out, so stop it! Look, ahead of us we can see the tail of* your *entourage disappear around the next corner, each time we make a turn.*"

My lips were moving and I mumbled a little as I started to tell Henri something.

Lorethe, walking next to me, jabbed me with an elbow. "Don't mumble. I like it better anyway, when you speak to her out loud."

"Oh, sorry. Listen, Henri," I said aloud, somehow directing my words both to these lips, for Lorethe's benefit, and to my distant brain, for Henrietta's. "When did you see a Boris last?" I drew forth a quick image of the henchpair, because I wasn't sure if she knew about them, or if she'd connected the name *Boris* to them after seeing them on her own. I couldn't remember if we'd discussed them at all, back in her ward unit.

These reluctant but obsessive entourages made me nervous. We hadn't really planned on this phenomenon.

Plan? Well, whatever fragile, half-formed plan we did have.

At the rate the trailing throngs were growing, it might not be long before we ran into the tail of their comet, and Myrt and Henri were mingling into the tail of ours. The military medical conspiracy hadn't foreseen this either, come to think of it.

"No, haven't seen one of those," she whispered into my brain. *"Not since yesterday, anyway, before I di — "*

"Don't think about that." This time I interrupted her. "*I* don't want to think about that, and if *you* think, *I* think. Listen, if Boris hasn't seen you yet, I want you to play dead."

"Don't think about that. You won't even let me say the word, and in the next sentence, you tell me to play dead. Listen now, I've been dying for a while, *Morton*, and I don't like it, but I'm used to it. I can mention it without getting weirded out. If anything, not being dead right now is the weird part, because *I* did it, and whether you're ready, or even if you're not, I'll say it. Ready? I died."

"Yeah, good point. Sorry. Are you talking out loud so Myrt can hear?"

"Yes. Let me rephrase your conceptual scheme: If one of us isn't moving, or only moving on wheels, and sometimes it's one of us and then next time the other, they won't know, or can't be sure, if there are two of us active, or just one, or less than one. Myrt? Yes. Yes. Okay. Oh, you can't hear him. Yes, it's not like a phone. I know, you can't overhear another person in the background. Duh. Myrt's scouting, scrounging up a gurney or a wheelchair. He thinks it's a good idea. I'm not so sure."

Before long, they'd found and swiped an idle gurney outside one of the visitor lounges temporarily doing dialysis duty, and we'd begun spotting — or caching — other bits of patient transport here and there for when it was our turn. during this time, we the comets continued to circle, and the disconnected tails followed, and lengthened. All the while, our minds were a badminton game, batting back and forth, a feathery light and airy series of thoughts, with a bouncy rubber base and resounding, *thwacking* rhythm.

"*Morton?*" I said. "Did Lorethe tell you that's my name?"

A giggle swirled at my brain. A telepsionic giggle, when minds were closely intertwined, proved a tickly thing — shivery, like a cold bolt of mercury shooting up the spine, and then swishing around the lobular cortices until it dissipated. We hadn't had much opportunity to explore that in the present grave circumstances.

That galvanizing giggle turned into whispered words that dug and teased. "No, *you* did, and I think it's a dang good thing. Anything you know, I know. Anything you remember, it's accessible. It may be a useful thing, too. Who knows when we'll get this sorted out? Could come in handy — "

I didn't have time to think much about sharing my world with an eleven-year-old girl, about knowing her dreams and secrets, or her knowing mine. We were getting focused, not just wandering around anymore. We seemed to suddenly have a plan, of sorts, and having located the necessary equipment, we were about to make our final twist.

Chapter 55

Something weird was going on.

I had this feeling of energy growing, but at the same time, everything seemed to be slowing down, churning down, as though something were holding back this massive buildup of energy. We didn't want to catch up with the brownian dozens that tiptoed up ahead, trying not to catch up with Myrt and Henri. The dozens behind us — maybe a hundred, maybe more — milled up and back, surging then dawdling, as if part of a hive mind, like six-leg social-insect colonies, cresting and waning but never getting any faster, slowing even. I couldn't see it, but I could feel it, hear it.

In a world where people can become famous for being famous, a crowd can form with no purpose but crowding. This one, though, had some purpose — vague, perhaps, but there. That vague energy in the atmosphere had grown, and everybody could feel it.

I kept in touch with Henri, and Myrt and Lorethe texted via their mobile phones now and then, because sometimes we couldn't talk out loud. After all, at first Henri, then I, was possumming in a rolling chair or gurney, taking turns being dead, for Boris... and Boris.

We'd been working on a wrinkle, and now, with the lengthening entourages threatening to blend, we needed to put the wrinkle in gear, to see if we could push confusion to another — no, to a *whole nuther* — level.

Lorethe and I had sped up slightly, while the other end of the yin-yang double tail had slowed just right. Thus, as the trailing crowds built to a tidal surge, Myrt and Henri approached one of the stairways just as we were about to pass the entranceway to the spiral atrium ramps.

Instead of continuing around the circuits we'd been using to follow each other, we led our mob past the ramps to some little-used stairs next to a bank of elevators, stairs that led down to the first level of basement.

At the same time, Myrt, half-a-hospital away, pushed the wheelchair with my body, and Henri's intellectual leadership, through the fire door into another stairwell, and ascended toward the upper floors.

We went down two levels, to the basement containing some administrative offices, the morgue, engineering, and the staff cafeteria.

Meanwhile, the Myrt-Henri entourage re-emerged on level two, where the maternity clinic was a self-contained, sealed-off ward. They'd actually led their group along a length of uninterrupted wall before passing several waiting areas, some nursing administration, and finally turned back into the *general population* section of the wards, where the sick people and their families were nothing special—just your average ailers, fractured clavicles and fibulas and diverticulitis, introverticulosis, concussions and organ murmurs, bowel blockages and bile pertussisage.

The chasing-comet tails had been pursuing each other in a counterclockwise direction on floor one, right above the ground level. At the sub-ground level, we continued in the same counterspin. On floor two, our counterpartners—Myrt and Henrietta—did a half-circuit, entered another set of stairs, and descended to the first level. They bumped the empty wheelchair down the steps for later use, but meanwhile *reversed* their spin, now moving clockwise. Since they pulled the reverse with a change in levels, the transition was smooth and likely didn't seem of much significance to the following throngs. Or maybe it seemed very significant. What matters is that they went along with it, herd mentality living up to expectations.

We moved toward each other now, rather than following heads-to-tails, making the two crowds approach each other quite rapidly, though on different floor levels. Within ten minutes, the two moving groups were quite literally one on top of the other.

That's when we, together, coordinated the convergence. They led their entourage down a short skyway, and then directly down the spiral ramps to the ground floor.

We emerged from the basement, a roiling serpent of humanity disgorging from the stairwell behind us, into the middle of the opposite dragon's *tail*, in the airy, high-ceilinged, dancing-light space called The Atrium.

We were weaving two streams of curious humanity into a single uncoordinated and inchoate tapestry. Together, Henri and I had also initiated a sequence designed to escalate this mild confusion into a roiling mayhem.

Somehow, we had coordinated it, each of us diverting a little stream of our interwoven mentalities to a strange and separated objective. This probably would not have been possible for me to do by myself, or her by her herself. It took both of us, probably because of a rule, a restriction, something inherent in the powers and abilities that I'd discovered and begun to explore, and at which Henri already seemed destined to surpass me. We could, it seems, each control one body, and we could sort of share control of two bodies because we'd never quite, somehow, in the strange circumstances that had brought us to this juncture, closed off the channels, the shimmery silver cords that ran from our spirit minds to our original home beings.

While we were both quite aware of the "rule," the inherent impossibility of multiplicity, the fundamental *one-soul/one-body, one-to-a-customer* nature of existence in our spiritual and physical universe, we both realized that by crossing our souls over and discovering this residual telepathic connection, we had also freed something up.

Though not strong, and not precise, it might be enough.

"*C'mon, help me out,*" she said.

She had the dog's head and forequarters roused, with that small percentage of leftover power that she could afford to project out away from our hospital maneuvers, and I followed her lead and shot my own attentions out there too. She had "borrowed" my own thoughts, my fleeting memory of a dead dog, a concept discarded when I'd been desperately seeking a body, *any* body, when I couldn't locate my own.

"*C'mon! I can't do it by myself,*" she beamed.

I went in, merged into *dog flesh,* and immediately felt 10% or so of my spirit weighted back, oddly devolved, somehow diminished and empowered at the same time by a sense of canine flow.

Not human, but not wild. Domestic, but instinctive, with other senses, an alien envelope, paws, jowls, and snout.

We did a mental mutual nod. This was why it was even remotely possible: a simpler being—simpler control system, instinct and reflex.

"I've already got the front," she said, "But it's all I can do to lift the head and front legs."

"So I'm the back end," I said aloud.

Lorethe, striding behind me as she pushed the wheelchair, leaned over and looked looked into my face, occupied by Henri, as if I were making a joke.

We approached the Atrium through a short corridor, with tall windows on one side and blonde wood-paneled walls on the other, but a piece of my mind, and an intertwined bit of Henrietta's, lay focused in a damp and shady thicket, where a tangle of honeysuckle and thorny wildberrybush had made a quiet place to die for a

Border Collie Dachshund Terrier mutt, who'd breathed his last almost a week ago in that little hedge tangle between a healthcare parking lot and one of the older postwar suburban housing developments in the area.

Left brain? Right brain?

In a canine nervous system, I didn't know which section operated the hindquarters, but that's where 10% of my attention was working, and it didn't matter because Henri got the head and paws up and had started dragging my end. All I had to do was start those motions.

Make the helfers springy, shin muscles tight now, left, right, left, right....

I just had to make my weary mind, deep inside a borrowed canine brain, ride an imaginary bicycle, and we were underway. It's snout wiggled under summer's green foliage tent, with its poles of bramble and its tarp of suckle, and we were out and free, scaling the rise to the edge of the parking lot.

All I have to do!

"Hey!".

I was getting a little feisty, and had our hind-end somehow up and walking level with our front end, which probably looked... interesting, like a dog walking forward and backward at the same time, and making progress sideways while it was at it.

If anybody's sitting and waiting in a car for a spouse to come out of a dermatology session or a B12 shot....

I caught a quick wisp of crosstalk just then, and saw a blurry snapview for a moment, through a dog's dead eyes routed through Henri's senescent visual verve. A woman leaned against the hood of a minivan, lighting up a long white slim one. I also noticed, before Henri shoved my vision access aside, that the woman was applying the flame to the middle rather than the tip of a specimen of Virginia's longest and slimmest cigarette.

"Hey!" Henri beamed again, with some english on it this time.

I fell into line, or at least attempted to approximate the *following* segment of a dog's perambulation, rather than competing with the snout for preeminence in forward motility.

We were just getting the hang of it when we reached the nearest entrance to the connected Medical Office Building, and ducked behind those bushy plantings that decorated such inside/outside transitional spaces, in their carefully curved puddles of brown-black mulchbark.

It was only a minute or so before the door opened and a man came out, and then, with a stumble and a shuffling convulsive peristalsis of getting the thing going again, we'd managed to somehow get this little quadruped corpse through the door before it closed on our decomposing tail.

We then trotted on down the hall of Medical Office Building III, better known among the initiated as M.O.B. Three, or MOB3.

Chapter 56

A mutt trotted through the office building halls, dead, its musculature and vital liquids a bit rearranged by more than a week of side-laying gravity, insects and their larvae, and microbial decay.

Trotted? More like gyrating. Somewhere in between, perhaps. Gyrotrotting?

I'd been a man, a son, a brother, a boyfriend, a mate, a husband. I could have perhaps been a father, and by some definitions perhaps I was, for a very short time — another story.

Some people say things happen for a reason. Some even say everything does. We've all heard people say this, because a lot of people do. Some believe it, even.

Well, now, with my more recent experiences, while I hadn't exactly been a woman, I'd experienced some first-person semblance of that perspective, as well as that of a volunteer fireman, a storyteller, story listeners, a backhoe operator, a grandfather, a grandmother, an organized criminal, a guy named Mike, and another guy nicknamed Duck, with his fighting waterfowl tattoos, and a dozen other people — people once full of life, but no longer.

Nobody, except a dog, had ever been a dog, but, together with a little girl having extraordinary abilities and talents that far surpassed my own, I had now, in a small way, known doghood.

As those two large swirling retinues came together from behind us, and as we entered the Atrium leading our fan posses, we slowed down to let it all synchronize.

We slowed down, then stopped. I was a female child in a wheelchair. Across the airy space were a man and a boy, the boy pushing a gurney, the man lying upon it.

The boy pushed the gurney hard, then stood and watched it roll away.

I felt Lorethe's hands on my shoulders, her standing behind me. "See you soon," I said in Henri's whisper.

With that, she pushed the chair firmly, and I rolled into the open space, toward the oncoming gurney.

Rolling forward, I saw, across the Atrium, the people surge behind and around where Myrt stood. Then he'd melted into their middle, behind the forefront of the crowd.

I turned my head and looked back at Lorethe for one more moment. Her face tightened with worry and trouble, and then she too shuffled behind the surging bodies and faces of others.

The surge suddenly stopped. On both sides, a kind of *hurry up and wait* settled in, probably because this was a *Rumor, Fear, and the Madness of Crowds* crowd, inspired by *rumor* to be here, propelled by a collective *madness*, and halted now by a gestalt *fear*.

The groups remained kinetic, milling and popping behind their barrier layers—the front crust that held them back, the crust of fear and hesitation.

Yet the irritation that finally unleashes or releases pent-up pressure can come from anywhere.

As we rolled across that space to meet each other, a knot of uniforms formed, with some uncertainty, near the wide stretch of glass where the vestibule had a row of alternating revolving and wheelchair-accessible transparent doors. Their unauthoritarian uncertainty probably had more to do with the lack of clarity regarding their purpose here, rather than crowd-control challenges. During our last confrontation, the authorities had been uncertain too, but uninformed; now they knew; they had seen the dead active and erratic. They remained uncertain, nevertheless, still not knowing the best weapon, the most effective tactic, against a revived corpse.

The atrium space wasn't exactly quiet at that moment, or during those moments, but a certain stillness had gathered, an evaluative quelling of the crowds. It seemed as though their contained energy could just burst forth again at any instant, or continue to build pressure, or just keep flowing together with no clear motive or predictable outcome. Things might get ugly... or not.

The irritation that finally broke everything up was... a sound.

It sounded like a laugh, or laughter, at first. Maybe. Or maybe it was a scream.

No. Laughter.

The crowd fell quieter as the sound, whatever it was, grew. It floated behind and above the sounds of people, of many nervous and excited people, muttering and milling and whispering. It was low and high at the same time, repeated, giddy and insistent and hoarse and clear. Yet it wasn't laughter at all, or screaming. It was one, then several, then many, then multiple voices.

Crows.

Above us, the skylight bubbles had been removed by the S.W.A.T observers, and of course the earlier crowds during our first showdown had bulged through parts of the glass panels out front. Thus, the Atrium had truly become an open air site, sounds and atmosphere mingling freely to the interior from outside.

I hadn't *called* them — I didn't know how to do that — but here they were.

Crows, like other birds, mean something when they caw, and unlike some flocking birds that have a rank-and-file instinctive sameness in their social collectives, crows are oddly and disturbingly humanlike in their speech, their social interaction, their individuality. They watch, they scheme, they remember, they get emotional. Some birds have a few calls, while crows have a whole vocabulary — barks, squawks, laughs, annoyance, irritation, celebration.

As the noise grew, becoming clearer and louder, it became a raucous, organic cacophony of big black bird assembly, resounding through the breezeway and hovering up above the open skylights. They'd come to watch, perhaps, or listen. Crows always have their own reasons, so there must have been *something* here for them.

It was time, but time stood still.

This can happen to anybody, anytime — moments that seem to slow down and come to a dead halt — but it was easy for me. I was, for those stopped-time moments, remembering Babby's ending to the little fable of the vole and the ground squirrel, the muskrat and the groundhog and the beaver, the mystery quest across the meadow and back.

Why had I thought back to it? Perhaps the crows had triggered it.

In Babby's resolution, when all the little creatures had returned to where it had all started, returning and regrouping to ask the vole why he started across the meadow in the first place, the little rodent was nowhere to be found — just a few bits of stray fur. They all looked at each other, and all around, and at the sky. Then they all went their separate ways, home.

Time started up again, and a wheelchair was rolling. I sat on it, and rolling toward me on the gurney was my body, and behind us, on each side of the Atrium space, Lorethe and Myrt faded back into the crowd. The crows barked and laughed and cried. The uniforms loaded their gas cartridges, fire hoses, rubber projectiles, or whatever they were readying, and just before the gurney and the wheelchair came together, they slowed almost to a stop.

Then they bumped, and everything was still, though we could hear the crows out in the sunlight.

A ripple moved through the people. With it came a chain of shouting, which became an icy, wordless, mounting scream. When the ripple became running, we knew our wrinkle was underway.

We were behind all of it. It was *our* wrinkle.

Even the dog had come, the dead dog. An inkling lingered in there—several, actually. They were simple: a food bowl, dented scratched red aluminum, a hated neighbor kid who threw acorns, some cats, and dogs that lifted their legs on top of his territory markings.

How irritating.

A name inkled in there too: Soames.

Soames had arrived.

Chapter 57

There came a moment when we knew. We could see it., like one of those crowd waves in a packed stadium, or a school of fish or a flock of birds, when a little flaw in the flow suddenly and decisively altered the trajectory of the whole group, or maybe even a cry of *fire* in a sold-out movie theater. Or gunfire.

Screams, laughter, vomiting sounds, crashings, feet running, stomping sounds....

Even before the parts of the crowd nearest us, centered there with our gurney and chair, knew what was happening, because the rest of the hundreds in the room had focused on this new spectacle, they had already craned their necks and moved their feet to jostle toward whatever had drawn this new attention.

Soames.

Although Henri and I couldn't see the dog yet with our borrowed eyes, we could see, of course — *dog's-eye-view* — with the little parts of our own spirits that controlled and accessed the animal's nervous system. As a result, we could time it just about perfectly.

And we did. Indeed, a moment ensued in that whole open atrium of people — patients, Elvis fans, cops, firemen, doctors, lawyers, Indian chiefs — when not a single pair of eyes rested upon us.

By that time, Soames had been running quite amok under and among about half the perimeter crowd. Not only did Soames have dog dish and acorn and territory inklings, but he had animal instincts that kicked in quite easily. Then as stimulus came in, he continued to kick in reaction. He'd started out sniffing, wagging, lifting leg, and generally checking things out, with our disgusted guidance, of course. Then, as the screams and kicks of revulsion started up, Henri and I struggled to keep head afore haunch as we darted little Soames from group to group, and as group collided with group trying to stay ahead of our little Soames in abject terror.

Somehow a little ex-sweet creature, a pet, a symbol of suburban domesticity like a puppy, with its cuteness inverted, transmutated into an exaggerated horror, and the human mind rebeled, revolted, revulsed—especially when already filled to brimming beyond stimulus overload.

Meanwhile, unseen and unremarked due to the Soames distraction, the other 90% of me and Henrietta climbed off the gurney and rose from the wheelchair. Hand in hand, we slipped into the crowd and walked toward the service hallway and service elevator, where we'd agreed, if all went well, to meet up again with Myrt and Lorethe. We needed to get a little distance from the clutches of Scutcheon, find a third host, and swap back to our own bodies.

And from there? We had plans in place.

Yet, alas, all did not go well.

It's always family—family that binds us, family that unites and collects and defines and validates us. If we'd asked the assorted family members that, through some unfathomably unserendipitous channels, were fated to assemble and obliterate all our half-baked and nearly fruited schemes, *they* being a father and a brother and a mom and an estranged wife, *they* undoubtedly would have congratulated themselves on their well-done, heroically achieved, last-minute collective and contributory saving of the day.

Whereas the father thought he'd rescue his beloved terminal daughter, he'd in fact snatch me from the jaws of victory. The wife thought she'd help the authorities rescue some remembered or idealized version of me from some mental illness-induced crime, but she'd help Henrietta get away. The brother thought he'd get even with his sister Lorethe for betraying him, and for her looser affiliation with his loose affiliation with a military contractor. Myrt's mother, the pulmonologist sleep doctor, had already collected him too. Probably just as well, because a kid could get hurt in those weird crowds and all.

After Soames helped us help ourselves to sift into the crowd, Henri and I, still swapped, managed to get to the arranged meeting area by the main bank of elevators. We turned the corner in the corridor, and there stood Lorethe arguing with her brother, the loose affiliated one who had blamed her for losing the safe combination when their father had died. Seeing them, we turned to run because, knowing his connections with Scutcheon, we couldn't linger. As soon as we rounded the corner, though, hearing Lorethe and her brother in pursuit, each for their own reasons, we saw the other people we both recognized. Of course, this particular estranged wife and bereaved father recognized us, but didn't—couldn't—know we weren't quite ourselves. We were literally each other.

Family is like a force field, or a freeze ray. Whether or not there are such things as force fields or freeze rays matters not, because family always matters intangibly anyway.

In this case, wearing Henrietta's body and seeing Anne Marie, my wife, looking at my body, but poor Henri in there looking back at her, and seeing Henri in there seeing her father, looking at me in her body....

I froze. We froze, too long. Then we ran, but of course we both wondered, including to each other across our mental crossconnection, why our family people were together like that. It turned out to be simple coincidence, all too common, but a coincidence, of course, that led to a botching up of things. We ran, and suddenly one of Scutcheon's Borises stood there in the hallway, as did a Zombie hunter with a shotgun, and the next thing we knew, things somehow got scrambled. Emotions tossed and turned, and confusion took over.

Then, before we could re-coordinate, Lorethe and Henri had managed to pair up and had vanished—Henri's mind, my body. Trailing the crows, they'd somehow made it out to the little blue Toyota—a good thing, perhaps.

They got away, somehow.

Little me, in Henri's body, did not. *Somehow.*

Henrietta's father was a rather athletic dude who'd somehow never been properly informed—*ahem*—of her revival. The Scutcheon team got away with explaining it to him as a miraculous recovery, *after* he'd managed to pull off a rather rude kidnapping-style snatching... of *me.* I ended up trapped between *"Daddy"* and one of the Borises, and his fatherly display of tears and affection mortified me.

Now I was her, alone and secured in her little suite, with her B2ST and 1Direction posters on her walls, with her laptop and her music thing and portable speakers. And hospital lockdown kept me here.

And I found three diaries.

Chapter 58

What could I do?

The first diary was already full, written in a girl's cramped but dainty script, with erasures and strikeouts, starts and stops. I looked it over, then read it. Yes, the first thing I did was read little Henri's story, her diary, her private business.

Of course, our marginally mixed minds had already spilled and slopped a lot of our individual privacies back and forth, from me to her and vice versa, so... well, we gave me permission.

She had been sweet and sad, vibrant and full of young life. With our intermittently intermingled minds, it was kind of interesting, reading her story, especially when a little part of her wandered back in to comment on what I was reading. She would clarify what she felt about her mom, still striving to parent, but perhaps trying too hard not to be too soft; or how much fun she had with Myrt wandering the facility; or that weird old guy who seemed to be everywhere in his wheelchair, talking to everybody, especially the really sick ones.

We actually had quite a chuckle over that last one.

The other two books were empty, so I wrote in one.

As time passed, I had a few sessions, interviews with Scutcheon, right here in my suite lockdown, but I didn't say much. I didn't break character, so he wasn't sure whether I was her or me in here. If I kept him guessing, maybe that would buy time for the others as they headed west. Sometimes I just told him to go away, that I was writing my *What I Did On My Summer Vacation* essay.

When Daddy visited, I mostly let Morton curl into a little dormancy alcove just inside her right ear, and let Henrietta take over from wherever she was out there with Lorethe. That got harder and harder to accomplish as time passed, though, and distance. Sometimes I just faked it. Angry, resentful little 'tween wasn't that hard to approximate, because it mostly involved shut-down body language, curt answers, and petulant expressions.

Full Circle

All of this — the entire thing — came from that borrowed diary, from a borrowed hand.

My handwriting is the same, pretty much, as Henri's, so I suppose, when this is over and some of the crazier incidents begin to fade, or get glossed over a bit, then they'll say, *"Look, what a brilliant little girl, creating a first person character, male, older, metafictional even. Look, she's given a slight male boldness to the handwriting in this* second *volume, the fantasy..."*

Right. Sure. Well, anyway, here we are. I've been writing in this blank book for a few hours a day, and I just now noticed that this second diary wasn't *quite* blank, after all. There's a poem she wrote here, near the back, and I'm just reaching it as I write this....

> *I stand within a circle that I drew*
> *Drawn upon a plain far, and wide*
> *And using all the colors that I knew*
> *I tried to paint everything inside.*
> *But even in my circle things I see*
> *Colors that weren't placed upon my brush*
> *And misty, distant things are telling me*
> *I was drawing with a stick, upon the dust.*

Why would she do that? Skip 150 pages and put the poem way inside, near the back?

Fewer and farther between now are her spirit visits, when a bit of her comes back, ethereally. They, Lorethe and Henrietta, are coming back when things calm down. So she says.

With the crossouts and edits in the little diary lyric there, it's clear that she composed it while writing it, so maybe she just grabbed one of her journals and started writing without thinking much about it. She likely did it just a few days ago, at a low ebb, near the end, when she didn't really care which book, or what page, or who would read it, or if anyone would ever read it at all, even. Next time she checks in, I'll ask her.

Again, I feel the need to say this, one more time: I never intended any of this to happen. I didn't plan it, or want it. I didn't learn to like it, although once the pattern was established, I got used to it. Would anybody ever intentionally infiltrate their soul or spirit into the lifeless husk of a dead human being? I don't mean some fringe obsessed type, but your 99%, your regular people? Would an average person want to climb inside a dead camel to keep warm on a frigid night in an Arabian desert? A horrid concept, but a *survival* concept.

Well, this was like that, only worse, like a stumble. About to freeze to death, I fell into the camel. It made me better, so I tried it again, and it worked *again*. Then I just couldn't stop.

I couldn't stop? Well, I could have, actually. When I started this whole thing, my life had wound down. Among the inevitable losses that accumulate when a person's life is ebbing, mine were perhaps worse than average, and less than heroic. When I no longer had the strength to be strong, to be vital, to contribute to the buoyancy that would keep a marriage together, that keeps friendships afloat, that keeps life worth living... that's when I fell into that camel.

In doing so, the despair that destroys a life's buoyancy, that waterlogs those relationships and perforates the thin flotation membrane that keeps us fighting for life, was suddenly lightened.

When I started writing this, I thought it was survival that drove me, that I had this instinctive will to live, which kicked in when I thought I had a chance. It appeared when the strange ability to use death to preserve my life presented itself, and I seized upon it.

But... it really wasn't *life*, after all, that *kept* me going, that *kept* me striving, that made me fight the darkness and cold. Most everything had already fallen apart, leaving precious little to fight *for*. All was already lost. *Nearly.*

Until Lorethe came into the picture.

So no, it wasn't survival. It wasn't *life*.

It was *hope*.

So Lorethe and Morton are out there, traveling west, pursuing whatever dream we had, perhaps altered a little. Playing the high-hat? Maybe. I still feel a little of it, of their life, but it's fading too.

I'm not sure what I'm going to do. Scutcheon has things he wants me to do, if I refuse, I don't think I'll last very long. Daddy wants me to, of course, but I don't know. I'm tired.

W. TOWN ANDREWS

About the Author

A native Pennsylvanian, Town Andrews has lived and worked in several western states and the Philippines. He speaks multiple languages, including fluent Spanish and Visayan. Working, reading, parenting, linguistics, history, music composition and performance, and travel have all influenced his storytelling. His career has involved the building trades, agriculture, marine sciences, developmental distilling, theater musicianship, and marketing functional fluids to manufacturers and engineers.

"I love my work. But for fun, I write these stories."

For more, please visit W. Town Andrews online at:
Website: www.UnheardOfBooks.com
Publisher Website: www.EvolvedPub.com/WTownAndrews
Facebook: @W-Town-Andrews
Twitter: @ATownAndr

What's Next?

W. Town Andrews is fast at work on his next novel, but as it remains in the early stages as of this printing, he's hesitant to share too many details... yet. One thing we know for sure: you're going to love that one as much as you loved this one. So please stay tuned to developments and plans by subscribing to our newsletter at the link below.

www.EvolvedPub.com/Newsletter/

More from Evolved Publishing

We offer great books across multiple genres, featuring hiqh-quality editing (which we believe is second-to-none) and fantastic covers.

As a hybrid small press, your support as loyal readers is so important to us, and we have strived, with tireless dedication and sheer determination, to deliver on the promise of our motto: **QUALITY IS PRIORITY #1!**

Please check out all of our great books, which you can find at this link: **www.EvolvedPub.com/Catalog/**

Thank you!

CPSIA information can be obtained
at www.ICGtesting.com
Printed in the USA
BVHW030354070519
547541BV00002B/4/P